DEVIL IN TARTAN

This Large Print Book carries the
Seal of Approval of N.A.V.H.

THE HIGHLAND GROOMS

DEVIL IN TARTAN

JULIA LONDON

THORNDIKE PRESS
A part of Gale, a Cengage Company

GALE
A Cengage Company

Farmington Hills, Mich • San Francisco • New York • Waterville, Maine
Meriden, Conn • Mason, Ohio • Chicago

LIBRARY OF CONGRESS CIP DATA ON FILE.
CATALOGUING IN PUBLICATION FOR THIS BOOK
IS AVAILABLE FROM THE LIBRARY OF CONGRESS

ISBN-13: 978-1-4328-5055-5 (hardcover)

Published in 2018 by arrangement with Harlequin Books S.A.

Printed in the United States of America
1 2 3 4 5 6 7 22 21 20 19 18

CONTENTS

DEVIL IN TARTAN 7

GLOSSARY 493

For Ann Leslie Tuttle

Some writers spin gold with every word they write. Others (me) always need a second eye. I've had some good editors along the way, but Ann Leslie is one of the best. She helped me shape this series of books set in 18th century Scotland with a lot of heart and wisdom and I will always be grateful for her sharp editorial eye.

Mackenzies of Balhaire

John Armstrong, *Lord Norwood*

Anne Armstrong

— Knox Armstrong *(bastard son)*

— Bryce Armstrong

— Margot Armstrong, b. 1688

m. 1706

Arran Mackenzie, 1680

Conall Mackenzie

— Cailean Mackenzie, b. 1711

m. 1742

Daisy Bristol, b. 1713
Lady Chatwick

(Previous marriage)

Georgina Mackenzie, b. 1747

Ellis, *Lord Chatwick*

m. 1751

Avaline Kent, b. 1732

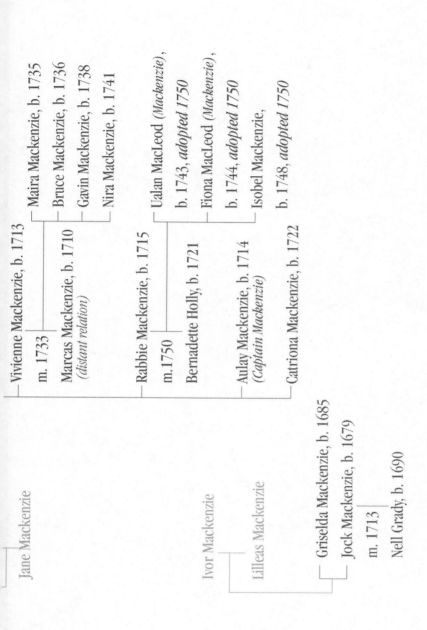

Jane Mackenzie

Vivienne Mackenzie, b. 1713
m. 1733
Marcas Mackenzie, b. 1710
(distant relation)

Maira Mackenzie, b. 1735
Bruce Mackenzie, b. 1736
Gavin Mackenzie, b. 1738
Nira Mackenzie, b. 1741

Rabbie Mackenzie, b. 1715
m.1750
Bernadette Holly, b. 1721

Ualan MacLeod (Mackenzie),
b. 1743, adopted 1750
Fiona MacLeod (Mackenzie),
b. 1744, adopted 1750
Isobel Mackenzie,
b. 1748, adopted 1750

Aulay Mackenzie, b. 1714
(Captain Mackenzie)
Catriona Mackenzie, b. 1722

Ivor Mackenzie

Lilleas Mackenzie

Griselda Mackenzie, b. 1685
Jock Mackenzie, b. 1679
m. 1713
Nell Grady, b. 1690

CHAPTER ONE

*Lismore Island, The Highlands, Scotland,
1752*

The Campbell men landed on the north
shore of the small Scottish island of Lismore in the light of the setting sun, fanning
out along the narrow strip of sand and stepping between the rocks and the rabbits that
had infested the island.

They were looking for stills.

They also were looking for a ship, perhaps
tucked away in some hidden cove they'd
not yet found. The stills and the ship were
here, and they would find them.

Duncan Campbell, the new laird of Lismore, knew that his tenants — some two-
hundred odd Livingstones — were gathered
to celebrate *Sankt Hans,* or Midsummer's
Eve, a custom that harkened back to their
Danish ancestors who had settled this small
island.

The Livingstones, to the Campbell way of

thinking, were laggards and generally far too idle . . . until recently, that was, when it had come to Duncan's attention that this hapless clan had begun to distill whisky spirits without license. He'd heard it said in a roundabout way, in Oban, and in Port Appin. Livingstones were boastful, too, it would seem. Rumor had it that an old Danish ship had been outfitted to hold several casks and a few men.

Where the Livingstones lacked godly ambition, the Campbells fancied themselves a clan of superior moral character. They were Leaders of Scotland, Pillars of the Highlands, Ministers of Social Justice, and they distilled whisky *with a license* and sold it for a tidy profit *all very legally.* They did not take kindly to illicit whisky that undercut their legitimate business. They were downright offended when someone traded cheap spirits against their superior brew. They disliked illegal competition so much that they took great pains to find it and destroy it by all means possible. Fire was a preferred method.

The Campbell men creeping along the beach could hear the Livingstone voices raised in song and laughter, the strains of a fiddle. When night fell, those heathens would be well into their cups and would light a bonfire and dance around it. Bloody drunkards. But alas, the Campbells did not make it more than a few dozen steps into their search when they heard the warning horn. It sounded so shrilly that it scattered rabbits here and there and, frankly, made Duncan's heart leap. He hardly had a moment to collect himself before buckshot whizzed overhead.

Duncan sighed skyward. He looked at his escort, Mr. Edwin MacColl, whose clan inhabited the south end of Lismore, and who was diligent in paying his rents and not distilling whisky. Duncan had pressed the very reluctant Scotsman into service by threatening to raise his rents if he didn't lend a hand. "That's it, then, is it no'?" he asked MacColl as another shot rang out and sent up a spray of sand when it hit the bit of beach. "They've seen us and warned the others."

"Aye," MacColl agreed. "They keep a close eye on what is theirs. As any Scot would," he added meaningfully.

Campbell recognized the subtle needling, but there was no opportunity to remind MacColl that illegal whisky was bad, very bad, because four riders appeared on the hill above them with long guns pointed at their chests. Naturally, Miss Lottie Livingstone, who, as daughter of the chief here, ran wild on this island, led them. If she were *his* daughter, Campbell would have taken her in hand and ended her feral behavior tout de suite.

"Laird Campbell!" she called cheerfully, and nudged her horse to walk down the grassy slope to the beach. "You've come *again*!"

Campbell groaned. "Must it be so bloody *difficult* to root out corruption and illegal deeds?" he muttered to MacColl. "Must the most beautiful lass in all of Scotland be the most unruly and untamed of them all?"

Apparently, Mr. MacColl had no answer to that, and in fact, he turned his head so that Duncan could not see his face. Duncan rolled his eyes and addressed the woman who lived like an undomesticated cat on this island. "Hold your fire, aye, Miss Livingstone? I am your laird after all!" As if that needed explaining.

"How can we help you, laird?" she asked.

"No' you, lass. I'll have a word with your father."

Her eyes sparked, and above another glittering smile she said, "Oh, but he'll be delighted, he *will*."

The lass had a way of giggling sometimes when she spoke that made Duncan wonder if she was laughing at him or was just a wee bit off her head. He called in his men, and motioned for them to follow along as he and MacColl trudged up the hill toward the Livingstone manor.

If they couldn't find the stills and Livingstone would not own to them, then by God, Campbell would inquire about the past due rents. He'd have something for his trouble.

CHAPTER TWO

Two weeks later
The North Sea
The wind out of the west was light, but brought with it heavy clouds. Nevertheless, the *Reulag Balhaire* was sailing along just as she ought to be, the sedative dip and rise of the ship's bow into the rolling waves a steady reminder that all was right.

Captain Aulay Mackenzie listened to the sound of his crew calling out to each other as they manned the sails. He closed his eyes and felt the mist of the sea on his face, the wind ruffling the queue of his hair. It was days like this — well, he preferred those glorious, sunfilled days — but days at sea when he felt most himself. When he was most at home. He was in command of his ship, of his spirit, of his world. It was, perhaps, the only place in his life that was so.

It had been too long since he'd been at

16

sea — a few months, but to him, a lifetime. Aulay chafed at life at his family's home of Balhaire. He had lived his entire adult life at sea, and every day away from his ship was a day something was missing. He was useless at Balhaire. His father was chief of the Mackenzie clan. His older brother, Cailen, was his father's agent, his face to the world. Rabbie, Aulay's younger brother, managed the day-to-day business of the sprawling estate of Balhaire, along with his youngest sister, Catriona. His mother was engaged in the social aspects, as was his sister Vivienne. And Aulay? He had no useful purpose there. Nothing worthwhile to occupy his days. He was merely an observer on land.

His father had begun the Mackenzie sea trade when he was a young man, and it had flourished under his clever eye, and as his sons grew, with them as well. Their trade had suffered in the wake of the Battle of Culloden some seven years ago. After the brutal defeat of the Jacobite uprising, the Highlands had been decimated first by English forces, and then by economics. The new economy was moving the Highlands from small croft farms to wide-ranging sheep herding. Great numbers of Highlanders, having lost their livelihood, were leaving for greener fields in Glasgow and beyond.

The Mackenzies of Balhaire had not been involved in the conflict, but nonetheless, they'd lost half their clan to it, had seen their livestock and a second ship seized by the crown. Still, they'd hung on to this ship and with it, a dwindling trade. With the last round of repairs, his father had wanted to end their trade business altogether. "It's no use," he'd said. "It costs more to sail than we bring, aye? We've lost ground to the MacDonalds, we have."

Aulay had panicked slightly at such talk. He didn't know who he was without a ship. He didn't know what he'd do.

But then a miracle had happened. Aulay, chafing at the loss of some trade, had gone in search of more. He'd struck an agreement with William Tremayne of Port Glasgow. William was an Englishman, but he was an agent with goods to trade and in need of a vessel to carry them. Aulay was a captain with an empty ship. It seemed a perfect match. And yet, his father and brothers had argued against the deal. It was too much risk, they said, to carry another man's cargo. Aulay had assured them there was no risk. Was he not a fine captain? Had he not delivered and brought home countless holds full of goods? He had prevailed in the end, but his father's skepticism was quite evident.

This was his maiden voyage for Tremayne. The ship was loaded with wool and salted beef, in route for Amsterdam and then on to Cadiz where they would load cotton for the return.

The men aboard were in high spirits, as Mackenzie seafaring was their livelihood, and they needed the work. So was Aulay in a fine mood. He'd not been to Amsterdam in some time, and there was a wench there, a lass who had eyes like two obsidian rocks and a lush mouth upon whom he intended to call.

He was thinking about the way she moved beneath him when a *boom* startled him. It sounded a bit like thunder, but not quite that.

"Got a light on the starboard side, captain!" one of the men up on the masts called down.

Aulay turned to the starboard side and was joined by his first mate, Beaty. It wasn't a light, precisely, but a glow. "That's fire, aye?" he asked Beaty, who was peering through a spyglass.

"Aye," Beaty grunted.

"Wind is rising, too," said Iain the Red, who had come to the railing to have a look. "They'll be naugh' they can do to stop the spread if it rises much more."

"*Och,* she's sailing toward land," said the wizened old swab, Beaty. His looks were deceiving — he was thick and ruddy, but still as nimble as he'd been as a lad some forty years ago. He hiked himself up onto a batten of the main mast, one arm hooked around a thick rope in the shroud as he held the spyglass with the other to have another look. "She's sailing at five, six knots if she's moving one. She'll make landfall ere it's too late if the cap'n keeps his bloody head."

"Is there a flag?" Aulay asked.

"Aye, a royal flag, Cap'n. Ship looks too small for navy, it does, but that's the Union Jack she flies."

Aulay gestured for the spyglass. He hopped upon the mast shroud with a sureness of foot that came from having spent his life at sea and peered into the thickening gray of sky and ocean. He could make out men trimming sails to better catch the wind while others lowered buckets into the sea and threw water on the flames to douse them. Ships didn't generally catch fire on their own, not without a strike of lightning or some such, and they'd not seen any hint of that. Aulay studied the horizon, casting the spyglass in the opposite direction of the burning ship's course, trying to discern wave from sky —

"Aye, there she is, then," he said. He'd marked another, smaller ship. It appeared that it had lost the top half of its main mast. He pointed and handed the spyglass to Beaty, then hopped down from the shroud.

"My guess is a fly boat," Beaty said, peering at it.

"A fly boat!" Iain exclaimed, snorting at the idea of the small Dutch ship. "Ought no' to be in open sea, no' a fly boat. They're for sailing the coast, they are."

"We're no' so far from the coast," said someone else. "Perhaps she's adrift, aye?"

Aulay glanced around at his men, who had gathered round to have a look. It felt good to be on board with them again. It put him in good spirits, in need of a bit of adventure. "Shall we have a look, then?"

The *Reulag Balhaire* was not in the business of saving other ships. It was generally considered unwise to approach another ship unless one was prepared to have a hull shattered by cannon fire. But their curiosity was aroused. The burning ship was just a spot in the distance now, so they'd set course for the starboard side of the smaller ship, a gun pointed at the forecastle in the event there was trouble.

Aulay watched the smaller ship slowly come into view, its outline muted against the darkening sky, the clouds weighing down on the masts. It wasn't until they were almost on the ship that they could see it was listing.

Iain the Red was studying it as they approached. "No' a fly boat, no," he said. "A *bilander.*"

"A *bilander*!" Beaty blustered. "What nonsense!"

Whether a fly boat or *bilander,* neither were particularly well suited for the open seas. "Is there a flag?" he asked.

"No." Iain the Red paused, then laughed. "Look at them now, trying to lower the sail." He laughed again with great amusement. "They look like children romping around a bloody maypole! Look at them trying to untangle those shroud lines, aye? They're twisted up every which way — *oof,* there went one, down on his arse!"

The men gathered at the railing to watch, and laughed at the blundering of the crew on the other ship as they tried to free a sail from a broken mast with what looked like a lot of pushing and shoving. "Aye, give it over, Iain, lets have a look," one said, and they began to pass the spyglass around, all of them doubling over with mirth.

The spyglass came back around to Iain, but when he held it up, he stopped laughing. *"Diah, de an diabhal?"* he exclaimed and lowered the instrument, turning a wide-eyed look to Aulay.

"What, then?" Aulay asked, feeling a mild tic of alarm, imagining a gun pointed at them, or a pirate's flag being raised.

"A *lady,*" Iain said, as if he'd never seen one.

A lady? It was not unheard of for one to be on the high seas; wives of captains sometimes sailed with them. If it were anyone else, a lady of importance, she'd not be sailing on a rickety boat like that.

"In a proper gown and *everything,*" Iain said, his voice full of awe.

Aulay didn't know what a *proper gown* meant to Iain, so he motioned for the spyglass to have a look. He could scarcely make her out, but it was definitely a woman standing at the railing, holding a white flag that almost matched the color of hair that whipped long and unbound about her face. There were a few men beside her, all of them clinging to the railing, all of them looking rather desperately in the direction of his ship.

Aulay instructed Beaty to maneuver closer, and when there was nothing but a

23

small bit of sea between the two ships, the men's frantic attention to the sail on the other ship was forgotten in favor of lowering a jolly boat down the hull. There was more chaotic shoving among them until four men scrambled down a rope ladder into the boat and began to row with abandon toward the *Reulag Balhaire.* The woman remained behind on the ship's deck with a few men, including one that was the size of a small mountain, towering a head above all the others.

When the smaller boat reached them, one of the men grabbed on to the rope ladder to steady them, and one rose to standing, bracing his legs apart to keep his balance. *"Madainn mhath,"* he called up, and with an affected swirl of his hand, he bowed low. And very nearly tipped over the side when a swell caught him unawares.

"Scots, then," Beaty said. "That's something, at least."

"We are in need of your help, kind sirs!" the man called up, having managed to right himself. "We've been set upon by pirates, aye?" He spoke with a strange cadence, as if he were a town crier delivering this news to a crowded venue.

The men did not carry swords or guns that Aulay could see. It seemed all they could do to keep the jolly from tipping too far to one side. "That ship flew the colors of the king," he called down.

The spokesman looked startled. He squatted down to consult the other men in his small boat. A flurry of shaking heads and talking over one another ensued, until the man stood up again and said, "She flew no such flag when she fired, on me word, sir! She fired with no provocation from us!" He pressed his hand to his chest quite earnestly.

"No' bloody likely," Iain muttered.

"Why do I feel as if I am watching a theatrical performance?" Aulay asked idly. "What do you think, then, Beaty? Could a freebooter put his hands on a royal flag?"

"More likely a privateer," Beaty said, referring to those private ships holding a royal commission. "They're no' above a bit of pirating, are they? Might have nicked a flag, I suppose."

Perhaps. It was hard to argue who'd advanced on whom when they'd not witnessed it. But it seemed unlikely that a privateer or pirate would have engaged this ship. It was too small to hold anything of quantity or value.

Aulay leaned over the railing. "What have you on board that invited attack?"

"Naugh' but a lady, captain!"

"Who is the lady, then?"

That question prompted more spirited discussion on the jolly boat.

"What, then, they donna know the lady?" Iain snorted.

Once again, the man straightened up, put his fist to his waist and called out, "Our Lady Larsen, sir! We are carrying her home to her ailing grandmamma!" He paused, put a hand to his throat and said, "Tis a journey of *great* and *intolerable* sadness, as the lady's grandmamma is no' expected to live!"

Larson. Aulay did not know the name.

"An ailing grandmamma my arse," Beaty muttered.

Aulay was likewise suspicious. These men seemed to have no idea what they were doing, who was on board, or even how to mount a sail and sally forth to dear old Grandmamma. Moreover, the man had the peculiar habit of speaking as if he were acting in a play. "Where is your destination?" Aulay called.

"Denmark, captain. Her grandmamma is a Dane, she is, but we are Scots, like you."

"Never knew a clever Dane," Iain mused. "No' a single one."

"Aye, she has the look of an heiress," said one of the crew, holding the spyglass to his eye. The man next to him punched him in

26

the arm and grabbed the spyglass as if he'd been waiting too long for his turn and was cross about it.

Apparently, the men had been passing it around to view the woman while Aulay, Beaty and Iain focused on the men below.

"Been sailing long?" Beaty called down.

"A day," the man said.

"No, lad, I mean, what sort of seaman are you, then?"

"Well that's the interesting thing, sir, aye? We are no' seaman. No' a one of us a sailor, save our captain. We're but Christian soldiers on an errand of mercy. Able-bodied, aye, willing to try. But no', as such, sailors."

"Bloody damn curious," Beaty muttered, his thick brow furrowed.

"Agreed," Aulay said.

Billy Botly, the youngest and smallest of the crew, was the last to receive the spyglass, and he had to fight for it. He was so slight that a good, strong wind would knock him overboard if he weren't careful, and as he swung one leg over the edge of the hull to have a look, Aulay feared precisely that. "Aye, an *heiress,*" the lad said, a wee bit dreamily.

Aulay reached over Billy's shoulder, took the spyglass from him and had a look himself. The lady was still standing there, still clutching the white flag against her chest, her hands crossed over it as if she feared she would lose it.

He lowered the spyglass again and peered down at the man. "Aye, and what do you want from me, then? I've no time to ferry anyone to her ailing grandmamma."

His crew chuckled derisively in agreement.

"The ship, sir, she's taking on water, that she is. We'll no' last through the night."

"Should no' have sailed in a ship no' meant for open water, then," Beaty called down. Apparently, Beaty was the only man aboard who was not moved by the sight of a comely lady in dire circumstances.

"Aye, but we've the miss and her father, wounded in the fight, he was. She's no one to look after her."

"You expect me to do the looking after?" Aulay asked and laughed roundly with his crew. He was bound for Amsterdam, and he'd not be late. This voyage was crucial for his family, and he firmly believed it had the potential to grow into something quite lucrative for the Mackenzies, in spite of his father's misgivings. After years of scraping by, Aulay was resolved to prove they could restore their trade.

"Just need a port, sir, that's it," the man

called up as he gripped the hem of his waistcoat in a nervous manner. They all seemed slightly agitated, each of them stealing looks at their damaged ship, as if they expected her to slip under the water while they had their backs turned.

"You'll make landfall by night," he called to them. "Go back the way you've come, aye? That's what your attacker has done. You've two good sails yet and the wind will carry you if you trim them properly. *Gun déid leat,*" he said, wishing them the best of luck, and turned away from the railing, his intent to be done with this unusual event at sea.

"Captain, sir!" the man shouted frantically. "She's taking on water too fast, can you no' see with your own eyes? It's a *miracle* of *heaven* that you've come at all, and we *rejoice* in our fortune! We were drawing straws to see who would take the lady and her father in the jolly and who among us would be doomed to *drown*! Will you turn your back on us now?"

"Aye, Cap'n, she's sinking," Billy said anxiously.

"What is the matter with him, then?" Iain asked curiously, eying the man in the boat. "Why does he speak in that fancy manner?"

Why indeed did he speak in that manner,

29

and who set sail with no experienced hands? It all seemed rather odd, but as Aulay was mulling it over, they heard a groan of wood from the other ship. The winds were picking up, and a strong wave had rocked it, making it list even more. He lifted the spyglass. The woman was clutching the arm of the mountain of a man beside her.

Bloody hell. The ship was sinking.

"How many of you are there?"

"Ten!" the man said.

One of the other men punched his leg and spoke. They exchanged a few words and then he said, "I beg your pardon, only eight!"

"Are they so inept they canna count the souls on board?" Aulay muttered.

"Fools," Beaty agreed.

Aulay debated. He was a man of the sea and he understood that sometimes, the sea won. All of them, to a man . . . well, with the exception of Billy, perhaps . . . understood the risks involved every time they made sail. The thrill of that risk drove them. But there was something about that woman clinging to the man across the way that tugged at Aulay's conscience. An unwelcome and disturbing image of his younger sister, Catriona, popped into his head, and he inwardly shuddered at the thought of her standing in that lady's shoes. "Verra well," he said. "Bring the lady and your men, then. Bring what provisions you have, aye? I donna intend to feed the lot of you. And you can expect to work for your passage."

"Of course. *Thank* you, captain, thank you," the man said, and quickly motioned for the men to row.

As they turned the small boat about, banging into the ship's hull as they did, Beaty sighed loudly and gave Aulay a sidelong look.

"What, then, you'd have the lady drown?" Aulay asked.

"No!" Billy cried.

"No," Beaty admitted reluctantly. "But there are too many of them, and one of them so large that he'll be as much trouble as three, he will. Where will they sleep, then? Have we enough water for them all? And what of these fools?" he asked, gesturing to Aulay's crew, all of them still at the railing, still chattering about the woman. "You'd think they'd never seen a lass."

"We'll put them in the hold with a night guard, aye?" Aulay said.

"Shall we arm ourselves?" Beaty asked.

Aulay glanced at the listing ship. "They are no threat to us."

31

Beaty's response was muttered under his breath.

It took two trips to bring all of them. When the first batch of men was delivered, along with a crate of food, Beaty demanded irritably, "Why'd you no' bring the lady, then, if you're so fearful of her drowning?"

"She willna come until her father can be brought," said the man who had first spoken to them from the jolly.

They watched the second batch of men come, and when they were delivered safely on board, they stood with the first batch at the rail in an anxious cluster, their eyes on the jolly as two of them returned to the listing ship.

Not one of them looked like a sailor to Aulay. Most of them didn't seem to have their sea legs, stumbling and banging into each other as the ship bobbed on the swells and they sought their balance. It was all very odd. He was impatient, too — the transfer was taking far too long. The *Reulag Balhaire* had to keep tacking around to keep from drifting too far from the smaller ship. Aulay watched the progress of the last few. The enormous man who had remained behind with the lady singlehandedly lowered a figure in a rope sling to the waiting boat. Next came the lady, climbing down the rope ladder with surprising agility. She leaped into the boat, foregoing any of the hands offered up, then turned her head up to direct the larger man. He began to make his way down, too, but much more clumsily — lumbering, really, appearing to have trouble fitting his feet into the slots along the ladder. When he at last made his way into the boat, the inhabitants had to fan out to both sides to keep the small boat steady and accommodate his girth, and the boat itself seemed to sit lower in the water as they began the laborious progress across.

As the small boat neared the Mackenzie ship, all the men strained to have a look at the woman. She kept her head down, her attention on the injured man. The only distinguishable thing about her was the unbound hair. Long hair that looked almost as white as snow, a beacon against the gray sky and sea.

When the boat came alongside the ship, Aulay's men crowded around, each juggling to be the one to help the lady up, and if pushed aside, hanging over the railing to have a look. Two men came aboard first, and together, they lifted the injured man with a pair of ropes. There was quite a lot of commotion as that man was carried off to one of the cabins. Aulay's men scarcely gave the injured man a look — they were clearly far more interested in the ascent of the woman, all of them craning their necks, and some of his crew swaggering about the railing like roosters as they called their encouragement to her.

Aulay saw the crown of her head as she hopped over the railing and onto the deck. *"Madainn Mhath,"* she said, as if she were greeting guests at a tea party. The men crowded closer.

"*Och,* let the lass breathe, then," Iain the Red said crossly. "Billy, lad, give the lady room."

"Are you all right, then?" asked Fingal MacDonald, one of Aulay's crew.

"Verra well, thank you." Her voice had a pleasing lilt to it. "If you please, sirs, might you step back a wee bit, then? I canna move."

"Give way, give way!" Iain shouted at them.

There was a shuffling, but none of his men gave an inch to another. Iain shoved one man aside, and when he did, Aulay caught a glimpse of an elegant hand as the woman pushed hair from her temple.

"You're unharmed, are you?" Beaty asked, and judging by the concern in his voice, Aulay guessed his disdain for this rescue had completely dissipated.

"Oh aye, thank you," she said. "I've had quite a fright, that's all."

"You've quite a lot of blood on your gown," Beaty said.

"Do I?"

Her lyrical voice was oddly accented, with a slight hint of a Scots brogue and a proper English accent. It reminded Aulay a wee bit of his mother, who was English by birth but had lived in Scotland for nearly forty years now, and had a similar accent.

"Aye, indeed I *do,*" she said, sounding surprised. "Never mind it — I fear more for my father."

At that moment, the lumbering giant came over the railing, and it felt almost as if the ship tipped a wee bit. "What am I to do, Lottie?" he asked. "I donna recollect what I'm to do."

The giant of a man sounded like a dullard.

"Stay close," she said sweetly. "You're all so verra kind," she said to Aulay's men in that lilting voice. "I should like to thank your captain, aye? Might you point him out?"

There was a lot of shuffling about, muttered *pardons* — a word, incidentally, Aulay had never heard his men use before. But these men, as rough and bawdy as any he'd

35

ever known, seemed almost bashful now. They were stumbling over each other to allow the lady to pass.

When they'd cleared a path, Aulay instantly understood what held them in such thrall. The first thing he noticed about her was her hair, a thick wave of unbound silk, the blond of it so light that it reminded Aulay of the color of pearls. Next, her eyes, large orbs the same color as the warm coastal waters of the Caribbean Sea. Plump, rose-colored lips that could bedevil a man. Her almost angelic beauty was as surprising as it was incongruent next to the men in her company. This young woman was *bòidheach.* Beautiful. To his eye, a pulse-fluttering sight.

Something strong and strange waved through Aulay. He felt himself standing on the cusp of something quite big, as if part of him hung in the balance. He innately understood the feeling. It was something he'd experienced the first time he'd ever been on a ship and had known that would be his life. Or the first time he'd ever lain with a woman. Aulay just *knew.* He was not one to flatter unnecessarily, but he was bedeviled.

As she approached him, her warm blue eyes fixed on his, that strange feeling of intoxication waved through him again. Her cheeks were pinkened from the wind and from her scrambling about, and her hair, *Diah,* her *hair* — it was falling wildly about her face in ethereal wisps. She wore a gown of silver silk over a blue petticoat, the stomacher cinched so tightly that it scarcely contained plump breasts.

Beaty pointed at Aulay, apparently incapable of speech, and even Aulay, who had heretofore thought himself inured to the effects of beautiful women after spending his life in so many ports of call, was a wee bit tongue-tied.

"Captain," she said, and dipped into a curtsy. "*Thank* you."

Aulay slipped his hand under her elbow and lifted her up with the vague thought that she ought not to bow to anyone.

The ship pitched a little, and she caught his arm as if to steady herself, her fingers spreading over his coat and squeezing lightly. "You've my undying gratitude, you do," she said. "I donna know what we might have done had you no' come along to rescue us." She smiled.

An invisible band tightened around Aulay's chest and his breathing felt suddenly short. He realized that hers was not a perfect beauty, but taken altogether, she was one of the most beautiful women he'd ever seen.

"You'd no' believe what we've been made to endure this day," she said, and pressed that slender, elegant hand to her heart. "On my word, I thought we'd perish. You've saved our *lives,* good sir!"

"Who have I the pleasure of saving, then?" Aulay asked as his gaze traveled over her face, to her décolletage, her trim waist.

"Oh dear me," she said, and smiled sheepishly as his men closed in around them, straining to hear. "The ordeal has robbed me of my manners, it has. Larson, sir. Lady Larson."

"Madam," he said, and bowed his head. "Captain Mackenzie of Balhaire at your service."

"Balhaire, of course!" she said delightedly. "No' an angel from heaven then, but the Mackenzies are legend all the same." She smiled again with sunny gratitude.

Aulay was confused by the notion of being called an angel and the idea she should know his name, but again, he felt strangely and uncharacteristically tongue-tied.

"Did you see them, then?" she asked, pushing more hair from her face. "The pirates?"

Her eyes, one slightly larger than the

other, were unusually bright, sparkling like a clear spring day.

"Thieves, they were. They attacked us without reason." She turned slightly, addressing all the men. "There we were, sailing without a care and getting on verra well, mind, as we've little experience at sea. Save our captain, of course," she said, and gestured to a man with narrow shoulders and hips. He clasped his hands behind him and bowed gallantly. "When suddenly, out of the mist, a much larger ship appeared and was bearing down us."

"How did they make contact?" Aulay asked curiously.

She turned those shining blue eyes to him again. "With a *cannon*!" she said dramatically. "We did naugh' to deserve it! We had scarcely noticed them at all, and then, *boom!*" She threw her arms wide, and her breasts very nearly lifted from her bodice, and all the men swayed back, as if expecting them to launch. When they didn't, his men quickly shifted closer.

"My poor father has been badly injured with a wound to his torso," she added, her smile fading.

"And so have you," Beaty said, pointing to a rip in the fabric of the skirt of her gown and the bloodstains around it.

She glanced down, to where he pointed. "Oh, aye, indeed. I'd forgotten it in all the confusion."

"Ought to have a look at it, Miss Livingstone," said one of her men, who stood somewhere behind the crowd of Aulay's men. "Gangrene and the like."

Gangrene. Aulay rolled his eyes.

"Gangrene!" she cried, alarmed.

"I think you need no' worry of that," Beaty said, glancing peevishly at whoever had said it.

Lady Larson suddenly leaned down, gathered the hem of her skirt, and lifted it to midcalf.

Aulay's men surged forward like a wave of cocks and balls, their gazes riveted on her leg, and the little boots and stockings she wore. "I donna see it. I suppose it's a wee bit higher still," she said, and much to Aulay's surprise, she lifted the hem to her knee.

He was completely devoid of thought in that moment. She lifted the gown higher still, past the top of her stocking, so that they could see her bare thigh, the flesh pale white and as smooth as milk. There was indeed a small gash there, but neither very deep or long, and certainly not one that could account for all the blood on her gown.

The lady glanced up at the men, and her

gaze settled on Aulay. "Do you think it is *verra* bad?" she asked prettily, practically inviting him to have a closer look as she thrust her leg forward. "Can any of you *see*?"

Aulay never had the opportunity to answer. A sudden and loud explosion from the other ship startled them all — at which point, Aulay suddenly recalled that the difference between a *bilander* and a fly boat was that a bilander generally carried a small gun or two.

Before he could utter a word or a command, he was struck from behind with such force that he was thrown to the deck and his wits were knocked from him. He instantly tried to stand, but the ship felt as if it was spinning, and he couldn't seem to move his legs properly. He managed to claw his way up to his knees, then looked up, saw the luminescent blue eyes of Lady Larson gazing down at him. She smiled ruefully and said, "I am so *verra* sorry," and kicked her knee squarely into his jaw with the strength to send him backward.

Aulay grabbed for the railing to pull himself up. He found his footing, was reaching for her when he was struck on the head once more.

The last thing he could register before

everything faded to black was that after all these years, he'd at last been felled at sea. Not by battle or storm, but by a woman.

CHAPTER THREE

When the *Margit* had set sail from the shores of Lismore, it had never occurred to Lottie that a scant two days later, she would have somehow become a pirate — at least that's what she thought she should be called after what she'd done.

The bedlam had settled, and the Livingstones had won the battle, such that it was. She and her clan had caught the unsuspecting Mackenzies so completely off their guard. What stretched before them now was disaster on a scale so vast, Lottie still couldn't catch her breath. A sharp pain kept pulsing at her temples as she tried to sort through it all. How in God's name had they lost one ship and stolen another all in the stretch of a day?

That had most certainly *not* been the plan.

She gazed down at her wounded father. They'd put him in the captain's cabin for want of any other suitable place. The forecastle held two Mackenzie men and one Livingstone, all of them injured, but none of them mortally, thank the saints. Morven, the closest thing to healer the Livingstones had, was sure of it.

Her father, however, was not so fortunate. Lottie could scarcely look at his gray pallor without feeling bilious, and even more so when she looked at the blood that soaked the bandages they'd put around the gaping hole in his torso.

He was groaning now, reaching for Lottie's hand. And everyone else? The men who were still on their feet and crowded around her? They were all offering their varied opinions about what they ought to do, then looking to her to choose. All of them but Gilroy, the captain of the *Margit* and her father's friend of more than forty years. He stood at the porthole, watching his ship pitch and roll and drift away, its bow under water.

"What do we do now?" asked Norval Livingstone.

Diah, but Lottie's head hurt. She wished everyone would stop looking to her to solve everything. Could they not see she'd made a mess of things thus far? The terror and panic that had shot through her when Gilroy shouted they'd taken a shot to the bow and were taking on water had blinded her to all common sense. They didn't know who attacked them, they didn't know why, and had only one gun on board to fight the larger ship, one they scarcely knew how to fire. But fire it they had, and the cannon shot had hit something explosive on the other ship and had sent flames shooting into the air. All quite by accident — she thought it nothing short of magical that they'd hit the ship at all. Just as quickly as it had come upon them, that ship turned about and fled toward Scotland.

She should have done what Gilroy advised once the fighting had ended and the other ship had fled. She should have agreed to let the crew draw straws to see who would accompany her and her father back to Scotland on the jolly boat, while the others tried to sail the listing ship back to shore. But then someone had shouted another ship was approaching, and her father had begged her not to turn back and Lottie had come up with an impetuous, foolish, *dangerous* plan that she prayed would save them all.

It was so absurd that she still couldn't believe it had *worked*.

"Aye, well then, Gilroy, what do you see?" asked Duff MacGuire. He was the resident thespian of the Livingstone clan and had played the part of spokesman on the jolly when the Mackenzie ship had come to their aid.

"It has begun to rain," Gilroy said flatly. "And my ship has sunk."

He turned his back to the porthole. There were lines on his face Lottie had never seen before. "We should no' have sailed her," he said morosely. "I said as much to Bernt, I did, but he convinced me ours was a noble endeavor. *Diah,* she's gone now."

"I'm so verra sorry, Gilroy," Lottie muttered.

"I donna like it," Drustan said, his voice full of panic. Lottie's younger brother was rocking back and forth on his heels, but because he was so unusually large, he kept knocking into the table. She put her hand on his arm to calm him, but he was staring with horror at their father, a bead of perspiration sliding down his temple. He was confused. But then again, poor Drustan was always confused. He'd been born with the cord wrapped round his neck and had very nearly died. He'd never been quite right.

Lottie's mother had always said Drustan was special in ways unlike anyone else. "Mark me, that lad has a brilliance in him. We've just no' discovered it yet."

"Donna worry about Fader," Lottie said

to Drustan. "He's quite strong. You know that he is. He's sleeping now because Morven gave him a sleeping draught so that he might heal, aye? You and Mats go with Gilroy now. There's much work to be done." She looked to Gilroy for confirmation, but the man was studying his feet, lost in thought.

Mathais, Lottie's brash and youngest brother, moved to her side, his chest puffed like a fat pigeon. He'd only recently turned fourteen years to Drustan's twenty years and her twenty-three. He had the heart of a warrior, but was still a child. He declared, "*I'll* go, Lot. You need no' send Drustan. He'll only be in the way, he will."

Lottie was too despondent to argue. "Aye, go," she said, waving a hand at Mathais. "Take Drustan with you."

Mathais rolled his eyes.

"Gilroy?"

"Hmm?" He glanced up.

"Should no' someone sail the ship, then?" she asked gently.

His brow furrowed as if the thought had just occurred to him. "Do you mean to say no one is sailing her?"

"Well who would sail it, Gilroy?" Duff asked with exasperation.

"Bloody hell, have we all lost our minds?"

47

Gilroy demanded sternly, and began to make his way out of the overstuffed cabin.

Mathais pivoted about to follow Gilroy and tripped over his own feet, which seemed to grow another inch each week. Drustan, who towered above them all, hurried behind Mats as if he was afraid he might lose him.

That left Duff and Robert MacLean with Lottie. Mr. MacLean was the one who kept the Livingstone books. In other words, he was the one who came round once a week to explain to Lottie and her father that their funds were dwindling. He was revered among the Livingstones for his creative accounting capabilities. "We should turn back, ere it's too late," she suggested to them.

"Nonsense!" Duff said. "We're no' three days from Denmark. Your father would no' abide it if you turned back now, what with all we've done."

"But his injury is *severe,*" Lottie said, swallowing down a swell of nausea, having seen the gaping wound in his belly. But she could not seem to swallow the bit of hysteria that followed.

"Morven is as good a healer as comes from the Highlands, aye?" said Mr. MacLean. "He canna have better care at Lismore. And besides, Lottie, Bernt wants you to carry on, does he no'?"

She didn't want to be reminded of the horror of this morning, but nodded that yes, he had told her in no uncertain terms to carry on. "But we canna keep him here in the captain's quarters." All three of them glanced around to the figure in the corner of the room, the captain of the *Reulag Balhaire,* bound and gagged and shackled to a desk that had been built into the wall, and at present, very much unconscious. He'd sustained a few blows, but it was the tincture Morven had managed to pour down his throat that had stopped his shouting and cursing. "Me granny always said this would put a horse on his rump," Morven had said, shaking his head at the vial he held, clearly in awe of its powers as the captain had sunk into the depths of oblivion.

"Leave him be, Lottie," Duff said. "The forward cabin is full, it is. It's either here, or below decks, which is currently occupied by angry men bound to each other and under guard. If you remove your father to the hold, he'll rouse them all to a fever, mark me."

"Donna fret for the captain, lass," Mr. MacLean had said. "He canna cause you harm now."

The three of them looked at the captain again. "Will he be all right?" Lottie asked.

"He'll be right as rain," Duff said with authority Lottie wasn't sure he possessed. "I reckon the captain's pride will suffer more than his body."

Diah, his body. When Lottie had first laid eyes on him as that sea of ogling men had parted, she'd been struck by how devilishly handsome he was. There he'd stood, quite resplendent in his trousers, with no coat or waistcoat, but only a lawn shirt, open at the collar. She'd not expected such a virile man to be captain of this ship, but someone more like Gilroy — older and bonier. And yet it wasn't his bonny looks that had made her heart leap so, but his eyes. It was the way he'd looked at her, with such heated contemplation that she could feel her skin blistering beneath his perusal.

"It's heartless to bring him so low as this," Lottie muttered, and turned away from the stunningly attractive man in chains, lest Duff and Robert see her guilt . . . or favorable regard. " 'Tis crime enough that we've taken his ship without his consent. I'd no' like to add injury or insult to it."

"*Och,* the deed has been done, lass," Duff said dismissively. " 'Tis no' a free society we've begun here, is it? He'll do as he's made to do, he will. What choice has he?"

Duff was right, of course, but that didn't

stop Lottie from feeling incredible remorse for what had happened. She didn't want to do any more to the men of the *Reulag Balhaire* than what she and her men had already forced on them. Oh, but this voyage had been badly conceived! They were in the midst of a living nightmare.

"Well then, we ought to be about helping where needed," Mr. MacLean said. "I donna trust Gilroy in his present state of mind." He glanced at Lottie. "You'll be all right, will you, lass?"

She looked at the unconscious captain, at her unconscious father, and shrugged. "Apparently so."

"Verra well, then," Mr. MacLean said, and opened the cabin door. "Someone will be just outside at all times," he reminded Lottie. "You need only call, aye?"

She watched them go out.

Silence. Blissful, golden silence. Everything had happened so fast! If she'd only had a wee bit of time to consider all the possibilities. But she hadn't, and not one man had disagreed with her plan. She needed time to think, to reassess, and thank heaven, for the first time since sailing from Lismore, Lottie was alone.

Well . . . not *alone.* But quiet.

She sank onto a chair, suddenly aware of

51

the heaviness that pervaded every limb, exhaustion settling in. She crossed her arms on the table, lay her head down on them and closed her eyes . . . but visions of the day plagued her mind's eye.

It was a *catastrophe* — there could be no other word that would adequately describe it. It had really begun a fortnight ago, in the early evening of *Sankt Hans,* the annual celebration of midsummer. The Livingstone clan had been preparing for a play, one written and produced by Duff. Duff fancied himself quite the actor, and he'd rallied a few members of the clan to join his theatrical troupe. There were six of them set to perform when they heard the warning horn from Old Donnie. He lived on the tip of the island just across the loch from Port Appin, and it was his job to sound the horn if anything or anyone should come to the island.

Everyone had frantically begun to gather up incriminating whisky jugs. "What of the play?" Duff had wailed unhappily.

It just so happened that Lottie's horse, Stjerne, was still saddled from her participation in the pony races, and when she saw Norval and Bear Livingstone leap to their horses, she joined them. It was the way of things on Lismore — she was always in the thick of things.

She'd not been the least surprised to find Laird Campbell, his periwig tightly curled and overly powdered, skulking among the rabbits. It wasn't his first attempt to find the stills. Naturally, Mr. Edwin MacColl, the chief of the clan who inhabited what the Livingstones considered to be the good side of their island, would accompany him.

Lottie had always liked Mr. MacColl as long as he stayed on his end of the island. He was a widower, his children grown and married with children of their own. He was older than Lottie's father, but still had a broad chest and thick, snowy brows that slid up when he smiled wistfully at Lottie as he was wont to do.

But his visits to the north end had become all too frequent of late, and quite recently, he'd suggested to Bernt that Lottie might make him a good wife. *"I've a nice house for her to keep, plenty of food for the table,"* he'd suggested, apparently considering these two facts to be his better points of persuasion.

Lottie had not been surprised by the offer. Frankly, on an island where unmarried lassies were not plentiful, every man seemed to believe himself her perfect match, just as her mother had predicted, God rest her soul.

Her mother had warned Lottie of her allure to males. "You're a beauty, lass, and men are drawn to beauty to their own detriment like moths to light, aye? You must no' allow them to turn your head with bonny words and empty promises. You *must* be diligent in seeking the man who honors you for your heart and no' your face, then, do you understand me? And beware your own father, lass — aye, he loves you, more than life, he does, but he's easily persuaded by the promises of others."

If her mother's words hadn't sufficiently cautioned her, Anders Iversen, her one and only lover, had driven her mother's point home.

Anyway, when Lottie had discovered the laird sneaking about, she'd escorted him to her home and had winced when her father emerged from the house a bit crookedly, a signal that he'd had too much drink.

"Ah, Laird Campbell. *Fàilte!*" her father said with great congeniality. No matter what trouble, he was always a jolly, carefree man. Lottie had come off her horse and had started inside with the men, but the laird had turned abruptly and said, "If you would, Miss Livingstone, give the men an opportunity to speak plainly. This is no' the sort of talk appropriate for your ears."

Lottie had bristled and had opened her mouth to suggest that was for her and her father to determine, but her father had said, "Aye, of course, laird. Lottie, lass, go and . . . have a look at the celebration, aye?" he'd said, waving his hand rather dismissively at her as he'd seen the laird inside.

An interminable amount of time seemed to have passed before the laird and Mr. MacColl finally emerged from the house, bid her good day — Mr. MacColl with a sheepish smile — and had returned to their boat. Lottie, Duff and Mr. MacLean had gone to her father straightaway to hear the news.

Naturally, her father had been completely unruffled by the laird's visit. "He came about the rents," Lottie's father informed them, then chuckled irreverently as he bent over and reached behind the sideboard and produced a flagon of whisky he'd hidden there.

"I said we donna have what's owed, no' yet, but, I says to him, *this* . . ." He paused and rapped his knuckles on his head, "is always about its work."

"Diah," Lottie groaned.

"And the laird, he said, well has *it* worked out precisely when the rents will be paid?" Her father laughed as he poured tots of whisky around for them all.

"And?" Lottie pressed him.

"I said we'd have them in a month."

Lottie's belly had sunk. A month was bloody well impossible.

Her father had waved his hand at her crestfallen expression. "Calm yourself, Lot. We'll think of something. Anything will be a wee sight better than what Campbell suggested, aye?"

"What?" she asked. "What did he suggest, then?"

"*Och,* he believes I ought to consider MacColl's offer to take my daughter to wife."

Lottie had gasped. She'd felt a little faint.

"Well of course he did! I've the bonniest daughter in all the Highlands, I've heard it said more than once. Why, there's no' a lad on Lismore who's no' pined for her, eh, Robert?"

Mr. MacLean's face had reddened at once and he'd turned his attention to his tot.

"But as I told the laird, while they've *all* pined for her, she pays none of them any heed at all, on account of her broken heart."

"Fader!" Lottie exclaimed, and felt the heat of humiliation creeping into her neck. "My heart is no' *broken.*"

"The laird insisted I ought to do as Mac-

Coll had offered, and give you over as his wife, and in exchange, MacColl would pay our rents and oversee the Livingstones and thereby solve a host of problems from one end of the island to the other."

"That's *quite* a lot of problems," Duff mused.

"I feel rather ill," Lottie had said, and had sunk on to the old settee.

"I am an admirer of Edwin MacColl, that I am," her father had blithely continued. "He's a right smart fellow, I've always said. But I've as good a plan as MacColl." He'd downed his whisky.

The only problem was that when her father had a good plan, disaster almost always loomed. "What plan?" Lottie had asked weakly.

"I'm coming round to that," he'd said, holding up his hand. "The laird was no' yet done with me, no," he'd continued as he poured more whisky for himself, clearly enjoying the retelling of his encounter. "He said I was bloody impractical."

"He didna," Mr. MacLean had said flatly, sounding quite offended in spite of the obvious truth in the laird's statement.

"He mentioned the limestone kilns, and the flax weaving," her father had said with an airy wave of his hand, as if dismissing

57

those two disastrous endeavors that had each ended badly and at considerable cost to the Livingstones. Bernt Livingstone was a whimsical man, scattered in his thoughts, impractical, and was easily gulled into schemes that fleeced their coffers. Once, when Lottie was a girl, there had been some talk of a new chief. But in the end, the Livingstones revered the code of the clan — Bernt was the grandson of Vilhelm Livingstone, A Danish baron, who had fled Denmark during the war with Sweden with a sizable fortune. He was their undisputed founder, and therefore, Bernt the rightful heir and chief.

Lottie could still recall how her father had stood in their salon that afternoon, his legs braced apart, his eyes gleaming with his plan. She lifted her head from her arms and looked at him. He was sleeping deeply with Morven's tincture, free from the pain of the hole in his abdomen for the moment. She adored her father, but if there was one thing that sent her into fits of madness, it was his impetuosity. He'd squandered his inheritance on fantastic plans that had never come to fruition.

It was times like these that Lottie missed her mother the most. She'd been good ballast for her husband. She'd been gone for more than ten years, alas, death taking her and the infant daughter she'd given birth to when Mathais had been but a wee bairn, and Lottie only eleven years old herself. But her mother, Lottie had realized years later, had been prescient on her deathbed. She'd known she was dying, and in those final hours, she'd called Lottie to her, had clutched her hand with a strength that belied her frail state. "Your father will need you, *leannan,* as will the boys, aye? Heed me, lass — it will seem your life is no' your own, but you must swear to me now you'll no' forget yourself, Lottie."

"What?" Lottie had asked, grief-stricken and confused.

"Swear to me now you'll no' forget your true desires and what *you* want, aye? You deserve the best of life. It will seem impossible to you, it will seem as if there is no room for you, but you will have that life if you donna lose sight of *what* you want. Do you see, lass? Do you understand me?"

"Aye, Mor," Lottie had said, but in truth, she hadn't understood her mother at the time. She'd been overwrought with grief, had considered her mother's plea a fevered one. But her mother was right — from the moment of her tragic death forward, Lottie had been mother, daughter and mistress to her family. She'd tried to be the ballast her mother had been to a father who desperately needed it, but God in his heaven, her father made it difficult.

And now? She was sitting at the table of a captain she didn't know, in his private quarters on a ship she'd taken from him, all because of that damnable whisky, another of her father's bad ideas.

On the day of *Sankt Hans,* the laird had accused her father of illegally distilling spirits.

"Naturally, I denied it," her father had explained. "Aye, he was a bit of a bore, really, what with his talk of penalties and for avoiding the crown's taxes and undercutting a legitimate trade. He claimed that *his* clan was the only lawful clan with the right to distill and sell whisky, and I best think on MacColl's offer to save my bloody arse."

That was the moment Lottie had assumed all hope was lost for her and she'd have to marry that sheepish old man.

"Aye, and what had you to say to that?" Duff asked.

"I said, good luck to you, then," her father had said with a twinkle in his eye, and had laughed roundly.

No one else laughed.

"*Och,* look at you all now," her father had

said gruffly, disappointed in their reaction. "MacColl's offer is no' without merit, is it, *leannan*?" he'd asked curiously, as if the thought had just occurred to him. "He does indeed have a bonny house, finer than this. Twelve rooms, is it?"

"I donna care," she had said, flustered. "Do you think I can be persuaded with a few rooms? He's older than you, Fader. Would you have me give up the hope of children one day?"

"Donna fill your head with bees, *pusling*," he'd said jovially. "I ask only if you might consider it. Were it up to me, I'd no' give my one and only daughter, the bonniest woman in all of Scotland, to that old man unless she asked it of me. My plan is far superior."

Her father had a plan, all right.

His idea was to sell their whisky, once it had matured, in Oban, just across the loch from Lismore. That was where he'd met a man who dabbled in whisky trade, and knew where illicit spirits could be sold for a tidy profit. Lottie had lost patience with her father then — it was one thing to include all of the Livingstones in their secret distillation and plans for the whisky, but it was quite another to speak of it to strangers. It was little wonder Campbell was so suspicious — someone had been talking.

"Naturally, the Scotsman will have a wee bit of the profit for having arranged it, which is only fair, aye?"

"What do you mean, a *wee bit of the profit*?" Lottie had demanded.

"A mere twenty percent."

Lottie had gasped with alarm and outrage right alongside Duff and Mr. McLean. *"Twenty percent?"*

" 'Tis an *opportunity,* Lottie."

" 'Tis robbery, Fader," she'd said hotly. "For twenty percent of our profit he ought to arrange for us to dine with the king! And now there is a Scotsman wandering Oban who knows what we're about!" She'd fallen back against the settee and had flung an arm over her eyes rather violently as her mind whirled with the conundrum in which her father had put them.

"We canna sell the whisky in Scotland," Duff had said to Bernt. "There are Campbells everywhere, aye? They'll hear of it and toss us in prison and leave us there to rot like dead fish."

Her father looked properly chastised, and Lottie turned away from him. If they'd only put a bit of money into sheep, as *she'd* suggested, they'd have no need to distill illegal spirits!

"Lottie, *pusling,* donna be cross with me," her father had pleaded. "I've many mouths to feed and rents to pay. What was I to do?"

Well. There was a host of other things he might have done, but he hadn't, and once again, it was up to her to figure a way out of the disaster. She'd stood and had begun to pace, her mind wildly racing. "If we risk discovery by the Campbells if we sell the whisky in Scotland, then we must go somewhere else."

"Aye?" her father asked, his eyes widening with hope. "Where? England?"

"No, no' England," Duff said. "Campbells there, too, mark me."

Lottie could think of only one place she knew anything about at all, and that only from the tales of others, including the only lover she'd ever had. Lottie hadn't thought of Anders Iversen in a quite a while, really, and generally preferred not to think of him — she'd managed to put that unfortunate summer behind her. But who would help them now? Who else could they turn to? "Anders Iversen is the bookkeeper for the Copenhagen Company in Aalborg, Denmark, aye? And his father, the exchequer there, remember? The company trades in spirits — he told me so. Perhaps, with Anders's help, we might sell what we have to that company, aye?"

"Aye," Duff said, nodding. "I remember, spirits and tobacco, he said. *Diah,* Lottie, you've come up with a bonny idea, you have. Half of us on this island hail from Aalborg."

"Do you think Anders would help us, then?" she'd asked Duff.

"Why, of course he would," Duff said with great certainty.

"Are you no' forgetting a crucial detail?" Mr. MacLean asked. "How are we to get the whisky to Denmark?"

"We'll go by ship," Lottie had said. "On the *Margit.*"

"Gilroy Livingstone's ship? That old tub?" Mr. MacLean said with a snort.

"Donna let Gilroy hear you say it," her father had warned. "He's as fine a captain as any to be found in Scotland, and that tub is his pride and joy. "Lottie, 'tis a splendid idea, it is."

It was not a splendid idea, it was a rash one, born of desperation. She'd never met Anders Iversen's father — for all she knew, he might have died, or changed occupations. She'd had no contact with Anders at all since he'd left Lismore a year ago. "There'll be some cost to sail across the sea, there will, but we'll keep our twenty percent," she said.

"What of Anders?" Duff asked.

"He should be delighted to make the introductions if Lottie asks," Mr. MacLean said gruffly. "And if no', we'll impress on him that we need every cent."

"What a bonny and bright lass you are, *leannan,*" her father had said. "No man on this island deserves you. We'll all go, all of us, you and me and Mats and Drustan and a good crew." He hesitated, waiting for her objection. When she made none, he said quickly, "We must keep this close, aye?" he said. "The fewer who know what we're about, the less we must fret over wagging tongues."

Out of care for her father's feelings, Lottie had not pointed out how ironic it was that he should say that. At that time, she'd wanted to believe she could set another of her father's bad decisions to rights.

But now?

Now, she was very sorry she'd ever uttered those words, that was what. She'd never once considered they'd be chased, or set upon, or whatever had happened today, and she'd certainly never considered the possibility of taking a man's ship. She was full of remorse and guilt and terror.

She sighed and gazed at the man in the

corner. He appeared so peaceful in his oblivion. Pity that she should meet a true sea captain in this way. She would like to have been properly dressed, engage him in conversation about his travels. To perhaps trifle with him a wee bit. A girlish wish, foolishly fantastic in light of everything.

Lottie lowered her head onto her arms, her eyes squeezed tightly shut, determined not to allow tears to fall and torture her more. She had to *think*. She had to determine how they would get themselves out of this predicament with their heads on their shoulders. But her thoughts were drowned out by her heart pounding hard against her ribs with waves of remorse and fear.

CHAPTER FOUR

It was the rising swells that seeped into Aulay's consciousness, the familiar pitch and roll of his ship as it was tossed about in a storm. The pressing instinct to change the sails woke him. He was disoriented and groggy at first, his throat parched, his head aching fiercely . . . but he was increasingly aware of heavy rain pummeling the ship and lashing against the portholes, the crashing sound of waves hitting the forecastle and the impact of the blow.

Who is at the helm?

He tried to rise but his wrists were bound. He remembered he was on the floor of his cabin, his ankle shackled to a desk that was bolted to the floor. He was gagged, too, the cloth biting into the flesh at his cheeks. He managed to push himself up to sitting and sagged against the wall of his quarters, attempting to shake off the feeling of wool covering his brain. His wrists ached and were bleeding where he'd apparently tried to twist them free of the binds. His thoughts were so hazy that he couldn't recall how, precisely, he'd ended up here. He couldn't recall anything but the woman who had kicked him in the chin.

He blinked back the fog and looked around his cabin. His paintings on the wall, his books stacked neatly on the small bedside table. Familiar things . . . and there, in the middle of those familiar things was the woman, her head pillowed on her arms at his table. That bloody bonny hair had been the siren's call that had snared him like a slow sea turtle — *that* much, he recalled. Aye, he'd be pleased to attend her hanging, he would. He'd watch the lot of them swing for what they'd done if they made it to the gallows and not feel the slightest bit of unease about it. He preferred to kill them with his bare hands, particularly if even one of his men had been harmed. *Where are the men?*

He glared across the room at the lady, wondering how to navigate this predicament.

God's teeth, but he ought to swing alongside these thieves for having been so bloody stupid. He was a grown man, not a lad, and yet he'd behaved like one, fixated on the woman the moment he'd caught sight of her. He'd been stunned stupid by her beauty and his common sense had walked off a damn plank. He'd been transfixed with the creamy skin of a shapely leg as that gown had slid up and up, oblivious to what was happening around him, and practically salivating like a lad. It was a naïve mistake and he despised himself for it.

The ship lurched to starboard. *Bloody hell,* he needed her to wake. Aulay tried to shout, but the sound of his voice was muffled by the gag and the winds howling around the ship. He spotted a pair of his boots tucked in next to the desk. He rolled onto his side, and with his free leg, kicked them. They toppled over, but the soft leather didn't make enough noise to wake her. He looked up to the desk. There were several things there, including an octant and compass. Aulay slid his free leg beneath him and pushed up the wall to his feet. He hopped closer to the desk and with one swipe of his bound hands, he sent the instruments tumbling to the floor.

The lass's head snapped up with her gasp of fright. She jerked around, her hair flying, and stared at him, blinking, as if she couldn't quite place him. But she quickly gathered her wits and leaped to her feet and

69

backing out of his reach.

The ship suddenly rose up on a wave and just as quickly sank again, heeling right, and she was knocked off balance, crashing into the wall just below the porthole before catching herself on the sideboard. They would capsize if the ship wasn't sailed properly, and somehow, he needed her to understand that. He looked at his desk. He grabbed a quill in his fist, and fumbled with the lid of the ink pot, spilling some ink onto a map. He picked up a chart and wrote *reef.* He pushed it toward her.

She stared at him with those wide, Caribbean blue eyes. She pushed a tangle of hair from her cheek, then craned her neck to try and see what he'd written from where she stood. Of course she couldn't, and shrank against the wall. "I know what you must think," she said.

What a ridiculous creature. She could not possibly fathom that he was imagining that slender neck in a noose just now.

"But this is no' what it must seem to you."

Not what it seems? What it seemed was piracy. Was he not bound? Were his men not lost to him? Had his ship and his cargo not been stolen? Aye, *piracy* was exactly what it seemed.

The ship heaved again and she stumbled,

catching herself on the bunk. She put her hand to the forehead of the man who lay there, then pulled up the coverlet — *Aulay's* coverlet, thank you. His bunk, his bed, his linens, his pillow.

"We donna mean to keep your ship, on my word."

Aulay arched one very dubious brow above the other.

"Once we reach port, we'll return the ship to you as we found it, aye? You have my word," she said, and pressed a hand to her heart as if to pledge it before being tossed again by the ship's heaving.

Bloody ignorant wench. If he'd been able to speak, Aulay would have cursed her. There was no time for her excuses. He glared at her and pointed to the chart.

But she moved away from the chart, putting the table where he often took his meals with Beaty between them. "You need no' look at me in that manner," she said. "I know you're quite angry. On my honor, I canna convey how much I regret that it has come to this, aye? But we were taking on water, and we've a mission that canna be delayed. We were hopeless, and I'm afraid there was naugh' to be done for it. But that in no way eases my deep remorse, Captain."

Did she take him a fool? Aulay wanted to

strangle her. Unfortunately, the more important issue was the matter of the ship.

"As you can see, my father is badly wounded," she continued, ignoring his dark look. "They . . . they meant to draw straws to see who would drown and who would accompany us in the jolly, and I couldna bear the thought of it, aye? But then *you* appeared! Out of that gray mist, you suddenly appeared like an angel from heaven," she said, her voice full of awe.

The ship rose up; she was very nearly tossed into a chair. "Your crew is to be commended, Captain. You didna see them as you were unconscious, but on my word, they put a good fight, they did. We were armed, so naturally, we had the advantage."

He suddenly remembered Beaty asking if they ought to pick up arms and his nonchalance about it. Aye, he was going to kill her with his bare hands, limb by lovely limb. Aulay shouted through the gag, which was really more of a hoarse throttle, as the gag prevented the use of his tongue.

"*Diah,* of course, you want to speak," she said sympathetically. She glanced back at the man on the bunk, then at him. "If I remove the gag, do you promise you'll no' scream? It willna matter if you do — there's no one to hear you, really."

His heart raced wildly at that — what did she mean, there was no one to hear? *Where is my crew? Who is at the helm?*

"Aye, all right," she said, warily eyeing the ropes at his wrists and the blood on his cuffs, the shackle around his ankle. She winced at the sight of it. "How you must loathe us."

Loathing was too good for the likes of her. But Aulay maintained his composure with the hope she'd free him of the goddamn gag.

She approached him cautiously. "Ah . . . you're quite tall, are you no'? Will you bend your head, then?"

His glare only deepened, but he did as she asked, bowing at the waist like a bloody supplicant.

She worked at the knot of the cloth at the back of his head, her fingers brushing against his neck and tangling in his hair. The gag fell away from his mouth and he coughed when he was free of it.

She moved away from him, staring at him, eyes wide with what, fright? *He* was the one trussed up like a Christmas ham.

"Who is at the helm?" he asked hoarsely. "Is it my man, then?"

"Ah . . . no," she said, then turned and hurried to the sideboard, twice pausing to steady herself when the ship pitched beneath her.

"Who then?" he asked impatiently. "Whoever is sailing the ship must reef the sails."

"Pardon?" She'd reached the sideboard and was struggling to pour water from the ewer into a cup.

"If he's no' reefed the sails, he must do it now or we'll capsize. If he doesna know how to sail in these winds, give him my first mate. Beaty is his name and he can sail through the worst of storms."

She began the unsteady trek back to him, but with a sudden lift of the ship, she spilled quite a lot of the water onto the floor of the cabin. Another wave pitched her forward, and she caught herself on Aulay's arm, then quickly yanked her hand away, as if he might burn her.

"Do you *hear* me, then?" he demanded loudly. "We'll capsize if you donna do as I say."

"Gilroy is a captain," she said evenly, and tried to hold the cup to his lips.

Aulay jerked his head away from the cup, causing her to drop it. That distracted her, and he seized the moment and caught her by the throat. His wrists were bound, but he could still wrap his hands around her neck, could still squeeze the life from her.

74

She gasped, and tried to claw his grip free of her throat with one hand, her eyes bulging with fear. "I ought to snap your neck here and now, aye?" he breathed angrily. "Can you no' feel that we're tossing about like a child's boat in the bath, lass? Your captain doesna know how to sail it, and if you donna wish to drown us all, then by *Diah,* put Beaty at the helm."

Her eyes dropped to his mouth, and Aulay's fool heart skipped a single beat, but then began to race as he felt the cold steel of a gun suddenly jab him in the neck. "Let me go," she croaked, "or I'll blow your bloody head from your shoulders."

Aulay glared at her, and she glared back, her eyes an icy blue now, her cheeks flushed. Her lips had parted and she was choking. She was shaking. But she thrust the gun deeper into his skin.

"Do as she says, captain," came a hoarse voice from the bunk. "And we'll fetch your first mate, we will."

Neither he nor the woman moved. Her eyes narrowed, her brows dipping into a vee of determination. He slowly let go her neck, and she sagged backward, dropped the gun from his gullet. She clutched a small dueling pistol in one hand and pressed the other hand to her throat. She blinked and suddenly turned to the bunk. "Fader? How do you fare?"

"As poorly as a three legged horse. Donna tend me, *pusling,* do as the captain says," he told her. "Gilroy is a fine captain, that he is, but he's no' been a'sea in many years, and he's no' sailed a ship as fine as this, aye? Go, and see to your brothers while you're out."

She hesitated. She gave Aulay a dark look. But then she went, obedient, hurrying to the cabin door and yanking it open. A gale of wind and rain blew in as she went out, then was silenced when she pulled the door shut behind her.

Aulay fell back against the cabin wall, his breath short, his heart still beating rapidly.

"Donna blame her," the man said from his bunk. "My daughter is no' at fault for what has happened. The blame lies entirely with me."

"It lies with all of you, and you'll all hang for it," Aulay said flatly. "*All* of you."

The man said nothing more.

Aulay waited, pacing the wee bit of floor the shackle would allow him. He heard voices, but could not make them out, not with the wind howling and the ship groaning so loudly. But after an eternity, it seemed that the ship was pitching less.

Perhaps the storm was weakening. Perhaps she'd given the helm to Beaty.

It seemed as if hours passed before she finally returned, bursting into the cabin and slamming it shut behind her in the face of a gale. She was soaked through to the skin, her hair was plastered to her head, and her gown so wet and heavy that it dragged the ground and clung to the voluptuous curves of her body. Her gun, he noted, was tucked into the waist of her petticoat.

She went straight to the bunk and leaned over the old man, stroking his head. "You're warm," she said.

"Aye, I feel as if that old Mrs. MacGuire has put her boot through me head," he said.

"You're bleeding again, Fader. I'll fetch Morven, aye?"

"Leave him be, lass. He's needed on deck and he canna do more than he's done. If you've a wee bit more of the draught, however."

She slipped a hand into the pocket of her gown and withdrew a brown vial. She shook the contents, then lifted the man's head and helped him take the liquid. When he'd had enough, she held the brown glass vial up to the light from the porthole. "We've scarcely any of it left," she said, the worry evident in her voice.

"*Och,* we Livingstones are made of sturdy stock. I'll be quite all right," the man said, but Aulay could tell from the roughness in his voice that he was not all right. That was just as well, then — one fewer to hang.

She sat on the edge of the bunk, shivering, periodically clutching the edge of it when the ship surged up or down or right or left. Aulay relaxed a wee bit — he was confident Beaty was now at the helm, as the ship was riding over the waves instead of crashing headlong into them.

He slid down onto his haunches, watching her, his gaze on her long, elegantly slender neck, the soft slope of her shoulders. Aye, she was bonny, that she was, as bonny as any woman he'd ever seen in his life. He had the sudden image of her silky hair covering her face as she twisted on the end of a rope.

He seethed with fury. With her. With himself. But he had to keep his wits about him if he had any hope of persuading her to remove the shackle and the binds at his wrists.

The old man was soon snoring. The lass — the Livingstone lass, apparently — stood and moved wearily to the table. She kicked off her boots, then wrung the water from her hair and tied it into a knot at her nape.

And then, without compunction, she lifted her gown, put one foot onto a chair, and began to roll down a stocking.

Aulay was not happy to feel just as fascinated by this display of a shapely leg as he had been when she'd first come on board. God knew he'd known many audacious women, many of whom were closely related to him . . . but none like her. Not a single beautiful, gun-wielding, knee-kicking pirate. Not a single lass who could possibly steal a ship, press a gun into his neck and then brazenly undress before him.

What infuriated him most was that there was a part of his sorry self that was utterly aroused by it.

She seemed to sense his study of her. She turned her head and gave him a pointed look. Aulay shrugged. "What did you expect, then?"

"What did I *expect*? I *expected* this entire voyage to have gone quite a lot differently, that's what," she said crossly. She tossed one stocking down, then lifted the next leg and began to roll that stocking down.

Aulay tried not to look at her bare leg. Well. He didn't try very hard, really, but he had it in his head he ought not to look. "Who sails?" he asked gruffly.

"Your man. *Beaty,*" she said with exasperation, and discarded the second stocking just as carelessly as the first. "He was *quite* at odds with the idea. He scolded me right harshly for having taken the ship, he did, and in front of all those men, too, aye? But when I explained that his very own captain had asked it of him —" she paused to look at Aulay "— after swearing on my mother's grave that you were *verra* much alive," she added, sounding miffed that Beaty would dare to question her on that front. "When I promised him that you lived, and you yourself had asked him to take the helm, he softened a wee bit and agreed to go on deck with Gilroy and the others."

"And the rest of my men?"

"Your crew? They're well, they are. Mad as hornets, but well enough."

"No one hurt?" Aulay asked.

"Aye, well . . . three of them. Broken bones and the like. But we're looking after them properly." She yanked the fasteners of her gown and shrugged out of it, throwing it onto the back of the chair. Next came her stomacher. Astonishingly, she now stood barefoot in the middle of his cabin with nothing more than a petticoat, her stays and a chemise so sheer underneath that her breasts might as well have been exposed to him. She slipped her gun from her waist and laid it on the table.

"What in God's name are you doing?" he asked incredulously. He'd never seen a woman disrobe without hesitation or conceit, unless for his pleasure. Certainly not in circumstances like this. This woman was utterly beyond redemption.

She clucked at him. "If I remain in soaked clothing, it will be the death of me, aye? I donna have a proper gown or a dressing room, do I?"

Aulay couldn't help himself — he took in her figure. Slowly. Curve by delicious curve.

"Donna look at me like that," she said.

"What, or you'll shoot? What would you have me do, then? Fix my gaze on the wall?"

Her cheeks colored. She folded her arms over her body, which pronounced her perfect breasts to him even more, and shivered noticeably.

Aulay sighed. He was either a bloody fool or a great humanitarian, because he said, "My greatcoat is just there," and nodded to a series of pegs on the wall that held his clothing.

She looked over her shoulder in the direction he indicated, but made no move to get the coat. "No, thank you."

"Stubborn wench," he said irritably. "Watching you shiver like a wee waif makes it feel bloody well cold in here. Take it."

"That's kind of you," she said.

" 'Tis no' the least bit kind. I shall have you in good health so that I might see you hanged."

The color in her cheeks darkened. "Hanged! I told you we'd return the ship to you! Think of it as borrowing —"

"Save your breath for your judge, lass."

"Och," she said with a flick of her wrist. "Your pride's been wounded, that it has, and you're angry now." She took his coat from the wall and put it around her shoulders. "Thank you," she muttered.

His pride had been more than wounded — it had been destroyed. He leaned his head back against the wall and closed his eyes. He didn't want to relive his humiliation, but unfortunately, it was impossible to ignore.

He heard her moving about, the scrape of the chair against the wooden floor, and opened his eyes. She was not very big at all, he realized, smaller than average. "Where did you learn to kick like that, then?" he asked with irritable curiosity.

She sat on one of the chairs, her legs drawn to her. Only her toes were visible. "I didna know that I could," she said with a slight shrug. "Fear makes warriors of us, I suppose."

"Or fools," he said. He moved his stiff jaw around, but it resulted in an annoying jab of pain through him, serving only to remind him that he'd been undone by a woman.

"Are these your paintings?" she asked.

Aulay stiffened. She had turned, was looking at the wall where he'd hung a pair of his canvasses. More paintings were stacked behind an easel in the corner of the room. For this voyage, he'd hung a painting of the Mediterranean Sea, off the coast of Cadiz, a view of the sea over the bow of his ship. The water there was as blue as the lass's eyes. The other painting was of the Atlantic Ocean. Aulay had not ventured very far into that ocean, but he'd sailed it enough to have a memory of the setting sun.

His paintings were a private side of him. He didn't like to talk about them, didn't like to compare notes with artists he met from time to time. He rarely took his work ashore. He didn't need anything else to separate him from his brothers. Cailean and Rabbie were both strong, virile men. When they were children, the two of them would stage battles and Aulay would draw. His father used to exhort him not to waste his time on endeavors best suited for the fairer sex, and to pick up arms, to be more like his brothers. "Learn to thrust a sword, no' a paint brush, lad," he would say.

"Our Aulay is a gentle soul, darling," his mother would say, her intent to defend him. But she only made it worse. His father had no use for sons with gentle souls.

Aulay would not have said he had a gentle soul. All he knew was that the painting was something in him that needed to come out. It eased him. Still, art was for him, and him alone.

He waited for the remarks he knew would come.

"There's no' a soul in them," she said curiously, and stood up, moving to the wall to have a look.

"That's because they are paintings of seas, aye?" he said defensively.

"You paint the same sea every time? Only the sea?"

Only the sea? What was the matter with her? They were obviously two different bodies of water. "They are no' the same at all."

"Aye, they are. One is blue, but they look the same." She bent over and began to rummage through his other canvasses.

Aulay shifted uncomfortably. "Have a care!" he said sharply.

"More paintings of the sea," she said, as if

84

he didn't know what he'd painted.

"The sea is *never* the same from one moment to the next, is it? It turns over on itself, it does. The changes are so vast that at times, they are almost imperceptible. But they are no' the *same,* and you have no' been invited to inspect my things."

She lifted her hands in surrender. "But there are no people. No' even a ship," she said.

It was just his bloody luck to be humiliated by a woman who also happened to be an art critic. "*Diah,* you're a thief with no appreciation for art," he said dismissively.

"We're no' thieves," she said as she resumed her seat. "Had it no' been for our emergency, we'd no' want your ship if you presented it to us with ribbons tied to the masts," she said pertly.

Aulay snorted. "If you're no' thieves, then who are you?"

"It doesna matter —"

"Aye, on the contrary, it does indeed. You canna hide. I heard the giant call you Lottie when you came on board. The man there bragged of his Livingstone stock. You are Lottie Livingstone, no' Lady Larson," he said, spitting out the name. "Are you pirates, then? Is it my cargo you want?"

"Pirates!" She laughed, and her eyes

sparkled with amusement. "If we are pirates, captain, then we are the worst of all!"

"Then why have you stolen my ship?" he demanded. *Why have you humiliated me? Why have you ruined this chance to save the life I love?*

"We've no' . . ." She sighed and shook her head. "On my word, I tell you the truth, Captain Mackenzie. Please try and think of it as merely borrowing your ship, aye? I told you, we had no choice. You'll leave us at port and then . . . then go about your business."

She said it hopefully, as if she desperately wanted to believe that could happen. He was quick to disabuse her of that idea. "That's absurd. You surely donna believe that I'll no' avenge the unlawful taking of my ship, aye?"

Her hopeful expression fell. She looked at the old man. "Then what should I do?"

"Pardon?"

She shifted her gaze to Aulay. "I could use your advice, aye?"

Aulay scoffed at the suggestion.

"I donna know what to do, captain," she said, sounding a wee bit desperate. "I can scarcely believe what I've done. Tell me what to do — you're a man of great experience —"

"You honestly think I'll *advise* you?" he asked incredulously.

"No," she said, her brows furrowing. "But I hoped. I'm in water well over my head, I am, and I could use a wee bit of proper counsel. I've none, you might have noticed."

Hardly proper counsel, seeing as he was the one bound. But it occurred to him he could perhaps use this opportunity to his advantage. "Where are you bound, then?"

"For Aalborg."

Aulay's heart seized. That was the wrong direction. "Denmark," he said.

She nodded.

"Why there?"

"We've . . . we've something to sell," she said hesitantly.

"Aye, and what is that? The contents of my hold?"

"No!" she said, affronted.

"What else would you have to sell, then? What could you possibly have that must be sold in some small port of Denmark, other than what is in my hold?" he pressed her. "I'm carrying wool and salted beef. My hold was full before you tricked us with your . . ." He almost said hair. "Tell me the truth, lass — do you mean to sell it?"

"For the love of all that his holy, your goods are where you put them, aye? At least in part." She abruptly came to her feet.

"What do you mean, *in part*?" he demanded.

"There are crates yet," she said, waving off his questions as she began to pace. "Some of it . . . mostly wool, I think . . . well, it was lost because . . ." She gestured with her hand in a manner of someone searching for a word.

"Because?"

"Because there was some confusion on board among my men about where we might put our cargo," she said quickly. "I stopped them before they threw over more than a wee bit."

Aulay stared at her, trying to make sense of it.

"I beg your pardon, but there was quite a lot of panic," she said, and stole a quick glance at the man on the bed before moving closer to him to whisper, "Our ship was sinking. It *sank*."

"You brought your cargo on board my ship?" he asked, pushing to his feet. "What cargo? What did you bring?"

"*Sssh,*" she cautioned him, pointing at the bunk.

"Slaves?"

She gasped with indignation. "Of *course* no'!"

"What, then?"

"Things! Sundry things."

"*Liar,*" Aulay said coldly. "Sundry things that must be sold in a foreign port? Sundry things that have caused a flush to creep into your fair cheeks? Things that your dying father insists you carry on rather than return for help?"

"He is *no'* dying!"

"What is it you mean to deliver to Aalborg?" he pressed.

"It has no bearing on you —"

"It has *every* bearing on me, you wee fool! I would know what I carry on my ship, aye? I would know if illegal whisky is in my hold! I know a ship running from the excise man when I see it. That was a *royal* ship you set on fire —"

"*Entirely* accidental! And they fired first!"

"You'd no' be the first to run illegal whisky from Scotland's shores. But damn you, you are the first to throw *my* cargo overboard to make room for it!"

Her eyes darkened. "No' *all* of it. As I said, I stopped them. Most of what we brought is on your deck."

"*Mi Diah,*" he muttered and sagged against the wall. Now he was carrying illegal goods in plain sight? Aulay seethed with indignation. His was not the indignation of the righteous, no — it wasn't so long ago that his family had resorted to running goods around the royal navy and excise bounties the crown would impose on imports. They'd felt forced to do it, felt it was the only way they could provide for their clan in those years before the Jacobite rebellion, when the crown imposed a usurious tax their clan could ill afford on the most basic of necessities.

But they had *not* thrown over anyone's legitimate goods to make room, and they'd *not* stacked illegal cargo on their bloody decks! Worse, much worse, if Aulay lost this cargo, if he failed to do what he'd promised William Tremayne and deliver it to Amsterdam, he couldn't bear to think what might happen to his family's livelihood. He couldn't bear to think of the mix of anger and pity in his father's eyes.

He turned a cold gaze to the woman who was pacing, the hem of his greatcoat dragging the floor behind her. Her brow was furrowed and she seemed lost in thought. *Bloody whisky runners.* His mind raced with the necessity to free himself, to salvage what he could before all was lost.

The lass stopped pacing. She turned to face him, and damn her if she didn't look almost tearful. "*Help* me," she said softly.

"Tell me what to do!"

"Help you pirate my own ship?"

She groaned heavenward. "You'll have your ship as soon as we are to Aalborg!"

He stared at her, his thoughts racing. "If we are to Aalborg, you'll need my men to sail us there, aye? Best you bring Beaty in so that he might chart the course." That was a lie — Beaty could navigate by the stars overhead, and it was almost impossible to chart a course when the day was as bleak as this. For all Aulay knew, Beaty might have already turned this ship about. But he hoped she would give Beaty entry into the cabin.

She considered his suggestion.

"Of course, you canna be certain I'll no' chart a course that turns us about and sends us back to Scotland and into the hands of the crown, can you, then?"

She shot him a suspicious look. "You'll no' do that. You'll no' risk putting your ship into the hands of the crown. They'll no' believe you're innocent, no' with whisky on board. You need me and mine off your ship, I should think."

Clever and beautiful. But Aulay would see her brought to justice. And he would do it by taking full advantage of her naiveté.

"Aye, you're right, you are." He held up

91

his hands. "Untie me, and I will help you."

She blinked. She moved closer, so close that Aulay could see flecks of light gray in her pale blue eyes that, under different circumstances, would have tempted him. His gaze slid to her lips, succulent and pursed, and errant thoughts began to wander into places they ought not to have gone. This was the woman who had aggrieved him, had stolen his ship, had put his crew in peril. How could he imagine kissing her? He'd been addled by that blow to the head, clearly.

She seemed to know what he was thinking, because she smiled saucily and tilted her head back. He held up his hands to her so that she might release him. "I'll no' deny it, I need you, I *do,* captain," she said silkily, and a warm shiver ran down his spine. "But donna take me for a fool." She abruptly put her hands on his chest and shoved him away, then stepped back.

She took the greatcoat from her shoulders, slid one arm into a sleeve, and then the other, then buttoned the coat up to her neck so that she looked as if she was wearing a priest's robe. She picked up the gun from the table and slid it into the pocket before she shoved her feet into wet boots. "There are men to be fed, and my father needs a change of bandage." She moved to the door.

He realized she meant to leave him. "If you want my help, bring me Beaty," he said sternly.

She opened the door and went out. A moment later, he heard what sounded like a barrel or a crate being slid across the decking and shoved in front of the door.

All right, then, she was no fool.

Well, neither was he . . . all evidence to the contrary. He would help her, all right. He would help her right into the arms of the authorities.

CHAPTER FIVE

Lottie didn't care that the rain was slashing across her face making it difficult to see. She walked directly to the railing and gripped it tightly as she leaned over it, taking deep gulps of wet, salt-soaked air and, for a fleeting moment, toyed with the idea of lowering the jolly and putting herself in it and bobbing off and away from this catastrophe.

That man, her captive, had snatched the breath from her. She'd never looked into eyes so piercing or so shrewd, had never felt such restrained power in a man. There had been only a thin chain keeping him from flinging himself at her and strangling the breath out of her with one hand as he apparently wanted to do — she could see it in the way he'd glared at her. What in God's name possessed her to stick her hand into the fire?

She thought of his hair, streaked blond by

the sun, wild about his shoulders, having come free of its queue. She thought of the dark beginnings of his beard that framed a sensual mouth, even with his lips pressed together in an unforgiving line. She thought of the way he looked at her as if he meant to put her on a spit and roast her. Was it a sign of depravity that she wanted to be roasted by him? In spite of extraordinary and challenging circumstances, the thought caused her to shiver with a mix of thrill and fear. And perhaps the worst of it all was that she *did* need the counsel of someone like him.

"Lottie!"

She swayed backward from the railing and turned about as Drustan lumbered across the deck to her, his face twisted with worry.

"What is it, *mo chridhe*?" she asked.

Drustan slipped on the wet planking and grabbed awkwardly for the railing to keep from falling. "I donna know what to do," he said. "Mats, he hasna told me what I'm to do, but I'm no' to go up there." He pointed to the masts.

Lottie looked up — Mats was several feet above her, helping with the sails. "Good Lord," she murmured.

"I want to see Fader," Drustan said.

"Aye, I know," Lottie said soothingly.

Drustan was not adept at finding his footing when circumstances changed. Frankly, none of them were. "We'll see that all the men are fed, and then I'll take you to see him." She reached up and used the sleeve of the captain's coat to wipe rain from Drustan's face. "Come," she said, and took his hand.

They made their way to the quarterdeck, where Norval Livingstone stood guard over Mr. Beaty. Even with the relentless rain, she could hear Gilroy and Beaty arguing.

"I tell you, 'tis no' the way it's done," Gilroy said as Lottie and Drustan climbed the steps.

"Canna outrun a frigate without a gaff," Beaty said gruffly.

"I beg your pardon," Lottie said.

Both men had failed to notice her approach and jerked their gazes around to her, slinging water off their cocked hats and into her face. Lottie sputtered, wiping the rain from her face with her sleeve.

"You ought no' to be on deck," Gilroy said. "Look at you, soaked through."

"Are we bound for Denmark?" she asked, ignoring Gilroy, her eyes locked on Beaty.

Beaty glowered at her. "Beggin' your pardon, but do you think I canna find my way to *Denmark*?"

"Why should she trust you?" Gilroy demanded.

Beaty glared at him, too, cocked hat to cocked hat. "*You're* the one who has stolen *our* ship, and *I* am no' to be trusted, is that the way of it? I'm sailing her, am I no'? Sailing east, too, as anyone can plainly see."

Lottie could not *plainly see* it. Gilroy was right — she didn't trust Beaty. But neither did she trust her own instincts, and she was suspicious of Gilroy's. How could he possibly know which direction he was sailing in the dark and the rain? She could only hope that she was right, and that these men would not return to Scotland with the whisky on board. They'd have nothing to show for their own cargo, and she knew very well how the crown's authorities viewed Highlanders — all of them were suspect. They would seize them all. Privateers might do worse. If they were set upon by pirates or privateers, she'd have to give these men leave to take up their weapons, and she had no doubt what would happen to the Livingstones if it came to that.

All right, that was enough. She couldn't bear standing in this rain another moment. She would have to trust her instincts, no matter how ignorant they were. "I'll see to it that the men are fed," she said, wiping rain from her face again. "After which, Mr. Beaty, your captain wishes to speak with you, aye?"

"What? Lottie, 'tis no' wise —" Gilroy started, but she waved a hand at him.

"It's all right, Gilroy," she said calmly. "Come along, Dru," she said, and left the quarterdeck.

She and Drustan went down into the hold where the Mackenzies had been forced. It was dank in the hold, and the faint smell of rotting fish assaulted her senses. It was poorly lit as well, and there didn't appear to be any space that wasn't taken up with salted beef, wool or casks of whisky. Lottie could hear the raised voices of men coming from the stern. They were shouting at each other, in English and Gaelic, with a bit of Danish thrown in for good measure. She followed Drustan around a stack of crates to an area they'd blocked off to hold their captives. When she stepped into the light of a single lantern, all shouting stopped. The men stared at her for a highly charged moment, and then as if signaled by some magical siren, they started shouting at once.

Lottie threw up her hands. *"Uist!"* she cried. "Silence!"

Duff MacGuire punctuated her shout with a sharp whistle that caused half of them to cover their ears. At least they stopped shouting.

Lottie took a breath. "We mean to feed you and give you what you need —"

"What I need is to have these binds undone!" shouted one man, lifting his hands up. "A man canna even piss!"

"By all that is holy, I'll put me bloody fist into yer trap if you speak so in front of the lady again," Morven threatened.

"Ye canna expect us to eat with our wrists bound," complained another.

"You ate the bread we gave you well enough, aye?" Mr. MacLean snapped. The men began to shout again.

"Please!" Lottie cried. A sharp pain was once again throbbing at the base of her skull, but the men kept shouting and arguing with one another. Lottie took the gun from her pocket, cocked it and fired at the ceiling above them. The crack was deafening and splinters of wood and smoke rained down on them. Men ducked, their hands covering their heads.

After a moment of stunned silence, a Mackenzie said, "For the love of God, take the gun from her, ere she kills someone."

"I'll no' do it," Duff said. "She's a better shot than any man here, she is."

Lottie hopped up onto a crate so she

could see them all. "Listen! I know you're all verra angry, aye?" she said, breathless with anxiety. "All of us," she said, gesturing to all the Livingstones around her, "are verra sorry for the situation that has brought us to this —"

" 'Tis piracy!" The Mackenzie men began to shout again. "What have you done with Beaty? Where is Captain Mackenzie?"

"Let us see them!" someone shouted, which roused the rest of them to shout at her, too.

Duff held up both arms and whistled again. When they had quieted, he said grandly, "Say no more, miss. I've already told the devils what we're about, that I have."

"Why in the name of Hades do you speak like a king to his subjects?" groused a Mackenzie man.

"Perhaps because I've had the good fortune of receiving my theatrical training at the Goodman's Fields Theatre in London!"

"The what?"

"The *theatre*!" Duff bellowed, always quite impatient with any poor soul who did not hold theatre in the same high regard as he.

"All right, thank you," Lottie said, and moved in front of Duff before he commenced a sermon. "We'll bring food to you now, and on my word, we'll bring Beaty down so that you can look on him and know he is quite all right, aye?"

"And what of Captain Mackenzie?" someone demanded.

"Beaty will see him and he'll vouch that he's quite all right. But we must hold him close until we reach our destination. You'd do the same, would you no'?"

"We'd no' steal another man's ship!" said one crossly.

"Aye," she said. A thought popped into her head — she'd never known a man who did not respond to money. "That's why we mean to compensate you for your trouble."

Duff and MacLean gasped at the same moment. "Lottie —"

"We will," she said firmly. " 'Tis only fair."

"We lost six casks," MacLean muttered behind her.

"Aye, and we might lose all if we donna have a care."

"How much?" a Mackenzie asked.

"Five percent more than the wage your captain means to pay you." Her gut dropped a wee bit the moment the words were out of her mouth. She hoped that was not extravagant. Perhaps it was, as her men were gaping at her. And the Mackenzies looked confused. She'd spoken too hastily, perhaps, but she had to make it sound worth their while. Except that she really had no idea how they would pay these men, and she could see from the concerned look on Mr. MacLean's face that he didn't, either. *Diah,* she was beginning to behave like her father, making promises she couldn't possibly keep without thought. But the shouting had stopped and the men were looking around at each other, interested. It *did* seem only fair. It seemed the only way to convince the Mackenzies that they had not stolen their ship with ill intent. Well, she'd said it, and there was no pulling the words back into her mouth. If they didn't make enough from the sale of the whisky, there was another way to compensate them. Mr. MacColl was still on Lismore, still pining for her.

Her stomach did a queer little flip, and she swallowed down that thought. She couldn't think of that now and looked at Duff. "Have we something to feed these gentlemen?"

"Fish stew," Duff said. "Yesterday's catch."

"Stew? How will we manage?" she asked.

"With our hands and one at a time," said Duff. He reached up to put his hand on Drustan's shoulder. "And we've a lad who might crush the head of any man who tries to keep us from it."

"I donna want to crush heads!" Drustan exclaimed fearfully.

"Well I donna mean there will be an actual *need,* lad," Duff said.

"Morven?" Lottie said. "The dressing on my father's wound needs attention."

"Aye, I'll fetch a few things, then," Morven said and started for the steps up to the main deck.

"Fear no'," said Duff, bowing his head. "Drustan and MacLean and I will keep all in order." He cast a stern look to his captives.

"Bloody Shakespeare is serving us fish, lads," said a Mackenzie, and they laughed roundly as Lottie made her way out of the hold.

When she emerged on the deck, Lottie paused and adjusted the heavy greatcoat around her. The rain had turned to mist, but the coat she wore was soaked. What she wouldn't give for a hot bath and her bed to chase away the chill and this horrible day, to perhaps ease the ache in her head. She wondered, as she trudged along to the quarterdeck, if she'd ever have a proper bath again, or if this voyage would be the end of her. All signs pointed to the latter.

Well, she wasn't done yet. The day had been disastrous, but they were still alive, still had that damn whisky. As her mother always said, "One step before the next, and again." So . . . one step before the next. She withdrew her gun from her pocket as she started up the steps to the quarterdeck.

Norval was still standing guard on the quarterdeck. Gilroy had taken over the wheel, and Beaty was squatting down beside a small brazier where he held a stick with pieces of fish over a small flame. He glanced up as Lottie neared him, and even in the dim light, she could see him blanch when he saw her gun. He slowly rose to his feet, his eyes fixed on it. "What's that for, then?"

"Donna you mind it. Come with me, please."

Beaty snorted. "You mean to escort me with a gun to me head?" He laughed with great derision.

Lottie lifted the gun and pointed it at his head. Behind him, Gilroy's mouth dropped open in astonishment. "It's no' for your head, sir, but your captain's. If I see any trickery, he'll pay the price."

Beaty looked at the gun in her hand. Was it possible for him to tell the gun was empty? She'd shot its only bit of lead into the ceiling above the Mackenzie crew. "I could take that wee gun and toss you over with one hand, lass," he said darkly.

She knew that, quite obviously, but she called his bluff. She cocked the gun. "Try," she said.

Gilroy recovered from his shock and slowly smiled. "Did I no' say that you ought not to trifle with the Livingstones?" he asked proudly.

"I thought you were Larsons," Beaty drawled. "Have you lost your mind, lass?" he asked. "Have you no' put yourself in enough peril?"

"Aye, without a doubt, I have," she agreed. "But I'll no' allow *you* to put me in more peril. Come," she said, gesturing to the stairs.

Muttering beneath his breath, Beaty stalked toward the steps. She followed him to the captain's cabin with the gun pointed at his back, but he wasn't terribly intimidated, apparently, for he entered the quarters in something of a snit, striding inside and pausing in the middle, his legs braced apart, his hands on his hips, surveying the lay of the land.

"What the devil?" Bernt said from the bed, and tried to rise up on an elbow.

"Please donna tax yourself, Fader," Lottie said with the pistol pointed at the captain.

"We've a wee bit of business, that's all."

The captain was leaning casually against the wall and glanced insouciantly at her gun. "You've no' been threatening my men with that wee gun, have you?"

"Aye, she has," Beaty said. "Pointed it right at my head, she did."

"Here he is," she said to Mackenzie. "You asked for him. Now speak."

"Where are your men?" he asked, undaunted, unhurried. "Surely one of them can come along to hold the gun for you, aye?"

"I donna need anyone to hold it. My men are feeding *your* men," she said pertly.

"Put away the gun, lass," he said. "Beaty will do as I say. Put the gun down."

"Tell him, then. I donna know which direction he sails, so tell him," she demanded.

"You can tell by the prevailing wind, aye?" Mackenzie said calmly, and lifted his bound hands. "East," he said, pointing in one direction, then arcing his hands to the opposite direction, "to west." And then he said something low and rapidly in Gaelic.

Had she been tricked? Lottie's temper flared; she lifted the empty gun and sighted it between the captain's eyes.

He didn't as much as flinch. In fact, he

arched a brow as if amused by her.

But Beaty flinched, throwing up his hands as if to stop her. "There's no call for that!" he said anxiously. "You'd no' shoot an unarmed man, lass!"

"She'll no' use it," the captain said.

He was not the least bit afraid of her. He probably didn't believe she knew how to use a gun properly. Men were always assuming things they shouldn't. She knew how to fire a gun, for God's sake. She was only missing a bullet.

"Put it down, Lottie," he said calmly. "We're wasting time, aye?"

"We're to use given names now, are we? I'll put it down when you explain to Mr. Beaty that we are to sail to Aalborg, and I can see with my own eyes that he's no' sailing us straight into the arms of the king's navy."

Again, the captain spoke quickly and softly in Gaelic. Whatever he said caused Beaty to give a slight shake of his head. Lottie panicked — her knowledge of Gaelic was limited to a few words and phrases. The Livingstones generally spoke English, except for the older clan members who spoke the language of the Danes. *English!* she said sharply. "You must speak English!"

Mackenzie looked almost amused. "English, then," he said graciously.

"Do as she says, aye?" her father said roughly from the bunk. "My daughter is as fine a shot as she is bonny."

The captain said something else in Gaelic; Lottie cocked the gun. The captain kept his gaze on her gun but leaned over and pointed to something on one of the maps.

"I'll blast a hole in you, I swear I will," Lottie said sharply.

"She looks a wee bit mad," Beaty said nervously.

"Mad? I look *mad*?" Lottie said. What shreds of patience she might have been clinging to were lost. "I suppose were *you* the one holding the gun, you'd look perfectly reasonable! Why is it man's unfailing belief that if a woman is anything less than demure and silent, she must be mad, but —"

"Lottie, lass . . ." her father said.

"Men think themselves so bloody superior," she snapped. "Come, Beaty, before I demonstrate just how *mad* I am. What would you do, were you me? My father wounded, my men without knowledge of the sea —"

"You should no' have pirated a ship, then!" Beaty said indignantly.

The captain said calmly, "There is no

need to argue, aye? Have you paused to consider, then, miss, that if you blast a hole in me, there will be a heavy price to pay? My men will go along with your thievery as long as they know I'm your captive. But if I'm dead?"

If he were dead, they'd all be dead — no one needed to tell her so. Lottie could well imagine the carnage, beginning with Beaty, who would not hesitate to snap her neck. Mackenzie knew this. He knew that her gun was merely display and really no use to her at all in this circumstance. *Diah,* but her heart was pounding so hard she could scarcely hear her own thoughts. "You donna frighten me, sir."

"Do I no'?" he asked congenially, as if they were playing a game. "Then shoot me."

"*Och, pusling,* before you shoot him, the tincture Morven has given me has no' dulled the pain. Might there be some brandy about?"

"Pardon, what?" She was so intent on the captain and the quicksand she found herself in, that at first her father's question didn't make sense.

"Brandy," he said again. "I could use a wee dram, that I could."

Lottie looked at Mackenzie.

He sighed at the imposition. "In the

109

sideboard, below."

Lottie moved backward, keeping her eye on Beaty, and bumping into the immovable table. Beaty looked terribly confused, his gaze swinging between her and his captain and her father. Lottie managed to keep the gun trained on Mackenzie as she dipped down and opened the cupboard beneath the sideboard. She took her eyes from him for a brief moment, reaching inside the cabinet for a half empty bottle of dark amber liquid. She noticed a neat stack of lawn shirts, trews and trousers. Lottie grabbed the bottle, closed the door and quickly stood.

Beaty leaned toward the captain and said something quite low.

"English!" Lottie shouted.

Beaty lifted his hands. "I need a wee bit of help setting a course for Aalborg, aye? 'tis the cap'n's head that can work out all the figures — no' mine."

"No," she said as she skirted around the table with a bottle of brandy in one hand and the gun in the other. The throbbing had started up in her neck again, and her arm was beginning to burn from holding the gun aloft. She knew that it wobbled, and she could see the captain had noted it, too.

"Ah, there's an angel. Thank you, *pusling,*" her father said, and with a shaking hand, took the bottle she held out to him.

"You ought to put the gun down, Lottie," Mackenzie said. "You'll lose all feeling in your arm if you donna. You'd no' want to cause injury to yourself."

"Uist," Lottie said, warning him to be quiet.

He smiled wryly and asked, "What is the penalty for piracy, Beaty?"

"Hanging, sir."

"We're no' *pirates,"* Lottie said irritably.

"What is the penalty for holding a captain with a gun against his will, Beaty?" he asked, his gaze on Lottie.

Beaty paused to consider it. He shrugged. "Hanging. Or walking a plank."

The pain in Lottie's head began to shift to her belly.

The captain made a *tsk, tsk* sound. "You should no' have picked up the gun, then, aye?"

Her father, who had taken two healthy swigs of the brandy, suddenly chuckled. "Aye, he's a clever one, Lottie, this captain. He means to unnerve you. He canna know that you're no' easily disheartened."

Ironically, Lottie was feeling quite disheartened at the moment.

"Donna pay him any heed, *pusling."* Her father paused to take another healthy swig of the brandy. "*You* have the gun and the ship, aye? If you so desired, you could shoot them both and toss them to the fish and the crew would be none the wiser."

Lottie turned her head and stared at her father.

"By the bye, captain, your brandy is excellent."

"My intention is only to help," the captain said. "As you've said, you're in a wee bit over your head, aye? I'd no' like to see you on a plank."

"I'd rather hang, were it me," Beaty opined.

Lottie swung the muzzle of the gun from the captain to Beaty now. "All right, then, you've seen your captain and now we'll go below to tell your men he is very much alive, aye? Come now, before I find a plank for *you.*"

"Aye, go, Beaty, lest they deliver us into the depths of the sea," the captain said. "And God help them find Aalborg if they do." He smiled.

Bloody hell, but this man had her at sixes and sevens. Beaty started for the door, but paused to speak in Gaelic to Mackenzie.

"Now," she said sternly.

Beaty opened a door, and Lottie fell in behind him. She glanced at the captain as she followed Beaty out, and the man had the audacity to smirk. *Smirk.*

That's what she got for asking for help.

CHAPTER SIX

"My daughter, she's made of strong mettle, that one. Never known a woman like her. No' even her mother, God rest her soul."

She was a fool, and Aulay was on the verge of suggesting the old man was demented, but the door flung open and men began to stream into the room, led by the giant — the same one that had knocked the life from Aulay — who had to duck his head to enter. Two others followed him. They walked past Aulay without so much as a glance.

He wanted some explanation about who these people were, why they were crammed into his cabin, and what the bloody hell was wrong with the big one. He reminded Aulay of a bairn in a man's body. He was rocking back and forth on his heels and moaning as he stared down at the man on the bed. The younger one stood with his back to the wall, his legs braced apart, his jaw set, as if he was determined not to show the least bit of emotion. Aulay recognized himself in the younger one — he'd been that lad many years ago. He had two warrior brothers who had commanded their father's attention and respect with their physical prowess. He had two sisters who'd been the jewels of his father's eye. And he, third of five, had gone unnoticed unless he was behind the wheel of a ship. It was strange to think of it now, but at that age, Aulay had struggled to find the attention and praise in his family or clan. He was the quiet one, the studious one, the lad who pursued painting. It was hard to be noticed by the others, and he'd felt entirely inconsequential in the world except when he was at sea.

The third man in his cabin, of middling age, was a physician or healer of some sort. He examined the old man's wound.

The old man wanted a report of all that had gone on since they'd come aboard. The lad attempted to report, but the giant kept speaking over him, expressing his vociferous and sincere desire to go home. But when the physician removed the bandaging from the old man, the giant began a keening cry that startled Aulay . . . and no one else.

Moments later, the lass returned. The giant called her name, and she went to him, putting her arms around him, holding him close like a mother would hold a child.

"Drustan lad, calm yourself," the injured man said, and groped for the giant's hand as the healer finished removing the bandages from his torso. "It's no' but a bad gash, aye?"

Lottie leaned over the physician. Whatever she saw caused her to gasp aloud.

"Aye, what is it, then?" her father asked.

"What? Nothing!" she said, fooling no one.

"Now, now, donna the lot of you fret," the old man said. "A wound always looks worse than it is. Is that no' so, Morven."

"That is *no'* so," the physician said.

"You know verra well what I mean," said the old man. "Look at your long faces! I'll be right as rain!" he said irritably. "Why, I scarcely feel a thing, thanks be to the captain's fine brandy."

Aulay suppressed a groan. That was expensive French brandy, the last of what he and his brother Cailean had smuggled into Balhaire a few years ago.

"Have you any more of it?" the healer asked.

"Aye, there's a good lad, Mats, hand him the bottle."

"I'll need fresh water as well," the physician said, and Lottie went at once to the sideboard to fetch it, returning with the ewer.

The physician poured water directly into the brandy bottle — so much that there would be no salvaging the brandy. He shook the bottle to mix the contents, then put his hand on the injured man's leg. "Steady yourself, Bernt," he said, and poured the diluted brandy onto the wound.

The old man howled with pain, which startled the giant, and he, in turn, shrieked like a banshee. When he did, the youngest of them threw his hands over his ears. "By all that is holy, Drustan, donna do that!" he shouted. "It hurts me bloody ears!"

"I've made a sleeping broth," the physician said, nonplussed by all the shouting and screeching. "It ought to keep you from this world for a few hours, Bernt. You need to sleep, aye?"

"What if he dies?" the giant asked tearfully.

"I willna *die,*" the old man said sternly. "A small wound canna kill a Livingstone, lad."

"We'll need a clean bandage," the physician said. All of them looked at Lottie.

"Aye," she said, and without the slightest compunction, went to the cupboard beneath the sideboard and removed one of Aulay's shirts.

"I beg your pardon — *wait,*" Aulay said, but of course she paid him no heed, and handed the shirt to the physician. He tore the shirt into strips, then employed the two younger men to help him bind the old man's abdominal wound.

When the bandaging was done, the physician picked up a bowl. "This is the sleeping draught." He held it up like a vicar would hold a cup of wine at communion.

"Aye, let's have it, then," said her father. "I've got an awful pain, that I do."

Lottie lifted his head and the physician helped him drink from the bowl.

"All right, then, lads," her father said with a sigh when he'd finished. "You heard Morven — I'm to sleep now. Do as Lottie says, aye? But go now; let your old father rest. I'll be good as new when we reach Aalborg."

"I donna like to be here," the giant said to no one in particular. "I want to go home to Lismore."

"We'll be there soon enough, lad," the physician said, but Aulay saw the man exchange a look with Lottie. He doubted his own words.

Lottie kissed first the giant, then the younger one. "Mind you do as Duff or Mr.

MacLean tells you," she said to them. "If they donna need you, find a place to sleep. We've a long voyage ahead of us and I'll have you rested, aye?"

"But what of you, Lot?" the youngest one asked.

"I'll stay here, with Fader."

The young man glanced at Aulay and frowned. "What of *him*?"

All heads turned toward him. "We've no other place to put him," Lottie said with a shrug.

"I donna like to be here," the giant said again.

"Aye, I know," she said soothingly, and rubbed his arm. "None of us do."

"*I* do," the younger one said as he bumped into a chair on his way out. "This is a bigger ship than Gilroy's, and it's much faster. I should like to be captain of *this* ship one day."

"That post has been taken," Aulay reminded the lad as he reached the door.

The young man shot him a wide-eyed look and disappeared out the door.

"Keep an eye on your brother!" Lottie called after them as the giant followed.

"I *always* keep an eye," Aulay heard the younger one say in a tone that suggested he believed he was very much put upon.

"He ought to sleep like the bloody dead for a few hours," the physician said as he went out. He paused to look at Lottie. "You look like death, lass."

"Thank you," she said, and pushed wet hair from her face.

"Is there no place you might sleep, then?"

"I'll sleep here," she said.

The physician looked at Aulay.

"He'll no' disturb me," she said before the physician could remark. "He can do no harm, bound up as he is."

"Well," the physician said, then shrugged and went out. *"God nat,"* he said, wishing her a good night, and went out.

"God nat," she answered, and closed the door behind him.

Her expression instantly crumbled into exhaustion. She sighed wearily and turned her back to the door. She unbuttoned his greatcoat, shook it off, and returned it to its peg. She stood in her stays and chemise and a petticoat that was soiled at the hem and soaking wet.

She looked even smaller than before, her shoulders stooped, as if the events of the day had worn her down. The lass reached for her gown, laying her hand on it in several places, but apparently found it too damp. She walked to the bed and picked up a blanket that lay at the foot, and threw it around her shoulders. She paused to lean over her father and stroke his brow. "Aye, he's sleeping well now," she said wearily. "I would that the same could be true for me." Aulay had the impression she was speaking to herself. She moved away from the bunk and wandered to the far wall, studying the two seascapes that hung there. She touched one with her forefinger, tracing over the ridges in the paint. "The sea is so blue in this one," she said wistfully. "I should like to see water so blue one day."

That was unlikely, given the fate that awaited her.

"Where is it?" she asked.

Aulay looked at the painting. His talents did not adequately capture how blue the water was at Cadiz. "Spain," he said. "The Mediterranean Sea."

"Mediterranean," she murmured, as if testing the word. She dropped her hand. "I must take advantage of your hospitality again, captain."

"Hospitality? You confuse captivity with hospitality. What now?"

She opened the cupboard below the sideboard and dipped down.

"If it's more brandy you want, you'll no' find it," he said with an edge of irritation.

But it wasn't brandy she was after. She removed one of his shirts. And then a pair of trews. "I'm sorry for it," she said ruefully. "But I'm chilled to the bone and I desperately need dry clothes."

She took the blanket from her shoulders and draped it over her chair, then kicked off her wet boots. One slid along the cabin floor and reached the door. She put her pistol on the table, then putting one foot in a leg of the trews, and then the other, she struggled to pull them up beneath her petticoat without revealing any part of herself to him. When she had them secure, she removed the petticoat.

Aulay couldn't help but ogle her. The trews were too big for her smaller frame, and yet he could still see her figure, could still visually trace the shape of her legs into a heart-shaped bottom. He could still feel the rumblings of physical desire for this wee thief.

She glanced at him and frowned. "What, then?" she asked impatiently.

"A wee bit too big," he said. "But a better fit than I would have expected." He took in the full length of her. "*Much* better," he said. "You ought to make a habit of trews."

Lottie blushed. She picked up his shirt and unfurled it.

Aulay was beginning to enjoy this unexpected event. "This will be a wee bit trickier to don, aye?"

She looked around the cabin, presumably for a place to hide.

Aulay slid down the wall onto his haunches. "We donna stand on modesty on this ship," he said. He balanced his bound hands on his knees in anticipation of her disrobing. "Aye, but this is a bright spot in an otherwise bloody awful day."

"Will you turn your back?"

"No."

"I believed you a gentleman, Captain."

He shrugged. "Tis my cabin. My clothes. If it's privacy you want, you should have pirated another ship."

The lass frowned darkly. She put the shirt aside and began to work on the laces of her stays, but seemed to struggle with them. "My fingers are numb," she muttered as two spots of pink appeared on her cheeks.

"Come closer and I'll lend a hand," Aulay suggested. "I'm a bit of an expert with laces."

Her cheeks colored even more, and she yanked harder on the lace she was working, managing to pull it free. She hesitantly removed the stays and draped them over a chair. Now she wore nothing but the thin chemise, through which Aulay could see the arousing shadow of her breasts, the darker shadow of erect nipples. "You're certain, are you, that I canna be of assistance?" he asked wolfishly.

She turned her back to him and quickly pulled the chemise over her head and tossed it aside.

Aulay devoured her bare back with his gaze, studying every facet. The small knots of her spine. The curve of her waist into her hip. The gentle slope of her shoulders and the way her hair, bound up in a loose knot, brushed against her skin. She put her arm over her breasts and turned slightly to pick up his shirt, but he could still see the soft underside of her breast, her softly rounded abdomen. His blood was warming, inflamed by the sight of her enticing figure. It made him cross with himself — he ought not to admire her, his enemy, and yet, how could he not? She was beautiful — her shape, her creamy skin, her silken hair, all of it. She was terribly, undeniably, infuriatingly arousing.

She picked up the shirt and put her back to him again. She was taking her time, deliberately moving lazily now, obviously aware of the effect she had on him. He watched her stretch her arms up and into his shirt, then let it slide down her arms and over her head. She turned around. "How is that, then?" she asked as she rolled the hem and knotted it at her waist.

"Bloody well bold," he said.

"Aye, and what's wrong with it?"

"Nothing at all." His gaze slid to the opening of the shirt, the vee of which dipped well into her cleavage. His shirt was almost as thin as her chemise — he could still see the shape her breasts and imagined them filling his hands, his fingers curled into firm, plump flesh.

"I will thank you no' to look at me in that way," she said, and picked up the blanket, throwing it around her shoulders again before sitting in a chair.

"What way is that?"

She lifted one leg and rolled up the trews to her ankles. "As if you've never seen a woman before," she said, and rolled up the second leg before peeking up at him. "In spite of all the stays you've unlaced."

Touché. Aulay couldn't help but smile. "I've no' seen a woman as comely as you," he admitted. "What do you expect of me? You take my ship, my brandy, my clothes. You disrobe no' three feet from me, and expect me to close my eyes?" He shook his head. "I'm no' a dead man. No' yet."

A smiled shadowed her lips.

"Were I you, I'd wear precisely that on your next bit of piracy. Perhaps men will drop their swords on command."

She stood up and walked to his sideboard. "You weren't even wearing a sword," she said. "I wonder how the day might have gone had you been armed." She glanced over her shoulder and arched a brow.

He didn't need the reminder. He'd not worn a sword because it hadn't occurred to him to arm himself against what looked like a congregation of pilgrims without any notion of how to survive at sea.

She picked up his razor, put it down and picked up his soap. "And besides, there will be no more *piracy* for me," she scoffed. "I'm to hang. Remember?" She picked up his comb and returned to the table with it.

"Oh, I remember," he said, and watched her pull her hair down from its knot. Thick tresses tumbled over her shoulders. Even when wet, her hair seemed to glisten.

She began to comb it, starting at the bottom and working up. She mesmerized Aulay. He'd seen his sisters at their toilette, but he'd never really *watched* a woman comb her hair. Not like this, not in a manner that seemed so highly erotic.

When she'd worked the tangles out of it,

she braided her hair, using one long tress to bind the end. She returned his comb to the sideboard, then looked Aulay over. "You should rest now, aye?"

He chuckled. "Sleep is no' possible, lass. No' while my ship is in your hands. No' while you make generous use of my closet. I'd no' want to miss another disrobing."

She sighed wearily. "It is impossible to convey how much I should like to put this ship into your hands and remove it from mine," she said. "And return your clothes and anything else we've made use of." She walked to the foot of the bunk where her father lay, and crawled onto the small space at the foot of it. "I'd return your bloody ship and your clothes here and now if I didna have such desperate need for them." She curled up beneath the blanket. Her braid lay like a silk ribbon across the dark brown of the blanket.

"What of me, then?" Aulay asked. "Am I to be denied food and a chamber pot?"

"Pardon?" She lifted her head to peer at him.

"Supper," he said impatiently. "A chamber pot. I need to —"

"*Och,* you need not explain it." With a weary groan, she pushed herself up and brought her legs over the side of the bunk.

She braced her hands on either side of her knees and stared at him as if he were an unruly child.

He held up his bound hands. "I'm your captive, lass. You have a duty to tend to me as the rules of war demand."

"Rules of war!" She clucked her tongue. She pushed herself to her feet with some effort, gathered her discarded boots, then took his greatcoat from the wall once more. She picked up her gun, slid it into the pocket, then shuffled to the cabin door and opened it.

"Lottie," he said.

She paused. She slid a sidelong gaze to him.

"Something warm, aye? And some ale."

She pressed her forehead to the edge of the door with a sigh. "What more, captain?"

"Nothing," he said.

She started out the door.

"A chamber pot!" he said.

He heard her mutter as she went out. He smiled to himself. He couldn't threaten her into untying him. He couldn't scare her, either, apparently. But he had strength on his side, and he was determined to exhaust her into it.

CHAPTER SEVEN

A half hour or more passed before Lottie returned to Aulay's quarters carrying a cloth bundle and in the company of two men. The men undid the chain at Aulay's ankle, hauled him up between them, then escorted him out "to take the air."

Aulay was relieved to be out of the cabin and breathed deeply of the salt air. In the wake of the storm, a blistering array of stars and the full moon lit the deck. He could see casks of whisky stacked haphazardly and tied loosely about the main deck. He was surprised they'd not lost them in the storm.

At the stern, a man casually held a long gun and smoked a cheroot. Beaty was at the helm with two Livingstone men, in deep conversation that seemed, from a short distance, almost friendly.

When Aulay had dallied as long as he might, the men returned him to his cabin. As they moved up the few steps to the forecastle, the Livingstone physician emerged from the forward cabin. He backed out of it, really, and was laughing as he went. But when he turned about and saw Aulay, he quickly sobered.

"Who is within?" Aulay demanded.

"Wounded men, captain. One of ours, two of yours." He scurried down the steps past Aulay and his guards.

It was too casual. There was no tension — it was as if everyone had settled into this arrangement and had no objection to it. What had she done, entreated them? Played to their sympathies? Seduced them with her bonny face and beseeching blue eyes? Were they all as weak as he?

In the cabin once more, Aulay simmered as they shackled him like an animal. Lottie watched with heavy eyelids, her head propped on her fist.

"Now what?" asked one of the men.

Lottie yawned. "Rest, aye? But go now — I'd no' like Fader to wake."

Judging by the snores coming from the bunk, there was no danger of that happening.

When the men had gone, Aulay lifted his bound hands. "Untie me."

She sighed.

"How am I to eat, then?" he asked, gesturing to a hunk of bread, some cheese, and what looked like a cup of soup laid on top of his desk.

"Can you no' manage it?"

"*No,* I canna manage it," he said curtly.

She wearily lifted her head off her fist and stood, and seemed a little unsteady on her feet. She looked at Aulay, then the food. "At least you must sit, aye?" she said to him. "I'm at a disadvantage to try and help you, as tall as you are."

She picked up one of the heavy wooden chairs at the table and clumsily maneuvered it across the floor, positioning it next to the desk. She pretended to dust if off, then bowed low, sweeping her hand over it. "Your seat, captain."

He sat heavily, his stomach growling. When she didn't hand him anything to eat, he turned his head toward her.

Lottie was looking at his hands. She grimaced, then leaned over to have a better look. *"Mi Diah,"* She knelt beside him and touched her finger to a particularly raw spot on his wrist.

Aulay hissed with the burn of her touch.

"I should call Morven to have a look."

"You ought to take them off," Aulay snapped. "You've asked for my help, but keep me bound like an animal."

"You know I canna do that." She moved the food to the middle of the desk, carelessly pushing his papers and maps aside in the process, then dragged herself up to sit on it. Her legs dangled, her ankles crossed, her feet bare. She picked up the hunk of bread and tore two chunks from it, handing one to him, and popping the other in her mouth.

"Just how long do you intend to keep me bound, then?" Aulay asked before fitting the bite of bread into his mouth.

"Until we are to Aalborg."

"We're two days from Aalborg! I canna carry on like this. Leave me shackled if you must, but untie my hands."

She broke a piece of cheese and handed it to him.

Aulay caught her wrist and locked his fingers around it. She looked up with surprise. "I donna like to see you bound, but if I untied you, I'd have a mutiny. You're the only leverage we have, you are."

"You donna seem to me to be a demure wee lass who does as others bid her. If you want to see my wrists freed, then think of how to do it that spares you a mutiny."

She glanced away, but Aulay yanked her close. His gaze moved to her mouth. "*Untie me,* Lottie."

"I thought we had an understanding," she said.

"Whatever made you think we did?"

She leaned closer still, her face only an inch or so from his. She glanced at his hand, wrapped tightly around her wrist. Long, dark lashes fanned against her cheeks. "There are men just outside that door, aye?" she said softly. She lifted her gaze and locked it with his. "If I scream, they'll be inside so quickly that you'll no' have time to blink." She leaned even closer, her mouth now beside his temple. "I've brought fish stew. Will you eat a wee bit of it? Or would you prefer to feel the butt of a gun crack against the back of your head?"

Aulay turned his head, so that his cheek was against hers. The air around them seemed to crackle. A fire was brewing, and he couldn't say which of them burned brighter. "I canna be seduced, lass. No' with you, no' with food, no' with threats."

"More's the pity," she whispered into his ear, and sent an arc of fire shimmering down his spine to land squarely in his groin. She slowly leaned back and with her free hand, she picked up the cup from the table and showed it to him. "I'll need both hands if you're to drink."

Diah, but he was weak. Damnably weak.

He reluctantly let go her wrist.

She put the cup to his lips, splaying her fingers across his jaw to hold it steady. Aulay was too aware of her touch, of how light it felt against his skin, scarcely more than a whisper, yet hot at the same time. He drank the contents of the cup eagerly, as he was famished. A bit of it rolled down his chin, and she used the sleeve of his shirt she wore to blot it.

"You need a shave," she observed.

"Do you propose to hold a razor to my throat?"

"No' as yet," she said, and a smile flashed across her face.

Her bonny eyes were making it impossible to keep Aulay's rage billowing. Captivity, he was discovering, was exhausting. He felt himself on the verge of losing this battle of wills, of surrendering. Since he'd been strong enough to control the wheel of a ship, he'd been in command. He'd never *not* commanded the *Reulag Balhaire,* had never been at the mercy of another. It left him feeling small. His strength came from his command of a ship, of men. It came from the sea. It came from the smell of salt and the sound of the gulls and the constant roll as they pushed forward, and being denied access to those things weakened him. He felt a child again, pushed to the margin by stronger, more vibrant siblings . . . only this time, a wee lass had done it.

He needed a drink of something strong. He watched Lottie pull more bread from the stale loaf. "Have you any whisky?" he asked.

She smiled lopsidedly. "Quite amusing."

"Look there, in the chest next to the bed. There's a bottle of wine there."

"Oh?" She perked up. She slid off the desk and padded over to the chest and opened the lid. She retrieved a bottle and came back to the desk, uncorked it, fit it between Aulay's hands, then shimmied up onto the desktop again.

He took a long swig of the wine, and another, then handed the bottle to her.

She did not hesitate to put the bottle to her lips and drink just as long as he had before setting it aside and tearing off more bread for him.

Lottie Livingstone was a contradiction in many ways — graceful and fragile in appearance, yet obviously fierce and brave. She was the sort of raw beauty that real artists — artists better than him — would spend hours at their canvas perfecting. She ought to be studied and admired . . . but where were her admirers? What was she doing here instead of being held on a pedestal in some gentleman's eye, adored, admired and pampered?

He watched her drink more, then put the bottle aside so that she could hand him cheese.

He'd never been the sort to place a woman on a pedestal, had never met one that had sparked that desire in him. Had never been in one place long enough to feel that sort of desperate attraction. There had been nights, in ports far-flung, where perhaps he'd felt it for the space of a few hours, but it had never lasted longer than that.

No, the sea was his love. The world and all her beauty is what called to him. And yet, in a strange way, this woman called to him. The truth, if he could admit it to himself, was that he admired her. He was furious with what she'd done, but he admired her bravery. Her willingness to at least try. He wanted to know how it had all come to this. He wanted to understand her.

He ate the cheese, washed it down with wine, then asked, "How is it that such a bonny lass has come to be in my cabin, in my clothes, in command of my ship? We offered to take you aboard. There was no need to attack us, aye?"

She picked up the bottle and leaned closer to him, unaware — or perhaps very much aware — that the vee of his shirt afforded him a tantalizing glimpse of her breasts. "There was every need." She fit the bottle into his hands, then straightened up again.

"Tell me," Aulay said, and drank. "I should like one day to tell my children of the day I was captured at sea by a beauty, and I would know why."

"Donna call me that," she said abruptly.

"Beauty?"

She glowered at him.

Aulay shrugged. "Verra well. When I tell the story, I'll cast you as an old hag."

She suddenly smiled, and it lit her face. It lit the cabin. "I would prefer that to *beauty*," she said, as if the word offended her.

"You are the first woman I've ever met who did no' care to be considered beautiful."

She rolled her eyes.

"Tell me," he urged her.

She yawned. "You'll be disappointed, that I know, for you're a man of the world. We are only peasants and our dilemma is verra simple, it is. We've had hard times, we have, and we canna let the whisky go. It's all we have."

"What do you mean?" he asked, returning

the wine bottle to her.

"We've never been accused of refinement," she said with a snort.

Aulay didn't follow.

"There, you see? A man of *your* refinement canna understand. I refer to our circumstances at home."

"Lismore Island," he said. "The giant would that he were there now."

"Aye," she said, and rubbed her eyes. "Lismore Island, a wee spit of land on the western coast of Scotland, scarcely good for living at all. The south end is inhabited by the MacColl clan," she said, holding a hand out. "Where the fishing is quite good and the land arable. We have the northern end," she said, holding out her other hand, "good for naugh' but a few sheep, a few cattle and perhaps a wee bit of linen, but for the rabbits that have overrun us and eat our crops and burrow under our houses." She shifted her gaze to her father. "We donna earn enough to pay our rents, and our laird is quite unhappy."

"Who is your laird?" Aulay asked curiously.

"Duncan Campbell."

Aulay knew of Duncan Campbell. He'd become laird two springs ago when Jacobites who had not accepted the defeat of

Prince Charlie had murdered his brother, Colin. Aulay also knew him to be an ambitious man, as most Campbells were. They aimed to be the only licensed distiller of whisky in the Highlands, an end that they aggressively pursued.

"My father is our chief, aye? He's a wee bit starry-eyed." Her expression softened as she gazed at the slumbering figure. "He means well," she murmured and leaned against the wall, crossing her arms over her abdomen. "But he's quite careless."

"So you are determined to sell whisky to afford the tenant rents," Aulay said, filling in the pieces.

" 'Tis our only hope."

"Must you go to Aalborg?"

"How I wish I'd never said it!" she moaned. "But our laird, he suspects we were making spirits. He kept coming round, unannounced, to have a look. He inquired after us in Port Appin and Oban and he heard talk. We decided we had to sell what we had ere he found it and we lost all that we'd spent. But because he suspected it, and my father had recklessly talked of it around the island and in the nearest ports, we thought it no' safe to attempt to sell in Scotland or England." She dropped her gaze to her lap. "I was the one to suggest Aalborg, aye? My family and more of us on the island are descendants of Danes from Jutland."

Her rationale was not surprising to Aulay. Entire clans had been dispersed by the retribution heaped on the Highlands after the Jacobite defeat, and those that remained survived by any means possible. Even clans that had not taken the side of the Jacobites were suspect, and any whisper of it was all the English forces needed to raid cattle and villages. Livelihoods had disappeared and every remaining man, woman or child worked to rebuild and move on from those bleak years.

"So we made sail," she said. "There was no' a soul about, and yet, no' a day later, a ship flying the king's colors had found us, a tiny wee dot in a vast gray of sea against a vast sky of gray." She turned her gaze to Aulay. "Who *was* it?"

"Campbell, lass," Aulay said. He'd thought it a royal ship, but now, he had a different idea. "I'd wager he had someone watching you."

She sighed and closed her eyes. " 'Tis my fault, all of it."

Aulay felt a twinge of sympathy. He'd been chased a time or two, particularly in the years before the rebellion when he and his brother Cailean had smuggled in French goods. He knew how fear gripped a belly when a bigger, stronger ship gained on you. It was only because of his intimate knowledge of the Scottish coastline and his crew's ability to trim sails faster than most that he'd escaped when he had. "Your ship was too small, Lottie. The naval ship, its masts were taller, its sails fuller. You could no' have outrun it."

"Aye, so we discovered."

"They fired first?" Aulay asked.

She didn't answer right away, her gaze on her father. "He was concerned for me," she said softly, and drew her knees to her chest, her arms wrapped around them. "He was fearful they would catch us, and . . . well, the spoils of war, aye?"

Aulay said nothing, the thought souring his appetite.

She told him about how the blast that had hit their ship had knocked her father across the deck, and he'd been impaled with a piece of wood from the hull. "I thought he was dead. I turned about to fetch Morven, but another explosion came, and the top half of the main mast fell and scarcely missed us. And then another explosion, louder and more violent, only farther away.

I didna realize that we'd fired on the other ship."

She was speaking quickly, as if to purge it all from her memory. She told him how bedlam had followed, of how barrels of whisky rolled into the sea from a hole in the side of the ship's hull until her brother — Drustan, the giant, she said, threw himself across the hole and stopped them.

She told him that she'd turned her back on her father for only a moment, and he'd used that moment to yank free the piece of railing with his hands. She took another long drink of wine, then handed the bottle to Aulay.

"I tried to staunch the bleeding with my hands," she said, and stacked her hands on top of one another to mimic what she'd done. The color in her cheeks was rising. "There was so much *blood.* Then someone was pulling me away and Morven was there with a blanket or perhaps a bit of that mangled sail, and my father, he was pleading with me, 'donna let go the whisky, Lottie.' It was impossible to think. Everyone was shouting and the ship was roiling beneath my feet so that I could scarcely keep my balance, and my insides were being tossed about. I thought I would vomit." She laid her hand against her throat and released a slow breath.

She was still terrified — Aulay could almost feel it filling the room. Many years ago, he'd been caught by a particularly bad storm and had lost control of the rudder. They'd tried to manage it with the sails, but in winds that high, it was no use. With every wave that crashed into the ship, he thought he would draw his last breath.

He had awakened on deck the next morning to bright sun and a battered ship. One of his crew had gone missing, no doubt blown overboard. It was only by the grace of God he'd lost only one man. It had been the most harrowing night of his life.

"It was madness," she said. "My brother Drustan was quite upset, and as you've seen, he's no' right in his head. He can become . . . destructive," she said carefully. "And Mats! *Diah,* he believes himself to be a man, but he's *no'* a man, he's a lad still, and he canna save the world, no matter what he believes." She hopped off the desk and began to pace, rubbing her nape with her hand. "Gilroy said our ship was taking on water. The other ship was on fire, and they pulled around and sailed in the direction of Scotland. My heart was in my throat — I believed all was lost, we'd all drown. My father was cursing, trying to rouse himself when he could no' lift his head, and his face as gray as the sky." She shook her head and turned away from Aulay. "My father, he took my hand, squeezing as tight as he might, and said that I must pay him heed."

"I didna want to heed him," she said, clearly distressed. "I didna want to know how bad our circumstance. But he'd no' let me go, he kept gripping my hand, *squeezing* it," she said, shaking her hand. "He said, Lottie, donna lose the whisky, aye? If you lose the whisky, all is lost. There is no more money."

She seemed to be speaking more to herself, her gaze on the middle distance, as if he were not present.

"I didna believe him — how could it all be gone? But he swore he was telling me the truth. All gone."

She sank slowly onto a chair, her hands squeezed between her knees.

Aulay leaned forward. "Lottie, lass . . ."

She glanced up as if he'd startled her. "That was the moment we saw you," she said. "Can you imagine? At first, we thought it was the other ship, come round to finish us off. But it was *you.* You flew the colors of Scotland. It was a miracle."

Aulay frowned. "A miracle, was it? If you

believed it so, then why then did you deceive us?"

"Oh." She glanced at her hands. "You willna care for the answer."

"Tell me."

"Well. I tried to think what to do, but my father, *Diah,* he kept shouting, 'save the whisky, Lottie, think of the Livingstones we left behind, Lottie, they'll be sent from their homes if we donna pay the rents, Lottie.' "

Things were becoming a little clearer to Aulay now. She was not ruthless, but an inexperienced woman thrust into an untenable situation by her father and the men of her clan.

"And then it came to me — I knew how to save us all and the whisky. What we needed was another ship."

"Obviously."

She smiled ruefully. "Do you no' agree that it was a miracle of heaven that you came along when you did, captain?"

"No."

"I suppose it must seem unfair to you. But we didna know if you were friend or foe, and as Duff pointed out, it hardly mattered either way, for if you were a friendly ship come to help, there'd be no room with your cargo and our whisky. And if you were pirates? Or worse, *Campbells*?" She turned her hands palm up and shrugged. "In either event, we had no choice but to take your ship. Would you no' have done the same?"

"No," he said. "Did it occur to you, then, that you might have accepted our offer of assistance and asked about your cargo? We might have taken some of it. You might have even offered a small share in your profit to transport it, aye? Or you might have taken what we could hold and sold it in Amsterdam."

She gave him a contrite smile. "I knew you'd know what to do. Pity I didna seek your advice."

"Pity," he said crossly.

She leaned back, stretching her legs before her and crossing them at the ankles, as if the telling of her ordeal had settled everything for her, had absolved her of the sin.

"You've no' yet told me of your brilliant scheme to steal my ship. You didna appear to have any plan at all."

"Aye, that *was* the plan."

"Pardon?"

"I was to appear to be a damsel in distress, on a voyage with men who'd never been at sea, who didna know what to do. If you believed it to be true, which you did, we could board your ship without suspicion. Then, of course, the challenge was to

146

surprise you. But as it was the only chance we had, I let down my hair."

"You *let down* your hair?" he repeated incredulously.

She nodded. "My hair is what a shiny pebble is to a crow, captain. It was Duff MacGuire's idea that we all appear inept, which, frankly, we were. Duff is an actor — he told the men what they were to do."

Aulay was incredulous that they had crafted such a ridiculous plan. More incredulous that it had *worked.* He closed his eyes with a groan of indignant shame. "You have added grave insult to my injury, madam."

"It was Gilroy's idea that I bear a cut on my leg in the event we could no' surprise you straightaway. But we had no' the slightest hope that it would work. It was far easier than we could have imagined," she said, sounding perplexed by it. "None of you bore swords? Why did you no' bear swords or guns? And your men! They wouldna turn away from me."

Aulay felt utterly humiliated. His lack of foresight was astounding. Had he been away from the sea for so long he couldn't think?

"Does it no' seem utterly preposterous in the telling?" she asked curiously.

"Please, say no' another word. No' a single word."

She smiled sympathetically. "I beg your pardon, captain. But I do hope you understand that for us, it was either drown or . . . or borrow your ship. We had so much at stake."

"So do we, Lottie, aye?" he said angrily. "Did you consider it for a moment? Did you bother to think that you were no' the only one with so much at stake?" He shifted his gaze away from her, ashamed he'd been felled by a beautiful woman with a shapely leg.

"I regret the blow to your head the most," she added quietly.

Aulay gave her a sidelong glance.

"You were the only one who looked at me askance. The others, they looked at me as men always look at me, but *you* seemed a wee bit suspicious. And, well . . . poor Drustan doesna know his own strength."

"I beg to differ," Aulay said. "He appears to know it verra well." He wanted to murder something. His gaze traced over her body, down to her toes, and slowly up again. He had a fury rising in him that made him feel almost ill. He was a colossal fool, had made the mistake of a lifetime, and as he gazed at the very woman who had caused it to happen, his rage mixed with . . . desire. Lethal desire.

It was insanity to admire her for being so bloody audacious, for making a laughing-stock of him, but that's precisely what he did. Had he *ever* known a woman, or a man, for that matter, who could best him so? It was madness to imagine all the ways he would make her pay for what she'd done, and yet in the same thought imagine making love to her. But that was precisely what was in his head, imagining her without a stitch of clothing, how she would look beneath his body. How soft and warm and wet she would feel.

He'd lost his bloody mind.

He wished for sleep, to wake refreshed so that he might think again how to free himself of these goddamn binds. He stood up from the chair. "I'll sleep now."

She stood up, too, and watched him put himself down in the corner of his cabin and kick the chair away in frustration. He propped himself up against the wall and closed his eyes, unwilling to look at her bonny face another moment.

He heard her move the chairs around, heard her put herself on the floor next to her father's bed.

When he opened his eyes later, he was struck by how graceful she looked, curled with a blanket wrapped around her, that ribbon of blond hair snaking out behind her, that laughably small dueling pistol beside her.

He thought of how she would look in the days to come, when the authorities caught up to her. No matter the mad thoughts roaming about his head, he would not allow her to escape her fate for this. That was impossible. Pirates paid for their piracy, and audacious beauties were no exception.

CHAPTER EIGHT

Lottie was surrounded by wildflowers — the bright gold of gorst, the brilliant purple of thistle and heather, the rare lilac bind-weed. Flowers covered the meadow — which meadow, and where, she wasn't sure — but her horse, Stjerne, trotted confidently along, shaking his mane now and again with his pleasure at being in bright sunlight.

Lottie glanced back over her shoulder. Anders was riding an inky black horse and she laughed — he'd been trying to catch her for miles, but could never reach her.

She came upon a stream and dismounted to let her horse drink. She heard the black horse approaching and stepped out from beneath the boughs of a tree that stretched over the stream. She leaned up against Stjerne's side, his body warm and firm. Lottie watched the man ride into view, and realized, with an increasing race of her heart, that it wasn't Anders at all, but

Captain Mackenzie.

He was wet, soaked through. Wet *and* vexed, judging by his dark expression. His hard gaze slid from her face to her legs, and Lottie glanced down. When had she donned *trews?* She looked up, her pulse galloping, because his gaze was quite heated and locked on hers. She couldn't move. Her feet were stones, unmovable. She had no feeling in one arm, and the other was as heavy as a dead man. He leaned closer still, and his lips touched hers so softly that Lottie's heart stopped beating altogether. It aroused her, pooling warm in her groin, making her perspire in spite of the chill around her. But the kiss was rough and strangely tasteless, too, and something smelled like mildew . . .

Her eyes flew open. She blinked the morning blur away and slowly became aware of something at her back, something warm and firm. And against her mouth and cheek, the rough fiber of rope.

Rope? Lottie groggily pushed up onto her side and glanced over her shoulder. She suddenly recalled where she was and worse, realized that she had rolled into the captain's outstretched leg. Her mouth had touched the tail end of the rope that bound his hands. He sat with one leg bent at the knee, the other stretched in front of him and stared down at her with an expression that was quite smug.

Lottie banged her elbow in her haste to scramble away from him, rolling up onto her knees and pushing herself back. How on earth had she come as far as three feet to be resting against his leg like an old dog?

He glanced to his right; she followed his gaze. She saw instantly what had caught his attention: the gun. She must have kicked it or pushed it in her sleep. She dove for it, sliding across the wood floor and catching the butt of the gun just before him, managing somehow to roll to her side with it just out of his reach.

She came up on her knees again and whipped around. She was breathing hard with exertion and he . . . well, he was not. His expression had gone quite dark as he eased himself back against the wall. The smugness had turned into a wee bit of a smile, as if he was confident that while he'd lost this opportunity to have her gun, he would ultimately prevail.

How odd that part of her hoped he would. She had a sudden image of being taken in hand by this man, forced to atone for her crimes —

"Ah, there you, *mo chridhe,* my heart."

The sound of her father's voice startled

Lottie; she clambered to her feet, her traitorous heart beating hard against her ribs. Her father was sitting up on the bed at an odd angle. He'd bled through his bandage, but at least the gray pallor had gone from his face. His eyes were shining brightly. *Very* brightly, as if he'd had too much to drink.

"The captain and I thought you'd never wake, aye? Sleeping like the dead, you were. He's been out for a morning stroll, he has, and we've had a wee chat."

Lottie blinked, disoriented. What time was it? How long had she slept? Sunshine was pouring in through the portholes, casting shadows around her father. The ship, she noticed, was scarcely rocking at all.

"Look here, lass, I'm good as new, what did I tell you, then?" her father said with some effort.

"Are you?" she asked, moving to his side and smoothing the hair from his brow. His skin was damp to her touch. She opened the porthole so that he might have some fresh air.

"A wee bit of pain, as one might expect, having taken a bit of railing to the gut, aye? But hungry, Lot. Quite hungry, I am. I should think our good captain is hungry as well."

Lottie couldn't look at Captain Mackenzie. If he was hungry, he didn't volunteer it.

"I'll go fetch food for you, Fader."

"Aye, and bring Gilroy round. I'll have a word with him."

Lottie winced inwardly. She didn't relish Gilroy reporting that she had offered to pay the Mackenzie crew. Her father would be livid with her, but what was she to do?

"Go now, aye? We've only a day before we reach Aalborg and plans must be made." He thrust his finger into the air for emphasis, then winced with pain that it caused him.

"Fader, please, donna move," Lottie begged him. She turned away from her father, and her gaze landed on Mackenzie. His expression, other than being quite intent on her, was as impenetrable as it was searing, scorching her all the way through to her bones.

She quickly pulled on her damp boots and went out, careful to shut the door behind her. She stepped over Norval Livingstone, who had been put at the cabin door to guard it through the night. *"Norval,"* she whispered, shaking his shoulder. "I need you now, aye? Find Morven to tend my father."

Norval's response was a grunt. She continued down the steps. "*You!* Miss Livingstone!" She turned around just as Beaty vaulted down the steps from the quarterdeck. "We need men," he said curtly.

"Pardon?"

"*Men,*" he said again, as if she didn't speak a word of English. "We've sails and rigging that need work. We canna carry on like a wee rowboat can we?"

"Use as many of our men as you —"

"No' *your* men, madam! Do you no' understand, then, that *your* men are addlepated? They could no' raise or lower a sail if their life depended upon it."

She wished she could feel proper indignation at his characterization of her clan, but she happened to catch sight of Duff and his brother Edward behind Mr. Beaty. They were trying to pry open one of the whisky barrels with no success, and arguing as they went about it.

"Well then?" Beaty demanded.

"I canna simply free your men after taking such care to tie them up!"

"Hold your guns to us, I donna care, but I bloody well need men up on the rigging now!" Beaty demanded, his face red.

"All right," she said, throwing up a hand. "I need but a moment to —"

"Lottie? *Lottie!*"

She suppressed a groan and turned about as Drustan came barreling across the deck. "I want to go home now," he said. "I donna like it, I want to go home."

"I know, Dru, so do I," she said soothingly. "We've a day or two to Aalborg, then quick as a fox, we'll be on our way home."

"I want to go *now,*" Drustan shouted, and slammed his fist down on a barrel of whisky so hard that the top of it cracked, causing both Lottie and Beaty to jump. At the sound of it, Duff and his brother turned about, abandoned the barrel they'd been trying to open, and hurried forward.

Drustan was prone to violent fits when he was confused or frustrated, and sometimes, those fits were impossible to contain. Judging by the way he huffed now, Lottie feared such a fit was imminent if she didn't do something. "Would you like to see Fader?" she asked quickly to divert his attention.

Drustan jerked toward her with his fists clenched, blinking.

"We'll bring him some food, aye? Will you help me, then, Dru?"

Her brother nodded as his breathing slowed.

"Cracked the lid, you did, Drustan," Duff said, examining the top of the barrel. "Good

157

on you, then — we're in need of a tot or two to keep the Mackenzie men from revolting."

"Whisky!" Beaty cried. "I need those men working, no' in their bloody cups! Look here, I need men on the sails!"

Lottie could feel Drustan tensing beside her. "All right, all *right*!" she cried, and caught Duff's arm to have his attention. "Let him have his men, Duff," she said. "Remind them that they will be well paid." She felt anxious, too — there was too much happening, too many things to think of, and the fear of what would happen once they reached Aalborg was beginning to ratchet in her thoughts. "Keep guard, but let them set the sails."

"That is *most* unwise, madam," Duff said majestically.

"Please, Duff. We've a calm sea — we must reach Aalborg by the morrow or risk more trouble." She pulled Drustan around and made him move with her, leaving Duff's complaints behind her.

Mathais was below deck with Mr. MacLean. He was wet from the waist down, his dark blond hair sweeping across one eye. He was assisting in the delivery of breakfast to both the Mackenzie and Livingstone men. "Look what we caught this morning, will you," he said proudly, pointing to a fish that was at least as long as Lottie was tall. MacLean was hacking off chunks of it and throwing them onto a brazier. "I reeled it in myself."

"With a wee bit of help," MacLean wryly corrected.

"You ought to have seen me, Lot!" Mathais mimicked pulling in a line before taking a whack at the fish, slicing off a chunk of the meat, and tossing it onto the brazier.

The Mackenzie men, she noticed, seemed much more relaxed than the previous day. Quite congenial, really. Two of them were engaged in a lively discussion about the price of wool, of all things.

Lottie took some of the cooked fish and some ship's biscuits, and two flagons of beer, and left Mathais to hack away at the fish.

Morven was already in the cabin, leaning over her father, when she and Drustan entered.

"Ah, there's me lad!" her father said brightly when he saw Drustan.

"We brought you food," Drustan said.

Lottie closed the door, then made herself glance at her captive. He returned her look with such cool rancor that her pulse fluttered madly. He had a way of looking at her as if he could see her thoughts, her organs, her heart beating like a bloody drum. As if he could see her foolhardy regard for him.

She looked away from those piercing blue eyes and went to her father's bed, juggling the ale and food, and together with Drustan, served him some biscuits and fish.

Her father ate heartily. He licked his fingers as Mathais came in, banging into a pair of chairs in his haste to see his father and knocking one chair into the captain's foot without notice.

Mathais was eager to relate his fishing tale, and launched into it so loudly and without preamble that no one could squeeze in a word while Morven mixed something in a wooden bowl.

Lottie moved away from her father and handed the captain a biscuit. When he reached to take it, she noticed that the skin of his wrists looked much worse today. Raw, open wounds.

"Aye, and how did you know to fish the starboard side?" her father asked, interrupting Mathais before the lad succumbed from lack of breath.

"*Och,* Fader, I had a feeling, I did," Mathais said, hooking his thumbs in the waist of his pantaloons. "I had the idea from

the wind, and I said to the man in charge
— Beaty is his name — that I should think
there is some fish on this side of the ship,
aye?"

"Morven?" Lottie called quietly as
Mathais carried on. She motioned the
healer forward. She pointed to the captain's
wrists. Morven frowned at them.

"Can we remove the ropes?" she asked.

"Aye, if we donna, he'll suffer worse,"
Morven said grimly and reached for the
captain's wrists. He untied the rope and let
it fall. Palpable relief instantly washed over
the captain's face; he closed his eyes and
swallowed.

"Canna leave it," Morven said. "I'll see if
I've got something to make a salve. I'll
change Bernt's bandaging then tend to his
wrists."

As Morven moved away, the captain gave
Lottie a slight smile of triumph.

"Lottie? Lottie, where are you, *pusling*?"
her father called to her. "We've much to
discuss. Where is Gilroy?"

"Ah . . ." Lottie reluctantly moved away
from Mackenzie and his freed hands, but
took the rope and anything else he might
reach and use against her. "Gilroy is at the
helm, he is."

"We've to prepare for the landing on the

morrow," her father said, and slapped Morven's hand away from the bandaging around his torso. "Leave it, man."

"I ought to have a look, Bernt."

"Look at my appetite, lad, if you want something to look at, aye? I'm fit as they come. I've long enjoyed excellent health, have I no', lads? Aye, then, Lottie, Gilroy, he'll accompany you on the morrow. You'll need to bring along the Mackenzie captain, too," her father continued, as if it were a trifling matter. So trifling, in fact, that he paused to drink from the flagon of ale.

"Pardon?" said Lottie at the same moment the captain said, *"No' bloody likely."*

"You canna leave him here — we've no' enough men to guard him and the crew, have we?" her father pointed out. "His crew will no' act while we have him, trust me on this. They'll do as we say."

"They'll do as *I* say, and I'll no' go ashore," the captain said firmly.

"*Och,* but you will captain, you will. We'll hold your Beaty under threat of harm if you donna."

The captain suddenly surged to his feet with surprising agility. "You would add to your crimes by threatening my first mate?"

"Fader!" Lottie exclaimed. "How can we possibly command him if he is no' bound? I

162

can hardly walk through the streets of Aalborg with a bound man at my side."

"Gilroy will keep him under control," her father said.

"I'll go," said Mathais. "I'm *verra* good with a sword." He made a thrusting motion.

"No, Mats, no' you. You must remain here to help guard the first mate."

Mathais perked up at that.

"No!" Lottie insisted. She could imagine it — Mathais would get it into his head that he ought to use his sword at the slightest hint of provocation.

"Now, *pusling,* you canna go dressed as you are." Her father said. "What would our Mr. Iversen think of you then? Can you imagine, Morven, our Mr. Iversen having a look at his long lost love dressed as she is?"

Morven's jaw tightened.

Lottie could feel her face turn an appalling shade of red. It was bad enough that everyone on the island knew of her love affair. It was humiliating to be reminded of it at every turn. "I am *no'* his long lost love and I hardly care what he thinks."

"Of course you do, *leannan.* Why, he's the reason you suggested Aalborg, is it no'?"

Morven, she noticed, avoided her gaze. And the captain, well . . . she could feel his eyes boring through her back. He was probably imagining all sorts of scenarios just now, and probably all of them very near true.

"Our Mr. Iversen will be pleased to lend us a hand," her father blithely continued. "You were clever to think of it, *pusling.*"

"Will you no' refer to him as *our* Mr. Iversen? And I donna intend to see him more than a moment to ask if we might use his name. I've enough to do as it is."

"No? Well, I suppose it is time you put that unfortunate acquaintance behind you. Canna remain at my side all your life, can you, lass? No' good for a woman to be without a man."

"Fader!" She wished a hole would open in this ship and suck her into the sea's depths. What was more dismaying — that her father was speaking so carelessly of a painful time in her life? Or that Morven and *worse,* Captain Mackenzie, were on hand to hear it?

Her father said, "Look at her, then, the lass can scarcely bear to think of it. Aye, well, no man on the island can bear to think of it either, for it's ruined you for anyone else, *mo chridhe.*"

"That is *quite* enough!" Lottie snapped. What was the matter with him? He was never so careless with her feelings and yet seemed almost oblivious to them now.

What he said was true. Since Anders Iversen had come to Lismore and ruined her idea of anyone else, and worse, since Anders had *left* Lismore, she'd been the object of great speculation. He'd come in the spring from Denmark, a distant cousin of the family. He'd come when the meadows were full of wild flowers like those she'd dreamed about, and the sun bright but not too hot, and he'd swept Lottie off her feet with his dazzling smile and quick laugh and touches to her hand and face. After years of caring for her brothers and her father, of having no prospects that excited her, of being the object of desire of every male on that island, no matter their age or occupation or other entanglements, Anders had made her heart leap, and she'd fallen head over heels into infatuation.

Her infatuation strayed beyond moral decency into a more physical realm. She'd convinced herself that God had sent her the man she was destined to marry, that her lack of virtue was expected, given their mutual feelings.

Diah, she'd been so unforgivably naïve.

Anders revealed himself to be a bloody arse. What sort of man would turn his back on a woman after sharing such a profoundly intimate experience? What sort of man would not then offer to take the woman to wife, especially after giving her every reason to believe that he would? And yet, Anders had seemed surprised she'd even thought it. He'd taken her hands in his and said with grave earnestness, "Lottie, *søde,* I'm bound for home at the end of the month. I'm to take over my father's affairs. You *know* this."

Well yes, he'd said that in the beginning. But as passion between them had grown and swelled she had assumed things had changed. She'd always fancied herself too clever to be manipulated by a charming libertine. She was not very clever at all, as it turned out.

"You'll come with me," Anders had said, knowing full well she would not.

Aye, he knew her better than she knew herself, for that was the first time Lottie's idea of herself veered sharply away from who she really was. All her life, she'd wanted to step out into the world, to leave that island with its too many rabbits and too few people and live. *Really* live. To see the world, to fall in love, to have a happy, healthy family. But when it came down to a choice to be made, the painful realization had set it. She couldn't leave her father or her brothers, not really. They all needed her. They all depended on her. She knew it, and Anders, damn him, had known it all along. She could recall the way his smile had faded into dismay when he'd understood that she'd given herself to him because she loved him. It had not been a lark for her as it obviously had been for him.

Now, a year later, she knew the whisper on everyone's lips: what would happen to Lottie Livingstone? Should she not be married now, should she not be providing some man his blessed heirs and warming his bed and washing his linens and cooking his meals? Why was it that men were the only ones entitled to their desires in this world?

She looked up; her father was watching her with eyes so bright and glittering that they startled her. "*Och,* donna be downtrodden, lass," her father said. "Put your hair up and pinch your cheeks, don your gown, and you'll be as bonny as ever. He'll rue the day he left *you* behind."

"He didna leave me behind," she said, trying to salvage at least a piece of her dignity. "And my gown is ruined. It is torn and stained with blood."

"You'll find something on this ship to mend it, mark me. They mend sails, do they no'? A bit of soap ought to remove the blood — *oof,* Morven, must you prod so?" her father complained as Morven tried to look under the bandage.

"It needs changing, Bernt."

"I'll need something for the pain, then," her father said. "Burns like the devil, it does."

"Fader?" Drustan said nervously.

"Donna pay me any heed, lad," her father said to Drustan. "Tell you what — go ask Gilroy if you can be of any use. Go with him, Mats. Find the lad an occupation. Lottie, go along as well, and find a way to mend your gown. 'twas your mother's favorite, and mine, too."

Lottie gladly quit the cabin and the shrewd eyes of the captain. She followed her brothers to the door.

"Lottie," her father said, stopping her before she could make her escape. "You'll need to have the captain shined and polished as well, aye? Canna have him accompany you looking like a pauper. No' especially if you mean to see Anders. Now *there* was a handsome lad if I ever I saw one. Was he no', Morven?"

"Donna recall," Morven muttered.

"Well *I* do. Bonny as a man can be, I'll say that for him."

Lottie opened the door and walked out,

168

shutting it firmly behind her.

Unfortunately, she had no place to go and lick her wounds, so she settled on top of a whisky cask and watched the Mackenzie men up on the rigging changing the sails, chattering back and forth while the Livingstones guarded them from below. They all seemed rather friendly, and she couldn't help wonder if they hadn't hatched some sort of plan, if this wasn't the calm before the storm of revenge they meant to launch.

"Lottie."

She jerked around at the sound of Morven's voice. His brown hair stood nearly on end, and his beard was beginning to look unkempt. "You best find a physician when we reach Aalborg," he said grimly. "Bernt's wound, it doesna look good. I've given him the laudanum tincture for the pain so he'll sleep. But he needs proper attention."

"But you —"

Morven shook his head before she could finish her thought. "I'm no' a physician, Lottie. He needs a proper one. I've done all I can do, aye? I'll make a salve for the captain's wrists." He moved to leave her.

"Morven!" she said. "How will I do as my father says I must? I canna take Mackenzie with me! He'll escape, he'll seek authorities straightaway."

"Aye, you can," Morven said. "These men will wait for their pay and their captain, but if they have only one of those things, they'll no' wait long, do you see? You need to take him with you for our sake."

"And then what?" she asked. "If they wait patiently while we sell the whisky, and then again while we wait for someone to unload it from this ship, will they merrily make sail without us? How will we all return to Scotland?"

"You were right to offer them pay, you were. Coin is a powerful lure. I suspect they'll go along, aye. As for us, we'll be *rich,* Lottie. We can hire the best ship to return us home."

Rich! They would have enough to pay their rents to Campbell and a wee bit more to pay this crew. No one would be rich!

"I'll make the salve now, aye?" Morven said. He smiled kindly and patted her arm, then walked away.

Did any of them truly believe the Mackenzies would so easily forget what the Livingstones had done to them, even if they were paid? And what of the captain? She couldn't imagine that he'd forget a single moment. She saw the way he looked at her — he would delight putting the noose around her neck himself.

She shivered in the bright sunlight at the very thought of it. Until they had sold that blasted whisky, they were stuck. Lottie had no other viable option that she could see. She got off her barrel and went in search of something to darn her gown.

CHAPTER NINE

The raw skin of Aulay's wrists burned with the slightest movement. His discomfort had been made worse by the incessant chatter of the old man, but thankfully, he'd finally fallen asleep under the weight of his many words.

His sons had left, too, thank the saints. Between the boasts of the young one, and the fear of the giant one, and the many words of the old one, it felt as if the Livingstones had consumed all the available breath.

With the twin portholes open to allow a flow of air, Aulay could hear the men outside. He recognized the voices of more than one of his crew up on the rigging. That gave him some ease, knowing that his men were at work, trimming sails as Beaty needed, and sailing these thieves on to Aalborg.

He and Beaty had discussed it very briefly

in Gaelic when Beaty had entered this room. Aulay had told him the lives of the crew were the only thing that mattered to him; Beaty assured him he'd handle things on deck and see them safely to shore. Like him, Beaty was more concerned with the ship and their men than avenging what had happened. But some of the men were obviously free to work the sails, and Aulay could hope that meant there was something underfoot that would return his ship to him.

He felt utterly useless and increasingly frustrated by his impotence, an old, familiar feeling he'd often felt at home. A burden to them all, useful to no one.

The door opened, and the lass returned carrying the tools required for sail repair — a large needle, waxed thread, a brace to stretch the fabric. She also carried a small glass jar.

She put the things down on the table and with the glass jar in hand, she turned around to him. The gun, he noticed, was tucked into the trews she wore.

"Morven made this for your wrists," she said, holding it out. "Will you allow me to tend to you without trouble?"

"What trouble could I give you, then?" he asked irritably. "I'm hobbled like a hog." He waved her over, grateful for any relief she could give the burning skin around his wrists.

She placed the gun on the table and approached him warily, sinking down onto her knees beside him. She opened the jar, and a pungent smell made his eyes water. "What in the devil is that?" he complained, rearing away from it. "It smells bloody awful."

"Morven said he used a wee bit of fish entails —"

Aulay unthinkingly jerked his hands back, but she caught one and dropped a dollop onto the raw part of his wrist. He was set to protest, but she began to rub the concoction into his skin, her touch feathery light, and the relief to his skin was instantaneous.

He relaxed.

He watched her fingers move gracefully on his wrist. She kept her eyes on the task, but she was so close, he could see the translucence of her skin, the slight shadow of a vein at her temple, a gentle pulse at her neck. Her hair, though tangled and knotted haphazardly at her nape, looked like silk. He wanted to touch it, to feel it between his fingers. He leaned forward, his desire to at least smell it —

She stilled. "What are you doing, then?"

He didn't answer her. In spite of the harsh conditions, she smelled surprisingly nice.

She slowly continued working on his wrists, smearing more of the unguent on his flesh. She turned his hand over, and Aulay caught her fingers in his. Lottie arched a brow in silent question. He answered by tugging her forward until she was close enough to kiss. He wasn't thinking — he was wrapped in a cloud of her feminine scent, and his actions were divorced from his thoughts. He touched his lips to hers. There was stillness in her — when everything around him moved every moment of the day, he noticed stillness. She was quiet calm.

He moved his lips on hers, touched his tongue to the seam of her lips.

Her lips parted beneath his, and he felt the touch of her tongue to his. But Lottie suddenly receded from him like water. "You've gone off your head, you have."

On the contrary. This was the first he'd felt himself, a healthy, living breathing man, since she'd kicked him in the chin. But he eased back and took some pleasure in the pink blush of her cheeks. "Who is our Mr. Iversen, then?"

A blush deepened. "No one." She turned his hand over, palm up.

"Shall I guess, then?"

"No."

He cocked his head to one side to study the way her lashes seemed almost to brush against her cheeks as she worked on his wrist. "He treated you ill, did he?"

She clucked her tongue at him. "It hardly commands any thought at all to guess that, does it?"

"What happened?"

She returned one hand to his lap, dipped her fingers into the jar. "Why did you kiss me? 'twas only yesterday that you wished to see me hang."

"I still do," he said. "I can admire a woman, can want her, and still believe she deserves to hang." He smiled a little.

One corner of her mouth tipped up and she rolled her eyes, then started to attend his second wrist, her touch so damnably soft that it sent a sparkling little jolt up his arm.

"You deserve better, Lottie," he said. "You deserve a man who will treat you well, aye?"

She suddenly stopped what she was doing and sighed heavenward. "Do you think me a fool, captain? Do you think I donna know what you're about?"

Surprised, he asked, "What?"

"Flattery." She said it as if she was accusing him of violent assault. "I've heard quite a lot of it in my life, that I have, and I know its purpose." She turned her attention to his

wrist once more.

"For the life of me, I donna flatter you, lass, no' now, no' ever, aye? But I donna think you deserve to be treated ill."

She shook her head.

He impulsively touched her face, and that stillness came over her again. "What happened?"

She moved her head from his touch. "Are you married, Captain Mackenzie?"

"Aye. To a ship."

"Verra touching. But a ship canna keep you warm at night. Why have you no' taken a wife?"

"I beg your pardon."

"Ooh," she said, her brows rising with amusement. "You must believe that as *captain,* you're the only one who is allowed to ask questions of a highly intimate nature."

He shrugged at the truth in that statement. "I believe I have a right to know who holds me captive and why."

She puffed a thick strand of hair from her eyes and continued with her attention to his wrist. "Mr. Iversen has no bearing on why I am holding you captive, does he? Why have you no one here to keep your cabin tidy, then? Scores of captains are married and away at sea."

"Scores," he scoffed. "Most of the captains

I know are as married to the sea as I."

"You seem lonely, that's all. A man as accomplished and capable as you, painting views of the sea with no one in it. Have you never longed for a wife? For children who will bear your name?" A smile shone in her eyes. "You *obviously* long for the sort of company only a woman can provide, aye?"

"You are bloody well brazen," he said, a wee bit stung by her observation.

"Obviously so," she said, and shrugged, still smiling. "I only wonder why there are no lassies about for the handsome captain."

Why did he feel so defensive about her remarks? There was a time when he was a young man that it seemed every time he stepped off a ship, someone was inquiring about his intentions to wed. In the last few years, no one bothered to inquire at all. The only person who had thought there was even the slightest chance of it was the fragile little English flower, Avaline Kent, whom his brother Rabbie once had been engaged to wed. That lass had, inexplicably, fallen in love with Aulay while engaged to his brother, and had truly believed there was some chance he would return her affection. Ridiculous creature, she was.

He realized Lottie had finished tending to his wrists and was wiping her fingers, studying him. "You have a curious way of turning conversation around," he said.

"Did I offend you, then? I beg your pardon. I only meant it's odd that a man of forty years would no' have sought the companionship —"

"Forty years! I've no' reached my *fortieth* year," he huffed. He had three years before that momentous occasion and planned to cling to every one of them. "And I *have* sought the companionship of women, but not in the prim way you undoubtedly imagine."

She laughed, and the sound of it was like morning birds, cheerful and gay. "You might verra well be astonished by the things I imagine," she said silkily. "Look at you, then — one moment you're full of flattery for your captor, the next, you're fuming over some slight. Fickle, you are." She stood up.

Fickle? Aulay had been called many things in his life, but never *fickle*. "Now you must think *me* the fool, Lottie. Do you think I donna know that you are avoiding the subject of Mr. Iversen? Is the subject of him so verra painful, then, that you will avoid your answer by needling me?"

She lifted her head, looked him directly in the eye and said without emotion, "Aye, I suppose it is." She shifted as if she meant to move away. But Aulay caught her wrist, his fingers sliding across her skin, then lacing his fingers with hers.

"What are you doing?"

"You're no' the only one who understands," he said quietly.

She tried to yank her hand free.

"I understand you're as brazen as a red buck. You've been disappointed, and you'll no' allow anyone close because you fear it will happen again."

"You're as absurd as you are lonely," she said, and attempted to yank her hand free again. "I donna *fear* it — I know it will happen again. Men are, by their nature, disappointing."

But Aulay held on. And he smiled. Her eyelids fluttered as if she'd seen something she couldn't quite make out. Her hand relaxed in his, giving into him, and when she did, he released his grip of her. She slid her hand away, her fingers trailing over his palm and sending that alarming bit of sparkle up to his chest again. She took a step backward, tucked a bit of hair behind her braid. "Morven says I'm to let the unguent sit for an hour, then apply more," she said to the wall. She turned around and walked back to the table, moved some things around without purpose, then dropped her hand. "I best go and . . . and . . ."

She never finished her sentence. She simply walked out the cabin door.

He heard the cask roll in front of it once again, sealing him in here with a slumbering, dying, man.

The day wore on, a host of people in and out to see after the old man who, from Aulay's observation, was not on the mend, but on the decline. He slept quite a lot, moaned in his sleep, but when awake, he would somehow rally and begin to talk.

Diah, did he talk. He asked about pirates, if they should have fear of them sailing around the horn of Denmark. He asked what a ship like this cost a man of Aulay's stature? How long would salted beef keep? Did he know Victor Mackenzie of Oban? He was a fine fellow but missing an eye. His right one.

Aulay was allowed on deck thrice in the course of the day. It was a gorgeous day at sea. There wasn't another ship about, nothing but bright sunlight and a good stiff western wind to send them on. Beaty was on the quarterdeck with the Livingstone captain. It seemed, from a distance, as if some arrangement between them had been struck.

On his second foray, those Mackenzies who had been freed to work the rigging leaped down and surrounded him. His guards seemed not to mind.

"How do you fare, Cap'n?" asked Billy Botly, whose arm had been set in a splint.

"Keep your heads," he told them in Gaelic. "We'll be in port soon enough."

"No' right, Cap'n," said Geordie Willis. "No' right at all."

"No," he agreed. "We'll sort it all out, we will. But for now, you must do everything in your power to no' lose the ship."

Of course, they readily agreed. It was their only livelihood.

On the third outing, someone had been offended — he walked out to quite a lot of shouting about Scottish rogues and bastards in English and in Gaelic, and fisticuffs broke out between two men. But two Mackenzies pulled a third Mackenzie sailor back and chastised him for the fight.

That seemed odd to Aulay, but it wasn't until he'd been returned to the cabin that he realized why. His men did not like to see him bound . . . but they didn't attempt to do anything about it. They didn't attempt to take him, they didn't demand concessions. They didn't even *ask.*

What in blazes was happening? Had she really charmed them all? She was an astoundingly beautiful woman, they were all painfully aware of that, but surely that did not rob *all* these men of righteousness.

Speaking of that women, Aulay had not seen her since he'd unthinkingly kissed her. The physician had come to reapply the salve, then had wrapped his wrists in what was left of Aulay's shirt. Another man brought him food.

The sun had disappeared by the time Lottie returned to his cabin. She carried a bucket of fresh water, soap, and a soft rag. She didn't speak to Aulay, but settled in next to her father and bathed his face.

Her father tried to push away her hand, but he was losing strength. She dabbed the water onto his forehead while the old man muttered something about a cow.

She glanced over her shoulder at Aulay only once, perhaps to assure herself she still had a captive, and didn't look again until the physician appeared a quarter of an hour later carrying a cup, the contents of which smelled foul.

"What is it?" she asked, wrinkling her nose.

"A healing broth laced with laudanum."

He slipped his hand behind the old man's head and held the cup to his mouth, forcing it in between his lips. The old man sputtered and tried to turn his head.

"Drink it, Fader," Lottie said soothingly. "It will help you to feel better, aye?"

"Only a corpse would feel better after imbibing that," he said coarsely. "Where are my sons? Bring my sons."

"They're needed below just now," she said, and exchanged a look with Morven. "Please, Fader, donna speak now. Mr. Beaty says we ought to be in port by the morrow."

"Aye, as I guessed," the old man said, although it was impossible that he might have guessed anything in his current state. He shifted about on the bunk as if settling in for the night. "I'm lying here, useless to you all, but I can still sense how fast the wind moves us. Once a sailor, always a sailor."

"You were never a sailor," Lottie said sweetly.

"Aye, but I might have been," he said through a yawn. "I verra well might have been."

Lottie and the physician stood shoulder to shoulder, watching the old man for what seemed an eternity. Finally, they turned as one away from him.

"I've only so much laudanum, Lottie. He needs a proper physician."

"Aye," she agreed. "How will we pay?"

The physician shook his head. "I'll ask around and see if there is any coin aboard this ship."

He walked across the room to Aulay and went down on one knee to have a look at his wrists.

"There's no' a farthing in the pocket of any Livingstone," she said. She removed her gown from a peg on the wall.

"Perhaps a Mackenzie then," the physician suggested.

She snorted. "We've taken too much from them."

"They donna have a choice," the physician said. He rewrapped Aulay's wrists. "Healing nicely, it is," he said, standing up. "In a month, you'll no' recall it."

"I will recall it," Aulay assured him.

The physician stroked his chin as he stared down at Aulay. "Have *you* any coin, captain?"

"Morven!" Lottie said.

"He's bound to have a few crowns, aye?"

"No," she said sternly. "We'll no' ask it of him."

"I didna intend to ask," the physician said with a shrug, and gathered his things.

"Bernt ought to rest soundly until the mor-row."

He went out, and Lottie sank into a chair at the table. She picked up the heavy darn-ing needle they used to repair sails. She threaded it and began to try and push the thick needle through the fabric of her gown.

Aulay watched her for several minutes. "I could go for a dram of whisky, I could."

She paused and looked up. Then dropped her sewing to the table. "Aye. So could I. As it happens, one of the casks has been opened." She put the things aside and went out the door.

Several minutes later she returned with two wooden cups. She slid down the wall to sit beside Aulay, leaning up against the wall next to him. She stretched her legs out beside his and handed him one of the cups.

Aulay took a long draught, relishing the familiar burn in his throat.

Lottie sipped.

"You've charmed my men into working by offering them the whisky, have you? That would explain the fraternity."

"I didna charm them. I offered to pay them."

Surprised, Aulay turned his head to her. "Pardon?"

"I mean to pay them," she said, and

sipped again.

"Pay them . . . with what, then?"

"With the proceeds of our sale."

Aulay was shocked. No wonder there had been no attempt to free him. "What sum did you promise?"

She shrugged. "I donna know, exactly, but I promised to pay them more than your wage."

Good God, she meant to steal his men, too.

She laughed lightly at his thunderous expression. "Donna fret so, captain. They're still verra loyal to you, on my word. They've called us every name they can think of in Gaelic and in English. Beaty put an end to it — he told them to keep their heads as you'd said, that we'd settle up in Aalborg on the morrow if pirates didna snatch us first."

"Have you considered there is little to keep them from stealing your whisky when you weigh anchor in Aalborg?"

She frowned. "No, I have no' considered it. But we'll hold Beaty. And . . . we'll have you."

Aulay's brows dipped. *"No,"* he said firmly, then drained the rest of the whisky. It burned unpleasantly in his belly. "Go and sell your bloody illegal whisky if you like, but leave me out of it."

"I would if I could," she said. "On my life, I canna think of much worse than to drag you along."

"*You* canna think of worse?" he asked, incredulous. "I am astonished how you've come to view your thievery as just, and that I am somehow impeding your progress."

"Well, you *are*," she said matter of factly. "It will be a chore to have to watch you with one eye, dock thieves with the other and strike a deal with the Copenhagen Company all at the same time." She smiled at him. "So please, then, donna give us trouble."

"Ask all you like." He tossed his empty cup aside.

She nudged him with her cup, handing it to him. He grudgingly took it. "Surely you realize that the sooner we are done with the sale of our whisky, the sooner you might have your ship and be on your way. You will sail on to Amsterdam, your men will have full purses, and this will all be but a distant memory."

Aulay turned about so he could look her in the eye. "Lottie, lass . . . do you honestly believe that I will let you go?"

When she looked up at him, the low light of the candle made her eyes shimmer, distracting him from her ridiculous assumption that he would merely allow her to swan away in that torn gown of hers.

"I hope it," she said softly.

He impulsively touched her cheek with his knuckle, stroking it. "I'll no' allow your thievery to stand without answer. I'll be held responsible for the loss of my cargo, so you've left me no choice but to see you brought to justice."

She glanced at her father. Aulay stroked her cheek again, and she leaned into his touch. How odd, this conversation, he thought. He was speaking of bringing her to justice for her crimes when all he could think of was kissing her. Something was terribly off balance in him, and he didn't know how to right it.

"Take me, then," she muttered. "Bring me to all the justice you like, but let the rest of them go home to their families. No one wanted this."

Who was this woman? What woman offered herself up as the sacrificial lamb?

Lottie suddenly stood up. "You ought to rest, Captain. Come the morrow, you'll have quite a lot to keep you occupied." She walked back to the table, picked up her sewing, and began to struggle with a needle too big for her gown.

Aulay watched her from the shadows of

his corner. The way she bent her head, the wisp of hair that fell over her eye, all of it filled him with longing. He imagined standing next to her, a man in control of his destiny and his movements. He imagined them together at the helm. At a dance. In his bed.

At an altar.

He must be teetering on the brink of insanity. He was bound, his ship under the control of his enemy, of this woman . . . and he was thinking of bedding her. Of *more.*

He downed the rest of her whisky and turned his back to her, unwilling to watch her any longer, unwilling to see one more disturbing image in his head that involved her, and struggling hard against the pull into her web.

He dozed off, but he was awakened by the sound of water. He opened his eyes, blinking against the dark. He was still in his cabin, still shackled. The only difference was that the light had grown dimmer and he could smell rain through the open porthole.

Aulay groggily turned his head, and when he did, his heart lurched in his chest. Lottie was at the table, bare from the waist up. She was partially turned away from him as she dipped a cloth into a bucket, then cleaned herself. She stretched one arm up and bent it over her head, and stroked the cloth on her skin, slowly sliding it down her side before dipping it in the bucket again.

The sight of her bathing was erotic and made Aulay instantly hard. He imagined bathing her. He imagined taking that cloth and tossing it aside, of putting his hands on her breasts, his mouth on her neck and the concave of her belly. He imagined her naked, those two pools of her eyes shining with pleasure and propelling him to drive into her until she cried out with release.

Lottie turned her head to the side and stilled, holding the cloth against her breast now. She stood like that for no more than a moment, then began to rub the cloth in a circular motion over her breast.

Did she know that he watched her? She never looked at him, never turned her head toward him, and yet she moved the cloth in a sensual path over her body.

He would swear she was aware of his attention.

When she finally doused the light, he was so hard he ached.

Chapter Ten

Gilroy pointed to a ship in the distance that had trailed them around the tip of Jutland and the white sandy beaches of Skagen. "Pirates, I'd wager," he said, and propped his foot on a barrel, leaning onto his knee as he squinted into the distance.

"You'd be a poor man, then — that's the Danish Navy," Beaty said, and lowered the spyglass.

Gilroy chuckled. "That's no' a naval ship, lad."

"The hell you say. I've sailed these seas as long as I've been able to stand on me own two feet, I have, and I think I know a naval ship when I see one," Beaty shot back.

Lottie stepped between them before the arguing escalated. "How long to Aalborg?"

"An hour," Beaty said confidently.

"An hour and a *half*," Gilroy countered.

It was very little time either way. "Gilroy, might we speak, then?" Lottie asked, and gave him a meaningful look. "Will you gather the others? I'll fetch Morven — he's with my father now."

She returned to the captain's cabin just as Morven was peeling her father's bandage from his wound. Mackenzie was perched onto one hip on top of the desk, his arms crossed over his chest, watching.

Her father's pallor had turned a sickly shade of gray overnight, which Lottie desperately hoped was a lack of decent broth and sun and not a sign of worse.

"Lottie, *pusling,* is it you?" her father called, his voice hoarse and weak.

"Aye," she said, and went to his side. His gray skin was flushed, and she exchanged a look with Morven.

"Aye, he's got a fever, that he does," Morven said gravely. "He needs help."

"Donna bloody well bother the lass with talk of doctors," her father said irritably, but he grimaced, as if even speaking caused him pain. "She's to worry about the whisky, aye? If she doesna sell the whisky, it willna matter how many physicians you bring."

"Fader, I —"

"Donna take less than one hundred kroner per cask," he said.

She blinked. *Fifty* kroner per cask was too high. As if to confirm her thought, Mackenzie muttered, "One hundred kroner is impossible."

"I agree," Morven said.

"Donna listen to them! One hundred kroner and no' a pence less!" her father demanded through gasps of pain.

"But —"

Lottie was stopped from arguing by Morven's hand to her arm. He silently shook his head.

"Did you understand me, *pusling*?" her father asked. His eyes were closing.

"Aye, I do, Fader. One hundred kroner," she said softly, and squeezed his hand.

"Such a good lass you are, a bonny good lass," he muttered as he drifted into the cloud of his fever and the laudanum Morven had doled out.

"His wound is infected," Morven said as he gathered his things. He hesitated and looked at Lottie with such sadness that she flinched. "I canna do more for him, Lottie. Bring help."

That was a wee bit easier to ask than it was to do. Lottie had no idea how they would bring a physician to this ship, but she'd think of something. She *always* thought of something. Isn't that what they depended on her for? To think!

"Come," Morven said, and gestured with

his head to the door.

Lottie followed him out, past the captain with the smoldering eyes that seemed always to bore through her. She and Morven joined Duff and Mr. MacLean, Drustan and Mathais, and Gilroy.

"All is at the ready?" Lottie asked Duff.

"Aye," he said. "Gilroy will remain on board in command, and Beaty will be held as surety. Our lad Drustan and I will accompany you and the captain ashore," Duff said, clapping Drustan on the shoulder.

"I donna see why Dru may go and I may no'," Mathais complained. "I've as much to do with this as he."

"Dru must help us keep a close watch on the captain, Mats," Lottie reminded him.

"I donna want to keep an eye," Drustan said, fluttering his fingers. "I want to go home, Lottie."

"Aye, we all do, but first, we must find a physician for our father, aye? If you donna come with me, Drustan, how will I find a physician?"

Mathais hopped up onto a crate, wrapped one arm around the mast, and swung his body around. "I thought Gilroy was to go because he speaks Danish."

"Duff speaks a wee bit of Danish."

Duff held up his finger and thumb to

indicate just how wee.

"Keep an eye on our father while I'm gone, Mats." She glanced across the deck to Beaty. "Have you told him?" she asked Gilroy.

Gilroy winced and shook his head. "I've no' had the heart to tell him, no. He fancies himself in control of the ship and his men."

"Well, he is," said MacLean. " 'Tis a bloody miracle they've no' cast us overboard. We'd all be sunk to the bottom if we hadna promised to pay them."

"Perhaps *you* ought to tell Beaty," Gilroy suggested to Lottie.

"Me?"

"He'll no' lift a hand against you," Gilroy said.

Why must it *always* be her? "*Mi Diah,* you men!" Lottie huffed. "It's a wonder any of you have lived as long as you have without me to help you."

Gilroy looked as if he might tear up at her admonishment.

"I'll tell him," she said. "But *you* must ready Captain Mackenzie. He must be allowed to bathe and dress and shave. He canna go ashore looking as if he's our captive. He should at least give the *appearance* of being in command. Just . . . just please do it, aye?" she said, and set out, marching across the deck to give Beaty the news that now he'd be the one with a shackle around his ankle.

Predictably, Beaty did not agree with the Livingstone plan, even though Norval pointed a gun at his head the entire time he argued with Lottie about it. He made such a commotion that Lottie was forced to re-assure the Mackenzie crew that she had every intention of honoring her promise but needed to take certain precautions, as would they, were the situation reversed. Still, there was quite a lot of disgruntlement as Beaty stomped off in the company of Drustan and another Livingstone man to be bound up.

"I'd no' tell you false," she entreated the crew, clutching her hands together at her breast in a manner she'd learned at an early age men seemed to believe was a sign of sincerity, as they tended to rely upon what they saw and never really questioned it. She assured them that the sooner they were done with this business, the sooner they'd have their money and all the Livingstones off their ship.

"Aye, and what of our cargo? What are we to do with it?" Iain the Red demanded.

"You'll be on your way to Amsterdam," she said. "You'll collect two pays for this voyage."

The men looked at each other. "I donna believe it," Iain said. He was big, with thick, curly ginger hair that matched the curly beard he wore. "I've never in me life collected two purses for one voyage, have any of you?"

The answer was such a resounding *no* that Lottie felt a slight tic of panic. The Livingstone's entire scheme to sell this illegal whisky depended on her ability to convince every single man on this ship that this could be done. She noticed even the Livingstone men — whose guns were no longer trained on the Mackenzies, but used as staffs on which they might lean — were eying her skeptically.

"Aye, she speaks true," said the young man with a splint on his arm.

"What do you know of it, Billy Botly?" said one Mackenzie, and cuffed him on his ear. "You're scarcely more than a whelp."

"She's no' lied to us," Billy said. "Everything she's said, she's kept her word, aye?"

"The only thing she's said that matters is that she'll pay us, and *that* we've no' yet seen," someone shouted in the back.

"Aye!" shouted several of them.

Lottie felt on the verge of losing control of the situation, but at that moment, Captain Mackenzie emerged from his cabin with

Duff and Gilroy behind him.

A shock ran through her that ended in a shiver up her spine. His was a commanding figure; she wished she possessed even a wee bit of his confidence. He was dressed in the last clean shirt, and a waistcoat, pantaloons and stockings, and the greatcoat she'd worn. His hair was combed in a queue, his face clean-shaven. He looked somehow taller, and broader through the shoulders, and curse the devil, but he took her breath away.

He strode into their midst, and suddenly, everyone was cheering. He held up his hands and began to speak. Lottie stared at him, lulled by the deep, dulcet tones of his voice. He made the guttural Gaelic language sound almost lyrical.

"English!" she said, shaking off her infatuation.

He shifted a cool gaze to her. "Donna fret so, Miss Livingstone. I merely explained that they are to keep the ship ready to sail, that when we return, we will resume our voyage at once."

She didn't believe him, but whatever he'd said had calmed his men. Relief began to snake through her. "Only that?"

"No, no' only that," he said pleasantly. "I also swore to them that we would have our justice." He smiled.

Lottie should have been alarmed — at least think what her next steps would be — but all she could think was how his blue eyes glittered in the sunlight with defiance, and how that defiance made her feel warm and wobbly. A bit like she'd been struck and paralyzed by lightning.

He arched a brow, apparently amused by her perusal of him. "Do you no' wish to change your clothing, too?"

Lottie blinked. She nervously touched her hair, then said to Duff, "Mind you keep an eye," and whirled about, fleeing in mortification, aware that the men ogled her in her trews.

CHAPTER ELEVEN

The cabin seemed almost empty without the captain glowering at Lottie from the corner. Her father's presence, which had been so pressing two days ago, had also diminished considerably.

Lottie latched the door shut, then sat on a chair to remove her boots, listening to her father's labored breathing. She unbraided her hair and began to comb through it.

"Lottie? Is it you, *pusling*?"

She dropped the comb and turned around — her father was trying to roll onto his side, grunting with pain.

"Stay where you are, Fader," she said, and went to his bunk, helping him to right himself. "Turn your head, aye? I must dress. Aalborg is in sight."

He did as she asked, and Lottie quickly began to undress, slipping out of the trews first.

"Not a krone less than one hundred per

cask," he reminded her.

"Aye, I remember."

"If you canna find Anders or his father, the Copenhagen Company ought to have offices in the port."

"Aye," she said, and fastened her stomacher over her stays and petticoat.

"I would that it was me," her father said.

"Aye, I know," she said soothingly. She went to the sideboard and propped up the small shaving mirror. She wound her hair in a knot as best she could, wishing for Wee Mary, a tiny young woman who always helped her dress when clan business demanded it.

She wished for home. These last few days had tested her in ways she could not have possibly imagined. She wished for Lismore, for the rabbits, for the cozy manor house where they lived. That house had been her mother's pride, and Lottie had kept it in pristine condition, even doing some of the maintenance herself. The island had always seemed so small to her, so confining. She had wanted out in the world, to see what God had created. She had wanted to see famous sites, people who looked different from her. She wanted to know what women wore in high society, to ride in a proper carriage, to be courted by a man who was not related to her in some form or fashion. But today, all she wanted was her home. Her bed. Her horse, her dog, her freedom. Unfortunately, she'd made herself a prisoner of her own foolish decisions.

When she had her hair put up as best she could, she donned the gown, fastening it at the waist over her stomacher. It was tight, the fabric having shrunk, and it smelled of seawater and sweat. It was badly wrinkled and badly mended — the lace around one sleeve had come undone, and she was forced to pull the lace off the other sleeve to match. *Diah,* she looked a sight.

"Donna tarry, Lottie," her father said.

She glanced at her father over her shoulder. "Pardon?"

"Set your price and go. Donna tarry or they will try and drive it down, aye?"

"All right."

"We must have this done as soon as possible."

"We will," she tried to assure him.

"Those men in Aalborg, they'll see you —"

She winced. "Drustan and Duff will be with me." She sat on the chair to pull on her boots.

"You must think what you'll say to Anders. It must seem plausible. A handsome man

203

he was, but never trust a handsome man, lass."

What an odd thing to say. "I'll think of something," she said. *I always do.*

"Mind your mouth, as well, *pusling.* Think before you speak, aye? Men will —"

"I know, I *know,*" she said, and stood up from the table and moved to his bedside. She leaned over and kissed his forehead. His skin was hot, and she noticed the front of his shirt was wet with his perspiration, yet he was shivering. She didn't care about the whisky now — she needed to find a physician, someone who could help him. She pulled the coverlet up under his chin and tried to blink away the tears that had suddenly sprung to her eyes from nowhere. "I'll be needing your pocket watch, Fader."

He didn't ask her why. "Morven put it nearby."

She looked around and spotted it on a small bedside table, between a brass candle-holder with the stub of a candle in it, and a stack of leather-bound books. She picked it up. "Your father's watch, was it?" she asked, examining the carving in the brass.

"Aye." He smiled a little. " 'Tis the only thing I've left of him. He'd no' be happy to know what will become of it."

"I'm sorry, Fader." She tucked the watch

into her pocket and put her hand on her father's shoulder. "Rest easy. We'll return before nightfall." She leaned over him and pressed her lips to his burning forehead once more. But she couldn't see his face — her vision was blurred by her unshed tears. She gave him as reassuring a smile as she could manage and started for the door.

There were dark, monstrous thoughts creeping about her head — things could go terribly awry on shore. Or her father might possibly be beyond saving. If she thought of those things, she'd lose heart. She could only think what must be done today, one foot before the other and again.

If they ever returned to Lismore, she would single-handedly dismantle those bloody stills herself.

She'd almost reached the door when her father roughly called her name.

"Aye, Fader?" she said. He spoke again, but his breath was short and she returned to his bedside. "What is it?"

"I never wanted but to provide for our clan and our family, *pusling.* You must know it."

"Aye, of *cours*e I know it —"

He grabbed her hand with surprising strength that reminded her of the strength with which her mother had held her hand on her deathbed. "You and the lads, you're the only things that have mattered to me. The *only* thing."

"I know, Fader," she said gently. "We *all* know." She tried gently to dislodge her hand from his.

"On my word, I've done the best I knew how to do," he said tearfully.

She fell to her knees beside him and clasped his hand in both of hers. "I've never doubted it. Of course you did! Mats and Drustan and I know you have. We all know you have."

Tears were sliding from the corner of his eyes and disappearing into his matted gray hair. "I've made a bloody wreck of things, I have —"

"No! I'll no' listen to it, Fader. It's our lot in life, that's all. We were born to struggle. Our mother always said that if life came easy it would no' be worth living, aye? No matter what happens here, we'll be quite all right — we always are. *Always.* We have each other."

"Only because of you, *pusling.*" He squeezed her hand. "Aye, I've never spoken truer words. Where would we be without you, then? I love you, Lottie lass. *Tha gaol agam ort,*" he repeated in Gaelic. "A king could no' have sired a better daughter than

I have in you."

Tears were sliding down her cheeks, and Lottie swiped at them. "I love you, Fader. Now, keep your breath old man, until I've returned, aye? You may no' think so kindly of me if I return with less than you wanted." She smiled.

Her father didn't smile. His eyes moved over her face. "Have a care for yourself, and mind you look after the lads," he whispered roughly.

"Always," she said. She kissed the back of his hand and let it go. She smiled at him and walked out the door in her ridiculously damaged gown, her wet boots, and hair put up in a crooked chignon.

She was a sight, she knew that she was, and yet that didn't keep every head from swiveling toward her when she appeared on deck. They'd all gathered, apparently, to await her. "All right, all right," she said, her cheeks warming as she descended the stairs. "*Och,* I'm the same as I was before, aye?" she said irritably.

"Pardon, miss, but you're no' at all," said the young man with the broken arm. "You're *bonny.*"

"Have you no hat?" asked Duff, before Lottie could fret too much about what she must have looked like before she'd donned the gown. "Aye, Lottie, you'll be needing a hat," he said firmly. "That hair of yours shines like a diamond in a sea town and will attract more attention than you want."

"He's right," Mr. MacLean agreed, and handed her a flagon of whisky. She looked at it with confusion. "They'll want a taste," he said.

"A hat, Lottie!"

"I've no hat!" she repeated. "I've no' a proper gown or shoes, either, for that matter."

"In the cabin," the captain said. He was sitting on a cask, his legs crossed, as if he were a gentleman in a park watching the world pass. "I've a hat on the wall in the cabin, aye? Billy, fetch it for the lady, will you? And bring your greatcoat for her, too."

The lad took the stairs two at a time.

"A lot of fuss and bother," Lottie muttered. "I donna need a greatcoat —"

"Aye, you do," the captain said, and casually studied his hand. "For the same reason you need a hat. The gown fits you like a glove," he said, and lifted his gaze and let it travel the length of her body.

She flushed furiously. She knew he'd seen her in a state of undress last night. She knew he'd been watching her, and she, well . . . she hadn't minded it. She'd felt a strange

208

sort of shimmering in her blood, like grease on a fire, sparking and flaring and pooling wet in her groin. She had lingered too long in the task of bathing, pleasantly inflamed by his perusal.

The lad returned, bounding into their midst with surprising agility for having the use of only one arm. He handed her a cocked hat, one that was so weathered it had lost the sheen of its wool felt, and one side of the brim was sagging. She put it on her head, but it was too big, and slid down so that it sat just above her eyes.

"Aye, tuck your hair up, then," Duff said, eyeing her critically.

Lottie tucked as much of her hair up under the hat as she could while the men stood about and studied her efforts. She slipped on the threadbare greatcoat and Duff stepped forward to button it. He turned the collar up around her face. "The less anyone can see, aye?"

"That will do," she said, batting his hands away.

"Well then," the captain said. "Might we about the business so that I might have my ship returned to me?" he asked impatiently, and turned toward the railing as the boat was lowered to carry them to port.

Livingstones and Mackenzies alike gathered to watch them row to shore. The Livingstones called out their encouragement to them, and Duff, theatrical to the end, stood in the middle of their little boat and sang up to all the men that they would return by eventide. But the moment Drustan began to row, Duff was knocked onto his arse and his oratory ended.

The room in the boat was close, and once Mackenzie handed his oars to Duff, Lottie was forced to sit beside him in the bow. He kept his gaze on the port ahead, and she kept her gaze on the water, her nose wrinkling at the smell of rotting fish as they drew closer to shore. Gulls lined the quay, and people were so thick that she couldn't be certain it wasn't a crowd gathered for some event.

But more than the blue sky overhead, or the sound of the gulls calling to each other, or the voices of hawkers calling out their wares to be sold, Lottie was acutely aware of the press of Mackenzie's thigh against hers, the firm meat of his hip against hers. So acutely aware of it, in fact, that she shifted, trying to put some space between them. Mackenzie turned his head, his gaze sliding to the open collar of her coat, and the exposed flesh of her décolletage, then slowly lifting to meet her eyes. He was thinking of last night, too. She could see it in the blistering shine of his eyes. Maybe he felt the memory just as as she did, pulsing in every vein, rising rapidly to the surface of his skin, too, because he turned his head and looked away.

Lottie leaned over the edge of the boat and dipped her hand into the water and brought it to her cheeks, trying to douse the flame that was beginning to bloom inside her. And then she did something that surprised her — she touched his thigh. It was hardly a touch at all, really, just a draw of her finger down the side of it, a slow, light caress. She just wanted to touch him, to feel the strength in his legs and imagine them wrapped around her. She hardly touched him, but it felt as intimate as her bath.

You will do this now?

Yes, *now*. Life felt unsettlingly short suddenly, and who knew if there would be another opportunity? She had no idea what she might find on shore.

The captain pressed a clenched fist to his knee and Lottie touched him again, her finger tracing the same path.

Chapter Twelve

They docked the boat, then climbed the ladder to the quay. The giant went first, startling a few sailors who happened to be going by, followed by Lottie, then Aulay, and the actor last.

Aalborg looked to be a thriving port, with all the good and bad that went with it. The quay and the road that ran alongside the edge of it were thick with souls — dock-hands and sailors, dogs, and young lads who swarmed those who looked as if they had money, begging for coin. The scent of salt, fish and ash was pungent, the gulls loud. Carters passed them with carts full of fish, trailed by gulls looking for food. Old women hawked their wares, young women hawking their much different wares by hanging out the windows of bawdy houses, calling out to sailors who happened by.

The warehouses built along the road were squat buildings. Some of them housed official offices of the Danish crown. Others housed shipping companies.

Aulay should not have been surprised at how surefooted Lottie was, because this was not a small Scottish island. And yet she strode along confidently, her arms swinging at her sides and a flagon over her shoulder. She strode past a man lying face down in the gutter either dead or drunk; past sailors staggering down the street after what Aulay assumed was a long night of ale and women, their arms around each other's shoulders, singing in clashing keys and laughing uproariously. She even marched past two harlots who smiled wantonly and called to her in Danish, challenging her.

Lottie paid them no heed. She was made of iron.

Her brother, on the other hand, was so startled by all that he saw that he kept bumping into Aulay, kept muttering under his breath.

They did not walk along without notice — it was impossible to ignore the young giant with his snowy hair and extraordinary height and breadth.

At a corner where an alley met the main street, Lottie stopped, planted her hands on hips and looked around them. "How do we find Anders Iversen and a physician?"

The actor shrugged. The giant was distracted by a pair of women smiling at him from a window overhead. Lottie looked to Aulay.

"You're asking me?" he asked.

"Who else can help us?"

"I will ignore the irony of your request for my help and suggest you might ask at a duty and toll office, aye?"

"A splendid idea!" the actor proclaimed. He and Lottie looked around, studying the various buildings. "There," he said, pointing to a building that was a wee bit larger than others. *"Toldforvaltning,"* he said, reading the sign. "If I were to guess, and guess I shall, as I learned only the wee bit of Danish at me mother's knee, I'd wager it's a customs house or something like it."

"Good," Lottie said, and put her hand on his back. "Go and inquire after Anders. If they donna know him, then inquire after the Copenhagen Company. And a physician! If naught else, a physician, aye?" She gave him a push.

"Me, is it?" the actor asked uncertainly. He straightened his neckcloth before striking out, striding across the street and very nearly colliding with a cart laden with fish in his haste.

"What are *we* to do?" the giant asked. He

was rocking back and forth on his heels, his arm connecting with Aulay's back every time he surged forward, as if he had no sense of how large he was, how his body filled the space around him.

"We are to wait," she said.

The giant rocked again, knocking into Aulay again, so Aulay moved aside and put his back against the wall to wait.

Lottie chewed nervously on her bottom lip, her gaze fixed on the offices across the way. She was not thinking of him at all, and it occurred to Aulay that he could slip away. He could slip away, return to the ship, invent some excuse about the Livingstones still on shore, and take control. He could set sail, *now,* and hope that he might make up for lost time.

He considered it.

And then Aulay imagined something else entirely. Her finger, tracing a path down the side of his thigh. There was no mistaking what that was, no pretending she had innocently or accidentally touched him. He imagined tracing a line down her bare back. Perhaps a bit more slowly. A bit longer. Perhaps following that path with his lips. He was thinking of her naked body when he ought to be thinking of escape.

Aulay frowned. He didn't like the thoughts

215

stirring in his head. It was infuriating to him that he'd been seduced by his captor. He tried, unconvincingly, to justify not walking away because he meant to see her to justice. To abandon her in Aalborg would mean she would not be punished for her unspeakable crime against him. He tried to convince himself that he didn't walk away because it would be cruel to leave her and the giant to fend for themselves, with no notion of the world between them. As much as he wanted justice — and he *did* want justice — he was not a cruel man.

Aulay tried desperately to convince himself of anything but the truth, which was that he no longer knew what sort of man he was. Only a few days ago, he would have sworn to anyone he could not be taken by a lass, and yet here he was. Or that he could possibly harbor feelings of admiration — and yet he did. The last few days had changed him in ways he didn't like and didn't understand.

She suddenly jerked around, as if she'd just remembered her prisoner. Aulay smiled with amusement at her fluster. Her brows fell with displeasure. Just over her shoulder, he saw the actor emerge from the customs house, walking briskly toward them, almost running, and he pushed away from the wall.

"What news?" Lottie asked as the actor reached them.

"Well," he said, pausing to catch his breath, "the gentleman I spoke to said there are only two physicians known to him and neither of them mad enough to board a foreigner's ship."

"What?" Lottie cried.

"He has directed us to the Hospital of the Holy Ghost, he has, where Samaritans may be found. Somewhere there," he indicated, waving vaguely in the direction of the town sprawling behind them. "Quite a large place, he said. Canna miss it."

"No, no, no — we *must* find a physician!" Lottie said frantically.

"We'll inquire at the hospital, lass. I donna know what a duty agent should know of it, really."

"What else?" she asked.

"*Och,* 'tis no' good news," he said. "The gentleman claimed no familiarity with Anders Iversen —"

"But his father —" Lottie was quick to interject. "Did you tell him Anders Iversen was the bookkeeper of the Copenhagen Company, and his father exchequer?"

"Aye, I did," the actor said. "I explained to him that Mr. Iversen, whose company we verra much enjoyed last summer, had found occupation as their bookkeeper with the help of his father, who is exchequer and ought to be well known in this port. But he said . . ." He paused, took off his hat and wiped his forehead.

"He said *what*?" Lottie demanded.

"Well he laughed, he did, and said the name of the exchequer is Mr. Pedersen and had been for nigh on thirty years, and he'd never heard of Anders Iversen, no' in this town, nor had he heard of any company hailing from Copenhagen and to move aside, as he had more pressing issues than my ignorance."

Lottie gasped. The actor returned his hat to his head.

Aulay suppressed a groan of frustration. He was not surprised, given what he knew about the Livingstones. What in hell would he do with all that whisky on his deck? Toss it into the sea?

"That canna be, Duff," Lottie said, her voice shaking. "Anders would no' have lied —"

"Apparently, he did, lass, for he told me the same," the actor said. "But donna fret, aye? I would no' leave without a wee bit of information and merely explained to the man that we've fine Scotch whisky to sell, and he looked a wee bit pleased with it, he did, and said I ought to speak to Mr. Ingoff Holm. He said if there was good whisky to be sold, he'd be the man for it."

Lottie didn't respond — she stared at the ground, her brow furrowed.

The actor dipped his head to see her face and said carefully, "Lottie?"

"I beg your pardon," she said. "What is the man's name?"

"Ingoff Holm," the actor repeated. "You may find him in a private room at the Kajen Inn." He pointed at the inn at the very end of the road.

Lottie flicked a gaze over her brother, who was trying to coax a seagull to him.

"I'd no' seek this man, were I you," Aulay offered.

"Why no'?"

How did one explain a sailor's intuition? "It doesna seem right," he said with a shrug.

She nodded, then abruptly took Duff's elbow and pulled him aside. Aulay watched as the two of them carried on an animated conversation until Lottie turned about, and announced, "We've no time to waste." She hesitated, then said, "We've decided, Drustan, that you will carry on with Duff. You're to go to the hospital and find help for our father." She smiled.

Maybe the giant wasn't as addled as Aulay

had thought, because he was not fooled by that smile. "*No,* Lottie! I remain with you!"

"No' this time, Dru," she said firmly, and withdrew a watch from her pocket, and pressed it carefully into the actor's palm. She turned to her brother again. "Duff needs you. A physician might need a wee bit of persuasion to row out to our ship, aye? If Duff tells you to pick someone up, you must do it."

Aulay recoiled. "You're no' suggesting he force a man against his —"

"I am suggesting he help Duff," Lottie said curtly.

"But I should no' like to leave you with him," the actor said, and jerked his chin in the direction of Aulay, as if he was the cause of the debacle in which they'd put themselves. "I know you believe you can do all, Lottie, and *Diah,* you have, we'd be at a great loss without you, we would. But you're a wee thing, and he might try and . . . and well, *strangle* you, aye? He might attempt to throw you in the ocean and leave you there to drown!"

"No!" the giant said angrily, and turned with fury toward Aulay.

Aulay straightened up with mild alarm.

"Duff doesna mean that, Dru —"

"I certainly *do* mean it —"

220

"Duff!" She gestured to her brother, who was growing more agitated. "Think! If the captain returns to the ship without me, a battle will be waged, will it no'? He canna have his ship back without *me.* The man is no fool — he'll no' risk damage to his ship or the loss of his own crew."

The actor looked at Aulay, assessing him. "If you dare lay as much as a *finger* on her —"

"I beg your pardon," Aulay said evenly, "But you seem to have confused who has laid hands on whom."

"Duff . . . we've no time to debate it," Lottie said urgently.

The giant began to flap his hands and mewl.

Lottie caught her brother's face in her hands and forced him to look at her. "*Calm* yourself, Dru," she said. "You know that Duff will care for you as Mats does, aye? I need you to be strong. Fader needs your help."

At the mention of the old man, the giant seemed to rethink his anguish. "Fader needs me help," he repeated. "Fader needs me help."

"I'll see you verra soon," she said, and shifted her gaze to the actor. "Go," she said softly.

"Aye, come then, lad," the actor said, and put his hand on the giant's shoulder. He eyed Aulay darkly as they moved on in the direction of the town, the giant lumbering after him.

Lottie watched them go, her arms wrapped tightly around her, the lines of concern evident around her eyes. When the two of them had turned into an alley and she could no longer see them, she glanced warily at Aulay.

He shook his head. "You're a rare one, Lottie Livingstone. But bloody well foolish. If this man conducts his business in an inn —"

"I've no choice," she snapped, and turned about, facing the squat building the actor had indicated was the Kajen Inn. "I'm no' afraid, if that's what you think. No sir, I'm *livid.* I will abide many things, but dishonesty is no' one of them!"

"Pardon?"

"Mr. Iversen is no' in the post he claimed. Nor does the trading company of which he was so inordinately proud seem to exist. And I have chased across the North Sea because I *believed* him!" She glanced at him sidelong. "Donna fear, captain — I've my pistol."

"I donna *fear,* Lottie. And what you have

is a wee dueling pistol that would no' stop a man who means to do you harm."

Her eyes glittered with ire. She took a breath that lifted her shoulders and released it, and said, "Captain Mackenzie, I have a matter of hours — *hours* — to save our clan and my father. I mean to go to that inn and speak to Mr. Ingoff Holm, because I've no other option, and now I've promised no' one, but *two* crews payment. You may come with me, or you may return to the ship, I donna care."

Well, then. She was lovely when her anger was aroused. A fine wisp of her snowy white hair had come down from the hat, and quite unable to stop himself, he tucked it behind her ear, trailed his finger along the bottom of her lobe and down her neck before he dropped his hand. "Aye, a rare one, you are," he muttered.

"Will you come with me?"

God help him, but the sea in him was beginning to turn. The things he could see, the things he could count on, knew like the back of his hand, were disappearing, and parts of him that were new, raw and unused, were coming to light. Of course he was going with her. He gestured to the street before them. "After you, then."

"You do know that if you say a single word

to hinder me, I'll shoot you, and I'll no' miss."

Aulay arched a brow.

"I donna care what happens to me, but if you ruin this chance for us, all is lost for the Livingstones. I canna allow that to happen."

One side of his mouth curved into a smile. "Aye, lass, you've made that abundantly clear." She was mad to think she could stop him, or anyone for that matter. But he said agreeably, "I consider myself warned," tucked her hand in the crook of his elbow, and led her to the inn.

CHAPTER THIRTEEN

The public room of the inn was crowded. With its low ceilings and thick walls, the din was nearly deafening. What little light there was came from a pair of small windows at the street front and a candle here and there in wall sconces. The burning tallow did not mask the smell of damp rot. They had to maneuver through tables crowded with rowdy sailors and dockhands, brushing past greatcoats hung on pegs on the wall, women serving tankards of ale, and the occasional dog.

At the back of the inn, Lottie approached a man busy hanging empty tankards on hooks in the ceiling. "I beg your pardon?"

The man interjected a string of something in Danish.

Lottie blinked. "Ingoff Holm," she said.

The man pointed to one of two rooms off the public room near the kitchen.

Lottie and Aulay exchanged a look, but

Aulay put his hand to her back and guided her through the crowd to the first room. He knocked, and hearing no reply, opened the door. It was empty. At the next door, he heard a muffled reply to his knock. He opened the door and stepped into the room.

Two men were seated at a table, one of them was considerably older than the other, with a thick tuft of white hair that reminded Aulay of the snow that topped the Highlands in winter, and jowls that hung like small satchels on either side of his face. The other gentleman, tall and lanky, had not bothered to remove his greatcoat and cocked hat.

The older man watched them impassively as they stepped deeper into the room, and Aulay pulled the door to, shutting out the noise. Snowtop squinted at Lottie. *"Kvinde,"* he said. Whatever that meant, it seemed to amuse him and disgust him at once. *"Ja?"*

Lottie stepped forward. "Do you, by chance, speak English?"

The man looked her up and down, then slowly stood from his chair. He was a thick man, but a head shorter than Aulay. *"Ja."*

Lottie suddenly smiled — with relief or affectation, Aulay wasn't certain — but it had the effect of lighting that room. "If you please, I'm looking for Mr. Ingoff Holm."

226

"*Hvem?* Who?" the old man asked as he came around the table.

"Mr. Ingoff Holm," she repeated.

Just then, the door behind them swung open, and another man stepped in, ducking under the low header. He brushed past Aulay and eyed Lottie curiously. He smelled as if he'd not bathed in weeks. He muttered something under his breath in Danish and Snowtop responded without taking his gaze from Lottie.

"My colleague would like to know what is your business with Herre Holm?" he asked as the third man took a seat at the table.

Aulay's misgivings ratcheted. There was something sinister about these men and this room.

"I beg your pardon, but it is a private matter," Lottie said politely.

"There are no matters for Mr. Holm that do not include me, *ja?*" Snowtop dipped his head so he could see Lottie under the brim of her hat. "*Ja, meget smuk . . .* a pretty thing you are."

Lottie took a small step backward, bumping up against Aulay. "Is Mr. Holm about, then?"

The man glanced curiously at Aulay. "Why is the lady the one to speak?" he

227

asked, and to Lottie, "What is he, your mute?"

"I'm no mute," Aulay said, and moved, intending to step before her, but Lottie swung her arm down and clamped his inner thigh before he could make any progress.

"He's naugh' to do with this. 'tis my private business."

Diah, but her naiveté was on full display.

Snowtop sneered. "A woman with business." He settled back against the table, casually taking her in, as if she were a fat little lamb for sale. "No good can come of that."

Aulay ignored Lottie's insistent hand and put himself between her and the men, but the stubborn little wench pushed around him. The room was so small that there was no space between Aulay and the table, and she stood with her back pressed against half of him. "Is he here, then?" she insisted. "Mr. Holm?"

"Tell me your business and I'll tell you if he is present or not. How about that?"

"You may tell him I'm selling fine Scotch whisky —"

"Uist," Aulay said, warning her to say no more. The less this man knew, the better.

"You've brought fine Scotch whisky all the way to Aalborg, have you?" Snowtop asked, one brow rising. "Was it no' good enough for you Scots? Why would a pretty little miss bring whisky all the way to Denmark?"

"My family hails from Denmark."

"Ah," the man said, and looked around to his companions. *"Hun er dansk."*

The two men chuckled.

"And where is this whisky you'd like to sell?" Snowtop asked.

"We'll leave that for Holm," Aulay said, although it was fairly easy to guess that it was likely a Scottish ship in the harbor. He hoped Lottie did not offer which ship.

"I've a taste for Mr. Holm, if you'd be so kind as to bring him round," Lottie said primly.

The man clucked his tongue and shook his head. "That's not how we conduct our business, *ja*? I'll have a taste of it, and if I think it is as fine as you say, I shall bring you to Herre Holm."

Lottie jerked the flagon from her shoulder and tossed it at him. The man caught it deftly with one hand and grinned at her. "There's a good *pige,*" he said. He handed the flagon to the man behind him, who took the first swig, then passed it to the next man. He drank, too, then held the flagon out to Snowtop. That one held it up and said *"Skål,"* and then drank.

When he'd tasted it, the three men discussed in their native tongue. When it looked as if they'd come to some agreement, Snowtop tossed the flagon to Lottie and returned to his seat. "How much do you have?"

"Twenty-two casks."

He smiled in a manner that made Aulay's skin crawl. "Very well, then, miss. You may wait in the public room until Herre Holm arrives."

"Will it be long?" she asked. "We've others who are interested."

Snowtop chuckled. "Go and enjoy a tankard of ale *pige,* you and your mute. We'll summon you."

Still, Lottie hesitated. Aulay put his hand on her waist, forcing her backward and to the door, then taking her hand and yanking her out of the room.

"What are you doing?" she insisted, pulling her hand free when they were outside. "I donna trust him. I want to keep a close eye on that one."

"Thank the saints you donna trust him. He's a scoundrel, that one —"

"I know!" she said angrily, her eyes flashing. "You were no' to speak!"

He grabbed her elbow and yanked her close. "You hold my ship hostage with this farce, and I canna trust that you've enough sense to recognize a liar and a thief when you lay eyes on him."

"I'll no' leave," she said stubbornly. "He might be a thief, and then again, he might no', aye?" She pressed her lips together and stared down at her boots, her hands on her hips. "I am doing the best that I know to do," she said stiffly. "But I donna *know* what to do, Captain. I rather thought my father would be the one to sell it."

Aulay sighed. He brushed his knuckles against her cheek. "You do *ken,* do you no', that Snowtop is up to no good?"

"Snowtop?"

"The older man. You canna trust the word of a stranger in a strange port about who to sell your whisky to."

"What choice have I?" she said, her voice pleading. "*Please,* Captain, give me another choice!"

"It's too late for another choice, Lottie." Any reasonable choice should have been made on Lismore Island before they'd ever made sail. He muttered something about foolish women under his breath, but then wrapped his arm around her shoulders. "If you refuse to leave, then I'll have a pint for all my trouble, and so will you."

"I havena any coin," she said, allowing

him to lead her through the throng.

"Aye, Lottie, I am painfully aware you have no coin. Your lack of it has bedeviled me for three days now," he said, and took her firmly by the hand and pushed through that throng to a table near the kitchen.

He didn't notice the way she was looking at him as he pulled out a chair for her, but then he saw the shine in her eyes and felt the flow of something that felt intimate and slightly carnal between them.

He did not notice, at least not in that moment, that he had forgotten he was her captive.

Chapter Fourteen

A harried woman appeared tableside and spoke to them in Danish.

"Ale," the captain said, and held up two fingers.

"We've no *coin*," Lottie sternly reminded him as the woman went off to fetch the ales.

He cast an impatient look at her as he reached into the pocket of his coat and withdrew a small purse.

Lottie flushed with shame and slumped back in her seat. Her first foray into the world at large had been an utter disaster, but she'd hoped — *prayed* — that at least she could sell the whisky. Unfortunately, the events of this day had nearly drained her of all heart.

She removed the blasted hat and rubbed her eyes. Strands of her hair fell down around her face.

"What's the matter?" the captain asked, and reached across the little table to brush crumbs from her sleeve.

"What's the matter? Everything." She averted her gaze. "I'm ashamed," she said bluntly. "It's no' always been like this for us."

The captain did not speak, and when Lottie glanced at him, his attention was on something across the room. He didn't want to hear her excuses, of course not. He'd never be brought so low as this. She didn't want to hear her excuses, either — it made her feel weak, and she despised that feeling.

The woman returned with the ale, slapping down the tankards without care for how the ale slopped over the sides and spilled onto the crude wooden table. The captain handed her a pair of coins, which she quickly pocketed, then just as quickly disappeared.

Lottie had no appetite or thirst. She felt nothing but bone weariness. The captain, however, drank heartily from his tankard, draining at least half of it before he put it down. He looked curiously at her untouched tankard and gestured to it. "Do you no' want it?"

She shrugged.

He leaned across the table and made her look him in the eye. "Drink," he commanded her. "The Lord knows when you might have another opportunity this day."

Lottie glanced at the tankard.

He pushed the tankard closer. "*Drink,* Lottie."

She picked it up and sipped, but the ale tasted sour.

"*Och,* now is no' the time to be petulant," he said.

She put the tankard down. "*Petulant,*" she repeated irritably. "Should I leap for joy? Sing songs for you?" She shook her head. "You've no idea how hard it's been."

"You're right," he agreed. "Perhaps you ought to tell me."

She clucked her tongue. "You donna really want to hear it."

He gestured for her to continue.

"Verra well," she said. All at once, it felt inexplicably imperative that she explain to this man, of all men, why she had dragged him through this horrible, awful journey. "I love my father with all my heart."

"Aye. We all love our fathers," he said. He drank more ale and glanced absently about the room, studying the crowd, as if he expected this to be the whining of a female with no sense.

"No, I . . ." She found it difficult to put into words her complicated feelings about her father, about the role she'd assumed in her family, about the heavy responsibilities put on her shoulders at a very young age. "I mean that I *love* my father, but he's made life verra difficult. He squandered *everything*, all of it! He has made us this desperate."

He turned his blue eyes back to her, curious now. "What do you mean, everything?"

"His inheritance, aye? It was quite generous, enough to have kept us all his life."

Mackenzie looked baffled. Lottie was not surprised — the Livingstones did not present as a clan who had ever possessed more than a few coins to their name, when in fact, they had possessed quite a lot of them at one time. "His grandfather was a Danish baron, a landowner. There was war with Sweden, and he escaped with his wealth and settled on Lismore Island. When my father came into his inheritance, he had many ideas of how to increase it. Wretched ideas."

"Ah," he said. "What ideas?"

She couldn't possibly name them all, but one of her earliest memories was of an argument between her mother and father over his purchase of a carriage. The island was only four or five miles long, and there was no need for a *carriage,* not to mention the expense of keeping horses to pull it those few miles. "Many," she said. "Many implausible ideas."

The captain glanced down at his tankard. He was probably imagining the many ways a man could waste an inheritance. He was probably thinking how absurd was this clan, these Livingstones, squandering their fortune, stealing ships, believing liars. He was probably right in all his assumptions, and Lottie wished she could disappear. She didn't really know the Mackenzies, but she knew of their reputation. They were a powerful clan, a *smart* clan, who had weathered the rebellions and the economic troubles better than most. The very opposite of the Livingstones.

But when he lifted his gaze, Lottie was startled by the compassion she saw in his eyes. She had not expected that. "I should have paid more heed," she said. The admission of guilt that constantly pricked at her conscience spilled out of her. If only she'd not been so determined to ignore the sudden responsibilities she assumed after her mother's death and live outside of it. If only she'd stayed closer to home instead of running wild over the island, racing on her horse, taking up a lover. If she'd not done any number of things, if she'd done other things, but above all, if she'd paid her father more attention, she might have stopped him from losing it all.

"Paid heed to what?" the captain asked.

"My mother died when I was just a wee lass. Mats was only just walking, and Dru, he needed quite a lot of minding and always will, and I . . . I didna want the responsibility of it," she admitted. "God forgive me, but I didna want to be a mother or mistress of the house."

"Of course no'," he said, nodding as if he understood her. "As you said, you were a child."

Yes . . . but even at that age, she'd understood how reckless her father was. One winter, her father had come back from Port Appin with three geese. He'd been convinced to purchase them by a stranger and was excited for his plans to fatten them for a Christmas Day feast. "We'll feed the entire clan, we will, Lottie, and the flavor of it, you'll no' forget it," he assured her.

He'd prepared his own concoction to fatten them, based on God only knew what. For a full fortnight, the geese had wandered about among the rabbits. But then something began to change. They began to wobble like three drunken sailors. Their feathers molted. The first goose died a few days before Christmas and the other two were dead by Christmas Eve.

It was much later that Lottie discovered her father had included gooseberries in his concoction. Morven's grandmother, upon hearing this, had cried for the poor geese. Gooseberries, it seemed, were poisonous to fowl.

There had been many other instances like that in Lottie's life.

"I was a child, but I knew him," she said darkly. "I knew how he thought, and still, so many times I turned a blind eye and let the consequences fall where they would."

Captain Mackenzie put his arms on the table and leaned across them, his eyes piercing hers. "You are no' responsible for your father, lass — he is responsible for you, aye? Why have you no' married? A good man would provide for you and your brothers."

Because the men who had tried to court her through the years had never earned her esteem? Because she dreamed of something bigger and better than that life on that tiny little island, of towns like Edinburgh and London, which she'd only heard about, but imagined so vividly? Because she was aware of the burden of her father and brothers that would accompany her into any marriage? Or was it perhaps because she liked being the one in charge when it suited her?

The one whom everyone sought for an-swers?

"Surely you've been courted," the captain said.

"Aye," she sheepishly admitted. "But none of them ever really saw past my appearance. Verra much tongue-tied and . . . and *stupid,*" she said with some dismay.

The captain surprised her with a laugh. She'd never said these things aloud to anyone, and his charming, sincere smile buoyed her. "I've no doubt of that. You're a beguiling woman, you are. Look at me — I'm your captive now, all because I was tongue-tied and a wee bit stupid." He touched his tankard to hers and drank.

A wave of pleasure at his smile spun through her and curved on her lips. "Aye, but you didna trust me, it was obvious."

"I trusted you enough, apparently."

Lottie laughed. It felt strange in her chest, and to her ears. How long had it been since she'd laughed? She picked up her tankard and drank. The ale didn't seem so sour now.

The captain's gaze was sultry. "Aye, but you're bonny when you smile, Lottie Living-stone, that you are," he said softly, and her smile deepened. His gaze slipped to her mouth.

"Such flattery, Captain Mackenzie. Is it

possible you've warmed to your captor?"

His eyes sparkled with amusement. "Warmed to her, aye. But no' forgiven her."

"I'd be disappointed if you had."

He held her gaze. Lottie felt warmth spreading in her chest, felt the depth his gaze slipping into her person. "Now you must confess to me, aye? Why have *you* never married? You're verra handsome," she said, and he inclined his head in acceptance of the compliment. "And a *sea captain.* I should think that would bring mothers and their unmarried daughters flocking to Balhaire. I believe you're verra honorable when you're no' complaining about your circumstances."

One of his dark brows rose. "My *circumstances* are no' fit for a dog."

She waved a hand dismissively. "Why have you no' married?"

He shrugged. "I suppose I never met a woman that would tempt me to surrender the sea."

"The sea! Must you surrender for love?"

"Aye, perhaps. Unless there is a woman who should like to reside within a small cabin on the sea for days on end. It becomes quite close, would you no' agree?"

The ale must have gone to her head because she giggled. "I would."

"But it's more than that, I suppose. I've never been in one place long enough to court a lady properly." He drained the rest of the ale as if might wash away the rest of this conversation.

"Does your family no' insist upon it?" she asked curiously. "Yours is a powerful family. Do they no' want to make a match for their most splendid son?"

"Splendid," he said with a chuckle. "I've two brothers and two sisters who are far more splendid than me. My family has made our matches there."

She couldn't imagine anyone more splendid than Captain Mackenzie. She regarded his face, the square cut of his jaw, the softly feathered lines around his eyes from days spent in the sun. His hair, combed into a queue, was gold on his crown where the sun shone on it day after day on the open sea. She truly couldn't imagine that mothers weren't depositing their daughters at his feet. "Might I be so bold to inquire after your given name?"

"Miss Livingstone, are we so familiar?"

She giggled again. "We've shared a cabin for three days and you call me Lottie."

"Three days!" he mused, pretending shock, his eyes shining. "Then I agree, we should be more familiar." His gaze shifted to her mouth, and Lottie felt a stirring in her blood. "Aulay."

Aulay. She repeated it under her breath. An unexpected name for an unexpected man. "*Feasgar math,* Aulay," she greeted him.

He smiled and said, "*Feasgar math,* Lottie."

"Shall I tell you what I think?"

He swept his arm grandly. "Now that we are familiar, by all means, enlighten me."

"I think, had I no' kicked you at our first meeting, we might have been friends."

He arched a brow with surprise. But his gaze was so warmly inviting, that for a moment, Lottie could well imagine that they might have been. He reached for her hand, twining his fingers with hers. "I think we might have been more than friends."

Her heart leaped. And then it ballooned in her chest. *And now?* She was desperate to ask him, but she was no fool. She knew the sort of man he was — honorable. Lawful. He was a man who would protect his inheritance for his children and never squander it. He would never seize another ship. And he would not allow her to escape her crime, no matter the heat that seemed to flow between them. Strangely, if he'd been any other sort of man, she would not feel the sizzling in her veins as she did now. She would not hold him in such high regard.

He squeezed her hand, and Lottie wanted nothing more than to crawl onto his lap and put her head on his shoulder and feel his arms around her. She'd feel safe there. At ease. The pain in her head would go away and her heart would stop racing.

But then his hand suddenly jerked free of hers and he straightened in his seat. "Put on your hat, aye? And tuck your hair as best you can into it."

"What — ?"

"Be quick," he said quietly.

She followed his gaze toward the entrance. One of the men from the private room had sidled in, a sword at his waist. Had he been wearing one before? He was scanning the crowd, clearly looking for someone. As she donned the hat, the second man from the private room entered the inn and went in the opposite direction of the first. "Perhaps they've come to fetch us?" she asked with a hopefulness she did not really have as she tucked errant strands of hair beneath her hat. Two more men wearing swords entered the inn and stood near the door, as if guarding it.

"They've come to fetch us, all right, but I donna think it is with the intent of making a fair offer for your whisky."

One of the men began to make his way slowly through the crowd, studying every table, every group standing about, his hand on the hilt of his sword.

"Aye, you're right. They mean us harm," she murmured breathlessly, as her heart was suddenly pounding in her chest.

"When I stand, put yourself behind me," Aulay said. "We donna want to draw notice."

Lottie had been through enough in the last few days to know better than to ask a lot questions. The moment Aulay stood, she slipped in behind him, her hand clutching the back of his coat.

"Stay close," he said, and began to push through the crowd, his head down, moving toward the counter that separated the kitchen from the rest of the inn. When he skirted around a timber that braced the ceiling overhead, Lottie stole a glance at the men. The four of them had fanned out and were pushing through the crowd with determination.

Aulay startled her by suddenly reaching for her hand, yanking her in front of him, then pushing her through an open door. She stumbled into a kitchen. The man who had pointed to the private rooms earlier was filling tankards and setting them in front of a serving woman. He began to shout in Danish at Aulay and Lottie, gesturing toward the door.

"Pardon," Aulay said, and pulled Lottie along, darting past a woman plucking the feathers of a chicken, past chickens very much alive but in a crate, past a side of beef hanging from the rafters. Around two barrels of ale and another man who cursed them as they spilled out into the mews behind the inn.

Aulay dragged Lottie into his side with an arm around her waist, hurrying her along, forcing her to run. They turned into another alley, this one quite crowded with the townspeople going about their day.

"Where is your pistol?" he asked, glancing backward.

"Here," she said, her hand in her pocket.

"Give it to me — I might need to fire that one shot, aye?"

"Alas, I have already fired that one shot," she said, and handed him the gun. "It's empty."

"You fired — *when*? Never mind." He slipped the gun into the pocket of his greatcoat just as they turned another corner and entered a busy market street.

"Donna look up, but we've company."

She gasped. "Are you certain?"

"Quite." He dipped under a row of embroidered linens that had been hung for display and tugged Lottie into a darkened alley. He pulled her into a building, where the scent of horses was quite strong — it was a stable. There was only one horse that she could see, and it snorted at them as Aulay looked around. There was a small alcove at the front of the stable, a deck above it where bales of hay had been stored. Aulay pushed her into that alcove, turned her about and put her back to the wall, then held a finger to his mouth, indicating she should be silent.

That was impossible — her heart was beating so hard that she was gasping for breath. Her anxiety was not eased as she watched Aulay creep along the wall to the door. He kept himself against the wall, but bent his head around the frame to peer outside. Almost instantly, he jerked backward and sprang to where she was. He pushed her down into the hay, then lay before her and pulled enough hay around his body to shield them from sight.

She was pressed against him, her heart pounding so erratically in her chest that Lottie was certain Aulay could hear it and feel it. She heard a pair of boots scuff against the stone outside the stable, heard them pause at the open door, and held her breath. She expected to be caught at any moment, to feel the steel of a gun or knife press against her neck. Her pulse throbbed in her ears, and she had to keep swallowing down the breath she wanted so desperately to gasp into her lungs. She could hear nothing but the horse moving about, munching on straw. She was certain her heart would explode in her chest at any moment . . . but then she heard the boots on the stone again, moving away. The footfall was moving down the alleyway.

Aulay slowly came to his feet. He held out his hand to her and pulled her up. Lottie was panting, she realized, and a bead of perspiration was slowly sliding down her temple. She swallowed. "What do they want?" she whispered shakily.

"You. The whisky." His expression was quite grave, and Lottie suspected there was more he wouldn't say, but she knew. Those men wanted her whisky and they wanted her, just as her father had warned. She felt faint. She struggled to release her breath, she struggled to draw more in. She clutched at his arm, as she tried to force air into lungs that seemed to have collapsed on her.

Aulay frowned with concern. He slipped

his hand to the back of her head and pushed her head down so far that her hat tumbled to the straw at their feet. "Breathe," he said, holding her there. "Donna think, just breathe."

Somehow, Lottie managed to gather her wits and draw a single breath. And then another. When her breath was coming to her, she pressed up, leaned against the wall and closed her eyes. "I didna think . . . I never imagined . . ." There were too many thoughts racing through her brain.

He stroked her cheek, her arm. "Donna think of it, Lottie. I'd fight to the death before I'd allow them to harm you."

How could he say that? How could he even suggest it after what she'd done to him? She slowly opened her eyes and looked into his arresting blue eyes. He was concerned for her. She could see it in his expression, he was genuinely concerned. And there was more — he *desired* her. This was a much different look than the lust that had shimmered in his eyes the night he had kissed her. Lust, she understood. Lust had followed her about all her life — there wasn't a man who didn't look at her in that way. But as he touched her face with reverence, Lottie could unequivocally say that no man had ever looked at her with the sort of desire she could see in his face. His was the look of someone who desired a woman he cared about.

He bent his head and kissed her.

Just like that, the world turned upside down. Lottie reacted with all the yearning she'd felt since the first time she'd laid eyes on him, the first time he'd kissed her, the first time she'd seen him standing tall, dressed like the man that he was, not the man she'd forced him to be. His lips were the only bit of warmth in that stable, the only hope in her heart. He was kissing her, and everything else, all her troubles, all her fears, seemed to blessedly fade away.

He spread his fingers across her face to hold her as he deepened his kiss. She invited his tongue into her mouth, tangled hers with his. Her hand was on his arm, her fingers wrapped as far around the thick muscles as she could possibly reach. This was utter madness — they were being hunted, her father was gravely ill, Aulay would bring her to justice, and yet, she had never desired anyone as violently as she wanted him, now, in this stable.

Lottie's arousal was quickly scorching, burning in her blood, the tide of desire rising on a flood of emotions. She craved his touch, the strength of his body, the hard planes, the soft curves. She touched the corner of his mouth with her fingers, angled her head so that she could deepen this kiss between them, and pressed against him with her body. She could feel his hard arousal, could feel the tension of his desire, the restraint that radiated out of him. He slid his hand beneath her coat and around her waist, holding her tightly to him. *Don't let go, don't let go.*

But Aulay let go. He lifted his head and braced his hands against the wall on either side of her head. "We have to go, aye?" He sounded regretful as he brushed her hair from her face. "They are looking for us yet, so we must be quick now, *leannan,*" he said, using an old Gaelic term of endearment that glided down her spine.

Reality slowly pushed its way into her thoughts once more. She nodded and dipped down to retrieve her hat.

"What do we do now?" she asked as she fit it on her head and tucked her hair up underneath.

"Return to the ship. They'll be searching the ships in the harbor if they're no' already." He wrapped his hand securely around hers and smiled softly. "Ready, now?"

She was *not* ready. She would never be

ready. She would be content to remain in this stable with him for the rest of her life. *"Aye,"* she whispered.

He wrapped his arm around her waist, and hurried her out of the stable and into the alley. The sun glared on the world just as they'd left it. Whatever had just happened between them, whatever they'd felt, remained behind, in the shadows of that stable. Out here, Lottie's situation was just as dire as it had been a half hour ago.

Aulay's sense of direction was quite good, and he successfully navigated the maze of alleyways to return to the quay. Norval was there, pacing the quay, the little jolly boat moored to a post.

He instantly began to unwrap the rope when he saw them.

"What of Dru and Duff?" Lottie asked, looking frantically about for any sign of them.

"They're on board," Norval said.

"What? So soon? With a physician, aye?"

Norval didn't look at her, busy with his task of the boat. "A healer of sorts, aye," he said. "Will you get in the boat, Lottie?"

Thank God that at least that part of their plan had gone right.

"Has anyone else come by?" Aulay asked as he helped Lottie down into the jolly, then leaped in behind her. "Any men?"

"Aye, four men," Norval said, and pushed away from the quay, hopping into the stern of the boat and facing Lottie. He picked up a set of oars and in time with Aulay, began to row. "They look for a woman with white hair."

Lottie blinked. She should never have removed her hat at the inn.

Norval's gaze was penetrating. Did he fault her? "Aye, what is it, then?" she demanded. "I canna help the color of my hair."

"*Och*, Lottie," he said. " 'Tis no' your hair." He suddenly pressed his lips together, as if couldn't say more. His expression suddenly seemed strangely sorrowful.

"What is it Norval?" she demanded.

He shrugged, then glanced over his shoulder toward the ship and said no more.

But as they neared the ship, Lottie noticed that the men — *her* men, Livingstones — had gathered at the railing. They were watching them approach, which did not surprise her. But something seemed off. And then she realized there was no urgency in their movements. There were no shouts. No calls to them. They were silent, all of them, staring down at her.

She looked at Norval accusingly. "What

has happened?" she demanded, although part of her knew. Part of her was melting into palpable pain and dread before words could even be spoken.

A familiar sound reached her ears and her dread swiftly turned to heartbreak. She knew that sound — it was Drustan, crying out in anguish.

No one had to tell Lottie that Bernt Livingstone had drawn his last breath.

She knew.

CHAPTER FIFTEEN

The Livingstones fell apart at the death of their chief and their grief put a pall over Aulay's deck. They stood about with expressions that were a mix of confusion and torment, talking in low voices and glancing furtively over their shoulders as if they expected death to sneak up and take them, too.

Some of them were positively bereft. The actor openly sobbed as he spoke to Iain the Red about the old man.

Aulay made his way to the quarterdeck, unchecked, unchallenged. There was no pretense of captives or captors any longer.

The door to his cabin was open. He could see a small group of Livingstones gathered there, all of them in tears, all of them with a hand clamped on the shoulder of the next, or an arm thrown loosely around the next person's waist, their heads bowed.

Lottie was somewhere among them.

Aulay would never forget the sound she made when she realized what had happened. It wasn't loud, it was quite soft. But it was anguish, pure anguish — the sound of a heart breaking. She'd said not a word, but had climbed up the rope ladder like a monkey and disappeared before Aulay and Norval could set the ropes to raise the boat and climb the ladder themselves. Before anyone could say aloud that the old man had died.

Norval trailed behind Aulay now, as if he wasn't certain if he ought to guard Aulay or help him. Aulay caught Iain the Red's eye and gestured for him to join him on the quarterdeck. When Iain reached him, Aulay said, "Prepare to make sail."

"Pardon?" Norval said, looking between Iain and Aulay. Iain brushed past him to begin work. "On whose command?"

"On mine," Aulay said. "Tell who you must, lad, but heed me — if anyone needs persuasion that we must make sail at once, tell them that your mistress's scheme to sell your spirits has failed, and now, we've a group of thieves on our arse. We'll be lucky to catch a good wind and outrun them, but we must be quick."

"What is this about? What is he doing here?"

A man Aulay recognized joined them. MacLean was his name.

"He says we have thieves in pursuit," Norval said.

"Thieves? Why?"

"*Och,* for the whisky, man," Aulay said impatiently. "Did any of you truly believe you might casually sell it without question? Without an agent, without any knowledge but what someone had said in passing? I'd wager that now there's no' a man on shore who doesna know what is on this ship and that it is ripe for the picking."

"This is a trick!" MacLean said hotly.

"A *trick*?" Aulay repeated angrily. "You think that I would trick my own men out of the pay your mistress promised them? Do you think with a gun pointed at my back that I would somehow manage to unload the whisky from my ship? No, sir — the trick was done to you long ago by a Dane. The Copenhagen Company doesna exist. But what does exist is a den of cutthroat thieves who wish to turn your whisky into their gain. I need every man on deck to set the sails and prepare the guns."

MacLean blinked with surprise. But then he looked at Norval and said, "Do as he says. We all heard the man say they were looking for Scots on shore."

Aulay jerked around to MacLean. "What man?"

"The man who came for the physician Duff brought on board. It was too late, it was, as Bernt was gone . . . but the rower asked if we were Scotsmen and said they were looking for Scots."

"Have you seen anyone else?" Aulay asked.

The man shook his head.

"Gather your men. Tell them we sail and I am captain and to surrender their arms, aye?"

MacLean hesitated.

"Think!" Aulay snapped. "They are stunned by their loss, you canna sell your whisky, and you need us to sail this ship out of harm's way, aye? We can move ahead with speed, or we can tarry and engage in another fight, but this time, I assure you, we will win."

MacLean considered that a moment, then sighed with defeat. "Aye."

"Where is Beaty?" Aulay asked.

"I'll take you to him," MacLean said, and gestured for Aulay to follow him.

It was a ridiculously easy feat to overtake the Livingstones. Their fight, so brilliantly displayed when they'd first boarded the ship, had gone out of them with the loss of their chief. More than one merely handed a gun to a Mackenzie and put up his hands. Those in the captain's cabin didn't seem to realize what was happening on deck, and none of them ventured out to have a look.

Beaty was in the forward cabin, seated at a table, cards spread before him, his beefy hands on his knees. He was playing a wagering game with Billy. Jack Mackenzie, who had been injured in the initial attack, tried to gain his feet when he saw Aulay, but the wound was to his leg and he fell back into his chair.

"Cap'n!" Beaty said jovially. "I'd greet you properly, that I would, but I'm bound to this bloody chair."

"I see," Aulay said, and signaled MacLean to free him.

"The old man has passed," Aulay said as MacLean undid the chains. "The Livingstones have surrendered."

"What is this? Where are they?"

The booming voice of the actor could be heard just outside, and a moment later, he burst into the smaller cabin, crashing against the doorframe and throwing his body into the room as if he thought he was entering a fight. But seeing none, he drew up short and looked around him, confused.

"Have you no' heard?" MacLean asked.

"There was trouble at port," MacLean said. "We must make a play for open waters."

"*What* trouble?" Duff demanded, his gaze swinging back to Aulay. "There was no trouble. We fetched a doctor quick as a hare, we did. I gave them the name of a buyer —"

"A thief," Aulay said. "Men are looking for the whisky and they mean to take it."

"*Diah,* you donna say," Beaty said.

"I donna believe you," Duff responded heatedly. "I spoke to the lad in the customs office myself, aye? He gave me a *name.*"

"He gave you a thieves' den," Aulay snapped. "If you find my account lacking, you might inquire of your mistress."

The actor gasped. "I would no' *dare* impose on her now," he said with great indignation, as if Aulay had suggested bedding her.

He didn't need this actor to tell him what sort of state she was in. He had been in close company with her and her father for three days and knew how much she loved him. But death was part of life — people passed, and sails still needed setting, skies still needed watching, tides still came and ebbed. Time would not accommodate them to properly mourn the old man.

"Have we the necessary provisions to

reach Amsterdam?" Aulay asked Beaty.

Beaty shook his head as Maclean freed him from the shackle. "No' with so many men aboard, aye? We're already low on water."

"Scotland?"

Beaty thought about it. "If we head north, and catch a good wind, then aye. But any trouble at sea, and we'll find ourselves in a mare's nest, we will."

"Scotland, then," Aulay said without hesitation.

"What of the pay?" Beaty demanded.

"There is no pay," Aulay said impatiently.

"No pay!" Beaty echoed and stood, shaking out his legs. "And what are we to do with this sorry lot?" he asked, gesturing at the two Livingstones.

What, indeed. "We need them at present," Aulay said. "We'll need every able man, until we are certain no one follows." He and Beaty could discuss how to present them to authorities later. Right now, he needed their cooperation.

"You can keep the whisky," the actor offered. "Set us free in Scotland and keep the whisky."

Aulay snorted. "I donna want your bloody whisky — it is as useless to me as it is to you."

The actor winced. "*Och,* we're done, Robert," he said to MacLean. *"We're done."* He shifted his gaze to Aulay. "Unload the casks, then."

"By all that is holy, Duff, what is the matter with you, then?" MacLean exclaimed. "You canna throw overboard all that we've worked for!"

"Aye, and all that hard work has brought us naugh' but trouble, has it? First, with our laird, now with this captain and some Danish ruffians. Bernt was wrong," he said, and put his hand on the other man's arm. "Bernt was *wrong* and now he's bloody well dead."

MacLean closed his eyes a moment, then opened them with a sigh. "Aye," he said. "Get rid of it, then. Most of it, that is — save a cask for the lads. We'll need a few drams after the events of this wretched day."

Aulay didn't care to debate the fate of the whisky in that moment. "Make haste, lads, we weigh anchor within the hour." He had very little hope that they would somehow emerge from this debacle unscathed, but he had not time to contemplate it. He had a ship to put to sail. And he had to convince Lottie that her father would be buried at sea.

CHAPTER SIXTEEN

"We're moving, aye?" Mathais said, and stepped up to a porthole to look outside. "Aye, we're sailing."

"What?" Lottie found it a supreme effort to lift her head, which she had been resting against Drustan's much larger one. The poor lad had been crying the last hour, unable to harness his emotions, unable to understand what had happened to his beloved father.

The only difference between her and Drustan was that she understood what had happened to their father. But she could no better curb her emotions than he could.

She remembered the grief that had followed her mother's death, but she'd forgotten how wretched it had felt, how grief made her feel numb, as if there was no feeling in her limbs or her heart — all of it had been swallowed by her sadness. She'd been made deaf by it, too — she'd not heard a word of what anyone had said to her since returning from port, other than how he'd taken his last breaths with Mathais and MacLean at his side. There had been condolences, pats to her shoulder, kind words whispered in her deaf ears. Her spirit, her thoughts, her heart, had been utterly obliterated.

"We're sailing away," Mathais said again. "Where are we bound?"

Lottie didn't care. It hardly mattered now. All she wanted was for her father to wake up, to tell them he had a new plan, to laugh at their tears and remind them that if the English and the Jacobites couldn't kill him, neither could a piece of wood. "Come away from the window, Mats," she said wearily.

But her father would never wake, and it was her fault. She could scarcely look at her brothers, she was so filled with guilt. She should never have mentioned Aalborg. She should never have played into her father's grand scheme. She could have destroyed the stills, she could have agreed to marry MacColl — she could have done so many things. But she'd let a whisper of Anders Iversen enter her thoughts, had believed she had the answer. How easy it would be, she'd thought.

She should have known it would all end

in colossal failure.

She shouldn't have gone ashore this morning. She should have left the whisky to the men and stayed by her father's side. Maybe she would have noticed him failing. If she had, she might have summoned Morven before it was too late, maybe kept him alive until the doctor had come.

An enormous, indefatigable force of exhaustion from grief and guilt was pushing her down and flattening her into nothing.

"What are we to do?" Drustan asked her. Again. His question repeated over and over, her answer not satisfying whatever it was he needed to hear from her.

"We're going home," she said.

"Is that where we're sailing, then?" Mathais asked, turning from the porthole.

She didn't know where they were sailing, she didn't care, and could scarcely feel the gentle rock of the ship beneath her. Her mind was perfectly blank. The only thing she was truly aware of was the terrible ache in her head and her chest. Like a vice, squeezing the life from her. *Let it.*

The door swung open and startled the three of them. Aulay strode into the room. He had removed his coat and waistcoat and had rolled up his sleeves. He wore a sword at his side, and his hair, so perfectly groomed this morning, was wild about his shoulders. His gaze moved from Lottie to the lifeless body on the bunk. He swallowed. "Lottie . . . lads. I offer my deepest condolences," he said, bowing his head a wee bit.

She pressed her lips together and nodded as another stream of tears fell from the corners of her eyes. It seemed impossible there was anything left, but here the tears came, unbidden, unwanted. She wished she could fall into his arms, she wished he would hold her while she sobbed away whatever was left of her spirit.

Her tears agitated Drustan — he suddenly stood up and went to his father's body, which had been wrapped in a coverlet. Drustan kept trying to unwrap the body. Lottie leaped to her feet as he tried again. "Stop that. Stop that now," she said harshly.

Her tone only increased his agitation, and Drustan began to wail.

"*Diah,* will you cease that wailing!" Mathais cried, slamming his hand against the wall.

"*Dru!*" Lottie said tearfully, and rose up on her toes, wrapping her arms around Drustan's neck as sobs wracked his body again.

"Look away, now. Look away, *mo chridhe.*" He buried his face in his hands and sank down to the floor, unable to cease his wailing.

"By all that his holy, make him *stop*!" Mathais shouted. "Is it no' bad enough that he's left us? Must we listen to that as well?"

"Mats, please," Lottie said, but her voice sounded hollow, devoid of proper emotion. She couldn't bear their grief, not this time. She couldn't bear her own. "We all come to acceptance the best way we can," she heard herself say as she caressed Drustan's head.

"Well *I* have come to acceptance," Mathais said, and moved so suddenly that he banged into a chair; it fell backward with a crash. Mathais was suddenly breathing hard, as if he'd run a great distance. Lottie sensed he was on the verge of exploding with rage and frustration. She let go of Drustan and put her arms around Mathais. The poor lad sagged, dropping his head onto her shoulder, his lanky arms loose around her waist, and fresh sobs racking his body.

Lottie squeezed her eyes shut and let him sob until he could no longer cry. He slipped away from her, falling raggedly into a chair at the table.

She braced her hands against the table and drew a deep breath. They were quite a trio, she and her brothers. She drew another deep breath . . . and slowly became aware of another in the room.

She'd forgotten Aulay. She pushed herself up and turned around.

His gaze was full of sympathy. "Are you all right, then?" he asked quietly.

No. She was at sixes and sevens and felt as if she were spinning out into darkness. She shrugged indifferently.

He took a step forward. "I would no' intrude on your grief, Lottie, but I must speak with you."

"Now?" she asked weakly. Whatever it was, she had no capacity to hear it.

"Aye, now."

She sighed. "What is it, then?"

Aulay glanced at her brothers. "Privately, if you please."

Privately. Lottie glanced around the room, looking for something. A cloak? A wrap? Anything to delay a private conversation she was certain she didn't want to hear.

She glanced down at her rumpled gown and rubbed her damp palms against the soiled, torn skirt. What a fright she must look — her eyes were swollen from sobbing, her skin undoubtedly as splotchy red as poor Mathais's. Her hair, a bird's nest, was partially falling down her back. Had she looked such a fright in the stable? *The stable.* How long ago that seemed! Like a dream, a pretty little dream while her father was dying.

Tears welled in her eyes again, but she swallowed hard, rubbed her palms on her skirt again, then forced herself to move woodenly around the table. She paused to put her hand on Mathais's shoulder. "I'll return directly, aye? Stay with Dru."

Mathais folded his arms across the table and laid his head on them.

Lottie brushed carelessly against Aulay as she moved past and out onto the landing. On deck, Mackenzie and Livingstone men were moving about, many of them up on the masts, shouting at each other as they rolled sails.

She folded her arms tightly across herself and made herself look at Aulay.

"Lottie, *leannan,* I'm so verra sorry —"

"No, donna say it, please," she said, closing her eyes a moment. "I'll fall to pieces if I hear one more condolence."

Aulay said nothing.

"You could no' have been surprised by it," she said.

He scrutinized her face a moment, as if uncertain what she wanted from him. "No."

She had not been surprised by the news, either. Shocked to her core, yes. Devastated beyond understanding, certainly. But not surprised. A part of her had known when she'd left her father this morning that it would come to this. Perhaps not as quickly as it had, but a part of her had known. She looked away, feeling the burn in her eyes again.

"Have you eaten?" he asked.

She dabbed at one eye. "I could no' possibly."

"Drunk anything?"

"The ale at the inn," she said weakly.

"*Diah,* Lottie, you'll be no use to anyone if you donna mind yourself."

"I was no use to my father even in the best of health, was I? One might argue that I brought this on him. On us. On *all* of us," she said bitterly, and tightened her hold of herself. If she didn't, all the misery frothing in her would spill out and contaminate everything and everyone on this ship.

"You're no' to blame," he said quietly.

"I wish I could agree with you."

"Ah, Lottie, lass," he murmured, and caressed her arm. "Listen to me, aye? We must bury him."

We. He was being kind. How could he be so kind to her after all she'd put him through? She gave him a tremulous smile. "Please donna trouble yourself, Aulay. I know we must. We've a place on the island, next to my mother."

Aulay winced and shook his head. He wrapped his hand around her elbow and drew her closer. "I mean tonight."

Tonight. How could she bury her father tonight? Would they be in another port? She'd not leave her father in some foreign port! She opened her mouth to tell him so, but then understanding dawned, and she gasped, rearing back, away from him, repulsed. Enraged. *Horrified.*

"You canna leave him as he is," he said, his voice soft. "There is the issue of decay."

She whirled away from him, appalled, fearing she might heave. "Donna say another word!" she begged him, and pressed her hands to her abdomen to contain her distress.

"You've born quite a lot in your life, and you'll bear this, too." He stepped up behind her, leaned his head over her shoulder and said softly, "Your father would no' want to rot away before his children."

A swell of nausea overcame her. She pressed her fists into her belly, swallowing it down. Hot tears clouded her vision again. She wanted to say things, to tell Aulay that her father was a good man, that he didn't deserve this death. She wanted to say that she'd failed him, and for that, she would never forgive herself. But no words came out. She began to lean forward, as if pushed by an unseen force. She felt faint.

Aulay caught her with an arm around her waist and pulled her back into his chest, holding her upright. "Ah, *leannan,*" he said, caressing her head. "It will be all right," he promised her. "On my word, it will be all right."

He was wrong — it would never be all right. Lottie had failed to save her father and her clan and it would *never be all right.*

"We'll have a proper ceremony, aye?" he said soothingly into her ear. "I'll give you and your brothers a bit of time to prepare yourself."

How did one prepare to toss her father's body into the sea? She couldn't do it. She wanted to lie down and close her eyes until the pain in her heart and head eased. Forever, in other words, for the pain in her heart would never ease. "Is that why we've sailed? To bury him?" she asked tearfully.

But Aulay never answered her, because someone below began to shout for him. He let go of her, the warmth and hard wall of his body disappearing from her back. "Go, now, and tell your brothers. I'll send your actor up to help you."

Emptiness surrounded Lottie as Aulay

hurried down the steps and strode across the deck.

She watched him go. She could still feel his strength surrounding her, could still sense the small bit of comfort she'd felt with him firmly at her back. She thought of the way he'd held her in the stable — so tenderly, and at the same time, his hold unbreakable.

It felt like a dream. Everything felt like a sad, sweet dream.

CHAPTER SEVENTEEN

There was no wind to speak of as they made their way from Aalborg into Kattegat Bay, and progress was slow. The tiny pinprick of light behind them was also moving slowly, and had made no gains on the *Reulag Balhaire* for several hours.

Not one of the men who peered through the spyglass — Beaty, Gilroy, Iain the Red and MacLean — could be certain that a ship was actually shadowing them, or was merely headed for the sea. But the steady path of that ship and the timing of its appearance made it suspect in Aulay's mind. He didn't want to lose sight of it.

The sooner they had the burial done, the sooner they could turn their attention to outmaneuvering that ship.

He understood from MacLean that Lottie and her healer had washed her father's body. But with no winding sheets to wrap the body, and no mort cloth to cover him, they had used the coverlet and linens from Aulay's bunk.

"No coins for his eyes," MacLean lamented.

"At least we've got suitable weights," Beaty muttered as MacLean moved away. He and Aulay had agreed there was no reason to distress the Livingstones any further by explaining the body had to be weighted so that it would not go trundling off across the waves, bobbing along behind them in their wake. It was better this way — with the cloak of darkness, they'd not know what happened to their father's corpse, which seemed to be the kindest thing the Mackenzies could do for them.

The actor, Duff, and MacLean took on the task of fashioning a funeral bier from the spines of a whisky cask. The bier would hold the body as Aulay read the scriptures that would commend the old man's soul to God.

When all the preparations had been made, Aulay hung a lantern at the starboard railing in the same spot the Livingstones had come on board a few days ago . . . or had it been weeks? It seemed a lifetime ago in many ways. He sent MacLean to assemble the family and begin the procession, and signaled to Iain the Red's brother, Malcolm, to play the funeral dirge on his pipes.

The Livingstone clan — those who weren't so far in their cups to impede their ability to walk — gathered solemnly, leaning against one another, staring morosely at their feet or the sky. Another set of them appeared carrying the bier between them, with the old man's body laid carefully on top. The bier was followed by Lottie and her brothers, walking three abreast, hands held.

Lottie had washed her face and braided her hair, and had dressed in Aulay's clothes once more. Her skin had an unearthly paleness to it that made her look wraith-like. Grief had a way of reducing a person to a shadow — Lottie seemed frail, nothing like the spirited young woman who had taken his ship.

When the men had placed the bier on the ship's railing, Aulay signaled Malcolm to cease the pipes. He opened the Bible his mother had given him on the occasion of his first voyage as captain. He recited the passages from rote, really, not hearing or registering the words. It was never an easy thing to give a body to the sea, no matter the circumstance. His mind wandered as he read. Was this the sum of the old man's life? To have squandered it in the chase of some ill-begotten scheme, only to be slipped into the dark waters of the sea?

He listened to the desperate sounds of the youngest Livingstone, trying so very hard not to weep. He listened to the keening of the giant. He glanced at all of the old man's children once or twice and despaired for Lottie. She stared straight ahead over the top of her father's body, her empty gaze fixed into the night's middle distance, her expression grim.

Aulay ended with Isaiah, "So do not fear, for I am with you; do not be dismayed, for I am your God. I will strengthen and help you; I will uphold you with my righteous right hand."

Judging by the lack of comfort on any Livingstone's face, Aulay wondered if any of them truly believed God had them in hand. All signs pointed to the opposite.

He turned to Lottie. "Is there anything more you'd like to add, then?"

She shook her head. Aulay nodded at his first mate. Malcolm began to play the pipes, and the Mackenzies lifted the bier and tilted it so that the body slid off and into the sea. The splash startled them all, and the giant began to sway, his moaning so loud that it arced over the small pipes. The Mackenzie men shifted uncomfortably, none of them understanding how to cope with a damaged giant.

Lottie linked her arm through the giant's and rested her head against his shoulder, whispering to him. After a moment or two of gulping his sobs, he stopped wailing and turned to Duff, who put an arm around his shoulders and led him away.

MacLean, unsteady on his feet, held up a flagon. "To the chief," he said. *"Slàinte mhath."* He took a good long swig, then passed the flagon to the next man as he dragged his sleeve across his mouth. And so it went, the whisky passed around, every man offering up a toast before drinking deeply from the flagon. But when it came to Lottie, she refused it, turned away from all of them, and disappeared into the dark.

Aulay was the last to receive the flagon. He drank, then gave the order the Livingstones were to be corralled. "Put them in the hold with a guard and a cask of their whisky," he instructed. The last thing he needed were drunkards careening around his deck. The more important question of what to do with the Livingstones in Scotland still loomed.

"What, why?" one of them complained as he swayed into his neighbor.

"You kept our captain tied like a roasted

pig. If he says you're to go down into the hold, then down you'll go," Beaty said gruffly.

There was some arguing about it, but the Livingstones were too drunk to fight and allowed themselves to be escorted, particularly with the promise of whisky.

With the Livingstone clan below deck, the Mackenzies began the arduous task of emptying and sinking whisky casks. They had made it halfway through those stacked on the deck when Beaty interrupted Aulay. "The ship, she's gaining on us, she is."

Aulay squinted into the darkness. He couldn't even make out the pinprick of light any longer. "You're certain, are you?" he asked as Beaty handed him the spyglass.

"Aye. She's tacked a wee bit east and north and caught a good wind, she has."

Aulay lifted the spyglass and spotted the hazy light in the distance. The ship had definitely gained ground. "Leave the whisky," he said. "Tack north, than east."

"Aye," Beaty said. "You ought to get some sleep, Cap'n, if you donna mind me saying. We'll need you when the sun rises. I'll fetch you if we need you before then."

Aulay reluctantly agreed. He'd reached the limits of his exhaustion, but he knew that what was ahead for the rest of the night was an arduous task, and come morning, he'd be fortunate if his men could keep to their feet. He would be no use to them if he were as exhausted as they would be.

He made his way to his quarters and entered without any thought other than a pressing desire to sleep. The interior was dark, the smell fetid. How long before the stench of death would be gone? Someone had closed the portholes and pulled the heavy linen drapes over them, as was the custom when a person died. They said it kept the ghost from escaping. In this case, the old man's ghost had nowhere to go and could not escape, so Aulay pushed back the drapery and opened the window. A bit of night light and the salty smell of the sea filtered in, enabling him to see better. He made his way to the next porthole, nearly stumbling over Lottie when he did. He had not seen her lying on the bare bunk, curled onto her side, her back to the door.

He pushed her feet aside and sat on the end of his bunk. "Have you eaten, then?"

"No," she said meekly. "I canna possibly."

"Aye, you can, if you donna wish to follow your father into the sea."

She gasped and rolled over, sitting up. "How dare you say such a wretched thing?"

"Lying here without food or drink? What

else am I to think?" He noticed some salted beef and a biscuit on the table beside his bunk that someone had brought her from the hold. How he would ever pay for the cargo they'd lost, he couldn't say. He'd think on that later — for now, he was exhausted and had a few days at sea ahead of him. And while he felt exceedingly sympathetic for the lass who had just lost her father, he had very little patience for anything that did not move them forward and away from the events of these last few days. What choice did any of them have?

Lottie pushed her legs over the edge of the bunk, bracing her hands on either side of them. He picked up the biscuit and held it out to her.

She wrinkled her nose. "I'm no' hungry."

"Eat."

She snatched it with exasperation.

Aulay went to the sideboard and rummaged around there until he found a candle. The light flared when he lit it. He looked at Lottie again. Her hair, unbound, fell long around her, almost to her waist, and framed her bonny face. Dark circles shadowed her eyes, as if she'd long been ill.

"Eat," he said again.

"It tastes like wood. Everything tastes like wood. I *feel* like wood." She took a small bite of the biscuit and made a face.

"It will have to do, lass. We've no' time to fish, and it looks as if we have a ship in pursuit of us."

She looked up with eyes wide with alarm. "The Danes?"

"I donna know," he said. "And I donna intend to let them get close enough to see who they are."

Her lashes fluttered and she glanced down at her biscuit.

She looked so forlorn that Aulay was suddenly overwhelmed with a desire to take her into his arms, to hold her, to lie to her and promise that all would be well. *Why am I so enticed by this lass?* She had likely ruined him and yet, he couldn't help but want her.

Sometimes, a man just knows.

He'd had the same ridiculous thought early at the start of their acquaintance, when she'd stepped on board his ship and had conquered him with her beauty and the spark in her eye.

"Can we escape them?" she asked.

"If we remain vigilant, aye. We had a good start on them, we did."

Lottie closed her eyes a moment, gave a slight shake of her head. "So much has happened."

Aulay put the candle aside, picked up the

beef, and handed it to her.

She took a bite. "Do you think you must account for your life straightaway when you die, or is there a wee bit of time for grace?"

"I donna know," he said, taking a seat beside her.

"Will you know the purpose of it all? Of this life? Will you know if it was worth the hardship?"

The lass was clearly tormented. She was so young, at least fifteen years younger than Aulay, and perhaps had never contemplated these questions before. Did anyone ever really know their purpose on this earth?

"Perhaps you ought no' to think of these things if they upset you, aye?"

"When I was a wee lass, only eight years, my father took me with him to Port Appin, and there we met a Scot with four ponies on a string, aye? I was quite taken with them, that I was, and particularly a black one. He had a wee star just between his eyes," she said, gesturing absently to her forehead. "My father said, 'do you want the pony, Lottie?'" She laughed ruefully. "What lass of eight would say no, I ask you? So he turned to the man and said, we should like a pony, and he offered him a price. The man said, *'why these are Percheron ponies,'*" she said, mimicking the man. "Spanish war horses, they are, the finest on a field of battle. My father didna question it, no' for a moment. He said, 'for my lass, only the finest pony. Percheron, you say? Spanish you say?' " She shook her head. "We returned home with that pony."

Aulay didn't see the point of her story. "He was kind to you, then," he said.

"That night, my father and my mother had an awful row about it. I heard them through the walls, shouting at one another about my pony. I thought my mother meant to send the pony away, but I'd already named him Stjerne. He's my horse to this day." She glanced at Aulay. "But he's no' a war horse. He's a Fell pony. An unremarkable Fell pony with a star between his eyes." She leaned forward. "Was that his purpose, then, my father? To make his children happy, no matter the cost? My mother adored my father, but he was so bloody impetuous, so careless with his purse, that they argued often. His carelessness hurt us all, it did. But this? *This?*" she said, gesturing around them. "This was all *my* doing, Aulay. He was careless, but I committed the greater sin, did I no'? I was arrogant. I thought I knew how to save us from his very bad idea of distilling whisky without license, and it cost my father his life. I could have set it all to rights and married Mr. Mac-Coll, but I would no' hear of it."

Aulay blinked — he hadn't realized there had been a marriage offer in the mix.

"I thought him too old, and I was selfish — I didna want to be his wife, I didna want to live in his house. In the end, I behaved in the same way my father behaved all my life — without regard for the consequence." She shook her head and turned her gaze away. "The worst of it is that I didna have the chance to apologize." She put the rest of the biscuit and salted beef aside, and with a weary sigh, lay down on her side. "What is *my* purpose, then, I ask you?"

"Donna weep," he said.

"I'll no' weep. I've wept all that I can, I have."

"Lottie . . . your father was a man, capable of deciding his own actions. You may have suggested this scheme, and no one could fault you for seeking a solution. But he took your idea. He knew the risks. He knew verra well what he did."

Her response was another sigh.

"Come, take the air, then," he said.

She shook her head.

He hooked his hand under her arm, drawing her up to a sitting position again. "You need air, and your men need a leader."

She snorted at that. "I'm no' a leader."

"Aye, you are. They are the captives now, and they are restless. They need you."

"Have Duff lead them, or Mr. MacLean. Anyone but me."

"I didna know your father well, but I know he thought you better than all of them put together, aye? He would have wanted you to carry on, Lottie, and you must. Your brothers are wandering the deck like the dead. Your clan is drunk and belligerent. I've lost enough time and money as it is." He caught her face with his hand and made her look at him. "Now is the time to be the man your father was no'. His purpose, whatever it might have been, is no' yours. *Your* purpose might be much greater."

She blinked. She smiled softly. "How can you be so kind to me, after all the misery I've caused you?"

It wasn't kindness, it was expediency. He was nearly certain of it. "I need you if I am to see us all safely home to Scotland."

"Aye, and what is to become of us then?"

It was a quandary of the highest order, and one Aulay hadn't yet sorted out. He would think of it when they were safely at Balhaire. "We'll decide when we reach Scotland, aye?"

She wrapped her fingers around his wrist

and closed them tightly. "Promise me, Aulay — promise me you'll give me the blame. Only me."

She was asking him to hand her over to authorities and no one else. If he had any doubt of it, she added, "I'm responsible for all of it. Let the others go free and I will gladly surrender, on my honor I will."

Something hitched with a sharp pain in Aulay's chest. He didn't want that. He wanted justice, but he couldn't bear to think of giving Lottie to the authorities. He stroked her cheek. "We'll speak of it when we near Scotland —"

"No." She pulled his hand from her face and grasped his head between her hands. "I beg you, make me this promise *now,* Aulay. Give me your word!"

Good God, this woman was remarkable. Who among them could make that sort of sacrifice? He peeled her right hand from his face and kissed her knuckles. He slipped a hand around the nape of her neck, and pulled her closer. Of all the women, of all the ones who might have snatched his heart, might have allowed him to see beyond the sea, it would be this one, this beautiful, doomed woman. He quite admired her in the moment, but blooming beside his admiration was grief. He knew very well what would happen to her if he agreed to it — she would likely hang; at the very least be remanded to prison.

Tears glistened in her eyes. *"Promise me,"* she whispered, and touched her mouth to his.

That tender kiss aroused him more than any torrid kiss ever could. Her fingers fluttered around his ear, her arm went round his neck. She moved her mouth on his, teased him lightly with her tongue, and Aulay's body, starved for a woman's touch, instantly ached for more. He took the reins of that kiss and moved to her neck. Lottie dropped her head back with a gasp of pleasure, and everything in Aulay ignited with white-hot, desperate anticipation. He smoldered, his body slowly turning to ash. He cupped her face and held it tenderly, but at the same time, he pressed her down onto the bunk. Lottie arched into him and pushed her thigh between his legs, pressing against an erection that was suddenly and powerfully present.

He paused to gaze down at her. Her pale blue eyes had gone dark with hunger he understood. What was he doing? Would he bed his prisoner? *Diah,* how deep this extraordinary esteem pulled between them.

She was looking up at him with an expression he did not understand. *"What?"* he whispered breathlessly as he caressed her head, her cheek.

Lottie put her hands on his chest and slid them up, to his shoulders, sank her fingers into his hair and answered, *"Everything."*

Aulay groaned. He kissed her cheek, her mouth. And then he reached for the hem of her shirt and untied it, slipping his hand onto her bare skin, over her ribs, to her breasts. He dipped down to press his mouth to the skin of her décolletage, kissing the swell of her breasts. Lottie sighed with pleasure, thrust her hands into his hair, and Aulay went spiraling into sensual havoc.

He pushed the shirt up and took her breast into his mouth at the same time his hands slipped into the waist of the trews and between her legs.

Lottie reached for the ties of the trews and pulled them free, pushing them down her hips, and Aulay abandoned himself. He was moving by instinct and sensation, his hands and mouth finding every place on her body that made her gasp with pleasure. He freed himself from his trousers almost desperately; his need to hold her and have her overtook every other thought. It was a need he'd never felt so sharply, had never experienced so deeply in his marrow. He hiked her leg up and pressed the tip of his cock against her on a moan of pleasure, sliding deeper, and then with torturous patience, completely into her, all the way to the hilt, before slowly sliding out again.

He began to move in her, his mouth on her mouth, on her neck, his hands on her breasts. Lottie's hands slid over him, her fingers digging into his flesh, urging him to move deeper into her. Wave after wave of sensual gratification rolled over him, spinning him like a top toward a release that was building to a ferocious crescendo. Lottie clung to him with one leg wrapped around his waist, her mouth on his skin. He was completely lost, more at sea than he'd ever been in his life, lost and clinging to the only thing that could save him — this woman, this astonishing woman. He could feel his deliverance mounting as she spread her arms and arched her neck, her eyes closed, letting him carry her along in his vortex of pleasure, washing this wretched week away from them. Nothing existed beyond the two of them, beyond her scent and the feel of her body around his.

When the vortex sucked them under, Aulay collapsed on her. For several moments they both sought their breath. But when they had it, Lottie cupped his face in her hands and kissed him gently. Reverently.

But the sound of one of the crew shouting up to another on the mast managed to slip into his consciousness, and Aulay remembered who and where he was. He suddenly broke the kiss and stood up, taking a step backward. Lottie caught herself on the bunk, breathing hard, her gaze fixed on him and filled with need.

How could he have done it? How could he have taken her like this, after all that she'd done, knowing that he would hand her over to authorities in a few days? "Clean yourself up," he said, his voice surprisingly hoarse. "Get some rest."

She didn't move. She remained braced against that bare bunk, watching him like a cat. *Wanting* him. He could plainly see her desire, could feel it mirrored in him, and God help him, it ran just as deep in him.

Righting his clothes, Aulay walked out of that cabin before he did something mad. His sorrow at what was to come was already closing in on him, squeezing him from all sides. Sorrow for her. For him. For what might have been before he'd had a chance to have it.

CHAPTER EIGHTEEN

Cold was seeping into Lottie's joints. She groped for the woolen plaid she'd found tucked beneath the bunk bed in the captain's cabin, pulling it tightly around her. It was as damp as everything else. With a sigh, she opened her eyes and blinked back her fatigue.

Drustan was beside her, snoring like her father once had. Pain sharpened around her spine, reminding her of her loss. Not that she needed any reminding — she'd dreamed of him for the last two nights. In her dreams, she was trying to catch him, but he was always just ahead of her, disappearing before she could reach him.

But there was one dream that stood out from the others — that was the dream where she caught up to her father, put her hand to his shoulder, and he turned with a smile and said, "I'm no' *dead, pusling.* I'm here with you now, am I no'?"

That dream had startled her awake.

Lottie pushed herself up and looked at the mound that was her brother on the floor next to the bunk. They were in the forward cabin now, where she'd decamped that night after Aulay had left her. She turned her head to the porthole and looked out at the sea.

She'd been completely undone by their coupling. He'd released her from misery, had shown her compassion and hope and a desire like she'd never felt in a moment she'd needed it the most . . . but that desire had faded away with the light of day.

It seemed so long ago now. A lifetime. She hadn't spoken to him since that night, and it surprised her that she should feel his absence so keenly. Perhaps as keenly as she felt her father's absence, but in a different way. She mourned her father, dreamed about him, missed his smile. But she craved Aulay like water. When she wasn't grieving her father's death, she was obsessively thinking about those moments with Aulay on his bunk, escaping from her grief, swimming headlong into another sort of grief entirely. She was desperate to remember the way he'd felt inside her, and the way he'd held her so tightly and carefully . . . and just as desperate to forget it.

Lottie was not an experienced woman —

her brief affair with Anders not withstanding — but she knew instinctively that there was something quite profound about their frantic lovemaking. At the very least, it was much different than anything she'd experienced with Anders.

It was funny how often she'd thought of Anders in the last year, but since she'd stepped foot on this ship, she'd scarcely thought of him at all. She wondered, as she gazed into a vast landscape of various shades of gray, what she might have done had she met Anders again in Aalborg. It hardly mattered to her any longer — with the perfidy she'd discovered in Aalborg, he had faded into nothing.

What time is it? She hated not knowing time, but it was impossible to keep track when one was at sea, particularly when the skies looked the same as the surface of the water. She drew her knees up to her chest and wrapped her arms around them. She felt oddly at peace. Fatigued, and full of longing. But the riot inside of her heart had calmed, the turmoil of having lost her father had begun to subside into acceptance. Her thoughts were turning to what lay ahead of them.

She yawned, stretched her arms overhead, then climbed off the bunk and over the sleeping form of Drustan. Mathais was in the other bunk. After their father's death, he had claimed to be made sick by the motion of the sea, but Lottie knew he was too proud to allow his grief to be seen. Yesterday, he'd gone out of the forward cabin and had made himself of use on deck, working hard until Duff had sent him staggering back into the cabin, where he'd fallen onto the bunk, exhausted, and into what Lottie hoped was a dreamless sleep.

A Mackenzie had been kind enough to bring her an ewer with some water, and a small bowl for washing. The water was dingy now, and it wasn't possible to change it, as the fresh water was being rationed. This, she understood from Duff, who fancied himself something of a seafarer now. He'd also explained to her that they had outrun the ship that had been following them.

"Turned round and went back to port, I'd wager," he'd said yesterday as they stood at the stern. "The Mackenzies are puffed up like dead bovines, what with their successful maneuvering, but Gilroy believes we might have tacked east to north and been quicker about it."

The ship suddenly rolled to the starboard side, and Lottie nearly lost her balance. The seas were rough and her sea legs, so sturdy in the first few days, were wobbly.

She washed her face and combed her hair with her fingers, then bound it at her nape. She hoped she was afforded the luxury of a bath before her trial, and some decent clothes for it. That was something else she'd become numb to — the prospect of a trial and punishment. Hanging or prison, whatever would happen, seemed so far in the distance and so impossible to comprehend that she couldn't feel anything for it. Just . . . nothing.

She grabbed the plaid from the bunk and wrapped it around her shoulders, and quietly quit the cabin.

The air was cold and wet, but a welcome departure from the hard sun and stiff wind they'd had for the last two days. More than once, she'd had to catch herself from being blown overboard. She would need to be vigilant today, too — the seas were rough and the ship was rolling and pitching with the swells.

She saw Duff on the deck below, arguing with a Mackenzie. She had always had a soft spot for the big man, and she would love him always for the way he'd taken Drustan under his wing. He'd kept a close eye on him, and had confided in Lottie that Bernt had asked him to keep Drustan in his care in the event of his demise. Lottie didn't know if that was true, or Duff's acting out his own grief, but in her despair, she'd been quite grateful for the help.

Duff had even cajoled Iain the Red into teaching Drustan how to whittle. Drustan was quite taken with it, worrying over a piece of the cask spine for hours on end. His distraction was a welcome relief to them all.

She looked toward the bow and noticed one of the Mackenzie men leaning against the mast step, his eyes closed. He was sleeping standing up! Duff had explained to her how arduous it had been to sail against the wind and to keep pace enough to outrun the other ship. The Mackenzie crew had worked round the clock.

As she moved cautiously across the deck, she was startled by the sound of pounding on the deck hatch that led to the hold below deck. Her men were held there, she knew, and, Duff said, quite restless.

She made her way to Duff's side. "What is that rumpus?" she asked.

"Your clan, aye?" Duff said, and slanted her a look. "They've drunk all the whisky below, slept it off, and now they want out."

"Can they no' come out, then? A wee bit of air would help soothe them, aye? They canna escape."

"While we work around them?" the Mackenzie man said, and snorted. "We've had twice the work because of them, and no pay, and we'll no' have them underfoot."

"Can we no' be of some service to you, then?" she asked.

The man grunted.

"Duff!"

The three of them turned about. Aulay was standing just above them on the quarterdeck, his hands braced against the railing, glaring down at Duff. "Can you no' control them?" he asked, gesturing to the hatch.

"What am I to do, then?" Duff shot back. "Our whisky is gone as are all our hopes, and they can find no joy in being locked away!"

Aulay turned his glare on Lottie. "Miss Livingstone," he said, quite formally, "Will you have a word with your clan and ask them to kindly stop making such a bloody racket?"

"What? Aye, yes — I will," she promised, startled by his outburst.

Aulay pivoted about and resumed his place at the wheel beside Beaty.

"Well," she said on a rush of breath.

"I'd take offense to that, I would," Duff

said. "But he's no' slept any more than the rest of them."

Lottie yanked the blanket tightly around her shoulders. "I'll have a word, then."

"I'd no' advise it, miss," said the Mackenzie man, but Lottie was already moving.

Beaty was at the wheel, and Aulay stood with one arm braced against the mizzen, staring ahead into the sea. He cast a look over Lottie, sweeping all the way down to her toes, then up again before turning his attention to the sea before them.

Well then — the man who had made passionate love to her had gone missing, apparently. "Can we no' help?" she asked.

"Aye, you can help by making them cease that ruckus," he said curtly.

The man she'd captured had returned and was as surly as he had been the first day of his captivity. "I meant with the sails, or on deck."

"No."

"Your men are in need of rest —"

"I am well aware of it."

Lottie's gaze narrowed. She moved closer. "What is the matter with you, then? I know we're a burden to you, but I —"

He suddenly spun around on her. "You've no idea what sort of burden you are, or how tall and wide your burden lies on my shoulders."

He said it so violently that Lottie took a step backward, shocked.

Aulay glared at her a moment, and then sighed to the sky. *"Bod an donais,"* he muttered. "Lottie . . . I beg your pardon. I donna generally release my frustrations on the fairer sex, but *Diah* help me, I donna know what to do with you."

He was confusing her. She didn't know what he meant. "I've kept away."

"That's no' what I mean," he said, his eyes piercing hers. "We've eaten what was no' ours to eat. We're almost out of water. We return to Scotland like dogs with our tails between our legs, and by all rights, you ought to hanging from the yardarm, aye?"

She flinched.

"But I donna know what to *do* with you and yours," he said.

Lottie's heart began to beat erratically. The ship suddenly rose up on a wave, then crashed down again, and he caught her waist to steady her. But Lottie could not be steadied and neither, apparently, could he. The cold hard truth of their situation had seeped into their membranes and was mixing with the desire in their veins. Esteem and thievery did not mix.

There was only one thing she could do, and that was to free him. "You know what to do," she said. "There is only one thing you can do, Aulay. I know it. I expect it."

Aulay blinked. His hand dropped from her waist.

"Give me leave to speak with my clan," she said quickly before he could say something to dissuade her. "We can help you, we can relieve your men, we can give you all an opportunity to rest, aye? It's the least we can do after all the trouble we've caused."

He pressed his lips together, exchanged a look with Beaty, then nodded. Lottie didn't linger. She found it painful to see him so conflicted over the grief she'd caused him. *Diah,* but they were sailing home on an ocean of grief, all of them, all of them full of sorrow for so many reasons. It was heart-crushing.

The Livingstones cheered when she appeared around the crates. They were all in their shirt sleeves, unwashed, boasting scraggly beards. "Aye, I knew she'd come to save us!" Norval shouted.

"Give us our freedom, Lottie," Morven said. "They've no right to treat us in this manner. 'tis no' gentlemen's rules."

"They are angry with us," she reminded

301

him. "And they treat us as we treated them."

"Aye, and we're angry, too, we are! They've thrown our whisky overboard!" shouted Gilroy from somewhere near the back.

"Have you forgotten that we threw their wool off to make room for the whisky?" Lottie reminded them. "And what good is the whisky to us now? It's caused more trouble than it ever might have been worth."

"What? *Why?*" asked Mark Livingstone.

Lottie stepped up onto a crate. "Lads, you know the Campbells will be as thick as a pack of wolves waiting for it, aye? And if no' the Campbells, then the crown. The Mackenzies must hand us over or be accused of collusion. We'll be caught one way or another, and then what?"

"We worked hard to make that whisky, Lottie!" insisted Mark. "Harder than we've worked at augh' else!"

"We did, aye we did," she agreed. "But it was always a risk, was it no'? We knew it could bring us trouble before we ever built the first still, aye?"

"We might have sold it yet!" Morven said. "The fault was in sailing to Denmark. We're no' sailors, no' one of us, save Gilroy."

Lottie winced with the painful truth in that. "That is my fault —"

"No, Lottie, the fault belongs to all of us," Mr. MacLean said. "Our choice was to sail to Denmark or lose the whisky ere we had a chance to sell it. All of you know it is true — we met and said these things ere we ever put a foot on Gilroy's ship. Have you forgotten?"

Mark looked as if he intended to argue, but Mr. Maclean held up a hand. "It hardly matters now, does it, then?" he implored them. "We are Livingstones. We care for our own. We must think ahead, not about the past."

"We ought to help them," Lottie said. "The Mackenzies are exhausted." There was grumbling, but Lottie was quick to put an end to it. "They have no' tossed us into the sea when they had every right! They've shared their provisions with us, and there are more of us than them! If you canna find it in your heart to help those who have helped us, then so be it — but I have given my word." Lottie said.

"Aye, we'll help," Mr. MacLean said, eying anyone who would disagree. "But I would know what we'll do when we return to Lismore. We've still the matter of rents to be paid."

"Lottie, will you marry MacColl, then?" Norval asked her bluntly.

The question twisted like a knife in her gut. She looked around at the men standing before her. None of them seemed surprised by the question. "You all know of that?"

Norval shrugged. "He's made no secret of his esteem."

"You save us all if you wed him, Lottie," Morven said.

Well, then, they were back to the beginning, were they? She should have known that there had never been any escape from her being the price to be paid to save all the Livingstones. She'd been naïve to think that she could avoide it. "We canna speak of what will come next if we never reach Scotland, can we? At present, we need to help the Mackenzies. Set aside your pride at having lost and be grateful we've not been walked off a plank."

"Aye, release us from this hold before we all go mad," Mark said.

"Give me your word that you'll work, and work hard," she said. "Swear it!"

"Aye, we will," Morven said, and looked around at his clan. "We *will*," he said, sounding as if he meant to convince the others.

"Dress, then, and I'll see you on deck."

She would marry MacColl, then. If, by some miracle, she escaped the gallows, she would give up her dream of seeing the world, perhaps of having children, and for the sake of her clan, she would marry him. It was, she thought, what her father would have wanted her to do. Perhaps she owed him that. To hang, or look at the walls of a cell, or marry an old man . . . none of it seemed better or worse than the other.

CHAPTER NINETEEN

Aulay was perched high above the ship, working to repair the top sail line that had whipped clean of its ties. Jack Mackenzie was Aulay's best sail man — he had an amazing ability to shimmy up the masts to the very tops when needed. But his leg injury had left Aulay without a necessary sailor on deck, and he'd had to climb up the mast to do the repairs himself.

He watched the Livingstones below him. They were working under Beaty's command, and in truth, it was a relief — his men were getting some much needed rest.

Yesterday had been cold and blustery, and today was bright and the wind calmer. Aulay worked for the better part of an hour, finishing the repair just as the sun began to slide into the horizon. He looked toward the setting sun and thought of painting it. A powder blue sky with streaks of gold, a muddy brown line that was the coast of

Scotland. *Home.*

This was the sort of seascape he loved, a vast canvas of water shining gold in the early evening light. Aulay retrieved the spyglass at his waist and looked out over the vista to study it, to remember it, so that he might paint it one day. That thin brown line would grow out of the water as they neared it, rising into sheer cliffs and rocks. The surface of the water would turn an undulating deep, dark blue in the moonlight, and the sky a tapestry of stars on inky black.

He guessed they had a day and a half of sailing, no more, before they reached Balhaire. They would sail between the Orkney and Shetland islands before turning south, down the western coast of Scotland, where his return would be heralded. As they maneuvered into the private Balhaire cove, a bell would sound, signaling their arrival. Mackenzies would begin to appear, a few at first, then groups of them, all of them hurrying the half mile or so from the castle and village that surrounded it, all of them eager to greet loved ones returned from the sea and the world beyond.

Aulay's father used to come out of the castle to greet him, but in the last few years, he had not — a bad leg ailed him and he seldom walked down to the cove now. No matter — his father always waited eagerly for Aulay in the great hall, his dogs at his feet, a fire in the hearth, a plate of food and a tankard of ale waiting for his son. His mother would be there, too. She had long ago accepted his love of the sea, although she never understood it. She was forever relieved when he walked into the hall, her beautiful smile illuminating the dark old castle.

His brother Rabbie and his wife, Bernadette, would have heard the bell, and would arrive just after him, coming from Arrandale with their children. His sister Vivienne, her husband, Marcas, and their brood would join the family in the hall, and his nieces and nephews would beg to know what he'd brought them. Catriona, Aulay's youngest sister, would run down to the cove, too eager to see him and hear his tales. She would trek up to the castle with him, her arm linked through his, peppering him with questions.

Catriona would have liked to have been someone like Lottie Livingstone, an adventurer, but her parents would never have allowed it.

Sometimes, Aulay's oldest brother, Cailean, and his wife, Daisy, would be in residence, having come for a month or so from England where they lived. They would greet him with their young daughter in Cailean's arms, their son, Lord Chatwick, in tow.

Aulay was allowed to play the part of prodigal son for a few days, returning to them with news of the world. For those days, he would be pampered and loved. It was the only way, he'd long ago discovered, to win his father's esteem. But slowly his family's life would return to the routine, and Aulay's star would fade under the blazing virility of his brothers, the chatter of his sisters. He would fade into the wall hangings, sitting quietly to one side, listening to the details of a life that did not include him any longer, wanting to retreat to his rooms and paint.

He kept his personal experiences to himself — the women, the wine. The exotic and the heart-wrenching situations he saw in every port. He kept his personal life separate from his family because he found it difficult to describe the sun to people who had only seen the moon. Nevertheless, Aulay had always enjoyed his homecomings immensely and looked forward to them with great enthusiasm — the same enthusiasm he held for the next voyage after that.

But this time, he dreaded coming home.

Understandably, his family would be devastated by his news — they'd all pinned great hopes on this voyage in spite of their great skepticism. Aulay had convinced them this launch was the rebirth of their trade, a path of return to their days of glory. What he would deliver was the news that they could lose everything.

The cargo must be repaid. He had to determine a way to do it, even if it meant selling his ship. The Mackenzies were not debtors, they were too proud for that. Not even in the meanest of times had they been in debt.

Despair twisted in his gut, and Aulay lowered the spyglass.

He had no doubt that his father would insist the Livingstones be brought to justice for the losses they'd caused the Mackenzies, and his brother Rabbie would agree. They lived by simple rules at Balhaire — one did not take what was not theirs, and if they did, there were consequences. Regrettably, consequences didn't simply disappear because Aulay had experienced something rather profound on this voyage. Their loss was not diminished because he'd happened to allow his heart to be filled by the woman who had taken their ship. *Bloody hell,* when there were women of every stripe in the world, why had he developed such esteem for the very one he could not defend?

He didn't want to think of it, or confront it until he absolutely must. It was tragedy enough that he couldn't rid himself of his more salacious thoughts of Lottie, much less her demise.

He went to put the spyglass away, but a movement caught his eye and he steadied the glass once more, shifting it slightly to the right. He could make out the topsails of a ship along the coastline.

He lowered the spyglass and started down.

On deck, Beaty reported that he'd seen the ship, too. "I'll keep an eye," Beaty said. "You ought to have a wee sleep now, captain. We'll reach the islands before dawn."

Aulay was grateful for the opportunity to rest and made his way to his cabin by way of the hold, where he helped himself to one of the last biscuits and some salted fish they'd managed to catch this morning. When he returned to the deck, the sun had all but disappeared into a ribbon of pink evening light. As he reached the landing of the forecastle, the door to the forward cabin opened and Lottie stepped out. She hesitated when she saw him, then looked back over her shoulder and carefully pulled the door to. They'd hardly spoken since he confessed he didn't know what to do with her. She looked better rested than she had in previous days, and the sun had put a rosy color in her cheeks. Her hair hung over her shoulder in a thick rope, and she played with the end of it, seemingly reluctant to move one way or another, to cross his path or step back into the smaller cabin until he'd disappeared round the corner to his own cabin.

"Is that where you've been hiding, then?" he asked, nodding in the direction of the first mate's cabin.

"Better there than at the top of the mast, like you."

"You spied me there, did you?"

"*Spied* you? I thought you meant to leap to your death what with all the trouble."

He could not suppress a sardonic chuckle. "If I intended to leap to my death, I would have done it long before today, aye?"

That earned him a wee smile. "Aye." Her gaze fell to the biscuit and fish he held.

"I owe you thanks," he said, and slipped past her, intending to walk on to his cabin.

She looked at him with surprise. "For what, then?"

"For convincing your men to work. You were right — they've been a great help to us. My men are rested."

"I think you are the first to ever suggest that the Livingstones have been helpful," she said wryly. "We're a hapless lot, captain. I thought we'd drive poor Mr. Beaty to drink."

"I'd no fret about that," Aulay said. "Beaty will search high and low to find something to drive him to drink."

Lottie's smile deepened.

Aulay gave her a nod. His head told him to go, to politely end this conversation, and he walked on, but as he rounded the corner, Lottie took a small step forward and said, "Will you avoid me forever, Aulay?"

His heart leaped ahead of itself. "I've been commanding a ship," he said, although that excuse sounded quite hollow to his own ears. He was still moving, a sort of half walk, half hesitation. "I mean to rest now, aye?" he said, and made himself walk on to his cabin. He opened the door and walked inside, put his food on the table.

"Have you perhaps determined you ought no' to put yourself in the company of a woman who will face a judge?"

He turned to the door. Lottie was standing there, her body silhouetted against a dark blue sky. Aye, it was something like that, some regret eating at him, tearing him apart from the inside out, and once again, he was astonished that she seemed to understand him. "What are you doing, then?" he asked. "Do you attempt to persuade me to be gentle with you when the time comes?"

"Will you?" she asked.

He shook his head. "It willna be up to me, lass."

"Then no," she said, and smiled a little. "May I say something?" she asked.

Aulay leaned back against the table and motioned for her to continue.

"I think you are a kind man, Aulay Mackenzie. But you are a wronged man, there's no denying it, and 'tis I who have wronged you. I'll go to my grave regretting it. But you must know that I . . . how I . . ." She paused, seemingly unable to find words. She sighed. "I would that you know how much I've come to *esteem* you."

Aulay had not expected her to say that, nor had he expected the words to softly wrap around his bruised heart.

" 'Tis no' a proper thing to say, I know. You're a gentleman, a man of the world you are, and I'm a lass from a wee island. But I'm running out of time to do things properly, and I'll have you know how I hold you in my highest regard. You've shown me kindness I didna deserve."

Aulay was momentarily at a loss for words.

But Lottie had found her words, and she stepped into the cabin. "These last days have been frightening, and devastating . . . and exhilarating and *remarkable,*" she said earnestly. "I've lived an entire lifetime in a matter of days."

He understood her sentiment completely — his own eyes had been opened after thirty-seven years.

"I've changed in so many ways, Aulay, and no matter what awaits me, I find it impossible to contain my feelings, aye? I've no' always confessed my true feelings when it mattered most, but now I know — I canna leave you without saying that I *esteem* you," she said, her hand pressed to her heart. "Beyond my wildest imaginings."

Her voice broke, and Aulay moved before he thought, taking her hand, pulling her into the cabin and into his embrace, heedless of others who might see them. He pressed his face into her hair, inhaling her scent. They'd been days at sea, and yet she smelled sweet to him, felt soft and warm. Everything about her was, in his eyes, perfection.

Lottie slipped her arms around his waist and whispered, "I've longed so for you to hold me."

"Lottie." His head clashed painfully with his heart. Lottie had captured him in body

and spirit. But he also loved his ship, and his life at sea — it was all that had mattered to him until a few short days ago. He didn't know what mattered any more. He couldn't fathom what he had to do in Scotland, how he'd be forced to avenge his ship, his life, his good name.

None of it made sense. None of it seemed right. No matter what path he chose, it was the wrong one. He couldn't even say with certainty if she was sincere now, or if she meant to seduce him into freeing her.

"I thought you hated me," she muttered.

"*Hate* you? I could never hate you, Lottie. No matter what else, I could never hate you." *I love you. Can you no' see it? Can you no' see the source of my torment? I love you.*

He picked her up, kicked the door shut with his heel, then turned her about and sat her on the table. He kissed her as he slipped in between her thighs. She wrapped her arms around his neck and returned his kiss with vigor, stoking a hot, intense flame in him that he'd be a fool to touch.

But Aulay was weak — he not only touched that flame, he let it consume him.

His hands wandered over her body, down her arms, up her torso to her breasts. He cupped them in his hands as he kissed her. He could feel a strange tightening in his chest — he was not a superstitious or sentimental man, but he felt something pulling them together, some force greater than the both of them locking its arms around them. He was, for better or worse, connected to this woman in a profound way.

She shifted, pressed against his hardness. She was not shy, which made Aulay want her that much more. So many deep-seated emotions were bubbling up in him, surprising him. He wanted to hold her, to protect her. He wanted to make love to her, to be inside her. But a nagging thought kept pressing against his wildly beating heart, trying desperately to slow it, to slow him.

She raked her hands down his chest, and Aulay caught her hands. "I donna want to give you false hope, Lottie."

Her eyes shimmered in the low light. With desire. With need. "I donna care —"

"You *do* care — you, of all people, *must* care. No matter what happens between us, it doesna change the truth of what we both must face. Do you understand, me?" he asked, and caught her face between his hands, forcing her to focus on him. "Tell me you understand what I say, *leannan.*"

"Aye, I understand," she said solemnly, and carefully brushed aside a thick strand of his hair from his eyes. "I'm no' a fool,

Aulay. I understand the stakes. But if my life as I know it is to end, one way or another, I will have it be worth the judgment. Do *you* understand?"

She touched him far more deeply than he would have believed his heart could be touched by sentiment. His emotions were roiling again, waves crashing through him, each one rising higher than the last, falling harder and faster. She'd sparked a helpless and powerful need to feel her body beneath his, her heart pressed against his chest.

Aulay moved his hands over her shoulders and down her sides, untying the knot in the tails of the shirt she wore, then lifting it over her head. He picked her up off the table, put her on her feet and unlaced her trews. They fell and pooled at her ankles, and she stepped out of them.

She was stunning, a vision of feminine beauty with heavy breasts, a curve of waist into hips, and long slender legs. Aulay's blood was rushing in his veins, and he quickly removed his clothes as she unbraided her hair and let that glorious curtain fall around her shoulders.

He gathered her up, kissed the hollow of her throat, then groped for his greatcoat and threw it onto his bunk before laying her down on top of it. "*Diah* help me, Lottie, but you've bewitched me, that you have," he said, and kissed her lips. "I am your servant." He kissed her cheeks, her mouth, her neck, and moved down, to her breasts.

She slid her fingers into his hair, arching into him. "I donna want a servant — I want a lover."

He'd thought he couldn't be more aroused, but she sent him higher. He wanted to explore her, every muscle, every patch of soft skin. He wanted to absorb the feel of her body into his so that he'd never forget it. He would fill her with his desire, would show her what it meant to love in a life worth living, to know what it felt to be loved. He *did* love her. In these moments with her, he knew that he loved her.

A deep sigh of pleasure escaped her; she dug her fingers into his shoulders as he moved his attention to her breasts. She arched her back into him, her legs moving against his, pressing against his erection. He slid his hand down her body, over the flare of her hip and her leg, and then between them.

Lottie's breath quickened, warm against his cheek. Aulay moved from the primal place that resided in every man and pushed her thighs apart with his knee, then pressed against her. She caught his face in her hands before he entered her, staring into his eyes, searching for . . . what? He was beyond control, lost in the ecstasy of her, impatient to carry on.

Lottie smiled. She kissed him, raking her fingers through his hair.

"Aye, what?" he whispered a wee bit desperately.

"*You,* Aulay. You're what."

He sank into those words. He moved his hand down her body, skimming her breast, her abdomen, and caught hold of her hip as he slid his body into hers and began to move.

This was not like their frenzied coupling of the other night, when they'd been driven by a lust born from heartbreak. This was greater than that — this was a coming together in a more primal sense, a man and a woman performing an ancient dance of being one. She had possessed him, and he possessed her, his strokes urgent, his desire swelling and taking ravenous shape.

Lottie gasped with her release; Aulay lost himself in his own. He sought his breath, clinging to the sensations of their coming together for as long as could. But at last he did prop himself on his arms and gaze down at her, pulling a thick strand of hair from her face.

Her eyes were closed, her expression one of utter happiness, free of pain and worry. She had never been more alluring to him.

"Tha thu breagha," he murmured. *You are beautiful.*

She smiled, opened her eyes and touched her fingers to his chin, then kissed his jaw before pushing her face into his neck and shoulder and turning into him.

Aye, it was worth it, Lottie.

At least to him, it had been worth every moment.

CHAPTER TWENTY

Lottie woke up with a start.

She was still wrapped in the warmth of Aulay's arms — a safe harbor.

She carefully untangled herself, kissed his bare chest, and slipped off the bunk. Aulay didn't move — he was sleeping so soundly that she wondered how long he'd gone without sleep. She dressed quietly and quit the cabin. It was the middle of the night — there was no one on deck that she could see but a pair of Mackenzie men, one of them minding the wheel, one of them with a spyglass held to his eye. She wondered what he could possibly see in the light of a moon.

She snuck into the forward cabin and stepped over Mathais. Drustan had taken one bunk and she crawled onto the other. In mere moments, she had drifted into blissful sleep.

The sun had risen when she woke again. Lottie stretched, happy as a new bride. She felt sated. She felt *loved.* Not in the way gentlemen generally professed their affection for her while looking at her with a bit of a leer in their eyes. But *loved,* deep and wide, body and soul. She'd never felt so desired like this. As if he desired all of her, and not just her looks. Aye, those moments with Aulay had been worth every moment of her life thus far.

"Why are you smiling, then?"

"What? Pardon?" Lottie sat up with a start. She hadn't noticed Mathais was awake and dressed. He'd pulled his blond hair into a queue in the manner Aulay wore his gold locks at times.

"You were smiling in your sleep," he said, staring at her curiously. "Were you dreaming of *Fade*r?"

No. For the first time in days, not for one blessed moment. "Aye, I suppose I was," she lied. "Do you remember the summer he bred those pups to hunt the rabbits?" She smiled with the fond memory of the puppies romping around their small salon. Unfortunately, her father had brought home pups that were useless for hunting rabbits, but better suited to sitting in ladies' laps.

Mathais stared at her as if she were speaking Danish. He bounced a leg impatiently. "We've no time for talk of dogs, Lottie," he chastised her, and began to pace, full of nerves. "A *ship* is near us. Sailed all night to reach us, that's what Gilroy says."

"What?" She leaped to her feet and started to look around for shoes. "Whose ship, then?"

"That's the problem, aye? It's got no flags, no markers." He suddenly gasped. "It could verra well be a *ghost* ship."

Lottie had no idea what that was and had no desire to learn. "Where is Dru?"

"Where is he always, then? Sitting on a barrel, carving on a piece of bloody wood."

Lottie gave her youngest brother a sharp look. He shrugged sheepishly. "Well, he's taken no notice of the ship or anything else," Mathais complained. "Gilroy says it might be excise men," he excitedly continued. "Or a privateer. But it *could* be a ghost ship." He spoke with far too much eagerness for Lottie's tastes.

Her heart began to race with apprehension — this was exactly what had happened a little more than a week ago — a ship had come too close and they'd speculated about who or what it was. She located her boots and yanked them on, and followed Mathais out onto the deck. A few men were standing at the port side staring out at the ship. *Diah* but it was quite close, sailing in parallel to them. She could see men on board that ship, the guns pointed at them, and her heart jumped. *Not again.*

Livingstones and Mackenzies alike were scrambling to change sails and move crates and casks around on the deck, to pull guns into place. She leaped off the forecastle landing onto the main deck and ran to Duff, who was among those at the railing. She tugged on his sleeve to gain his attention. "Who is it? What's happening?"

"Canna say. But they are in dire pursuit of us, that they are."

She heard Aulay bark a command to two men up on the masts. She whirled around at the sound of his voice, seeking him, but at that moment, Drustan noticed something was amiss, and stood up from his crate and bellowed for Lottie.

Aulay's head snapped around. He looked at Drustan, then shifted his gaze to Lottie.

"Aye," she said, understanding his look — his command, really — and went to Drustan. Her poor brother, bless him, was confused and in the way of men who were working to keep ahead of the other ship.

"Take him below," Aulay said, and reached for the spyglass from Iain the Red.

"Who *is* it?" Lottie asked.

"I donna know," he said, and held the

spyglass up to his eye as he spoke to Iain in Gaelic. He handed Iain the spyglass then whipped around, nearly colliding with Lottie. "Lass, please, aye?" he said, gesturing to the hatch. "Take you brother and go below. We canna have the two of you underfoot."

She wished he would assure her, she wished she could assure him that no one was more willing to help than she, but he'd already moved on, shouting up to the men on the masts.

Behind her, Drustan knocked a cask that rolled into one of the guns. Lottie caught his arms and made him look at her. His eyes were unfocused, something that happened when the world didn't make sense to him. It was as if he disappeared inside himself. "I'm here, Dru. Where is your wood?" she asked, turning him toward the hatch that led to the hold.

Drustan looked down at his hands, his brow furrowed. "I donna know. Have I lost it, then?"

"Let's have a look below, aye?" she said. "If we donna find it there, we'll start anew."

"Here it is!" he suddenly shouted, having located it in his pocket, and allowed Lottie to steer him down into the hold.

After several days of housing too many

men, the hold had a certain stench to it. Drustan was quite at home here, apparently, for he plopped onto a pile of straw and began to work on his bit of wood, bowing over it, squinting as he carefully carved slivers from it, already having forgotten whatever had happened on deck.

Sometimes, Lottie wished she could live as simply as her brother — how bonny it would be. Unfortunately, she had nothing but worry to occupy her and all she could do was wait.

She paced endlessly. She went in search of candles to replace one that had burned down. She could hear the men overhead, sometimes moving things about, sometimes shouting. How much time passed? An hour? Four? It seemed an eternity before the hatch was suddenly thrown open, startling her and Drustan both. Mathais clambered down the steps, leaping halfway and landing squarely into their midst.

"What has happened?" she demanded.

Her brother was aflutter, unable to keep still. "We're to sail through the Pentland Firth!"

Lottie had no idea where that was or the significance of it. "Aye, and . . . ?"

"And it could be *quite* dangerous if you donna know what you're about. It's a bit of sea between the Orkney Islands and the mainland, aye? Sailors are meant to go between the Orkneys and the Shetlands, for the sea is wider there. The firth is narrow and the tides are fast, and that's why we'll sail it. Gilroy says if we enter the firth at the right time, the sea will sling us round the bend."

"What?" Lottie exclaimed. "What bend? That seems so —"

"Dangerous, *aye,*" Mathais said, his eyes gleaming with the prospect.

"And the other ship? Will they no' be slung as well?"

"Aye, they're *just* behind us!" Mathais announced.

"No, no *no,*" Drustan said. "I donna want another ship!"

"Aye, Dru, but you're no' to fret," Mathais said with great authority. "We'll beat them, we will. We will *win!*"

"We'll win!" Drustan shouted.

Lottie's breath was growing short with her nerves. "I must . . . I have to see with my own eyes, Mats. I have to understand what is happening. Stay with Drustan."

"But I'm to help!" Mathais exclaimed.

"Aye, and you will. But I must see!"

"No, Lottie, I donna want you to go up there. Stay here!" Drustan wailed.

"She'll come back, Dru, she always comes back," Mathais said impatiently. "Donna *weep* over it. I *hate* when you weep."

Lottie hurried up the steps before either one of them could stop her.

The wind had picked up and knocked her back a step as she emerged onto the deck. All around her men were engaged, pulling ropes, rolling sails or manning the yards. She picked her way through the throng, trying to stay out of their way, but finding herself in the wrong spot when someone shoved a crate and it narrowly missed knocking her right over the railing.

She climbed the steps to the quarterdeck, where Aulay, Beaty, Duff and Gilroy were gathered. Aulay stood at the wheel, his legs braced apart, his hair uncovered, whipped by the wind. She turned around to look behind them and gasped. The ship was closer than it had been earlier today. "What do they want?" she demanded of no one in particular.

"What do they ever want?" Duff said.

"You ought no' to be here now," Aulay said to her, sparing her a glance.

A strong wave knocked the ship to its right, spraying the quarterdeck. Lottie lost her footing and went down hard.

"Take the wheel, Beaty," she heard Aulay

say, and then felt two strong arms slide under her arms and haul her to her feet. Aulay marched her down the steps to the main deck. "Go below, *leannan.* I'll no' see you harmed."

He turned to go but Lottie caught his arm. "Aulay, I . . ."

"Save it," he said, not unkindly, but in the manner of a man who had much more important things to do than soothe her.

It was just as well. Lottie didn't know what she meant to say, really. *Sorry* seemed woefully inadequate. *Save us* seemed too bloody obvious. *Hold me, I'm frightened* was unfair.

Mathais was quick to hurry back up to the deck when she returned, disappearing through the hatch before she could speak to him. "Mind you have a care!" she shouted after him.

"Aye, aye!" he called down, and let the hatch door slam shut.

Lottie and Drustan went back to waiting.

Minutes turned to hours, long enough that Lottie twice replaced the candle in the lantern that swung from a beam above their heads. She found something for them to eat, but mostly, she moved restlessly about. Occasionally she looked up when she heard shouting. She watched Drustan cover his head when they heard a lot of movement above them, sounding like a herd of cattle charging. And then there was nothing but the creaks and moans of the ship moving through water.

She realized it was dark when the hatch opened and MacLean appeared, followed by Mathais. "We're to bring up food," MacLean said. His face was lined with fatigue, his clothing wet. Mathais was still filled with his youthful exuberance and was rummaging about the crates and boxes stored there. "I'm to bring whisky," he said grandly.

"Whisky?" Lottie looked at MacLean. "Have we won, then?"

Maclean snorted. "No' at all. They followed us into the firth. They lost a bit of ground, but they remain in the hunt, still matching us, move for move. Aye, but Mackenzie is the better captain, he is — he has sailed us through treacherous water without so much as a bump. When we round Cape Wrath, we'll hug closer to the shore. The ship behind us is bigger and canna go in as close. Beaty says there is no' a captain on the seas other than Mackenzie who can sail as close to shore without running aground." He picked up the last of the sea biscuits. "We'll lose them then. Come, then, Mats, let's bring this up, aye?"

The two of them left.

Drustan made himself a place in straw and settled in to sleep. He didn't seem to understand the danger they were in, which was a blessing, really. Lottie couldn't even think of sleep. Every shudder and groan of the ship, every bit of footfall overhead startled her. She moved back and forth between the stairs and where Drustan was sleeping, waiting. Her imagination soared wildly with ideas and scenes that seemed to grow more deadly as the hours wore on.

She became so lost in thought that she didn't at first realize she'd heard nothing above her for some time. She paused, listening. Not a single footfall, not a muffled voice. Her first thought was that pirates had snuck on board and murdered them all. Were she and Drustan destined to float along, forgotten or undiscovered here, until the ship capsized or they crashed into cliffs and drowned? Or was there an ambush waiting for them above?

She couldn't stand about like a lamb — she had to know. She looked upon Drustan, who slept soundly, then made her way to the stairs and crept up toward the hatch. She slowly, carefully pushed it open, an inch at a time. It was quite dark, but it was not night — a thick gray, fog engulfed the ship.

Lottie pushed the hatch open a wee bit more, and poked her head out. She was suddenly and violently pushed down, and whoever had done it came crashing in behind her, forcing her down to the hold's floor, and pulling the hatch shut very quietly. Lottie caught herself on a post and whirled around. "For the love of God, Duff, you scared me half to death!" she exclaimed.

He lifted a thick finger to his lips. "No' a word, Lottie," he whispered.

Her heart vaulted into her throat. "Have we been overrun by pirates?"

He shook his head. "They canna see us in the fog. But we can hear them. They are passing us, and we must be as quiet as the dead until they've gone," he whispered.

Lottie brought her hands to cheeks, pressing her fingers hard against her skin to keep from screaming with the anxiety that was ratcheting up in her.

Duff turned his attention to the closed hatch door. Lottie dropped her hands and looked up, too. They stood together, staring up, both of them straining to hear something, both of them waiting for someone to open the hatch.

"What is it?" Duff hissed.

Lottie heard it then, too — a soft pattering overhead.

"Rain," she whispered.

Duff frowned. "That means the fog will lift soon."

The pattering was light at first, but suddenly the rain fell heavy, falling in a deluge on the deck.

"I'm going up," Duff said.

"Lot? I canna see you!" Drustan cried.

"I'm here, Drustan," she said. She watched Duff go up, desperately wanting to go up with him, but unable to leave Drustan. She could never leave Drustan. Hadn't that been her mother's favorite refrain? *Donna leave Dru.*

"I'm hungry," he said when she came to his side. He was clutching his carving to his chest. A gull, she'd noticed, and a rather good one at that. "I'll see what I can find, aye?" she said, and dug in the crate for anything to eat and finding nothing but sour ale.

Drustan drained the flagon. "But I'm hungry, Lottie."

"Soon, Dru. You must be patient."

He suddenly looked up. "What's that, then?" he asked. "What's that noise?"

It sounded as if someone were pumping water from a well. "The tide must be rising." Or was it going out? Why did no one come for them? If the ship had passed, why were they still locked away? The rain began to leak through the planks above them, and they moved into the center of the hold.

All at once there was a lot of shouting overhead. Drustan wailed beside her, frightened by the shouting. Lottie made out the word *heave,* and suddenly the ship pitched right so violently that it caught Lottie and Drustan unawares. She grabbed her brother and a post, and had hardly righted herself when the ship suddenly and violently collided with something. The force of it knocked her and Drustan to the floor. Lottie's hand landed in water, and when she turned around, she saw water rushing in from the stern.

Drustan cried out, groping for the post, hauling himself to his feet. Lottie managed to gain hers, too. There was a hole in the hull the size of a whisky cask. She shrieked with alarm and grabbed Drustan's hand. "Come! We have to go!" she shouted.

"No!" he screamed, and wrapped his arms around the post.

She tugged frantically at his arms and tried to unlock his grip, but Drustan refused to let go. She was no match for him — he was far too strong and she could not move as much as one of his fingers. "Dru! If we stay below we drown!" she cried, and punched him in the arm. "You have to *come*!"

He responded with a roar and squeezed his eyes shut.

Lottie gasped with the understanding she would go down with this ship. Drustan would not leave the post he clung to, and she would not leave Drustan, which meant she would drown. Panic clawed at her throat and her belly, threatening to erupt in bile. *"Please,"* she begged her brother. "I donna want to die, Dru! You must trust me, aye? Fader would tell you to do as I say!"

At the mention of their father, Drustan cut her a look. "I'm scared!"

"Aye, so am I! But I donna want to sink to the bottom of the sea with no hope! At least above we have a chance of surviving. Fader would want us to fight!"

"I canna swim!" he shrieked, and tears as big as raindrops began to slide down his face.

"We'll no' *swim,*" she promised him, her voice shaking as she caressed his cheek. "There are boats above, Dru, remember? *Boats!*" She hoped to heaven that was true, that everyone else had not deserted them. She gripped one of his large hands and managed to peel it from the post as water inched over their boots.

Amazingly, she managed to tug her reluctant brother to the stairs. He kept grabbing at things, trying to find something to hold on to, but her determination was making her stronger than she had ever been in her life. When they reached the stairs, she pushed him in front of her, yelling at him to go up, to open the hatch. "I'm frightened!" he shouted.

Diah, what was she to do with him? Lottie shoved around him. She scrambled up the steps and threw open the hatch, then just as quickly went down again and made him step in front of her. "Duff and Mats are waiting for you," she said breathlessly. It was a lie, but she had to do something to get him to move. She watched his hulking shape crawl hesitantly up the steps, then slowly disappear onto the deck. When she was certain he was out, she began to scramble up the stairs after him.

She was halfway up when the ship lurched and she fell off the stairs, landing on the floor of the hold on a knee. Wrenching pain shot up her spine, stunning her. She took several breaths to quell the nausea the sharp pain had caused her. Water had reached her fingertips, and through sheer will, she got on two hands and one knee and pushed herself to standing. She hopped to the steps and tried again. Her good leg onto a rung, followed by her bad. Then again, gasping with pain as she put weight on the bad to lift the good one up to the next rung.

She had made slow progress when a hand reached through the opening. "Give me your hand!" Aulay shouted.

Relief flooded her, and she grabbed his hand with both of hers. He yanked her up through the opening, pulling her out of the hold and setting her on her feet on the deck. Lottie's knee buckled in pain. "Can you walk?" he demanded.

She shook her head.

Aulay immediately swept her up in his arms and strode to the port railing. They'd already lowered the jolly and the *Reulag Balhaire*'s larger boat. "Help her down!" Aulay shouted. "She's injured!"

Everything was a blur from there. Lottie made it down the rope ladder with the help of two men, and was practically tossed into the jolly while the sea frothed around them and battered against the sinking ship. There were still men on deck as the jolly was pushed away and men began to row, straining to battle the waves. Lottie looked frantically about her, relieved to see Mathais and Drustan with her in the jolly, and behind them, Duff, too, who was helping two Mackenzie men row.

She twisted around to see the ship. It was listing horribly now, the main deck at a sharp angle. The ship looked close to capsizing. She couldn't see where the other men were, not in the great sheets of rain that came down, and she couldn't see what was happening on the deck. She went up on one knee to see, but the jolly rode up on a wave and came down so hard that she fell back and struck her head on the side of the boat.

"Hold her!" someone shouted, and a hand wrapped firmly around her wrist to keep her from tumbling into the water. *Drustan.*

When she tried to sit up, everything around her blurred. She couldn't tell sky from sea, and water was so rough and choppy that she was made quite ill. Everything began to spin away from her. She was reeling into oblivion, and she thought she would do anything to make it stop . . . including dying.

Her last conscious thought before she was spun into blackness was, where was Aulay?

CHAPTER TWENTY-ONE

Brine filled Aulay's mouth. He choked on it, sputtering it out of his mouth. Water was lapping around his body, getting in under his clothes, in his mouth and nose. He pushed up, his hands sinking into dark wet sand. He spit salt water from his mouth, and when he moved, he felt sand in every crease of his skin, rubbing against him.

Diah, but his head ached. A jib had come undone as the ship foundered and had hit him square in the side of the head.

He rolled onto his rump, gasping for air, and looked around him. The tide was coming in, pooling where he'd been lying. The bodies of men were scattered across the sand like so much seaweed, all of them utterly spent from a harrowing twenty four hours. There was the giant, sitting up, his legs crossed beneath him, his face tilted up to a perfectly brilliant blue sky.

Aulay slowly came to his feet, unsteady at

first, but finding his balance.

There was Mathais, on his back, gulping like a fish for air. The actor and MacLean, and the rest of the Livingstones, all accounted for. Iain the Red was leaning over his brother, who was retching. Beaty, shaking the water from his hat, which he'd somehow managed to keep on his head. Billy Botly with his arm in a splint, who looked no worse for the ordeal. Geordie Willis and even Jack Mackenzie with his injured leg, leaning up against a rock, speaking quietly.

And there was Lottie, lying on her side, her back to the water.

Aulay turned to face the sea. A different sort of pain squeezed at his heart. There was nothing there, no sign of his ship. The sea, calm now, looked as empty as one of his paintings. A few crates and whisky casks were being carried along by the tide onto shore, but his ship was gone, sunk a quarter of a mile off the coast.

He climbed onto a rock and stared blankly at the sea, unable to fully grasp his loss. As the last of them had rowed away, he'd watched it go down, disappearing into tumultuous waves. The man he'd become, his entire adult life, had been forged on that ship and now it was all gone. His paintings, his books, his French wine, gone. The small knife he'd won from a French pirate, the instruments of sailing, all gone. The cargo he'd carried, the sails, the rigging the guns . . . gone.

That ship was everything he was, and he would never be the same again. He'd never *sail* again — how could he? The Mackenzies had scarcely afforded to sail this time, and now they'd have to make recompense to William Tremayne for his lost cargo. It would likely ruin them.

What Aulay dreaded most was his father's disappointment. Arran Mackenzie had steered the clan through the best and worst of times in the Highlands, and they had weathered it all, better than most. Aulay did not want to be the one to destroy what his father had worked tirelessly to build, in the twilight of his father's life. He'd seen gut-wrenching worry on his father's face too often in the last decade, and could not forget how skeptical he'd been of Aulay's plans to rebuild their trade. But when Aulay had set sail, his father had smiled more brightly than anyone. He'd seemed younger somehow, his features filled with hope and the excitement of a new beginning.

Arran had believed in his son.

The sea turns over on itself. Aye, Aulay's

own personal sea had turned over on him and washed him away. He was adrift.

And he was furious.

Fury was boiling in him as he stood on that rocky shore. It was a cauldron, near to the point of spilling over in hot, molten waves.

"What now, Captain?" Beaty asked, having come to his feet.

Aulay hadn't noticed Beaty at his side. He glanced over his shoulder — all of his crew was on their feet, watching him warily, as if they expected him to swim out to where his ship had gone down and stay with it after all.

"Break up the casks and crates as they come in, aye? Hide the boats. We'll walk over the hills to Balhaire. Let there be no sign of where we came ashore. Whoever followed us was quite determined, and I'd no' be surprised if they return to search for us now that the storm has cleared."

The effort to hide the evidence of their survival was particularly grueling under a hot sun and with no proper tools. Nothing was salvageable — the salted beef was ruined and thrown into the sea. The bales of wool absorbed so much water they sank on their own.

Two of his men had managed to flee the

sinking ship with long guns, and these they strapped on their shoulders in the event a Livingstone or two thought to run. All camaraderie between the two clans had been lost when the Mackenzies lost their ship and their livelihood. Yet in spite of their vigilance, two Livingstones managed to slip away. None of the Mackenzies had the patience to go after them, and no more of the Livingstones had the strength to run.

When the detritus from the ship had been cleared from the beach and hidden away, the group began their trek over the hills. Aulay guessed they were twenty miles from Balhaire, perhaps a little farther. They were exhausted and hungry, and because of a few injuries, progress was slow. Aulay noticed that Lottie was also limping, but she was walking, and declined Beaty's offer of a staff. She kept up to the pace of the men, save for a stumble here or there.

He kept his distance from her. He could not bear to look at her just now. Over the last several days, he had come to admire her, to even love her. But he could not ignore the fact that his ship, his life, was now completely lost to him because of her. The truth beat a steady drum with the ache in his head, throbbing with each step he took. How could he have thought any different? How could he have bedded the enemy?

They had walked for hours when they came to a small stream where Aulay and his brothers once fished as lads. It was a place to rest and drink.

On the bank of the stream, Beaty removed his hat, wiped his sleeve across his brow, and glanced sidelong at Aulay. "Have you an idea, then, where we are, Captain?"

How odd that he was captain no more. He pointed at the hill rising up across the stream. "Balhaire is on the other side."

"An deamhan thu ag ràdh," Beaty said, and shook his head. "I've never known a man who had a sense of direction as keen as yours." He bent down to drink, and Aulay wandered downstream a bit, to a rock that jutted into the stream. Beaty was right. As children, they'd explored the land around them, but even then, Aulay was the one they relied on to see them safely home. He always knew where he was because he always knew where the sea was.

He sat on the rock and tried to comb his hair with his fingers.

"Aulay."

He closed his eyes and swallowed, then slowly turned his head to look at Lottie. She was utterly bedraggled and still, quite beautiful to him. It was that beauty that had sucked him in, had sent him into a tailspin that had ended with something that felt as close to death as he'd ever come. His heart began to beat with his outrage, and he turned his attention to the stream.

"I am so verra sorry Aulay. For your loss. For everything. My heart is filled with so much regret."

He said nothing. Bonny words from a bonny lass. He wished he could despise her, but that was impossible. He loved her, no matter the devastation she'd caused. But he hated her, too. He was so furious that he was blinded by it, couldn't look at her without feeling his rage ratchet uncontrollably. He flinched when her hand touched his and he involuntarily yanked it away, and ignored the sharp intake of her breath at the slight, the slow release.

"I beg your pardon," she said, her voice low. "Have I offended you? I meant only to convey my sincere gratitude. "I think you are the best man I have ever known." She smiled sheepishly.

He suddenly wondered why she would say that now? Was it her attempt to smooth things over with him? Because she cared for him? Or because she cared for her own wee neck? "Go," he said, his voice belying the fury in his veins. "I donna want your damn flattery."

"Aulay!" she exclaimed. "Will you no' speak to me?"

"Speak to you?" he echoed, and made himself look at her. "Do you want me to *speak* to you, Lottie?" he asked, and the dam inside him broke. Raw fury, like so much sewage, began to spill through him. "Aye, I will speak to you," he said, and rose to his feet, towering over her. "I will tell you that I utterly rue the day I changed course to help you. You have *ruined* me," he said, thumping his chest. "Have you no' taken enough from me? Have you no' done enough damage to my men and yours?" His voice was rising, and he was quite unable to stop himself from shouting. His thoughts were roiling, and he felt almost outside of himself, as if the demon of his wrath had inhabited his body. Everything he had ever been, ever *would* be had been destroyed by her.

"Would you now have me soothe your tender feelings and tell you that it's all quite all right, that as long as *you* have your way it doesna matter that I and my men have lost our livelihood? That these men canna feed their families now? That your men canna pay their rents? Do you want me to find words that magically change the truth?"

"*Diah,* no! I —"

"If you want me to speak, madam, *that* is what I will say! And I will add that I wish I'd never laid eyes on you! I wish I'd never heard your name. God forgive me, but I wish I'd sailed the other way when I saw your bloody rotten ship, for if I had, I would have spared us all the disaster you have brought down on all our heads! Alas, I did no', but you may rest assured, I will do everything in my power to see that you are made to account for it."

"There is no call for that!" Mr. MacLean suddenly appeared and put his hands on Lottie's shoulders. She looked stunned. And broken.

Aulay realized that everyone had heard his diatribe and sprang from the rock, pushing past Lottie and MacLean. He called to his men in Gaelic to gather round, and warned them that when they reached Balhaire, they should not invite discussion about the Livingstones, and to have a care what they said about what had happened. "We'll not have anyone believing we had any part in the illegal trade of the Livingstones. The less we say, the less involved we are, and the less anyone will believe any accusations to the contrary."

"But we have them in our custody," Iain the Red pointed out. "Will we pretend we are ignorant?"

"They pirated our fecking ship, and we have that right to keep them in our custody," Aulay said curtly. "But donna mention the whisky, lads — men can be quite irrational when it comes to women, money or lost whisky."

"Will we accuse them of piracy?" asked Billy Botly.

Aulay looked around at his men and their haggard faces. He thought of how they must face their families now. "We will indeed," he said darkly, and whirled around, shouting in English, "Walk on!" and signaling for the party to carry on.

They were, all of them, completely spent when they at last reached the high street that ran through the village that surrounded Balhaire. They were stumbling along, mostly silent, too weary to speak and concentrating on putting one foot before the other.

A lass was the first to spot them, and with a shout of delight, she ran ahead of them up the road, calling for her mother with the news the ship had come home.

Moments later, the bell began to ring, signaling the return of a ship that was no more. People spilled into the street to call out their welcomes, some running toward them, eager to greet their loved ones. More than one slowed their steps when they saw the ragged crew, staring in shock and confusion.

Aulay's men were a wee bit emotional as would be expected, having survived the sinking of a ship. They began to fall out from the group, some of them to their knees with relief, others rushing to kiss their wives and scoop their children up in their arms.

Aulay halted in the middle of the high street with the Livingstones as the reunions played out around them. He was sickened by these happy homecomings, knowing that these families would expect their men to have returned to them with money in their pockets and trinkets for their children. They were expecting the means to put shoes on their children's feet or a winter's crop in their plots of land.

He needed a dram or two of whisky. He signaled the rest of them to carry on, up to the castle at the top of the hill. The Livingstones, too exhausted to do anything else, followed dully behing him. Aulay had lost half his men to reunions with their loved ones, but Beaty and Iain the Red, steadfast and loyal to him, brought up the rear.

Just as they reached the gates to Balhaire,

a rider came barreling around the corner from the road that led into the glens, moving too fast, too recklessly. Aulay's heart lifted. He knew only one person who rode like that — his younger sister, Catriona.

She reined up sharply with a cry of delight when she saw him, threw herself off the horse, and strode forward, her face a wreath of smiles . . . until she drew close enough to see him. "*Mi Diah,* what has happened?" she exclaimed. "You look a fright, Aulay, you do! Have you taken ill?"

"I'm quite well," he said. " 'Tis a long tale, lass, one I'll tell you with the rest of the family, aye?"

She cocked her head to one side and eyed him shrewdly, then put her arms around him.

"Cat, lass, I'm filthy —"

"I donna care." But she suddenly leaned to one side. "*Dè an diabhal,* who is that?"

Aulay didn't bother to look behind him. "Prisoners."

She gasped. *"Prisoners!"* she whispered loudly, and tried to get another look at them. Aulay put his arm around her shoulders and began to move her along toward the castle gates. He knew very well that if he removed his arm, she would put herself in front of the group and begin to ask questions.

She blinked her blue eyes with surprise. "I canna guess what you're about, Aulay Mackenzie, but I canna *wait* to hear it." She grinned, slipped her arm around his waist, and together they walked through the gates and into the bailey.

A groom was instantly on hand, and Catriona sent him to fetch her horse. The thick-planked double oak entrance doors to the old castle fortress opened and Frang, the family butler, stepped out onto the landing and bowed. "*Fàilte dhachaigh,* Captain. Welcome home."

"Thank you," Aulay said wearily, thinking of how close he'd come to never laying eyes on Balhaire again. "My father?"

"The laird and the lady wait for you in the great hall, aye?" Frang said. But he was looking past Aulay, to the group behind him.

Aulay reluctantly glanced over his shoulder. The Livingstones had crowded together and were looking around them in awe. The youngest, Mathais, who, he had to admit, had proven to be a good hand on deck, seemed particularly taken, and was pointing up at the turrets. Lottie stood next to the giant, her head bowed.

"Have you a plaid the lass might put

around her shoulders?" Aulay asked Frang.

"The *lass*?" Catriona dipped under his arm to peer at the group. "*Diah,* I had no' noticed that one of them was a lass."

"Aye, Captain," Frang said and disappeared inside. He returned in a few moments and wordlessly handed the plaid to Lottie. She seemed confused, but wrapped it around her shoulders as the party was shown into the cramped foyer. Aulay signaled them to follow him down a close corridor lit by a few tallow candles that made the air pungent.

The wind, a constant at Balhaire, groaned and rattled the old fireplace flues, but the gloomy corridor gave way to the great hall, where things were considerably brighter with its enormous windows that overlooked the sea in the distance. Great iron chandeliers hung above their heads, blazing with candles. Thick carpets muted the sound of many people and dogs and added some warmth to the room. At one end of the hall was a raised dais, a long table and upholstered chairs where Aulay's family took their meals. At the other end, a massive hearth. It was always lit, for even in summer these old stone walls trapped the cold.

Two dogs, napping before the warmth of the fire, came to their feet and loped forward with tails wagging to greet Aulay. But they quickly lost interest in him and moved on to sniff the rest of the group. The giant was delighted by them and went down on one knee to nuzzle the mutts.

"Aulay, *mo chridhe*!" his mother cried. She was seated next to his father at the dais, and she came swiftly down the steps, hurrying to meet him halfway in his progress toward them. Margot Mackenzie was an elegant, silver-haired beauty. She held out her arms to embrace him, and Aulay put his up hand. "Donna Màither, aye? I'm filthy."

"I will greet my son as I see fit," she said, and put her arms around him as Catriona had, hugging him tightly, enveloping him in the sweet scent of her perfume. But she abruptly withdrew, her nose wrinkled. "Oh dear," she said. "Have you come from a public house?"

He shook his head. "No, madam, but what you smell is whisky, aye."

"Aulay! How do you fare, my son?"

The Laird of Balhaire, Arran Mackenzie, did not come down from the dais due to a leg that pained him terribly, but he eagerly leaned forward across the massive dining table. "Are you well?"

No. He was broken in half. "Well enough, Athair, I am. There is much news to tell, but first, might we have some ale and something to eat?" Aulay asked. "It's been a long journey."

"Yes, of course!" his mother said. "Frang, darling, will you? There is stew, I think, and Barabel made the most delicious bread this morning."

Frang signaled a serving boy to fetch ale, and went out to instruct their kitchen.

"Please," his mother said graciously to the Livingstones. She had no idea who they were, but she'd never lost the decorum she'd been taught as a girl on an English estate. Anyone under her roof would be treated well, no matter what they'd done — a theory Aulay would soon test — and she invited them to sit.

"They're no' guests," Aulay said as she returned to his side and walked with him and Catriona to the dais. "They are in our custody."

"Custody?" his father repeated.

"Aye, Aulay, tell us!" Catriona said excitedly, and took a seat next to her father, leaning across to balance on the arms of his chair so she'd not miss a word.

Aulay had hoped for at least a glass of ale, but he knew his family, and they'd not leave it until he'd told them everything. He shoved a hand through his hair, made stiff

by the saltwater and the sun. "My lord, I
—"

" 'Tis my fault."

Aulay started at the clear, strong sound of
Lottie's voice. She'd walked up to the dais
without his notice, and stood holding the
plaid tightly around her shoulders, her hair
spilling over her shoulders. "My fault," she
said again.

Aulay groaned with exasperation. "For
God's sake, woman, if you donna mind —"

"I *do,*" she said insistently and set her
gaze on Aulay's father. "Everything that has
happened, all if it, 'tis my doing. 'twas I who
stole his ship, and 'twas I they pursued from
Aalborg."

"What? Aalborg?" Aulay's father repeated,
his wooly eyebrows cascading down in
confusion as he swung his gaze to his son.
"What, then . . . *Denmark*?"

" 'Tis my fault the ship sunk."

"What?" Catriona all but shrieked.

"For God's sake, allow me to speak!"
Aulay said sharply, and Duff stood up, putting his hand on Lottie's arm and drawing
her back.

But she shook his hand from her arm. "I
want to help, to explain," she said to Aulay.

"You've helped enough, aye?" he snarled.

" 'Tis *my* doing! At least allow me to

explain *why*!"

"It doesna matter why!" he said loudly. "You will kindly allow *me* to tell my family what has happened ere you begin your long and winding tale," he snapped.

She glared at him. He glared back. "Verra well," she said pertly. "But you canna stop me from saying that the Mackenzies have been naugh' but decent and kind and I have ruined that goodwill," she added, directing that to his family.

His family was, for the first time in his memory, collectively dumbstruck. They stared at Aulay then at Lottie, their eyes wide with astonishment.

"You said *sunk*," Catriona said carefully, breaking their silence. "What do you mean? *Precisely,* if you please."

"I mean that it sank to the bottom of the sea," Lottie said with great precision.

Aulay cursed under his breath. "That is *enough*! I am still the captain and you are *still* my prisoner!"

"Oh dear God," Aulay's mother said. She put a hand to her throat and slid into a chair next to Catriona looking as if she might faint. "Is it truly *gone,* Aulay?"

He swallowed down his bitterness. "Aye, Màither."

"But . . . but what *happened*?" Catriona

demanded frantically. "How?"

"Well, we were desperate," Lottie said, chiming in again. "I saw no other way, on my word I did no', but to take his ship as ours was sinking."

"Yours. Oh. *Oh!*" Catriona said, and laughed with relief as she put one hand on her father's arm, the other on her mother's arm. "I beg your pardon, then, I thought you meant to say that the *Reulag Balhaire* sank."

"That one too," Lottie said meekly.

"No," Catriona said, her gaze shifting to Aulay. "It canna be. Say it's no' so, Aulay."

"I canna say it, Cat, because it is so," he sadly admitted.

"I've seen two ships sink in as many weeks," Lottie continued, clearly unable to contain herself, "and for that, I present myself to you to be punished as you see fit, milord. These men," she said, gesturing behind her, "had naugh' to do with it. Only me."

"Well, that is *no'* true," Duff said haughtily. "I had a wee bit to do with it as we all did! You'd no' have managed to steal the Mackenzie ship without my performance —"

"Silence!" Aulay shouted, throwing up his arms and startling everyone. He was extremely unwilling to listen to the Living-stones debate who had the bigger part in destroying his ship.

The hall grew quiet. All heads turned to him. He looked at Lottie and pointed to one of the many tables below the dais. "Go. *Sit.* No' another word from any of you, aye? No' a bloody word, or I'll hang you in the bailey myself. Do you understand, then?"

Lottie bit down on her lower lip as if trying desperately to keep words from slipping off her tongue. She nodded curtly, tightened the plaid around her shoulders and returned to the table, Duff behind her. The sound of chairs scraping on the floor filled the room as the Livingstones took seats.

Aulay glanced up at his father. He'd remained silent, but his impenetrable gaze was locked on his son. Aulay could guess what his father was feeling. Disappointment. Rage. Incredulity. With a weary sigh of defeat, Aulay climbed the dais and leaned over his father to hug him.

"My heart is glad to have you home," his father said. "An eventful voyage by the sound of it."

"Aye, quite," Aulay agreed, and took a seat beside him. A lad appeared with a pitcher of ale and some cups. Aulay helped himself, filling a cup, draining it thirstily. He filled it again.

"It's true, then, darling?" his mother asked carefully. "The ship is truly sunk?"

Aulay nodded numbly, unable to say the words aloud, and burning alive with shame. He slowly, wearily, told his family what had happened these last many days. How the voyage had started off well, with good wind and clear skies and high spirits. They'd seen it as an omen. He told them how they'd seen one ship sailing away with fire on its deck, another ship listing.

"You saw a royal ship, prowling for illegal trade," his father confirmed. "I've heard it is to be scuttled."

So it had been a royal ship after all.

"Aye, and then what?" Catriona asked.

Aulay told them how the *Reulag Balhaire* had changed course to investigate the listing ship, discovering it was smaller and ill suited for open sea. How the crew had appeared so hapless that it was clear they would all drown. "We invited them on board," he said. He did not mention how he'd been struck dumb by the sight of Lottie, how her beauty had put him back on his heels. Or that he'd been wholly unprepared for an attack, because he'd been too bloody arrogant to suspect them of any trickery.

He told them they'd been ambushed and his men corralled, and he himself shackled and bound. His mother shot a dark look to the Livingstones, but his father remained impassive, listening closely. Aulay explained that in spite of their chief's mortal wound, they had set course for Aalborg, where they believed they could sell illegal spirits.

"Why Aalborg?" his mother asked.

"Their laird, Duncan Campbell, suspected them of illegal distillery, and they believed their whisky could no' be sold in Scotland because of it." He shrugged. "They are Danes by lineage and have relations there."

"Well?" Catriona asked. "Did they sell the whisky there?"

"No," Aulay said, and related what happened in Aalborg, as well as the death of the old man.

"Oh dear," his mother said, and cast another long look at the Livingstones. "A wretched ordeal for them."

"Aye, but what of Aulay?" Catriona asked. "They bound him like a dog."

"For which I cannot forgive them," his mother said. "But look at them. They are young, these Livingstones. They must have been devastated by the death of their father."

Catriona leaned forward and whispered, "What is wrong with the big one?"

"A bad birth," Aulay said.

"What happened then?" Aulay's father asked.

Aulay told them the rest of his wretched tale. The flight from Aalborg and the decision to return to Scotland. The chase down the Scottish coast into the fog.

"Who?" his father asked.

"I donna know. There was no flag, no markings."

His father leaned forward. "And the ship? How was it lost?"

Aulay had sailed this coast more times than he could count, but that fog, damn it, had rolled in so quickly, and so thick, that he'd lost his way. He admitted this to his father. He said that had he been at sea, he would have held course, but that he'd been sailing too close to the shore to avoid the other ship, and when the storm blew up, he couldn't keep her from the rocks.

When he'd finished, his family fell silent. Catriona slowly leaned back in her chair, resting her head against it, staring at the ceiling. His mother reached across her husband for Aulay's hand and squeezed it.

His father didn't speak, but stared down

at the Livingstones, his jaw working in a clench.

Would he ever have his father's forgiveness? Aulay wanted desperately to ask for it, to hear his father say that he was forgiven for what he'd done, forgiven for ruining them. But his father did not offer forgiveness. When at last he turned his gaze from the Livingstones, he rapped his knuckled absently on the table. "We'll discuss what is to be done with Rabbie on the morrow, aye?" he said.

Aye, of course — he'd hear from one of his better sons.

"We'll hear what the Livingstones have to say for themselves," he added, and gestured at the lot of them, eating stew as if they'd just crawled out of the desert after forty days and nights. His father looked at Aulay pointedly. "We canna allow this crime to go unanswered, can we, then?"

Aulay's heart squeezed. It had been so full of fury, but now it felt as if there was nothing left. Not fury, not hope, not acceptance. Nothing. "No. Of course no'."

"Will you send for a justice of the peace, then, Pappa?" Catriona asked.

"We'll decide on the morrow," the laird said. "I want to think on it and have Rabbie's opinion as well."

"They've been through quite a lot," Aulay's mother said, gazing at them below the dais.

"They're no' strays, Margot," his father said curtly. "And they've caused us an insurmountable loss, as you must see, aye?"

"I do. But it's been so very hard for so many in these hills, Arran. People have been forced to do things they would never do."

"Aye, and we are included in that number, are we no'?" he asked, looking at his wife. She pursed her lips. "Margot, *leannan* . . . we've lost our best hope to return an income to us with the loss of the ship. We canna let it lie."

"I understand," she said. But she didn't sound as if she did. "Is there enough room for them in the gatehouse?"

"Aye," his father said. "Aulay, put them under guard."

"Aye, my lord," he said as Frang appeared to place a platter of food before him. But he'd lost his appetite. Perhaps because Lottie was in his line of sight, scarcely touching her own food. Aulay felt a little sick — sick at all that he'd lost, sick at what he feared he might lose yet.

Chapter Twenty-Two

In a small room with a single window, Lottie was introduced to the most glorious thing she'd ever seen: a bed. A proper bed, with real linens and even a pillow. And what's more, Lady Mackenzie had insisted a bath be drawn for her.

Lottie had not argued. She was too exhausted and too heartbroken to care about anything other than a bath and a bed.

Servants arrived with a tub, buckets of hot water, and in the company of the young woman who had greeted Aulay at the gates. She was obviously Aulay's sister — there was a strong family resemblance in the golden hair and blue eyes. She was carrying a basket, which she placed at the foot of the bed. "You'll need a change of clothing, aye?" she said, gesturing to the basket.

"Ah . . . aye, thank you," Lottie said, feeling suddenly ashamed of her appearance. "I canna thank you enough for it."

"No," the woman said coolly. "I donna suppose you can." She folded her arms, leaned insouciantly against the wall as the servants filled the tub, and eyed Lottie closely, like a crow, as if she'd never seen a woman in such a state before.

When the servants had finished the chore, they went out, but Aulay's sister remained.

"Ah . . ." Lottie gestured feebly to the tub.

"You donna strike me as bashful," his sister said. "Go on, then." She moved to look out the window at the hamlet rooftops as Lottie disrobed. "You've no' asked my name, so I'll tell you. I'm Miss Catriona Mackenzie, Aulay's sister, aye? You may call me Catriona if you like. I canna abide all the Miss This and That."

"I'm Lottie," Lottie said, and tossed her trews and shirt onto the floor. "Lottie Livingstone. You resemble, him, you do," she said, and stepped into the tub. She closed her eyes on a blissful sigh as she sank into the bath. It was pure luxury after the last week.

"Here."

Lottie opened her eyes — Catriona was standing beside the tub, holding out a bar of soap. Lottie reluctantly took it, wondering why Aulay's sister should linger.

Catriona strolled around the room as

Lottie bathed. "There's to be a meeting on the morrow. Two of my brothers and my father will determine what is to be done with you and your clan." She glanced over her shoulder at Lottie. "Does it frighten you, then?"

Lottie remembered how fear had choked the breath from her in those moments she thought she would drown. She shook her head. "I'm a wee bit uneasy, I'll no' deny it. But no' frightened." She began to wash her hair.

"Funny, but I thought you'd say that." Catriona stopped her wandering and turned around to face Lottie. "How did you do it?"

"Pardon?"

"How did you steal my brother's ship? He's one of the finest captains on the seas, and 'tis no' only me who says it, aye? Everyone on Skye would say it as well, and the MacDonalds are no' easy with their praise, they're no'."

"Ah . . ." Lottie still didn't know how she'd managed it. "We, ah . . . we planned to do it."

"It would no' be so easy."

"No," Lottie said softly. "I, ah . . . I distracted them."

"How?"

Lottie could feel her cheeks heating and

averted her gaze, then gestured vaguely to her face.

"Pardon?" Catriona asked.

Lottie made a circular motion around her face again. "I distracted them."

Catriona's brows dipped. Lottie waited to be ridiculed, or worse, censured for it. But Catriona abruptly laughed. "Are gentleman no' the most ridiculous creatures? Such slaves to beauty they are."

The heat in Lottie's cheeks intensified. "While I . . . distracted them, my brother struck him from behind. You might have noticed him — he's rather big."

"Oh, aye, he's your brother, is he? What ails him?"

Catriona was very direct, which, in any other circumstance, Lottie would have very much admired. But at present, she wished Catriona would leave. "He was born with the cord about his neck. He's never been right."

Catriona sat on the end of the bed. "How *tragic* for your family. For your *mother*! Does she wait for your return?"

Lottie shook her head. "She died in the course of bearing my sister."

"Oh," Catriona said contritely, and glanced at her hands. "My condolences. Well! I donna know what will happen, but the ship is lost and the cargo we held was no' ours, aye? We canna replace it and now we have a large debt we didna have before. Everyone is verra angry just now."

"Aye," Lottie said softly. "I understand."

"Nevertheless, my father is quite fair."

If he were a fair man, he'd see them hang for it, for that was the only fair thing. The only fair thing would be for the Livingstones to pay the Mackenzie debts, but that was as laughable as it was impossible.

Catriona leaned across the space between them and lifted a wet strand of Lottie's hair. "I've never seen such a color, in all my days I've no'. No wonder Aulay was stricken." She dropped Lottie's hair and smiled.

"He was no' *stricken,*" Lottie scoffed. "He was the only man on that ship who seemed suspicious of me."

"That is what constitutes stricken for my brother. I've never known a lass to catch his eye. He's had his courtships, aye, and I've heard from Rabbie — that's another of my brothers — that he has no' lacked for the attention of the fairer sex. But Aulay likes his solitary life, I think. He prefers to be free to sail the seas and return to us every now and again. The good Lord knows that when he's here at Balhaire, he canna stay for long. He's always been quite desperate to be out again."

"He is married to the sea," Lottie said, thinking back on their conversation.

"Pardon?"

"Nothing," Lottie murmured. She thought of the seascapes he'd painted, of the places he'd been. She had taken that from him and she couldn't bear that she'd hurt another person as she had clearly hurt him. She would give anything in her power to make it right.

Catriona tilted her head to one side. "You are a beauty, that you are. Pity," she said.

Lottie flushed.

"I mean pity that you'll no' be at Balhaire for very long. I should like to learn how to steal a ship. It can be so tedious here."

"Borrow," Lottie said, and closed her eyes.

"Pardon?"

"I borrowed it," she said.

"Hmm. My brother would disagree," Catriona said. "He said you are the worst sort of thief, for you pray on the weakness of men."

Lottie's eyes flew open, but Catriona had moved to the door. "Sleep well, then."

Did Aulay really believe that she'd prayed on his regard for her?

In spite of the anxiety that filled her, Lottie slept heavily. Her body had given out, but her heart and mind plagued her with dreams. She was in the water, trying to reach the shore, or her father calling down the hatch for her to come up before she drowned, but she was unable to reach the steps. And then there was a dream in the space between sleep and waking. It was Aulay, crouched on a hill above her, his hand extended to her, his smile broad and inviting. "Come now, lass, come with me," he said, and as she slipped her hand into his, his smile became a snarl. "You will hang for what you've done."

Lottie awoke from that dream with a tear sliding from the corner of her eye. She held him in such great esteem that it was physically painful to have destroyed the thin thread of trust they'd had between them. She hadn't deserved his trust at all, but he'd been generous, far more generous than she might have been in his shoes. She'd destroyed that. He was right — she had ruined everything.

She tried to think, tried to determine a way the Livingstones could pay the Mackenzie losses. Did Mr. MacColl have that sort of fortune? If, by some miracle, she could escape the noose or incarceration, could he set the debt to rights if she married him?

All that thinking made her head ache, and Lottie finally rose from bed. She dressed in the gown Catriona had given her, a gray muslin over a white petticoat and a silky white stomacher. It was a plain day gown, but after her two weeks on the sea, Lottie felt like a queen in it.

Catriona had also left her a hairbrush and hairpins, and even a bit of rouge. Lottie was deeply mystified by her kindness, but grateful for it. She brushed her hair, then pinned it back from her face but let it fall down her back. She left off the rouge, however, as two weeks in the sun had left her with all the rosiness she needed.

When she was fully dressed, she walked down the hall to the rooms where the rest of the Livingstones had been shown the night before. She found Mathais dressed in clean clothes, too, and Drustan in a clean lawn shirt.

"The lad said they couldna find anything but a shirt for Dru," Mathais said.

Drustan didn't seem to mind. He was sitting on a bed, bent over a piece of wood in his hands. Mathais noticed Lottie's interest and said, "Iain the Red brought round a bit of wood for him. His gull is quite good," he said, and held it up for Lottie to see. "He's carving a ship now."

Lottie checked on the other men — all of them in clean clothes, all of them groomed, all of them hungry. She volunteered to inquire after the guard if they might have a wee bite.

Lottie went to the door that led into the bailey and knocked lightly, then carefully pulled it open. Much to her surprise, Aulay was standing on the other side of the door with the guard. She gaped at him, unable to speak at first. He was clearly rested, his hair combed into a queue, his jaw clean-shaven. He wore a plaid, which had been banned by the king, with a coat and waistcoat and *ghillie brogues.* He was the picture of strength and virility, and Lottie's blood began to race. He was a devil in tartan, and in spite of herself, she smiled broadly, a wee bit like a mad woman.

Aulay did not smile. "I've come to fetch you," he said. "My mother should like to see you all returned to good health with breakfast."

Lottie nodded. Whatever was swimming in his clear blue eyes made her feel weak and fluttery. It was not esteem — it was the shine of enmity. "What?" he demanded, growing irritable with her intent study of him.

Lottie was reminded of another time he'd

asked her what, and she'd said everything. He was *everything.* "Well . . . I should verra much like to kiss you, that's what."

His gaze darkened. "My father and brother are waiting. We'll receive you once you've broken your fast, aye?" He turned around and strode away from her.

Lottie's heart deflated until there was no life left in it. Aulay had lost all regard for her, and it hurt.

They were fed a king's breakfast with fresh eggs and ham, soup and cheese, freshly-baked bread. "What do you think, is it our last meal, then?" Duff asked curiously as he stuffed more bread into his mouth.

Lottie's stomach turned, and she put down her fork.

"Beg your pardon."

She glanced up — the butler was standing at the end of their table. "Aye?"

"Miss Livingstone, Mr. Duff Livingstone, Mr. Robert MacLean and Mr. Gilroy are to accompany me to the laird's study, aye? They rest of you shall return to the gate-house where you will wait until further notice." He gave them a curt nod of his head and stepped back, waiting for them to do as he instructed.

"Sounds a wee bit formal, does it no'?"

Mr. MacLean muttered.

"I donna see why I'm no' allowed to come," Mathais complained. "I helped take the ship as much as anyone."

"Donna be daft, lad," Duff said, chuffing him on the shoulder. "Do you think this is to be a *feill*?" he asked, referring to a Highland festival.

A guard appeared to march them off to the gatehouse, and Lottie, Duff, Mr. Mac-Lean and Gilroy followed the butler down a darkened corridor to a pair of oak doors. He opened them, stepped inside and bowed. "The Livingstones, milord."

Lottie was the first to enter, determined to accept the blame for all of it. But when she stepped inside, the room stopped her midstride — she'd not expected it to be so large or so grand. There were large windows along one wall, framed with heavy velvet drapes. A hearth with a cheery fire chased the damp, but the most striking thing was the wall of books. So many books! It was what she imagined a king's room to look like.

The other thing that startled her was how many people were in the room. The laird and his wife, of course, as well as Catriona. Aulay stood at the hearth with a man with rich brown hair who was a wee bit taller and broader. That man stared at Lottie in a manner that she was very much accustomed to, but then suddenly glanced away, to a woman seated in a chair nearby. There was another couple, the lady on a settee, the gentleman standing behind her.

"Miss Livingstone," the laird said. "You will pardon me if I donna rise, aye? My leg pains me. You've met my wife and daughter. Might I also introduce my son Rabbie Mackenzie, and his wife, Mrs. Bernadette Mackenzie."

"How do you do," the woman said in a crisp, English accent.

How did she do? She was shaking in her borrowed slippers, hoping there was something to which she might cling to keep from collapsing.

"My daughter Vivienne and her husband, Mr. Marcas Mackenzie," the laird continued.

"Madainn mhath," the woman said.

"Madainn mhath," Lottie responded, her voice scarcely above a whisper.

"You may introduce yourself, then," the laird said.

Lottie curtsied and introduced the Livingstones, who stood behind her in a half circle, none of them coming any deeper into the room.

"I'd like to ask a few questions, if I may?" the laird continued and gestured to a chair at his desk. "Will you sit, then, Miss Livingstone?"

Lottie glanced at the chair. She clasped her hands before her to hide her trembling and said, "If you please, milord, I prefer to stand."

One of his bushy brows rose above the other. "Verra well. You may begin by explaining when you first saw the royal ship in pursuit?"

So it had been a royal ship. Lottie exchanged a worried look with her men.

"Shortly after we came round the Orkneys, sir," Gilroy said, stepping forward. " 'Twas my ship that was lost."

"What caused the altercation between you and the royal ship?"

Gilroy looked at Lottie.

She cleared her throat. "We carried illegal spirits, milord. Spirits we'd distilled, aye?"

There was a rustling in the room, and the laird glanced at his sons. Aulay's expression remained impassive, but his brother was gaping at Lottie, either appalled by her audacity, or that she'd admitted it.

"If I may?" Lottie asked. The laird nodded. "We've a new laird on Lismore Island, Mr. Duncan Campbell, aye? He's raised our rents, and we canna afford to pay them. My father . . ." She paused, swallowing down a lump in her throat, the wound still so fresh. "May he rest in peace," she added softly. "My father had the idea that as we could no' produce our rents by our usual means, which is to say, a wee bit of farming or fishing, that we might do it with whisky."

"Illegal whisky," the laird unnecessarily reminded her.

"Quite."

"Did you know, then, that the Campbells are engaged in the legitimate end of the whisky trade?" he asked curiously.

"Aye, milord."

The laird looked again at his sons.

Lottie felt strangely at ease, somehow calmed by the truth. It was easier to just say it, to admit everything they'd done, than try and hide aspects of it to make them look at least somewhat justified. So she forged ahead. "Our laird Campbell, he suspected what we were about, that he did. He meant to find the stills, but we had them hidden verra well. Still, he kept coming round, kept looking, and we knew it was only a matter of time ere he found them. We decided we ought to sell what we had."

"Why Denmark?" the laird asked curiously. "God knows there's enough of a market in Scotland, aye?"

"Aye, milord, but we thought it no' safe, no' with Mr. Campbell's suspicions and his eyes everywhere. We . . . all of us," she said, gesturing to her companions, "are descended from the Danes. A man had come from Denmark last summer and mentioned that he had worked with a trading company in Aalborg that traded spirits and tobacco."

"You were sailing to Denmark when the royal ship met you, then."

Lottie nodded. "They came round, signaled for us to drop our sails. When we did no', they fired on us," Lottie said. How odd that the memory was so vivid in her mind, but seemed like almost a lifetime ago now. It felt like a story she'd once told. So much had happened since that day.

"And you fired on them?" the laird asked.

"Aye," Lottie admitted. "On my honor, I donna know how we managed to strike them at all, much less cause a fire. None of us are sailors."

"I'd say you're a better shot than sailor, I would," the laird said. "The ship had to be scuttled."

"Bloody hell," Duff muttered behind her.

"So, then, while you were taking on water, along comes the *Reulag Balhaire* to your aid, and you determine the best course of action is to deceive the captain and his men and take control of the ship, is that it?"

Lottie winced. She glanced at Aulay. "We didna mean to keep it," she said softly. "We meant to . . . to borrow it, more or less."

"Borrow it," the laird repeated. "How in hell do you borrow a ship?"

Her cheeks felt as if they were burning. "Aye, well, we tricked them, milord. We had nothing but that bloody whisky, nothing to our name, and verra few options." She paused, swallowing down the bitter truth that she had chosen the wrong path. She should have accepted her fate as a woman and a daughter of the Livingstone chief and accepted MacColl's offer. Her regret knew no depths. She cleared her throat. "We stood to lose our land to the laird and decided, as a clan, that we ought to sell the whisky. We never meant to do more than take our whisky to Aalborg and sell it and return the ship to the captain as we found it."

The laird leaned back in his chair and templed his fingers. "Either you are the most naïve lass I have every encountered, or verra canny. Anyone may call a deed what she likes, aye? But in the end, 'tis your actions that speak. You took our ship without consent. And as a result, it is now lost to us and at considerable expense."

Lottie's pulse began to pound in her ears, dreading what he would say next.

"This morning I sent a messenger to Port Glasgow with the news that we'd lost the ship. I sent another messenger to request a justice of the peace. He'll hear our complaint and determine what is to be done with your clan, he will. We might expect him in a fortnight."

"It was all my doing, milord," Lottie said. "Not theirs."

"No' true," Mr. MacLean said. "We all had a hand in it."

"Aye, but I am the one who commanded it, in the name of my father the chief," Lottie said.

The laird put his hands against his desk and pushed himself to stand. "Do you bloody fools think I care who of you made the decision? You *all* participated, and you'll all be judged for it. You'll remain here, under guard, until the justice of the peace arrives. You are forbidden from leaving Balhaire."

Lottie's breakfast began to rumble disagreeably in her belly. She put her hand on Mr. MacLean's arm to steady herself. "We'll return to our rooms, then?" she asked uncertainly.

"I think that best," the laird said coolly, and waved a hand, dismissing them. Lottie gave him a small curtsy, then turned around, gesturing her men to the door. She stole a glimpse of Aulay just before walking out of the room.

He was standing at the windows, his back to her.

CHAPTER TWENTY-THREE

The most pressing issue for the Mackenzies was how to pay for the loss of cargo. "This is precisely what I feared, aye?" Aulay's father said when they'd reviewed the books. "We were in no position to assume that risk."

Aulay bristled, but held his tongue. His father might as well announce his disappointment in Aulay before his brother Rabbie and brother-in-law, Marcas.

"We are agreed, then?" Rabbie asked, pressing forward. "We'll see if we have any interest in the cattle, and if no', we'll put Arrandale on the market." Arrandale, the house Cailean had painstakingly built with his own two hands, where Rabbie and Bernadette and their children lived now. Either solution was so substantial that Aulay's head spun with the enormity of it.

Even worse was the worry that etched itself into his father's features as the day wore on. It aged him, and when he closed his eyes to rub his temples, Aulay felt shame upon guilt surging through him.

That evening, he rode to Arrandale with Rabbie to see his nieces and nephew and Bernadette. And, truthfully, to escape the worry and weariness in his father.

"You astound me, Aulay," Bernadette said, embracing him at the door. "No matter how difficult the voyage, you always emerge from it unscathed."

"Unscathed?" Aulay said and laughed derisively. "I've lost all, Bernadette."

"Quite the contrary. You saved every life on that ship, didn't you? You are to be commended."

Commended. What a strange word. If anything, Aulay felt utterly diminished by what had happened.

After Bernadette had retired for the evening, Rabbie produced a bottle of whisky.

Aulay rolled his eyes. "Is that a jest, then?"

"For God's sake, 'tis no' Livingstone whisky," Rabbie said cheerfully, and chuffed Aulay on the shoulder. "*This* whisky is the best Scotland has to offer. From Skye."

"Skye?" Aulay said, and looked up, confused. He wasn't aware of any legitimate still on the Isle of Skye. "MacDonalds'?"

"Aye." Rabbie laughed. "Did you think

they'd allow the Campbells to have the trade? They've a few of their own hidden stills. More than a few, as it happens." He laughed and winked at Aulay as he poured a tot for him, pushing it across the table. "Speaking of well hidden . . . I've no' seen a lass as bonny as the Livingstone lass, on my word, I've no'. No' even my own wife, who is bloody well bonny."

Aulay swallowed the whisky.

" 'Tis hard to believe she's remained tucked away on a tiny little island. By all rights someone ought to have come along and married her, aye? I'm a wee bit surprised the *Sassenach* didna discover her after '45."

A cold shiver ran down Aulay's spine. He couldn't stand to think of that. He didn't know what Rabbie suspected, but he'd not mentioned anything between him and Lottie. Not because it was an emasculating tale — although it was definitely that — but because it felt too personal. She had single-handedly destroyed his life and at the same time, shown him a side of himself that went so deep that he still couldn't make sense of it.

"Will you be all right, then, brother?" Rabbie asked.

The question surprised Aulay. "All right?"

He thought about that. "There is no use for me here, Rabbie. I've no use beyond the sea, have I?"

Rabbie leaned over and squeezed his shoulder affectionately. "I once stood in your shoes. I thought my life was no' worth living."

"Aye, I remember it well."

"But it was, lad. I had to fall to the bottom of the well and crawl back up to learn it, but *Diah* save me, I crawled to where I ought to be." He gestured to the house around him. "I canna imagine life without Bernadette and the bairns, aye? And yet, if you'd asked me a year ago, I'd have said you were mad."

"What do you suggest, then — that I marry Bernadette?" Aulay asked with a wry smile.

Rabbie laughed. "Donna doubt that there is more to life than what you've always known, that's what I mean to say."

Rabbie meant well, but the words quietly infuriated Aulay. Rabbie had not lived in anyone's shadow. "You climbed out of your well onto dry land," Aulay shot back at him. "It's a wee bit different for me, is it no'? I canna exist without something to buoy me."

"You can exist on land," Rabbie said evenly. "You're no' a bloody fish, lad."

"Where?" Aulay suddenly shouted, casting his arms wide. "Here? With you? At Balhaire? And do *what,* pray tell?" he said, and slammed his hand down on the table, rattling the cups.

Rabbie was stunned by his outburst.

"Rabbie?" It was Bernadette, come from her room, peering curiously through the door at them.

"Pardon, *leannan,*" Rabbie said, his eyes fixed on Aulay. "We've had a wee bit too much whisky, we have."

"Hmm," Bernadette said, and disappeared again.

Rabbie waited until he could no longer hear Bernadette's footfall, then leaned across the table. "You'll find your way, Aulay. You've somehow forgotten it, or lost it, but there is more to this life than painting on a ship in the middle of nowhere."

Aulay suddenly surged forward and snatched the whisky bottle from the table. "I'm seven and thirty, Rabbie. There *is* no more to my life. The sea is all my life has been and I'm to simply put it behind me and find something else to occupy me?" He filled their tots and refused to discuss it further.

He awoke at sunrise with an aching head and the unsettling weariness of another restless night. It felt as if ants were crawling on the inside of him, an uncomfortable feeling that could not be doused, no matter what he did.

Lottie had shadowed his thoughts through the night. As angry as he was, as desperately as he wanted someone to pay for his very dear loss, he also wanted to be near her. It was a heartbreaking, maddening need that ate at him, and he couldn't stop it.

He recalled her standing before his father, never wavering, honest about what they'd done, and why. She'd looked his father in the eye and put the blame on her own shoulders. She could have done anything else — cried, begged, lied. But she'd stood up stronger than many men he knew. It was another thing to admire about her.

His fury dulled.

Frang met Aulay when he returned to Balhaire. "Your mother bids me tell you that the Mackenzies will dine with guests this evening."

"What guests?" Aulay asked as he moved to pass the butler.

"The Livingstones, then," Frang said.

Aulay stopped. He stared at him. "Is my lady mother mad?"

"I'd no' be at liberty to say, Captain," Frang said with a bow.

There was no need — Aulay was acutely aware of the answer.

He retreated to his rooms. He wished he had a canvas, something to do with his hands. Unfortunately, his paints had been on board the *Reulag Balhaire.* He spent a restless day, wandering about the grounds, imagining wandering about every day for the rest of his life. He toyed with the idea of approaching the MacDonalds to run one of their ships with the whisky they were distilling illegally. It was hardly the sort of life he wanted, always sailing one step ahead of the crown . . . but an experienced captain such as himself could demand a higher wage for such risk.

The idea of having to resort to it, of having no other foreseeable options, left Aulay in a foul mood, his ire stoked again. He was entirely impotent, a man in a desert, stumbling about with no sense of direction, riding a wave of fury and lifelessness.

He dressed for supper in a formal coat and plaid. When he entered the great hall, the atmosphere seemed too festive to him. It felt a wee bit like a celebration. It was anything but a celebration — it was a wake.

Most of the Mackenzies were in the hall, as well as the crew of the *Reulag Balhaire.* It was the clan's custom to dine together most evenings in the great hall. All who could come, including friends such as Lizzie Mac-Donald, a particular favorite of Catriona, who had come from Skye.

The Livingstones came last, gathered together like so many frightened sheep. They caused quite a stir when they entered, as word of the ordeal at sea had spread.

And then there was Lottie. She was dressed in a gold silk gown with tiny seed pearls embroidered down the panels of the mantua and the cuffs of the sleeves. He recognized that gown, and looked at his older sister, Vivienne, with a questioning gaze.

Vivienne smiled prettily and shrugged. "Why no'? After bearing four children, I can no longer wear it. She's bonny, aye? It looks much finer on her than it ever did on me."

Bonny was an inadequate word. Ravishing was more apt. Aulay was reminded of why he'd been so bloody dumbstruck when he'd first laid eyes on her.

More people came into the hall, and soon, Aulay could scarcely hear Vivienne speaking to him. He kept his gaze on the crowd below the dais. The Livingstones sat alone, and most of the Mackenzies paid them no heed, other than to cast a dark look in their direction from time to time.

Aulay couldn't keep his eyes from Lottie. He wanted to speak to her, to touch her. He wanted the circumstances to be entirely different. He was not a vengeful man, but he was quite certain he could never forgive her.

He wished he could claw out of his well, but in his version, he'd come up from the hold of a very big ship, and she'd be on the deck. *Diah,* he'd turned into a maudlin, overly sentimental man. Is that what the loss of his ship did to him?

His mother suddenly tapped her spoon against the goblet of wine. The fiddlers stopped playing and his father stood. Everyone stopped eating and the hall grew quiet, all eyes on the laird. Even the giant seemed to understand he was to pay heed.

Aulay's father held his goblet aloft. "A tragedy has befallen us in the loss of the *Reulag Balhaire,*" he said solemnly.

There was a murmur through the crowd, and several glances thrown in the direction of Aulay.

"Aye, but 'tis no worse than the tragedies that have befallen us before."

"No' true, laird!" someone shouted from the back. "The source of our tragedy dines at our table!"

"*Och,* Charlie, they are fellow Scotsmen, are they no'? They've suffered as we have, and they did what they had to do. Was it no' so long ago, then, that we avoided the excise men? Leave them be — they'll pay the price for their crime, they will. But we'll no' allow their foolishness to bring darkness to us. No' *us.* We are Mackenzies!"

"Aye!" Iain the Red shouted.

"We are *Mackenzies*!" his father said again, only louder.

"Aye!" more men shouted.

"We are *strong,* and we persevere!"

"Aye! Aye! Aye!" The room began to shout their agreement, cups banging the tables. The Livingstones looked around them uneasily. Only Duff was smiling. The giant had covered his ears, and the young whelp Mathais had picked up a cup and was banging it, too, as if he were a Mackenzie.

"Music, Malcolm! Give us the pipes!" Aulay's father bellowed, and resumed his seat. His wife beamed at him, her mission of this gathering clearly accomplished in her husband's speech — rally the clan.

In the midst of the shouting, Aulay's gaze met Lottie's. She smiled uncertainly, then glanced away.

He sighed. His heart had dried up and cracked, a ship's hull left too long for repair in the sun.

The music began and several Mackenzies were quick to dance a reel. Aulay watched from the dais, drinking his ale in a vain wish to drown his thoughts, if only for the space of an evening. But then Aulay noticed, through a haze of a wee bit too much ale, something that required his immediate intervention. Men — *Mackenzie* men — were looking at Lottie. And he could see that Iain the Red and Beaty were bating young Billy Botly to invite her to dance. He could see Charlie, who had just spoken out against the Livingstones, eye her and very nearly lick his chops.

That would not be born. Aulay had his own issues with the Livingstones, and Lottie in particular. But he'd be damned if any other Mackenzie would touch her. He came to his feet and strode off the dais, tankard in hand, down to the table where the Livingstones were seated, staring down Billy Botly who dared to approach. The lad turned about and scurried back to the laughter of Beaty and Iain.

Lottie glanced up, startled by the sight of Aulay suddenly looming over her. "Captain Mackenzie?"

Aulay was aware that everyone in the hall was watching him, whispering. Well then, he'd done it, and he'd come down from the dais. "Miss Livingstone, will you do me the honor of a dance?"

"Oh! Ah . . ." She glanced around her.

Good God, she'd not *refuse* him —

"Aye," she said, sounding as if she were agreeing to stick her hand in a flame, and rose from her seat. Aulay offered his hand; she hesitantly slid hers into it. Her small, elegant hand. A memory of that hand caressing his face flashed across his mind's eye, and he closed his fingers around hers as he led her to the area cleared for dancing.

They joined a reel. Lottie was a spirited, graceful dancer, but her movement seemed almost wooden. She didn't smile, she scarcely even looked at him. He missed her smile, he realized. The brilliance of it, the way it radiated into his heart.

Diah, but Aulay had never had so many treacly thoughts or flowery metaphors in his mind. He'd had too much ale, that was what. He was not this utterly besotted fool.

When the dance came to an end, Aulay said, "Shall I bring you an ale?"

She was looking at his neckcloth. "No, thank you, then. Thank you for the dance, Captain." She dropped her gaze and bobbed a curtsy, then turned about and headed back to her clan.

Many eyes followed her, Mackenzie and Livingstone alike as he stood stupidly in the middle of the room. When she reached her clan, all of them smiled, every man. The woman who had kicked him, had held a gun to his head, was the bright star among them, the light under which they all blossomed. Could she really be both women? More important, could Aulay be so wholly aroused by both of them? *Damn her.*

He returned to the dais and drank more ale, sullenly watching the dancing. Lottie didn't dance again and, in fact, none of the Livingstones did. They remained huddled at the table, warily watching the Mackenzies around them.

Aulay's mood turned blacker. What did they have to be so bloody gloomy about? They were being treated like kings.

The evening, like so many nights at Balhaire, began to draw to a close in the wee hours of the morning. There were only a few left in the hall when Aulay, swimming in his cups, stepped off the dais and walked to the Livingstone table. Lottie was still there, her head propped on a fist, her finger tracing a line around the rim of her cup.

She straightened when she saw him and put her hands demurely in her lap. Aulay was suddenly sick of ale and set his tankard aside. "Did you enjoy the evening, then?" he asked, aware that his tone was accusatory. That had not been his intent.

"As well as one might, under the circumstances, aye," she said. "We are most grateful to you and your family for it."

He inclined his head in acknowledgment, but this evening had been planned in spite of his feelings about it.

She stood up. "I ought to retire, aye? I should have gone with the others, but I . . . I enjoyed the pipes, I did."

The pipers had stopped playing a half hour ago, hadn't they? Aulay couldn't remember. "Where is your guard?" he asked, looking around the room.

"On my honor, I'll go straightaway to my room."

He flicked his gaze over her. "I'll escort you," he said. His sense of outrage had been sufficiently drowned for the evening.

"Are you certain? You've made it right clear that you canna bear the sight of me."

He flinched inwardly. He could not recall all that he'd said that afternoon after the ship had sunk, only that his speech had been full of rage. "I am a gentleman," he said, and bowed over his leg in an exaggeratedly drunken manner, then offered his arm. She did not take it, but clasped her hands at her back and walked beside him.

They stepped into a bailey awash in moonlight, the sort of night Aulay most loved on the sea, when the light of the moon illuminated the water's surface and reminded him of just how vast the earth was.

"I think the way the night light shines on the surface of the sea is quite bonny, too," she said.

Startled, Aulay looked at her. He was just drunk enough that he hadn't realized he'd actually paused to look up. He took a moment to admire how the moonlight made her hair almost glow. "How do you know what I'm thinking?"

"You painted it. Several times."

He looked at her mouth, her lips darkly plum in the moonlight. "You made a greater study of my paintings than I knew," he said, and began to walk.

Lottie did, too. "I found them fascinating."

"You found them empty," he scoffed.

"I never said such a thing. I said there were no people in them. But they were no' *empty,* Aulay. They were your view of the world and they were beautiful. You're verra talented, that you are."

Something in him shifted a wee bit off

center. He'd assumed she couldn't appreciate his view and he wasn't entirely certain she did now. "Do you mean to flatter me, Lottie? It willna change anything."

"*Flatter* you?" she stopped walking and turned around to face him, her hands on her hips. "That is the second time you've accused me of it. I have no need to flatter you, Aulay."

"No need? Then tell me, madam, what was your intent on the day my ship sank when you began your speech about what a good man I am, aye? Did you no' mean then to ingratiate yourself to me so that I'd no hold you responsible for it? Did you think me so utterly besotted that if you fawned I'd forgive you for the loss of my ship?"

She gaped at him. "I never believed for a *moment* you'd forgive me. *I* would no' forgive me! I will go to my grave regretting it!"

"Then what was your point?" he snapped.

She sighed. Her shoulders sagged. "Do you think me so heartless that the days on your ship meant nothing to me, then? My *point* was to tell you that I esteemed you. That my regret was as deep and as wide as is the ocean of my regard for you. I've never known a man like you, Aulay Mackenzie.

You have my complete, incandescent esteem."

His drunken heart began to thrum in his chest. "Then you are mad, Lottie. I am the man who was taken by a lass, who couldna save his cargo, or his ship or his clan, aye? There is naugh' to esteem."

Her eyes widened. *"Aulay,"* she said, and touched his arm, her fingers sliding down to his wrist, and tangling with his fingers. "How *wrong* you are! How verra wrong you are. Aye, we caught you by surprise and we took your ship. But you bore that captivity with more grace than a dozen kings. You *helped* me, in spite of what I'd done, in spite of what you'd already lost. You were kind even when the worst had been done to you. You *saved my life* in Aalborg, when you were well justified to have left me to the wolves. You brought us back to Scotland, and when it looked as if all was lost, as if we'd all be caught and accused, you saved us all again. Aye, you lost your ship, and for that I am so verra sorry. But *you* saved us all, Aulay. You put those souls ahead of your own, and you are, you truly are the best man I have ever known, a remarkable, decent, kind man. All I wanted to say that day was I will always hold you in my heart."

His heart began to spin. He was spinning.

He had needed to hear those words more than he might have guessed. He tucked his arm under her elbow, drawing her forward. "I am furious," he said.

"I know."

He cupped her face with his palm, gazed at the smattering of freckles that had appeared in the last few days. At the long dark lashes and brows that contradicted the pale color of her hair. At the intense blue of her eyes. "I donna trust you."

"Entirely reasonable, aye? But I've confessed it all, Aulay. It is out of your hands."

His gaze fell to her mouth.

"Do you want to kiss me?" she whispered, lifting her face to his.

"Do you want to be kissed?"

"Desperately."

He twisted her around and put her back against the wall of the gatehouse. He braced his hands on either side of her and leaned in, his lips only a whisper from hers. He felt restless, his body's desires drowning all rational thought.

"Kiss me," she said.

He bent his head and casually ran the tip of his tongue along her bottom lip. Lottie sighed softly. Aulay had hardly touched her, and yet it felt like the most sensual, decadent moment he'd ever experienced. He lifted his hand to her jaw and angled her head just so, catching her sigh of pleasure as it passed through her lips. He drew her bottom lip lightly between his teeth and teased her body forward by slipping an arm around the small of her back.

She opened her mouth to him and her hand found his waist, clutching at his coat as if she feared he might slip away. Aulay's kiss was slow and thorough as his hand explored the shape of her body.

Lottie moaned into his mouth at the slow torture, fanning the fire that was smoldering in him. Aulay was of a mind to carry her into that little room in the gatehouse and have her there, but the sound of footsteps began to filter through the carnal fog that had enveloped him, and he reluctantly, regrettably, lifted his head.

Her lips glistened in the moonlight, and she looked up at him with such desire and affection that it made him feel a wee bit dizzy. He stroked her cheek with his knuckle and unwillingly stepped away to open the door to the gatehouse. "Sleep well, *leannan*," he murmured.

She slipped inside, but once in, she turned around, walking backward, her eyes fixed on his, her smile luminous, before she disappeared into the shadows.

Aulay returned to his rooms, and sent the sleepy lad who appeared to inquire as to his needs home to his bed. He didn't bother to undress and collapsed onto his bed and pillowed his head with one arm, gazing out the window at the starry night. His thoughts were far from Balhaire, but for once, they were not on the sea. They were on a tiny island called Lismore.

He would be eight and thirty in a month, a confirmed bachelor, a man of the world . . . and for the first time in his life, he fancied he might be in love . . . with a woman he wasn't certain he could trust and could not have.

CHAPTER TWENTY-FOUR

With the exception of the first night when she'd fallen into bed and had collapsed into exhausted sleep, Lottie had spent every night since tossing and turning, awakened over and over again with the ache of missing her father, or worry of what would happen to her, or fear of what would become of her brothers, of the ways she might make this right, if given the opportunity.

But in the last few nights, she'd been awakened by an unsettling case of desire.

Now was not the time to indulge in a fantasy about Aulay Mackenzie, and yet, she did. Over and over. What was she to do? Sit in a corner and mope all day as she waited for the arrival of the justice of the peace? These could very well be the last days of her life, or at the very least, the last days of her freedom. By all that was holy, she would not end without having experienced love — real, raw, expansive love.

It was the best distraction she could hope for.

As the nights slowly gave way to day in the endless wait, the endless rumination, the endless review of all the possible scenarios, Lottie would wake, dress in one of two day gowns Catriona and Vivienne had loaned her, then go and tend to her clan.

They had settled in at Balhaire perhaps too well — Mr. MacLean missed his wife and children, and had made use of the library to write letters to them. He proclaimed he'd deliver them personally after they appeared before a judge, but just in case, he'd extracted a promise from Billy Botly that he would see them delivered if Mr. MacLean did not go home again.

Duff missed his wife and children, too, but he had discovered an unlikely friend in Iain the Red, who, as it turned out, had once thought of being an actor. One night at dinner, the Mackenzies and Livingstones were treated — or tortured, depending on one's perspective — to a reading of a sonnet performed by those two.

Gilroy and Beaty spent quite a lot of time wandering about the bailey, arguing about various things. Ships. Winds. Whether or not the Jacobite rebellion had begun in the Hebrides or the Highlands. They were like

an old married couple with nothing important to bicker about, but determined to
bicker all the same.

There was another curious development
that warmed Lottie's heart — Lady Mackenzie had taken an interest in Drustan.
There was something about the regal lady
that soothed Drustan, and more than once,
Lottie had found him wandering around
after her, picking up a chair and moving it
at her direction, or helping her draw open
draperies.

"Drustan," Lottie whispered one morning, and gestured for him to come away,
fearing that he was bothering her.

"You will not take my helpmate from me,
Miss Livingstone," Lady Mackenzie had
said, and smiled fondly at Drustan. "We've
forged our acquaintance quite well on our
own, thank you."

"But he —"

"He is a help to me," she'd said flatly, and
made a shooing motion at Lottie. "Go. Walk
on, now. Take in the sun, but leave us be."

When Drustan wasn't following Lady
Mackenzie around, he was carving, and at
last, Mathais had found something to admire about his brother. He eagerly showed
the carvings to Lottie — a gull, a ship, and
Drustan's latest, a dog that looked exactly

like one of the mutts that was constantly underfoot in the great hall. The most amazing thing about Drustan was that between Lady Mackenzie's need of him and his newfound talent in carving, he was much less prone to fits of frustration. Her father had always said that Drustan was too simple to be of any help to anyone. Perhaps her father had been wrong about that, too.

Mathais and Morven had passed the time pretending swordplay in the bailey. Rabbie Mackenzie happened to see them and invited them to learn real swordplay. Apparently the Mackenzies had long been known for training Highland soldiers. Mathais was beside himself with glee, and every afternoon, he returned to the gatehouse, sweating and dirty, his eyes gleaming, speaking rapidly about all that he'd learned as he thrust his phantom sword here and there around the little room Lottie used.

Lottie herself had been taken under the wing of Catriona and her friend, Lizzie MacDonald, a frequent visitor to Balhaire. The two of them liked to gossip about all the gentlemen in and around the Highlands. Lottie guessed Catriona to be close to her thirtieth year and wondered why she'd not been married off. She was the daughter of a powerful laird, quite bonny and spirited.

How had she avoided it? Catriona doted on her nieces and nephews and sighed with longing when one of the women from the village brought her newborn bairn around to be admired.

"One day, I should very much like a bairn," Catriona said wistfully, then smiled at Lottie. "I've no' given up hope. Have you?"

Lottie's face must have fallen, for Catriona suddenly gasped with alarm, and her cheeks flooded pink. "I beg your pardon, Lottie! I do so beg your pardon," she said again, mortified that she would mention a happy future in the face of a trial.

Lottie didn't see Aulay as much as she would like. Apparently, he spent quite a lot of time with his father. "Examining the accounts," Catriona said ominously. "We owe so *much*."

One afternoon, however, Aulay sought Lottie out. He wanted to take her and Mathais down to a cove. "We're no' to leave the castle walls," Lottie reminded him.

"What, then, have you lost your daring?" he asked, arching a brow.

No, she had not.

Aulay showed her and Mathais a path that went around the village, through a small forest, and down to the beach. The land jutted out into something that resembled a comma, providing a natural shelter in a cove that was large enough for ships. "Imagine it," he said, sweeping his arm to the water. "We once had two ships moored here." He dropped his arm and stared at the water, as if seeing those two ships, long gone now.

Lottie folded her arms around her belly. It never failed — every time his ships were mentioned, she felt a wee bit ill.

Aulay crouched down on the sand and pointed across the water. "There, do you see?" he asked. "A red mark, halfway up."

Lottie squinted. She could see it — red markings that looked like writing.

"Our initials," he said. "I swam there on a dare from my brother Cailean and climbed up with a bit of paint in my pocket."

Mathais gasped. "How did you do it?"

"I was a good climber, aye?" Aulay said, and laughed.

"I was challenged like that once, to jump from a cliff into the sea," Lottie said absently. "The cliff was ten feet high, perhaps a wee bit higher. But I didna account for my skirt. It came up around my head and verra nearly tumbled me upside down."

"We had to pull her out of the water," Mathais added. "It took four of us."

Lottie laughed at the memory. Times had

been hard on Lismore, but they'd also been blissfully free. How odd that the freedom she'd had there had felt so confining. It didn't seem so now.

They walked along the water's edge, picking up shells. Mathais boasted that Rabbie Mackenzie had said he'd make a good soldier, and he'd be willing to train him when the time came. "That's what I've long wanted to be, aye?" he said.

Lottie looked at him with surprise. "I've no' heard you say so!"

"I rather thought you'd no' approve and insist I am needed at home. But I must be me own man, Lottie. That's what Rabbie says, aye? Every man stands on his own two feet and faces the world." And then he promptly backed up over a rock and tripped, righting himself just before he would have tumbled to the ground.

"A lad canna face the world if he's on his arse," Lottie muttered out of Mathais's hearing, but Aulay heard her, and had to turn his back to them to hide his laughter.

They strolled along the shore toward the path leading back to the castle, but once they began the steep climb, Lottie paused and glanced back at the cove. So did Aulay. "What will you do now?" she asked. "Will you have another ship?"

His jaw clenched. "Unlikely," he said tightly. "What we have will go to pay the loss of cargo. There'll be nothing left for a ship."

Lottie said nothing. Her guilt choked all words of condolence from her. And she did not like to think about what was glaringly true — she'd done to Aulay what her father had done to his family. She'd lost his livelihood with foolish choices. But Lottie thought she might have divined a way to fix it, at least in part, should she be granted the opportunity. The opportunity, it seemed, would be the difficult part.

Whatever Aulay thought of her now, for the space of one idyllic afternoon, his anger had subsided. She tried to imagine them together like this always. She tried to make it into a dream she could hold and keep. But it was impossible. There was a cloud over that dream that was growing darker and darker as the date with the justice of the peace loomed.

One morning, Lottie woke up with a start, her heart pounding. She'd had a thought in the last minutes of her sleep, the sudden reminder that in three days time the justice of the peace was due to arrive to adjudicate her taking the Mackenzie ship. In practical terms, that meant any day now, really, as no one knew precisely when the judge would appear.

Any hope of going back to sleep was lost, so Lottie got up and dressed and went out into the bailey. It was quite early yet; the few souls she saw were servants preparing for the day's work. She made her way to the gardens, which she'd discovered early on. At least once a day she came to wander through the roses and rhododendrons. It was bonny here, tranquil. A tiny slice of heaven, as her mother used to say about her own garden. It was the only place in Balhaire Lottie could go to forget about her fate.

"You're about early."

She was startled by the sound of Aulay's voice and jerked around as he strolled into the garden, pausing to study a rhododendron that had grown quite tall. He was wearing the plaid again, his hair loose around his shoulders. He looked wild and untamed to her. Entirely seductive, overwhelmingly enticing. The devil in tartan again.

"Aye, and what brings *you* here so early, then?"

"You."

Her breath caught. She arched a brow.

"I saw you from the window." He paused just a few feet from her, but it hardly mattered the distance. There seemed always something so palpable when he was near, a raw need that buzzed between them. She knew that he felt it, too — she could see it in the way his eyes glimmered.

"Would you like a wee adventure?" he asked, and squatted down to pick up a long leaf that had fallen onto the path.

He didn't need to ask — of course she would like a wee adventure, anything to take her from her thoughts. "What sort?"

"My nephew, Lord Chatwick, has a hunting lodge no' far from here. It is closed for the season." He looked up from his study of the leaf. "It has a bonny view of the hills."

She'd seen the hills. She'd walked through them with him, to Balhaire. "I'm no' to leave Balhaire."

He slowly rose to his full height. "I'll see to it that you are returned in due course."

"Are we to walk?"

"We'll ride. I donna have a pony for you, but if you can manage it, I've a horse."

Her heart began to skip. She'd given her word she'd not leave Balhaire. What he was suggesting was different than a walk down to the cove, which was still in plain sight of Balhaire. "My brothers will —"

412

"Catriona will see to them, I've no doubt. Well, then?"

She would go, of course she would go, she would go anywhere with this man, for as long as she was able. "Then aye, Captain, I can manage a horse."

Aulay saddled two horses himself, and before anyone was about, before shop fronts had opened or anyone had appeared to break their fast, before Gilroy and Beaty began to argue, or Mr. MacLean wrote another letter to his wife, or Duff staged another play, Lottie and Aulay departed Balhaire on horseback.

They rode away from the sea and up a meadowed glen. After a half hour, she could see the glint of a loch in the distance, and as they neared it, a white manor house on the shores of the loch. "Arrandale," Aulay said, pointing to it. "Rabbie and Bernadette make their home there."

From there, he turned south, and led them onto a wooded path. It was dark and cool in among the trees, the path dappled by the sun shining through a thick canopy of branches. When they emerged into another meadow, she could see another house.

" 'Tis the lodge, Auchenard," he said.

"A *lodge,*" she said, her voice full of wonder. It was smaller than the others, but to Lottie, it was just as grand. "It's so beautiful, aye?"

Aulay dismounted on the front lawn, then held her horse as she hopped down. "It's quite big for hunting, is it no'?" she asked curiously.

"It was built by an English earl. They prefer grandeur to simplicity, aye?"

Lottie wouldn't know — she'd never met an Englishman that she could recall. It was one of the hopes she'd had for her future. She longed to see their grand houses, to see London, to see what proper ladies wore. That dream had crumbled along with her other hopes in the last fortnight.

He walked to the front door and tried it, but it was locked. "Rabbie keeps the house for Cailean and my nephew. Tight as a ship, it is. Stay here," he said, and disappeared around the corner of the house. Several moments passed before she heard some clanking behind the front door. It swung open and Aulay bowed. "Madam," he said, and gestured grandly to the entrance.

She stepped inside and looked around. The musty smell of the house, the sheets covering the furnishings, indicated the house had been closed for a long time. Most of the windows were covered, too, painted with soap. Aulay led Lottie down a dark hallway and into a larger room, which she supposed was the salon. The ceiling was several feet over her head, criss-crossed with thick wood beams. A massive hearth stood cold at one end, the smell of ash still quite pronounced. Aulay pushed aside heavy drapes from the windows, revealing a surprisingly fine view of a loch at the bottom of an overgrown green lawn. The surface of the loch was smooth as glass, glittering in the sun. Behind the loch, hills rose up in shades of dark green, gold and purple.

Lottie pressed a hand to her chest as she took in the beauty of the lodge's surroundings, awestruck. "I've no' seen a view as fine as this, on my word."

"Aye," Aulay agreed. But was not looking at the view. He was looking at her.

They continued their tour of the lodge, eventually wandering upstairs. The master suite of rooms had a similar view as the room downstairs. Aulay opened windows, pushing them out, allowing a breeze to waft in and settle the dust. "I've always longed to see grand places like Balhaire and Auchenard. I am grateful that I've had the chance."

Aulay walked up behind Lottie and wrapped his arms around her middle, pulling her into his chest and resting his chin on her head. They stood like that, gazing out at the pristine splendor of the loch and the land surrounding it. "Did you want to marry him?" Aulay muttered.

The question, apropos of nothing, surprised Lottie. "Iversen?"

"Aye."

She had wanted to marry him because she was supposed to be married, and her choices on the island had been rather limited. "Aye," she admitted. "If he'd stayed on at Lismore, I'd have married him, had he offered. But . . ." She paused, thinking.

"But?" he prodded her.

"I'm expected to marry, aye? I've avoided it on Lismore . . . selfishly," she said, swallowing that word. "But I have long wanted to go out into the world, to see all there is. I should be struck by God's wrath for it, but the truth is that I wanted to be free of the burden of my family. But when I had that opportunity, when Anders said I should come with him, I couldna leave them. And he . . . well, he knew me better than I knew myself, he did. He knew I'd no' leave them."

"Do you miss him, then?" Aulay asked.

Lottie shook her head. She had scarcely given him any thought these last few weeks. Once her horizons expanded, which they had, if only a wee bit in the course of this voyage, Anders disappeared into a bank of faded memories. Beyond the initial shock and swell of anger at discovering that Anders was not in Aalborg in the capacity he'd said, or any capacity for that matter, Lottie had forgotten him. "He was my first infatuation, and I thought I esteemed him more than I did, because I didna know better. I hadna seen the world. But he was no great love of mine." Her feelings for Aulay ran much deeper. And Lottie wasn't sure now that there wasn't a wee part of her that had suspected Anders wasn't the man he presented himself to be. Nothing overt, but a small feeling.

"Now that you've seen the world, what do you think?" he asked curiously.

She thought she should have married MacColl. But if she had, she never would have experienced the extraordinary feelings with Aulay. "I think I feel small in it." She turned around in his arms. "What do you think, Aulay Mackenzie?"

Aulay kissed her forehead. "I feel invincible in the world. It's at home that I feel small."

"Why?"

"Because I stand in the shadow of two brothers who were always a wee bit bigger than me, who followed my father into training soldiers. I was rather quiet, too, and my sisters, as you've surely noticed, are no'. I preferred painting to rough play, reading to talk. It was easy for me to be lost in the whirl around my siblings. But on a ship? I was the tallest of them all. I was the one my father noticed. I was the one everyone looked to."

"I would look to you on land or sea," Lottie murmured. How swiftly grief and guilt could weigh down on her these days. She bowed her head, resting it against his chest.

"I wanted to speak to you," he said, and slipped his hand under her chin and made her look up, studying her a moment. "Donna be uneasy, lass."

"Will I hang?" she asked boldly. "If I am to hang, I should like to know it, aye?"

"My father thinks no'. He thinks incarceration in Edinburra is more likely. There is the question of what your laird will want for the debts, but as for us . . . a loss of liberty, as it were."

Lottie pressed her lips together. She couldn't bear to think of herself locked away with thieves and debtors. "And my brothers? The others? What will become of them?"

"I donna know, lass," he said sorrowfully.

She knew what would become of them. She had worked it out, had discovered a way to pay back, at least partially, the Mackenzie debt, and provide for her clan at the same time. "What will become of you?" she asked.

His gaze dropped to her lips. "I donna know as yet," he said. "The MacDonalds are distilling whisky illegally. Perhaps they will need someone to transport it for them."

Lottie blinked. "You *wouldn't*."

"Aye, I would, if it meant returning to the family coffers what must be paid for the loss of the cargo. But it willna matter, Lottie. Nothing will matter."

"Why no'?"

He stroked her hair. "Because if you are gone, I truly will have lost everything that matters." He lowered his head to kiss her before Lottie could speak.

She wanted to argue, but something exploded in her chest when his lips touched hers. She realized she desperately needed to be held by him, to be touched, and filled. She needed to feel desired and wanted. She needed to feel his strength surround her and buoy her before she faced her punishment, and she responded with ferocity to that kiss that startled even her.

Aulay picked her up and twirled her around, pushing her up against one of the four posters of the bed. He smelled spicy and woodsy, his body hard planes and firm angles beneath her roaming hands, his scent of sea and woods. He was an elixir of lust.

He dug his fingers into the meat of her hips as he tangled his tongue with hers. It seemed as if a fire had flared beneath them and the flames were licking them from all sides. Aulay yanked the hem of her petticoat up and slid his hand between her legs. Lottie groaned with pleasure and grabbed his head between her hands to stop the kiss so that she might lean her head against the post and give in to the erotic sensation of his hand on her flesh.

Aulay picked her up with one arm around her waist and moved her to the bed. He fell with her onto its top and began to move over her body, his hands trailing his mouth.

Wildly pleasurable sensations glittered and spun through her veins. Lottie welcomed the weight of his body on hers, every stroke of his hands, every touch of his mouth.

He suddenly pushed up. "Take it off," he said breathlessly as he quickly began to disrobe himself.

Lottie slid off the bed and undid the laces of her gown. Aulay's frantic motions slowed, and he fell back against the bedpost, watching her intently, his gaze following her every movement, tracing over every bit of her bare skin as she revealed it to him. When she had removed everything and stood before him completely nude, Aulay held out his hand to her. It seemed so civilized after the heathen side of them had been writhing on that bed. But she slipped her hand into his and met his warm, dark gaze as he pulled her to the bed.

He buried his face between her breasts, took one in his mouth, then stood up and dropped his plaid. He was the most magnificent specimen of a man Lottie could possibly imagine, and she was savagely aroused. He reached for her, his fingers gliding over her skin, burying his face in her neck as he slid one arm behind her back and lifted her up so that he could move between her thighs. Lottie raked her fingers down his back to his hips, sinking her fingers into his flesh as he slid into her. She groaned like a wild animal as he began to move in her, then was quickly panting with the pleasure that was mounting in her. He kept his gaze locked on hers, his eyes the color of a blue-green flame, wild and intense and filled with molten desire.

His need sizzled through the tips of his fingers and his mouth on her skin; she could feel his gaze burn a path across her body, could feel the connection between them growing tauter. The climax they shared was as powerful as it was profound, both of them crying out with it.

This was what love was supposed to be. This was the way love was supposed to feel. And as Aulay collapsed beside her, she stroked his hair and said, "*Tha gaol agam ort*, Aulay. I love you, I do."

He gathered her in his arms, hugged her tightly to him, and whispered into her hair, "And I love you, Lottie Livingstone."

His admission spiraled down and around her heart and left Lottie breathless. She kissed his face, his ear, his lips. It had all been worth it, it had, to hear him say those words to her. No matter what else, those few words, his esteem, this look in his eye, had made it all worth it.

But as the heat began to ebb from their bodies, her euphoria began to ebb, too. Something about this extraordinary after-noon began to feel final. It was as if the promise of what could have been between them had sunk off the coast of Scotland, and this afternoon was the last bit of it to sink.

Aulay must have been thinking the same. He traced a circle around her bare breast and said, "I want you to escape."

She surely hadn't heard him correctly. "Pardon?"

"I canna save you, lass, no' this time. God knows I would if I could, but there are too many others affected, too many who have lost as much or more than I." He put his finger under her chin and turned her head to his. "It is out of my hands, aye? You must run. You *must.*"

She sat up and stared down at him in disbelief. "I'm no *coward,* Aulay Mackenzie! I'll no' run!"

He had the audacity to smile at her declaration. "Aye, lass, I know better than anyone that you are no coward." He took her face between his hands. "You owe me at least this, Lottie, aye? I've tried to despise you, God knows that I have, but I canna do it. I canna fault you any longer. It's madness, but I can only admire you and love you, and hopefully send you to safety. You *owe* me this."

"You donna think clearly!" she cried. "We canna escape — every Mackenzie of Balhaire knows who we are and from where we hail. What do you think, we'll get on another ship and sail back to Denmark? No! We'll return to Lismore and sooner or later, they'll come for us, they will."

"Lottie, heed me —"

She pushed his hand away. *"No."* She couldn't run. She'd done something awful and now she would stand up to what she did, especially knowing that running would only delay the inevitable and make it worse for all of her clan. She could see the pain in Aulay's eyes, could feel his despair. She pushed him onto his back and straddled him, then leaned over him, her hair falling around them and curtaining off the world. "No more talk. We've no' much time, aye?"

He put his hands on her breasts. "*Diah,* woman, do you ever abide what a man tells you to do, then?"

"That depends on what he bids me do," she said saucily, and silenced him with a kiss.

CHAPTER TWENTY-FIVE

Aulay didn't want to leave Auchenard, and put it off as long as Lottie would allow it, but eventually, he couldn't disagree — they'd been gone too long and he had to face reality. Lottie would be missed and his father . . . well, his father would demand an explanation.

As they approached the gates at Balhaire, unrepentant — at least he was — Catriona appeared, darting through the gates as if she were being chased. She glanced furtively around her as she hurried to them. But as she neared them, she slowed. She looked at Aulay, her eyes wide with surprise.

Lottie jumped off the horse before Aulay could help her, and nervously touched her hair. He had to admit he was rather clumsy when it came to assisting a woman to pin her hair — the result was a bit of a bird's nest.

"Where have you been?" Catriona demanded.

Aulay shrugged and loosened the harness on his horse in order to avoid his sister's shrewd gaze. "I thought Miss Livingstone would enjoy the gardens at Auchenard. Daisy is quite proud of it," he said, referring to his sister-in-law, who had done the work herself.

Catriona smirked. "Oh, that she is." She stepped forward, so that Lottie couldn't hear her. "But the gardens at Auchenard were cleared after a blight took her roses last spring."

Bloody hell. Aulay hadn't actually *looked* at the gardens. "Aye, that's what we discovered," he muttered, and looked his sister squarely in the eye, daring her to challenge him further.

Catriona was too cagey for him. She turned to Lottie, who had come around her horse. "How did you find the gardens at Auchenard, Lottie?"

"Oh! Aye, they were *bonny,*" she said. "No' as bonny as your mother's gardens, no, but all that color!" She shook her head as if marveling at it.

Catriona shot her brother a look. *"Color,"* she scoffed. "I should verra much like to speak more about the *gardens,* I would, but we've unexpected guests."

Lottie blanched. "He's here, then, the justice of the peace?"

"Worse," Catriona said. "Roy Campbell and his sons."

Lottie glanced at Aulay with confusion. "For us?"

"Perhaps you ought to return to the gatehouse, aye?" Aulay said calmly, but his heart was suddenly slamming against his ribs. There were a lot of Campbells in the Highlands, and perhaps it was nothing . . . but a call just now seemed suspect. Aulay put his hand on Lottie's elbow. "Stay there until someone sends for you, aye? Keep your clan in the gatehouse. Go, lass."

"Aye," she said, and turned away with a frown of worry.

When she'd gone, Aulay asked, "Why have they come?"

"I donna know," Catriona said as they began to walk toward the castle. "Pappa has ordered them a meal and has sent a lad after Rabbie." She paused at the gates and looked her brother up and down. "Best you go and comb your hair and change your shirt," she said, and disappeared inside.

A half hour later, Aulay entered the great hall to find his father and Rabbie seated at a long table in the company of three men. They rose as he entered, and Roy Campbell extended his hand. "Captain Mackenzie," he said jovially. "We meet again."

Aulay had no recollection of meeting this man. "Have we met, then?"

"You donna recall it? A few years ago, in Whitehaven."

Aulay suddenly remembered. Roy Campbell and some other men had fallen into their cups and were treating a serving girl ill. Aulay had intervened. It had ended with a black eye for him, but the lass had escaped their rough hands. "Aye, now that you mention, I do indeed," he said coolly. "What brings you to Balhaire, then? Our serving girls are our own, aye?"

Roy Campbell chuckled. "We've heard an interesting tale, we have, so preposterous that we had to come and hear it for ourselves, aye?"

"What tale is that?" Rabbie asked, his voice just as cool as Aulay's.

"My sons and I have come from Port Glasgow, aye? And there we heard that the mighty Captain Aulay Mackenzie had been overrun by pirates and had lost his ship and, moreover, had asked for a justice of the peace to be sent to Balhaire. *Naturally,* we were all astonishment at the news," he said, feigning shock, "particularly as this had come on the heels of another impossible rumor we'd heard about the Mackenzies."

"Aye, go on," Aulay said impatiently.

"Have you no' heard it, then? A ship flying the royal flag was sailing the waters off the eastern coast, it was, on the hunt for pirates and whisky runners at our behest. You'd no' believe the scoundrels that try and steal our trade, aye? This particular ship happened upon a wee ship that ought no' to have been so far out to sea. There was a bit of skirmish, there was, and the wee boat was struck. But she hit the naval ship with a shot of her own and started fire on her deck, of all things. The captain was quick-witted, that he was, and he turned the ship about to save his men. But he saw a curious thing as he returned to shore."

"What?" Aulay's father said darkly, having no patience for Campbell's games.

"He saw a ship flying the flag of the Mackenzies sailing in the direction of the wee ship. To render aid, do you suppose? To salvage any cargo, perhaps? But what *cargo* might that wee ship have carried? Quite a mystery, is it no'?"

The Mackenzies remained silent. Roy Campbell looked to each one of them, expecting some answer. When he received none, he asked, "Might it have been *you,* Captain Mackenzie? You seem the sort to render aid. Might *you* have manned the ship that sailed to help the smaller one?"

Aulay steadily held the man's gaze.

Roy Campbell leaned across the table to look him in the eye. "The English donna take lightly to losing their ships, they do no'."

"Is there anyone who takes kindly to it?" Aulay asked.

"The bounty," one of the sons muttered.

"*Och,* I almost forgot, did I?" Roy Campbell said. "The *bounty.* Perhaps you might recall if you saw a wee ship on the North Sea when I explain."

"Then explain it, for God's sake," Rabbie said irritably.

Roy Campbell smiled. "We Campbells donna care if that naval ship sinks or floats or is hacked to bits to make tables, aye? Our concern is much more personal," he said, tapping his chest. "We are building a trade of fine Scotch whisky — a *legitimate* trade. We've all the badges and papers and what-not the crown requires, that we do, and we've gone to great pains to get them. What we canna and will no' tolerate are illicit stills that undermine our *legitimate* operation, aye? It makes us verra unhappy."

As if on cue, his two sons nodded.

"What has that to do with us?" Aulay's

father asked.

"When we heard the tale of the naval ship, we thought to ourselves, what would cause a wee ship to fire on a vessel of the Royal Navy?" he asked, tapping a finger to his head. "They must have had something on board they didna want the crown to find, would you no' agree?"

Aulay shrugged.

"We are searching the Highlands like an Englishman searches for a nit on his periwig to find the man who sailed that wee ship. We'll find him, too, we will."

Aulay hoped his expression did not reveal the thudding of his nerves.

"The crown has offered a bounty to whoever can bring in these thieves, aye? We Campbells have added to that bounty, for we would verrra much like to put an end to the bastards who undercut our trade."

"Your trade is being undercut across the Highlands," Aulay's father said. "But no' by us. What is the reason for your call?"

"The bounty is a good one, lads. A sum so dear that there are ships sailing around Scotland as we speak, looking for the culprits. And do you know that no' a fortnight ago, they verra nearly caught one? *Och,* but the ship eluded them. Or . . . did it perhaps sink?"

"I'll ask it again, I will," Aulay's father said. "What has that to do with us?"

"Would you care to at least know the bounty?" Campbell asked cheerfully.

"Of course we want to know," Rabbie said gruffly. "When you unwind a tale so fantastically, what do you think, then?"

"Five thousand pounds, it is," Roy Campbell said, and sat back to allow the surprise of it to sink in. "That's quite a lot of money, is it no'? What do you think, Alistair," he said, directing his question to one of his sons. "Would five thousand pounds build a new ship?"

"Perhaps no' all, but quite close, aye," Alistair agreed.

"All we would need from you, sir, is a name. Just the name of the scoundrel who sailed that wee ship. Whoever the bloody blackguard is, he canna escape the scuttling of a royal ship or the Campbells. If you donna tell us who he is, we'll find him eventually, so you might as well give us the gentleman's name, sir, and there you have it, enough money to build the ship you've lost."

Aulay's blood was racing hot as his head warred with his heart. He wondered what his father was thinking just now, if the name Livingstone was on the very tip of his father's tongue. He wondered if Rabbie desired to admit what these men suspected was true, to give them the name of who was responsible for the scuttling of that royal ship. If he did, the Mackenzies would have the money they needed to pay for the cargo they'd lost and begin the construction of a new ship. Without it, Aulay's only hope was that the MacDonalds would take him on, and he'd spend the next years outrunning the crown and privateers and Campbells like a bloody pirate just so his family could pay for what they'd lost.

Moreover, a justice of the peace was on his way. Which was worse for the Livingstones — the law? Or the Campbells?

But there was something else that was niggling at Aulay. Roy Campbell assumed that whoever had done this was a man. Not Lottie — a man.

"Well?" Roy Campbell asked Aulay. "Have you a name?"

"I would that I did," he said casually.

Campbell's gaze narrowed. "Perhaps you need to sleep on it. Perhaps you need to remind yourself why you sent for a justice of the peace, aye?"

"We sent for a justice of the peace because we lost another man's cargo," Rabbie said. "There's quite a lot to do about it."

Campbell's face darkened. "*Think* on it," he said again. "I'm sure it will come to you. But donna think too long — if you give the name to the justice, well . . . the bounty will no' include the Campbell part of it, and willna be enough to build that ship." He smiled, his expression unctuous. He rose to his feet. " 'Tis a new justice of the peace, aye? I hear he's no' as lenient as the last. Mr. Ross, he is."

"Ross!" Aulay's father repeated. "What happened to MacRay, then? He's been the justice of the peace in these parts for years."

"MacRay has been relieved of his duties, he has." Campbell smiled thinly. "Too lenient on the Scots, I've heard it said."

"What, then, Campbell, you'll no' stay for supper?" his father drawled as his sons came to their feet, too.

"No, thank you," he said. "We're to call on the MacDonalds. Perhaps they've seen something, aye? I've heard Miss Lizzie Mac-Donald is a frequent visitor to Balhaire. Perhaps she's seen something when ferrying back and forth."

"It would seem you've heard quite a lot said," Aulay's father said.

"Aye, milord. We pride ourselves on knowing our neighbors, that we do."

"Well, safe journey to you. Frang, see the

gentlemen out," he said, brooking no possibility of continuing this discussion.

When they had gone, the three Mackenzies exchanged a look. "Five thousand
pounds is a lot of money, aye?" his father
said to Aulay.

"Aye."

"The justice of the peace will arrive on
the morrow. The Livingstones will face the
consequences of their actions one way or
another," his father mused.

Aulay said nothing.

"God in heaven, donna look so woebe-
gone, lad!" his father said impatiently, flicking a wrist at Aulay. "As if I've asked you to
put your best dog out of its misery, aye? We
agreed, a wrong has been done to us and
there must be consequences. The only question is whether the consequences bring us a
bounty or no'. We could sorely use it."

"I donna disagree," Aulay said evenly. Not
out loud, he didn't.

"I donna trust the Campbells," Rabbie
said.

"Nor should you," his father agreed. "Aye,
but five thousand pounds would be a god-
send." He glanced at Aulay. "I leave it to
you, Aulay. You are the one who was
wronged and you will be the one to give
them her name. If you donna give the name

to the Campbells, the justice of the peace will determine her fate."

"I understand," Aulay said tightly. He understood far better than his father could begin to understand. "If you will excuse me?" He stood up and quit the room as quickly as he could without appearing to sprint. He felt sick to his stomach — it was churning with disbelief, with indecision, with despair. No matter what he did — give the Campbells her name, let the justice of the peace decide, or defy his father — someone would be hurt.

But it would be nothing quite like the painful shattering of his heart.

CHAPTER TWENTY-SIX

The news that the justice of the peace would arrive on the morrow was delivered to the Livingstones just before the supper hour. That effectively dampened their collective appetites, and they remained in the gatehouse, huddled together, their hands clasped, speaking of what they would say to the justice of the peace.

Lottie was determined — this was her cross to bear. "I am the one who put Aalborg into our thoughts! I am the one who said we must take the ship," she reminded them.

"Aye, but what choice did you have?" Duff asked.

"An obvious one, aye? I might have let the whisky go. I might have married MacColl." She might yet, if she could prevail with the justice.

"No, Lottie. You listened to Bernt," Gilroy said angrily. "Too many times, we *all* listened to Bernt!"

"What's done is done," Mr. MacLean said
solemnly. "Let's try and get some sleep.
Tomorrow might be a very long day."

They embraced, one by one, patting each
other on the back, not actually speaking a
goodbye out loud . . . but the word hung in
the air between them.

Lottie remained behind with her brothers.
She didn't know how to prepare them for
what would likely happen. "Heed me, lads.
I must go away for a time."

"No!" Drustan said instantly.

"Dru, *mo chridhe,*" Lottie said, and took
his big hands in hers. "Mathais will take
good care of you. So will Duff, and Gilroy,
and Mr. MacLean, aye? We Livingstones,
we stay together."

"But why will you no'? You've always
taken care of me, Lot."

She would not cry. She *refused* to cry.
"Aye, I have. But Dru, did you know, then,
that you can care for yourself?" He began
to shake his head, but she squeezed his
hands. "Think of it — you've been minding
yourself these last few days at Balhaire."

"Have I?" Drustan asked, frowning with
confusion.

"Aye," Mathais said. "I've no' shouted at
you once, have I?"

438

Drustan thought about that. "No."

Lottie kissed Drustan's cheek as he mulled that over, and turned to her youngest brother. "Mats, you're the man of the family now," Lottie reminded him.

"I *know*, Lot. Fader told me the same."

She smiled wistfully. "I would give anything were he here now, aye?"

"Me, too," said Mathais.

"Me, too," said Drustan.

When she finally left their room, she felt bone weary. She had one last thing she desperately wanted to do — she wanted to see Aulay before she was taken before the justice of the peace. She wanted to tell him again how he'd made her feel truly desired for the first time in her life — desired for who she was, and not her face. She wanted him to know that he'd made her feel as if every bit of her mattered, that she was not a prize sheep won in the bargaining.

She was pacing, thinking of how she might see him — would the young guard fetch him? Should she make an excuse for returning to the castle? — when a knock sounded on her door.

"Come," she said, assuming it was Mathais.

But it was not Mathais who walked through the door. It was Aulay.

He stepped inside and quietly shut the door. Lottie hesitated only a moment before she ran to him, leaping into his embrace.

He held her tightly, breathing her in, his big hand cupping her head and holding it against him. "Lottie . . . there is a boat waiting for you at the cove. Go now — the tide will go out at half past eleven."

"What?"

Aulay let go of her head. He lifted her hand and pressed some coins into it. "Put them in your pocket — you'll need them. You might have to bribe your way home, aye?"

"No!" she said, and tried to push the coins back into his hands. "I canna escape, I've told you. I'll no' make it worse, Aulay!"

"It canna be worse, *leannan,*" he said, and grabbing her shoulders, he dipped down so that he was eye level. "The Campbells are searching the Highlands now, and if they've no' already been to Lismore, they will be soon. Gather your men and go, dismantle your stills, make some excuse for the ship. There is a small door next to the gates. You know the path around the high street. You know how to reach the cove. Donna dawdle — if you miss the tide, you'll be caught."

"Aulay!" she said, suddenly tearful and afraid.

He held her face in his hands, his eyes raking over her face. "I told you this afternoon that you have taken everything I held dear, Lottie. You owe me this. You *owe* it to me to do the one thing I ask of you."

"I want to make it right," she exclaimed, panicked now. She had her speech planned.

But Aulay sighed sadly. He bent his head and touched his lips to hers. He kissed her so tenderly that she could feel her heart fluttering with it, pieces breaking off and falling away. "You canna make it right," he whispered. *"Go,"* he whispered. "And know always that I loved you."

He let go of her and opened the door carefully. He looked out, then disappeared through it.

He was gone.

Lottie pressed her hands to her abdomen and bent over in wretched pain. It felt as if someone had driven a stake through her and she lurched forward, caught herself on the single chair in the room, and slowly sat in it. She couldn't breathe. If she breathed, she would be sick. She braced her hands on her knees and tried to drag air into her lungs. How would she ever bear the agony of leaving him? How could she bear the anxiety of escape? There *was* no escape. No matter what she did, she would live the rest of her life tortured by thoughts of him.

But Aulay was wrong about one thing — she could make it right.

Aulay's father, his mother, Rabbie and Catriona were already at breakfast in the smaller family dining room when Aulay joined them the next morning. His head was pounding with anxiety, his heart numb. He'd never felt so odd in his own skin. How strange it was to think of all the times he'd feared he might be lost at sea, and yet, he'd never felt fear clutch his heart quite like this.

He guessed the justice of the peace's boat would arrive with the tide, just before midday.

"Breakfast, Captain?" Frang asked.

Aulay looked around at his family. None of them appeared as if anything was amiss. His mother was reading a book. His father was eating his breakfast. It was another morning at Balhaire.

"Aye, thank you," Aulay said. He took his seat at the table, poured ale from a pitcher and drank. He felt unusually parched.

He had just been served his meal when the young guard assigned to the gatehouse, Ewan Mackenzie, appeared at the door of the dining room. He looked nervous, and Aulay's pulse quickened. A good lad, Ewan, always wanting to do the right thing. If someone had told him to go and patrol the high street last night, he would have gone immediately. He would have taken his mission of keeping watch for Campbells quite seriously.

"Beg your pardon, milord," Ewan said, and began to nervously crush his hat in his hands.

Aulay's father flicked his gaze over Ewan. "Aye?"

"The Livingstones . . . they're gone, they are."

"Gone where?" his father asked, confused.

"I donna know where, milord, but they're gone from the gatehouse."

Aulay's mother looked shocked. She turned her gaze to her husband, who had leaned back in his chair, his brow furrowed in a frown. "Are you certain, then?"

"Aye, milord. They're no' in the gatehouse, and no one has seen them."

"Where could they have gone?" his father asked rhetorically, and shifted his gaze to Aulay.

Aulay casually bit into his bread.

"All right, then, thank you," his father said, and gestured for Ewan to take his leave. He shifted around in his seat to glare at Aulay. "How odd, is it no', that the Livingstones, who have enjoyed our company and our food for nigh on a fortnight, who have waited patiently for the lawful judgment of the justice of the peace for their crime, should leave now?" He leaned forward, his gaze piercing Aulay's. "Where do you suppose they went, Captain Mackenzie?"

That voice would have frightened Aulay as a lad. Not now. "I donna know. Far away, I hope."

His father looked at Rabbie, who shook his head. And then at Catriona, who was buttering a piece of bread. Thoroughly.

He made a sound of disgust as he looked to Aulay once more. "Of all my children, *you* are the last I would suspect in this."

"Arran, please," his mother tried.

"We have lost *everything!*" his father roared, and brought his fist down on the table so hard that plates and cups rattled into each other.

"No, my lord, it is *I* who have lost everything!" Aulay roared back at him. His mother gasped loudly. Catriona dropped her knife. "It was *my* ship, *my* arrangement, *my* livelihood that is lost! The only place I ever felt myself was on the sea! The only floor that I have ever commanded has been a deck! All my life, I have sought your approval. All my life, I have wished that just *once*, you would bestow your smile of approval on me! And you think *you* have lost everything?"

His family stared at him in shock, but the floodgates had opened. Aulay's father suddenly surged forward. "I donna know what you are nattering on about, but I *do* know that for the want of a *name*, we could have had a ship restored to us! To *you*! *You* could have restored your pride!" he shouted, shaking his fist at Aulay. "But as it stands, we will empty our coffers and borrow money to repay what we've lost for the mistakes *you* made! Am I the *only* Mackenzie who feels wronged? Am I the *only* one to stand among us and demand that justice be done?"

Aulay had never defied his father that he could recall, but he was unmoved by his father's speech. "It was my loss to bear, and I will bear it. But no one has the right to feel more wronged than me. *No one!*" he shouted. "And even I can see that to have them incarcerated or worse, *hanged,* will no' bring back my life! We've lost everything, aye. *I've* lost everything. But extracting a pound of flesh for it will no' change it —"

"Giving the name of who has brought us

so low is *no'* extracting a pound of flesh!" his father roared to the ceiling. "It is justice! It is living by the rule of law! It is what civilized people do!"

Aulay took a breath and forced himself to speak calmly. "Had they acted maliciously, I would likely agree with you, Athair," he said. "But they did no'. They made mistakes, that they did — but their intentions were never to harm anyone. Their intentions were to survive. Circumstances can make fools out of all of us, aye? Circumstances have made *me* the fool in this case. No' you."

His father groaned. " 'Tis the lass, is it no'? That bonny lass has caught your eye."

This was not a childish infatuation, of that Aulay was certain, and he would not reduce it to that to appease his father. "It is far more than that, and I think you understand it, aye? It is everything I've ever tried to be in this family."

"What?" his mother said in disbelief. "Well, I don't understand you, darling. You are our son. You are as cherished as anyone!"

"Màither," he said, and shook his head. "You canna understand the heart that beats in a man, aye?"

His father groaned and then cast his gaze to Catriona. "What have you to say?"

Catriona squared her shoulders. "I agree

with Aulay. Completely. They're no' bad people. I should rather arrange for repayment then see any harm come to them."

"Of course you do," the laird said irritably. "Rabbie?"

Rabbie glanced at Aulay. "I donna know."

Aulay shrugged. At least his brother answered truthfully; he could not fault him for that.

Frang stepped into the room. "Milord, the justice of the peace," he announced.

Everyone jerked toward the butler. "So soon?" Aulay's mother said.

"Aye, madam."

Arran Mackenzie sighed to the ceiling. "Show him to my study, Frang. We'll be along directly."

When Frang had gone out, Aulay's father rose to his feet and picked up his cane. "I'll forgive you this, Aulay. But I'll no' allow them to escape with their crime and pay no consequence. I will *no'*. We have been dealt a blow, *all* the Mackenzies, and it canna go unpunished. Come now, the rest of you. Let us make our case to the justice of the peace."

The justice of the peace, a diminutive young man with a hook nose, was pacing the floor when the family entered. His clothing was dusty, and he looked tired in spite of it being early in the day. He was in the company of a clerk, a thin fellow with a nervous habit of scratching his neck.

After the introductions were made — the justice of the peace, it would seem, hailed from the lowlands — the clerk looked at his pocket watch and nodded at the justice. "Well then, let's have it, aye? I've an agenda in these hills as long as a man's arm."

"Our ship was stolen —" Aulay's father began.

"Borrowed," Aulay's mother politely interjected. She patted her husband's hand. "It was borrowed, darling."

"It was *stolen,*" the laird insisted, "by another clan, aye? And as a result of their mishandling, the ship has been lost at sea."

"Aye, what clan?" the justice of the peace asked, and nodded at his companion to make a note. "The MacBeths, was it? I'm no' surprised. A pack of thieves, they are."

"No," Aulay's father said. "The Livingstones."

"Livingstone," the justice of the peace repeated. *"Livingstone."* He shook his head. "No' familiar with that name, I'm no'."

"Pardon, darling, but I think you have that wrong. It was Leventon," Aulay's mother said.

Aulay's brows rose. His mother's gaze

448

flicked over him, and he could have sworn he saw the barest hint of a smile.

"I beg your pardon?" his father blustered, his face going red. "It was *Livingstone,* for God's sake! By all that is holy they have been here at Balhaire for a fortnight!" He turned back to the justice of the peace. "They've escaped."

"From this fortress?" the justice of the peace asked, clearly surprised. "How, then? Did they climb the walls?"

His father's brows dipped into an un-amused vee. "Aye, it would seem so."

"Well, we'll find them, will we? From where do they hail? These thieves always return to their dens to hide like moles. It's incumbent on us all to root them out and dispose of them if we're to set Scotland to rights, aye? Where do they call home?"

"What do you mean, set Scotland to rights?" Rabbie asked.

"Well, it was the rebellion of Highlanders that put us back on our heels, was it no'? A lot of their sort still about."

"Lismore Island," Aulay's father said.

"Pappa, it was Linsfare," Catriona said, and looked desperately to Aulay. "I'm quite certain it was Linsfare."

"The Highlands donna need to be set to rights," Rabbie said. "And my sister is wrong as well. It was Lybster. I know verra well it was, as I have met many Leventons from Lybster."

The justice of the peace looked around the room with disgust. "I donna have the men to go here and there on a wild hare's chase!" he said. "Where do these . . . Leventons call home?"

"I would suggest you start in Lancashire," Aulay's mother said smoothly.

"England!"

"Yes, England. I personally conversed with the gentleman who fancied himself in charge, Mr. Charles Leventon, and he assured me they hailed from there. It's close to the sea, you know."

"For all that is holy," Aulay's father muttered, and sagged in his seat.

The justice of the peace's face was turning red. "Shall I suggest that when you have determined precisely where these *Leventons* have gone, you inform me when I return to your part of the Highlands next spring? I've no' the time for this confusion! If you've no complaint now, then donna waste my valuable time!" He stood to go, gesturing for his assistant.

"Spring!" Aulay's father blustered, but the justice of the peace was already moving, barking at his assistant to come along.

"We'll be gone from here by spring, pushed out by poverty!" his father shouted after the man.

Not that it helped. The justice of the peace was gone.

Arran Mackenzie glared at his family. "I've been betrayed by my own blood," he said. "I never thought I'd see it, that I did no', but aye, you've all betrayed me."

He pushed up, grabbed his cane, and stomped from the room.

None of them said a word for a long moment. None of them looked at each other until Aulay's mother said, "I'll go and soothe his ruffled feathers. He does hate to lose. Aulay, darling, you best think of what next."

"What have we just done?" Rabbie asked of no one in particular when their parents had left the room.

"Enraged our father. Set free the verra people who ruined us. Lied to a justice of the peace," said Catriona.

"Aye. And none of it will stop the Campbells," Rabbie groused.

Aulay knew that, too. But Roy Campbell thought he was in pursuit of a man. Not a wisp of a lass with hair the color of pearls.

CHAPTER TWENTY-SEVEN

The Livingstones reached Lismore Island at dusk the next day and were greeted by a dozen rabbits hopping around on the little strip of sand as they made their way up from the beach. When they'd crested the dune, Old Donnie sounded the horn, startling Drustan and causing him to wail.

Very soon, Livingstones were coming down the path to greet them. People were laughing, throwing their arms around them, kissing their cheeks. The commotion unsettled Drustan even more. "I want to go home, Lottie. I want to go *home*," he said, flapping his hands uncontrollably.

"Aye, we're almost there," she assured him.

"Where's Bernt, then?" called out a woman. She was one of three widows in their clan. All three had been frequent visitors to Bernt's salon, coming round with a pie, or to mend shirts that did not need mending. Lottie had hoped she'd not have to address her father's absence so soon. She needed to think. She needed to plan. But she knew these people — they would not rest until they knew what had become of their chief. So she slowed her step and reluctantly turned around to look at the crowd behind her. Her heart crawled to her throat. For all his faults, her father was a beloved man. "Have you no' heard from Norval and Mark, then?" she asked.

Everyone looked around them. "Norval and Mark were with you," someone said.

"They're probably hiding," Mr. MacLean muttered.

"Where is Bernt?" someone called.

"My father . . ." Her throat tightened, and she cleared it. How did one announce that their chief had passed on? "He's . . . well, he's dead." Her inelegant announcement was met with gasps and soft cries of distress.

"*Dead!* But how?"

Lottie's eyes began to burn with tears. "We met with a wee bit of trouble, we did. And we . . . we —"

"I'll tell them," Duff said firmly, and removed himself from the embrace of his wife and children and stepped before Lottie. "Allow me, Lottie." He turned to the group. "It's a *tale* as old as *time.*"

453

There were several stifled groans, but Lottie was grateful to Duff for sparing her the necessity of telling the story about their demise. Duff told it all right, on that grassy hill, with rabbits all around them. And when he was done, some were quietly weeping. Others were visibly angry. " 'Tis no' right," said Gavin Livingstone. " 'Tis no' right at all."

"What are we to do without a chief?" someone near the back shouted. "We must have a chief, aye? We've taken the stills as he asked, but he said we'd all be rich."

"What?" Lottie asked, lifting her head. "My father asked you to take down the stills?"

"Aye," said another. "The morning you left, he bid us take down the stills, and remove any trace so that no one could ever know. We didna need them any more, Lottie, for we'd all be rich."

"We're no' rich," MacLean said bitterly.

"The laird is to come Monday!" said a woman. "Who will answer for the rents?"

"We must have a chief," said another. "It must be Lottie."

"What? *No!*" Lottie exclaimed, and held up her hands. "No, I canna be your chief. Duff will take charge for now, aye?"

"For God's sake, no' Duff," Mr. MacLean

said. "He'd turn us into a theatrical troupe, he would. It *must* be you, Lottie. I daresay it *is* you. We all know you've been chief for a verra long time, aye?"

A chorus of *ayes* rose up to agree.

Panic rose so quickly that Lottie thought she might choke. *"No!"* she said again, and took several steps toward the small crowd, imploring them. "Do you no' see that I'm the *last* person who should be chief? I am the reason we sailed. I am the reason we took the Mackenzie ship! It is because of me that we've come to this terrible place, with no money, and no occupation, and no way to pay our rents."

"Aye, but you'll think of a way, Lottie," said Mrs. Livingstone Blue. Several heads around her nodded in agreement. "You always do. I've always said you're right clever, you are."

Lottie looked around at their hopeful faces. What was the matter with them? *"Och,"* she said, flicking her wrist as her father used to do at the lot of them, and whirled about and continued the march to the house, rabbits and people following behind her.

At the manor house, Lottie said, "We'll think on this again on the morrow, aye? But now, some rest."

There was some rumbling, but the crowd began to thin, gathering their sailors and taking them home. Lottie and her brothers went inside and she shut the door behind them.

They stood in the foyer, looking around them. "I never thought I'd see it again, in truth," Mathais said.

"Neither did I," Lottie breathed.

"I'm hungry," Drustan said.

"Aye, me too," Mathais agreed.

Lottie had no appetite. The last twenty-four hours had been an eddy of conflicting emotions, of despair and hope, of fear and utter relief. She was grateful for her freedom, afraid of being discovered. She'd found love with Aulay, and they'd parted so suddenly. He'd disappeared from her life almost as irrevocably as her father had.

Lottie went to her father's bedroom and opened the door, hesitating a moment before stepping over the threshold. Just inside, she found the stub of a candle and lit it. She held it up — his room was comfortingly familiar, essentially unchanged since her mother had died. And yet it felt strangely distant from the person she was now. That voyage had changed her in ways she didn't fully understand.

The spirit of her father was still very much

alive in these walls, as was her mother's spirit, and Drustan and Mathais and Lottie's, as well. But she felt herself miles and miles from here. She didn't know how she could return to being the woman who had left this island three weeks ago.

She picked up a wooden box and opened it, inhaling the scent of the cheroots her father had kept there. It was his scent, and the familiarity of it felt almost as if he'd wrapped his arms around her. She sank down onto his bed and curled onto her side and allowed her tears of exhaustion and loss and heartache to fall.

She awoke the next morning to the sound of birds chirping. Sleep and tears had made her groggy, and she slowly sat up, uncertain at first where she was . . . until she saw the rabbits through the window, come to devour what was left of the grass.

Lottie swung her legs off the side of the bed and rubbed her eyes.

She knew what she had to do. She'd known all along, but hadn't come to fully accept it until she'd found herself at Balhaire. It had taken her a grand adventure and deep loss to come to terms with it. "I've no' forgotten what I want, Mor," she said to her mother's departed spirit. "But I'm no' clever enough to achieve it."

She stood up and went to her room. She opened her wardrobe and examined the gowns there. She owned precious few, but the yellow one with tiny rosebuds and green leaves would do.

By midmorning, while her brothers still slept, Lottie had bathed and dressed, and had made the eggs she'd found in the hen house. She donned her sturdy walking boots, picked some flowers from the garden that the rabbits had not yet feasted on, and set out for the south end of the island.

An hour or so later, the MacColl house came into view. Her father was right — it was larger than theirs. It had six chimneys across the top, four of them with smoke curling out of them. The lawn was better tended than the Livingstone house. Well, in fairness, they'd never been particularly orderly on the north end of the island, but really, how *did* the MacColls keep the rabbits from destroying every green thing?

Lottie walked down the hill and went through the little picket fence, and up to the door. She drew a breath for courage and knocked. Before long, an elderly woman in a plain cap stood in the open door. *"Madainn mhath,"* Lottie said. "Might Mr. MacColl be at home this morning?"

"Lottie? Is that you?" Mr. MacColl suddenly appeared behind the woman and stepped around her. "Aye, thank you, Miriam, you may go." He turned a beaming smile to Lottie and ran a hand nervously over the silver hair on his head. "You've come back! I had some question of it, that I did, but here you are! Come in, come in, aye?" he said, gesturing for her to enter. "Miriam! Have we any tea? Bring some tea for the lady! And . . . and some biscuits!"

"We donna have biscuits, you know it well!" the woman shouted from the back.

"It's all right," Lottie said quickly. "Please, Mr. MacColl, donna go to any trouble."

" 'Tis no trouble for *you*, lass. I'm so . . . *pleased*, that I am, that you're quite all right. I had feared the worst."

"The worst?" she asked curiously. "Oh. I brought these for you." She held out the flowers to him.

Mr. MacColl looked at the flowers and his face lit with delight. He beamed. "Miriam!"

He took the flowers and ushered her into a room. "Please," he said, gesturing to a seat.

Lottie sat gingerly as Mr. MacColl bustled about, looking for something in which to put the flowers. She noted some touches of his life before his wife had died. A bit of china. Some bonny paintings on the wall.

But it was rather stark, really, and obvious that a man lived here without benefit of a female companion. Or children, his all grown and married now, with families of their own. Her heart ached a little for him.

Mr. MacColl returned to her side and sat on a chair across from her.

"You said you expected the worst?" she asked curiously.

"Oh, aye," he said, blushing. "I thought . . . I suspected, well . . ." He paused. He swallowed. He studied his hands, clearly searching for words.

"The stills are gone, Mr. MacColl," she said, taking advantage of his fluster. "My father, he ordered them taken down when we left. I'm glad they're gone."

He sighed with relief. "I am happy to hear that from your lips, Lottie, that I am. Naugh' but trouble, that. Gilroy's ship didna look seaworthy, and there was rumor of a wee bit of trouble on the North Sea. A ship that sounded quite like Gilroy's had fired on a naval ship and set it afire, which, again, sounded a wee bit like Gilroy, aye?" he said with a slight roll of his eyes. "And that wee ship has no' been seen since."

"So, you knew that we . . ."

"Oh, aye," he said, nodding. "I saw you go out, I did. Sailed right past us here on the south end."

There was no other way to the sea. They'd been such fools, the lot of them. "We thought no one had seen us."

"Oh, but we all did," Mr. MacColl said cheerfully. "Was your, ah . . . *voyage* successful, then?"

Lottie shook her head. "Quite the contrary. There was indeed trouble on the North Sea and Gilroy's ship sank."

Mr. MacColl's eyes rounded.

"We couldna find a buyer and lost our cargo . . . and we lost my father."

Mr. MacColl's eyes widened. *"Bernt?* The devil you say," he added softly, and moved to sit next to Lottie on the settee. He took her hand in his. "Lass, my deepest condolences. What happened, then?"

Lottie told him everything. *Every* thing. She left nothing out — from the fight with the naval ship, to stealing the Mackenzie ship, to Aalborg and the awful voyage home. She told him about the fortnight spent at Balhaire, and their escape. She told him about the Livingstone predicament, and the Mackenzies loss, and what she hoped to do to repay their loss, and what had brought her here. She talked so much that her head began to throb with all the talking.

When she had finished, Mr. MacColl

smiled affectionately. "Your father has long boasted that you were the brightest star on our little island, aye? He was right about that, he was. Of course I'll do as you ask, Lottie . . . but are you certain this is what you want, then?"

She laughed ruefully. "No' at all." She colored slightly and said, "I donna mean to offend."

"I'm no' offended, lass. I'm a wise old man. I understand you completely, aye?" He stood up. "Shall I come with you now?"

"No' now, if you please," she said. "I need a wee bit of time — I've no' told anyone. Will you come for supper?"

"I will."

She stood up and smiled at him. He took her hand and kissed the back of it, then smiled at her again. "You're a brave lass, no one can ever say you're no'."

Lottie wasn't brave at all. She'd just run out of options.

CHAPTER TWENTY-EIGHT

Catriona, bless her, did not need to be persuaded. She arrived at the cove at precisely noon, dressed for sailing and wearing the boots Aulay had brought her from Flanders a few years ago, carrying a small satchel. "We may be gone a few days. Are you prepared for it?" he asked her once more.

"Aye, of course!" she said brightly. "What else have I to occupy me, then?"

She was the first to board the small cutter Aulay had borrowed from the MacDonalds, having paid a call to them yesterday afternoon.

Iain the Red and his brother Malcolm had volunteered to sail them down the coast. They were fortunate to catch a good wind that sent them well along for the better part of the day. It was a stroke of luck that they reached Lismore Island just as the sun was starting to slide west. They put in at a small

dock on the southern end of the island, and
Aulay and Catriona walked on shore. After
they'd meandered down a path a ways, they
met a pair of shepherds.

"Feasgar math," Aulay said, greeting them.
"Might you point us in the direction of the
Livingstones?"

"North end of the island," one man said,
jerking a thumb over his shoulder. "Two
miles, perhaps a wee bit more."

Aulay and Catriona walked on. It was a
bonny evening, the sun casting gold shadows across the island. "I've never seen so
many rabbits," Catriona said with wonder.

Neither had Aulay. "The island is infested," he said as one hopped across their
path.

The rabbits seemed to multiply the farther
north they walked. They passed a pair of
cottages, and received hearty waves from
the inhabitants. They waved back. Eventually, the path took them up a hill. At the
top, they spotted a small manor house in a
picturesque clearing below them, and behind it, a sea loch. The house was surrounded by trabbits and was guarded by a
dog sleeping on the front step.

"Is that it, do you suppose?" Catriona
asked.

"We canna go farther north than this,"

Aulay said. "It must be, aye."

They walked down to the house, nudging rabbits from their path, then stepping over the dog, who did not move other than to roll onto his back and invite anyone to rub his belly, which neither sibling was inclined to do. They had other things on their mind.

As they stepped onto an old brick landing with some bricks missing from it, they could hear voices raised inside the house. Aulay smiled reassuringly at Catriona, but put his hand to the hilt of his sword and knocked. They could hear the heavy footfall of someone, as if they were both skipping and running to the door. A moment later it swung open and Mathais stared at them. "*Feasgar math,* Mathais," Aulay said.

"*Lottie!*" Mathais shrieked, and whirled around. "*Lottie!*"

"What?" she exclaimed, and popped out of a room just off the foyer. The moment her gaze met Aulay's, her hands fell to her side. She looked on the verge of tears. "Has something happened, then? Are they coming for us?"

"Rest easy, Lottie," Catriona said. "May we come in? I fear being eaten by rabbits, aye?"

"They'll no' eat you. They eat grass and such," Mathais said.

"Mats! Let them in, then, for God's sake. Come, come," she said, motioning them to enter.

Behind her, Drustan appeared. He instantly held up his latest carving. " 'Tis a rabbit," he announced. "I've a horse, a ship, and a gull. A dog, too, I do."

"A bonny rabbit you've got," Catriona said, and brushed past Mathais to enter the small manor. "Show me to a wee tot of whisky, will you, lads? 'tis no' easy to find Lismore Island, is it?"

Mathais trotted behind Catriona and Drustan as they disappeared into an adjoining room.

Lottie's eyes were gleaming with what looked like delight and fear and a perhaps a twinge of hope. "What are you . . . why are you here, then?"

"I needed to see you," Aulay said, and took her in his arms and held her tightly to him. The night he'd sent her away, he had believed he would never see her again, so to hold her like this was . . . remarkable. It felt right. It felt like home. He lowered his head and kissed her, savoring it. Until she pushed against his shoulders. "But *why* do you need to see me? Have you come to take us back? Has the justice of the peace —"

"No, it's no' that," he said. "As you know,

466

we were visited by the Campbells. But I didna tell you that there is a bounty. That's who chased us through the firth, aye? Bounty hunters."

"A bounty for . . . for *me*?" she whispered, the color draining from her cheeks.

"They donna know who, aye? But they are determined. They've added to the bounty the crown has offered and in exchange for the name of the man responsible, five thousand pounds is to be paid."

She blanched. "Five *thousand* pounds?"

"But they seek a man, Lottie —"

"Ho there! Anyone home?"

"Diah," she whispered, and pushed Aulay aside and stood in the door. "Mr. MacColl, *Feasgar math*! Do come in."

MacColl. Aulay remembered that name, and his heart gave him a painful start. Surely she hadn't . . . she didn't truly intend to *marry* him . . . did she? He forced himself to turnabout and came eye to eye with a man who was at least thirty years older than he. There were two more just like him, big, strapping Scots, like Aulay's brothers.

The man was eying him curiously, so Aulay thrust his hand forward. "Aulay Mackenzie, aye? And my sister, Miss Mackenzie," he said, when Catriona appeared at his side.

She dipped a curtsy.

"Ah, Mackenzie," MacColl said, nodding. "Didna expect you to come all this way." He chuckled. "Didna expect you at all, in truth. My sons, Orv and John MacColl. They've come along to witness, they have."

God, it was worse than he thought — Lottie had not wasted a minute. He looked at her. "You donna have to do this."

"I do," she said flatly. "Please, can everyone come into the salon?"

The MacColls followed her and her brothers into the salon, but Aulay stood rooted, stunned by this turn of events. Of all the things he'd imagined when he'd come for her, this had never entered his mind. Catriona elbowed Aulay. Her eyes were wide with shock, too. "*Diah,* Aulay! If there was ever a moment to speak your peace, now is the time." When he didn't move, she shoved him. "*Go!* Say something ere it is too late!"

Aulay strode into the room. "Pardon," he said. "May I speak?"

All eyes turned to him expectantly.

Why did he feel so at odds with his own mind suddenly? He couldn't seem to find the right words. He couldn't seem to find *any* words.

"Aulay?" Lottie prodded him.

"I donna know . . . I have this idea," he

said, gesturing to himself.

"Oh," she said, and exchanged a look with Mr. MacColl.

"My sea has turned over on itself, it has," he blurted.

He heard Catriona groan, saw the Mac-Colls exchange looks.

"Pardon?" Lottie asked.

"That is to say, I'm no' the man I was when you stole my ship."

"I prefer borrowed," Lottie muttered.

"I'm a different man, Lottie. That voyage has changed me, has changed my thinking about many things, that it has. Lottie . . . you made me different. You . . . you filled my canvas."

"Filled his what?" asked one of the Mac-Colls.

"I'm no' making sense, aye," he said, and nervously raked his fingers through his hair. "I am no' accustomed to such declarations."

"He's never been in love," Catriona offered.

Aulay's heart lurched. He leveled a gaze on his sister. "Aye, thank you, Cat, but I'll carry on from here if you donna mind."

He shifted his gaze to Lottie. He moved forward, reaching for her hands. "Aye, it's true, I've naugh' been in love ere now, and it has changed me profoundly. Lottie . . .

I've naugh' to offer you. The trade is gone, we're likely destitute —"

"I'd leave that part out of the declaration, were I you," Catriona muttered.

"But I love you, lass. More than the sea. More than my life. I donna want to be without you. I want to hold you close and care for you. I know this gentleman has made an offer of marriage and he looks a fine man, I've no doubt of it, but I *love* you."

"Diah," said one of the sons.

The rest of the room was silent. Lottie stood motionless for a long moment. "But what of the sea?"

"I donna know," he answered truthfully. "If I can gain another ship, will you no' come with me?"

"There are my brothers —"

"*Och,* they are welcome at Balhaire," Catriona said. "My mother misses Drustan dreadfully."

Lottie blinked. She looked stunned. Worried. Clearly at a loss for words, and Aulay's heart began to beat wildly, charging, preparing to be broken. But then a smile began to illuminate her face. The single dimple appeared, along with a glitter in her bonny blue eyes. And then she giggled.

Aulay groaned. "All right then, have I done it so badly? Is it so amusing?"

"On the contrary, that was the bonniest speech I ever heard, and I've heard every one Duff has ever made. But I donna mean to marry Mr. MacColl."

"What?"

"I mean to make him our new chief."

Bloody hell," Aulay muttered.

"He will buy what little we have, which I intend to give to you, Aulay. And then I intend to turn myself in."

"No!" cried Catriona, Mathais and Drustan at once.

"I didna want to tell you in this way, lads, but how can I live with myself if I donna? We stole a ship! We are the reason a royal ship was scuttled! And they'll no' stop looking for us, they'll *never* stop. I must stand up."

"You *borrowed* a ship," Catriona pointed out.

"Lottie, they donna know it," Aulay pleaded. "They seek a man."

"Aye, well that's just it, Aulay. I havena got a man to sacrifice."

"A man you say?" MacColl said thoughtfully.

"It doesna matter —" Lottie started.

"Aye but it might, lass," MacColl said, and looked at Aulay. "What man, then?"

"That, they donna know," Aulay said, and

471

related his conversation with Roy Campbell and everything they suspected.

When he'd finished, MacColl said, "I've an idea. One that might work for all, aye? Do you recall, Lottie, that after the rebellion, the English soldiers came round looking for Jacobites, aye? We had one or two, that we did. But we took care of it by hanging them."

Catriona gasped.

Lottie gasped, too, but in manner that suggested delight. "Aye, we did! I remember!"

"We're no' hanging anyone," Aulay said firmly.

"No. But we might have a funeral for one. The laird will come round on Monday, so we've no' much time," MacColl said, and began to lay out a plan.

CHAPTER TWENTY-NINE

Duncan Campbell's boots were wet, which annoyed him. There was nothing worse than clumping about in wet leather . . . unless one was using the same wet leather to knock the bloody rodent rabbits out of his path. "We ought to set fire to this island, one end to the other," he complained as the Mac-Coll lad reached him on the path. "Have you thought of that, then? A good fire that ought to take care of the problem."

The lad looked appalled. "What of our houses and sheep and our coos?"

Duncan shrugged. He was furious with his cousin Roy for sending him on one wild goose chase after the other. Roy seemed to think that one would find illegal stills by having a walkabout in the Highlands. It was hardly the way of things, and Duncan had been dispatched from Applecross to Inverness, as everyone was suspected of brewing spirits to compete with the Campbells.

"Where is your chief, then?" he asked the lad as he simultaneously knocked mud from his boots and kicked at a rabbit.

"Funeral, milord."

"Funeral? Whose funeral, then?"

"The traitor, milord."

"What traitor?"

"Donna rightly know. The chief said I was to fetch you."

"I am fetched. Take me to him," Duncan said, and signaled his men to remain with the boat.

He followed the lad down a wooded path, then up a hill to a small chapel. There were several people gathered there in the adjoining cemetery, and as they neared them, Duncan could hear a woman sobbing and wailing, unnecessarily loud, *"Me poor Davy!"*

MacColl was the first to greet him, striding down the path, his expression grim. "I beg your pardon, milord, that you should come at this inopportune time."

"What's so inopportune, then?" Duncan asked, squinting at the people gathered around what he presumed was a grave. "Who has died?"

"Aye, well, there was a traitor among us, Davy Livingstone, but he is no more."

"Davy," Duncan repeated. "I donna know a Davy." Not that he knew many of the Livingstones, useless lot that they were.

"Aye, no, you'd no'. He was no' a friendly lad," MacColl said. "But he was a devious one, as it happens. You were right, laird, you were. Bernt was making whisky, and Davy stole it right out from under him, he did."

Duncan blinked. "What?"

"He betrayed them all, the Livingstones," MacColl said darkly. "Stole their ship, their whisky, their chief, then fired on the royal ship. Aye, well, he came home to roost, that he did, and without Bernt. Bernt is gone, milord. But justice has been served."

"What?" Duncan all but shouted. He was shocked that his instincts about Bernt Livingstone had been right. What did it mean, *gone*? Would he have the bounty for having found the thief? And what of the praise his uncle, chief of all the Campbells in these hills, would heap on him? Duncan could well imagine the look on Roy's face, who did not believe Duncan would find any stills. But how in bloody hell was he to present his uncle with a dead man?

"Aye, no one is as shocked as his kin," MacColl said low. "We'd never have guessed it, no' a one of us, but it was wee Davy Livingstone."

Duncan was dumbfounded.

"Ah, you've come just in time, laird, that

475

you have."

Duncan turned around — it was Duff MacGuire, the *actor.* Duff handed him a dram of whisky.

"What's this?" he asked, and looked around Duff. That was when he noticed the roughhewn coffin, the freshly dug grave. He moved closer . . . and noticed the distinct smell coming from the coffin, too. That was death if ever he'd smelled it. Granted, he'd never smelled death, but that scent turned his stomach.

"To Bernt Livingstone," Duff announced. "Recently departed but forever in our thoughts." He lifted his cup. "Seems fitting we drink the whisky that ended Bernt's life, aye? To Bernt!"

"To Bernt!" the rest of them shouted, and drank. And then the sobbing commenced again.

"What in hell has happened here!" Duncan demanded, and whipped around to MacColl. "If there are two dead men, I see only one grave. Is it Bernt Livingstone you bury?"

"No, milord. Bernt was lost at sea. This is Davy Livingstone, who met justice for his crime," MacColl said, looking surprised by his outburst. "We had no choice, did we? He stole from his clan, he mutinied against his chief."

"I donna understand," Duncan said. "How?"

"Aye, it's true, laird," said a tall, lanky man. " 'Twas my ship he stole, took it with the blackguards he'd rounded up in Oban. A mutiny it was!"

"Mutiny?" Duncan's head was beginning to spin.

"Aye," said Mr. MacLean, the accountant. "He tricked our Bernt, he did. I beg your pardon laird, I'd no' speak ill of the dead, but you know verra well, I suspect, that Bernt could be a wee bit . . . overtrusting?"

"Aye," Duncan readily agreed. A fool that man was.

"Davy tricked him, convinced the old man that he might sell his ill-begotten spirits in Oban. In the dead of night, they took Gilroy's ship," he said, pointing at the tall, lanky fellow, "and loaded the wee bit of whisky Bernt had made in the stills, aye? And set sail for Oban."

"Oban," Duncan said.

"But Oban was no' his true destination," Duff said. "He and his lads took the ship out to sea, bound for Denmark, and there they fired on a naval ship, lost Bernt, and watched that old bucket sink."

"No' an old bucket," Gilroy muttered.

"Came limping home, he did, with naugh' to show for his thievery."

"And the stills?" Duncan asked.

"Destroyed, milord. After what happened, it seemed fitting."

Duncan suspected a trick. He'd never found the bloody stills, so how could he be certain they were gone? He couldn't. This sounded like a fantastic scheme Bernt Livingstone would concoct to avoid paying his rents. "How is it that I've never heard of Davy Livingstone, then?" he asked, eying them warily.

"Never around much, that one. Liked the public house in Oban. None of us knew him well enough to know he'd forged a bad agreement with Anders Iversen. None of us could have guessed he was bound for Denmark."

"Anders Iversen!" Duncan said. "Is that the man, then, that left Miss Livingstone high and dry?"

"Aye, one and the same."

"He did *no'* leave me high and dry."

Duncan twisted around. Miss Livingstone stepped out of the crowd, dressed quite somberly, her glorious hair piled up under a hat. "I knew him for a scoundrel in the end," she said. "Had I known that he and *Davy Livingstone* struck their wicked agreement, my father . . . my father would be alive now." Tears welled in her pretty blue eyes. "I should have known! I should have realized what my father was about and I should have stopped him! Oh, but he was concerned that you'd find our stills, milord, for you're a clever man, and my father realized the error of his ways. But it was too late! He feared you would punish us harshly, and the poor soul wanted only to save his clan." A sob escaped her throat and she bowed her head and began to weep.

"I would no' have punished you *harshly*," Duncan demurred, feeling uneasy, and reached out to pat Miss Livingstone woodenly on the shoulder. "I donna understand, yet," he said, moving away from her. Sobbing women unnerved him. "Why would this Davy fellow return to this island if he'd stolen your ship and your whisky and caused the demise of his chief, then?"

"Because the Campbells are searching everywhere!" Miss Livingstone wailed, throwing her arms wide. "Is it no' true? He had no place to go!"

The youngest son of Bernt Livingstone put his arm around Miss Livingstone's shoulders and pulled her into his chest, and she began to weep again quite loudly.

"Aye, but he should no' have come here,"

said MacColl through clenched teeth. "The men and women of this island willna stand for depravity. He was tried and judged for his crime, he was. He was hanged and now we'll bury him."

Duncan eyed the coffin. He eyed the mourners, all staring back at him. "How do I know it is Davy in there?" he asked, pointing at it. "Maybe you've hidden the whisky in there, aye?" he said accusingly.

MacColl looked at him as if were a precocious child. "Milord . . . you're far too clever for such a simple ruse, aye? It would be foolish for any of them to try, as a man of your talents would discover whisky there. On my word, the spirits the Livingstones produced has been lost and the stills destroyed."

Duncan agreed, he was too clever for that trick to work. Had he not just mentioned his suspicion? They'd be bigger fools than he thought to try and hide whisky right under his nose.

"If you like, milord, I can open the coffin," said a man with a bushy beard, and moved as if he intended to do just that. He hesitated, and winced. "Fair warning to you, aye? His eyes were plucked out by the crows. They made quite a mess of it, they did."

Duncan swallowed. "That is no' necessary," he said quickly. He tossed his whisky down his throat, then dropped his cup. It landed on a rabbit. God, he hated this island. "You've made everything verra difficult for me with your island justice, that you have," he said irritably. "I should have liked to present the culprit to my uncle so that I might have the bounty. Now he'll think I canna command the bloody lot of you. Where are my rents, then?" he demanded.

"I think we've come to an arrangement you might like," said MacColl, and gestured to the path. "The Livingstones have at long last come to their senses. Perhaps we might speak of it in my salon, aye?"

Duncan glanced at the gathered and the roughhewn coffin. "Anywhere but here," he said, and yanked a handkerchief from his pocket and pressed it to his nose. As they moved down the path, the mourners raised their voices in a hymn.

Aulay didn't know how long he paced, but he was certain there had been carpet beneath his feet when he started.

"What's that?" Catriona said, and vaulted from her seat on the settee, hurrying to Aulay's side.

"What?"

She put a finger to her lips.

Aulay heard it then — voices. Many voices. It sounded as if they might be shouting. "God in heaven, it's a fight," he said, and whirled about, prepared to go and assist.

"No, they're *singing,*" she said. "A hymn from the sound of it."

He recognized it them. They were singing, all right, and the sound grew louder, coming closer, and people began to appear from the woods, scattering rabbits like leaves, their arms linked, all of them singing and laughing.

Mathais was the first to burst into the room house. "It worked!" he shouted. "Campbell was utterly convinced!"

"The best performance was our own Johnny Livingstone," Duff said, coming in next with several more and bowing to a slender young man, who blushed at the praise. "The crows plucked out his eyes!" he said, and laughed uproariously.

"If you ask me, the best touch was the corpse," said Gilroy. "Mrs. Potter Livingstone was right — the mix of grass and kelp and seaweed makes an awful stench."

The Livingstones laughed roundly.

"And Duncan Campbell believed it," Aulay said incredulously. He'd thought the plan ridiculous, had argued against it, but had been overruled by the Livingstone clan.

"Aye, of course. There was a coffin before us, a freshly dug grave. Of course he believed it." Gilroy laughed, then clapped his hand on Aulay's shoulder.

"Where is Miss Livingstone, then?" Aulay asked.

Duff pointed out the window. She was walking down the path with Mr. MacLean.

Aulay strode outside to her. "Is it true?" he asked as he reached her. "Campbell has believed this nonsense and carried on?"

She lifted her shoulders in an incredulous shrug. "It's *true.*" Her sudden smile was brilliantly sunny and full of relief.

"Aye, now, donna fret, Lottie," Mr. MacLean said as he carried on toward the house. "We'll be quite all right under the MacColl banner. He's proven himself a good man, he has."

She watched MacLean walk away then turned her smile to Aulay.

He nudged a hare out of the way. "It's really true?" he asked again, unable to believe it. "Campbell believes you hung the traitor?"

She laughed. "He was appalled by it, and a wee bit miffed he'd no' have the bounty, but aye, he believed it."

"Bloody hell," Aulay said with wonder. He reached for her hand. "Well then, Miss Livingstone, now that it's done, and I've declared my intentions, it seems a good time to put it all behind, and look toward a future."

Her smile brightened and she shrugged a little. "Is it? Have you forgotten that I canna pay your debt? No' even with the sale of our house and livestock."

"I've no' forgotten."

"Do you still intend to sail a whisky runner?"

"That depends," he said, "on what my future holds."

"Well then, remind me of your intentions, Captain."

"Which part?" he asked, smiling, too. "The part where I declare I've no' a bloody thing to offer and that we'll be quite in debt and I canna show you the world? Or the part where I tell you I love you and will make you my wife?"

She slipped her arms around his neck. "I like the bit where you tell me your sea has turned over on itself, and you're no' the same man you were. And I particularly like the bit where you give me your solemn vow you'll never again mention the two ships I sank."

He laughed. "My sea has turned over on itself, lass, that is true, and I am a different man for it. A *better* man. A happy man." He was truly happy. He'd never believed he could find happiness without a ship, but he supposed he'd found a different sort of deck to stand on, a different sort of sea. One so vast and ripe with possibility that it would take the rest of his life to explore. "But you are mad if you think I'll never mention the two ships you sank," he muttered, and kissed her.

Lottie laughed into his mouth.

"What of you?" he asked. "What of your desire to see the world, then? I donna know if I can give that to you, Lottie.

She clucked her tongue. "I will see it," she said. "If I never step foot off this island again, I will see it through your eyes, will I no'? She touched her fingers to his lips. "You'll paint it for me."

He could not possibly love her more. "I will."

" 'Tis madness!" she exclaimed. "A pretend funeral and a verra real offer of marriage all in one day!" She kissed him again, much to the loud delight of the Livingstones who were gathered at the window, watching them.

It was madness, all right. Aulay might

never see the deck of a ship again, but his life would not want for adventure. His view of the world would never be empty again. He'd found the one to add to his seascape.

EPILOGUE

Three years later

The family had gathered in the cove on a brilliantly warm summer day to launch the new ship. It was not a very big ship, and in fact, could be counted on to hold nothing but perhaps a seashell or two.

But Beathan Mackenzie, son of Aulay and Lottie Mackenzie, was mightily proud of it all the same.

Aulay watched his son toddle after the ship on bowed, chubby legs, shrieking with delight as Aulay moved along in the surf to keep the ship from sailing off to sea. Beathan would be two years next month, and Lottie was expecting another child. Drustan had made the ship for his nephew, complete with sails and guns and even a few casks of whisky carefully carved and affixed to the deck.

" 'Tis a beautiful ship," Aulay's mother said proudly, her eyes misting a wee bit. She was very partial to Drustan. "He's got talents we've not yet discovered."

Mathais had come down to the cove to see the ship launch, in the company of Rabbie and his son, Ualan, who followed Mathais about like a wee puppy. Mathais had grown taller and fuller, and at seventeen years, Rabbie said he was one of the best with a sword and would be one of the finest Highland soldiers one day.

Bernadette and Catriona were walking together in the surf with Bernadette's daughters, their shoes off, their skirts held up so as not to wet the hem.

Aulay's father had come down, too, helped by two Mackenzie lads. He leaned heavily on a cane but stood tall nonetheless, breathing in the salt air, his gaze on the horizon. It had been two years since he'd come down, he'd said, since shortly after Beathan's birth.

"Aulay! Donna let him go so far!" Lottie called to him. She hurried forward to scoop her son up from the water where he'd wandered into the ankles.

"He's all right," Aulay said. "I'll no' let him float away, Lottie."

She kissed her baby's cheek and held him close. "I donna like him on the water's edge," she insisted. "A wave could come along and sweep him off," she said, and carried her son up the beach, cooing to him.

Aulay picked up the wooden ship.

"New mothers," his father said. "Wait until the next comes along — she'll breathe then, mark me."

Aulay smiled. He walked up to stand next to his father and gaze out at the sea.

"Do you miss it, then?" his father asked. "The sea?"

Of course he missed it. Sometimes he ached with longing for it. "Aye," he said. He missed it, but he'd found much more meaning in his life than he would have thought possible all those years on the deck of a ship. Since the *Reulag Balhaire* had gone down, Aulay had gradually begun taking over the accounting from his father. That gave Rabbie the freedom to work on their various enterprises. It was not the sort of work Aulay was accustomed to, but he didn't mind it. He'd been rather creative in finding ways to repay their debt to William Tremayne without selling property.

But more than anything, he'd found such happiness with Lottie, particularly now that they were all at Balhaire, that the rest of it didn't seem to matter as much. With Beathan's birth, Aulay had experience a burst of love and purpose beyond his wildest imaginings. William had, surprisingly, recently offered Aulay the use of another ship. Aulay had toyed with the idea of it. But for the first time in his life, he was hesitant to risk his life at sea, what with a beautiful wife and baby and another on the way.

And it was more than that. Something profound had happened to him on that last voyage. When his ship had gone down, and his life with it, it had been a turning point for him. Aulay didn't want to recreate what he'd had, particularly when he had realized that his dreams of revitalizing their trade was probably never going to happen in the way he'd hoped, not with their trade routes being encroached on every day.

He'd also slowly realized that his life at sea, so important to him, had been his escape. But it had not been a meaningful life. Yes, he'd seen many ports of call. Which meant he'd seen the inside of dirty taverns, had encountered rough men and hardened women. And every time he returned to Balhaire, he'd felt restless, eager to be gone again. But that was because his life had been empty. Lottie was right — the sea was the same. It was what was in his sea that mattered, and he'd nothing until she came along.

He glanced at his wife and son, who were

now walking hand in hand, the same pearl white hair. They stopped every foot or so to squat down and examine some find. Lottie seemed more beautiful to him now than ever.

He painted the world for her, just as she'd asked, drawing on memory of things he'd seen. She loved the paintings and would study them, asking him about this stroke or that shadow. He was grateful that their family fortune had improved enough that Aulay had surprised her on her birthday with plans to see London. Lottie was beside herself with excitement, really — when their next child was born and was strong enough to travel, they were accompanying Cailean and Daisy and their brood to London.

"I'm proud of you, son," his father blurted.

The admission startled Aulay. He turned to his father in amazement, baffled by why now, after all these years.

His father seemed to sense his confusion. "Aye," he said, his gaze still on the sea. "I'm no' verra accomplished with saying the things that matter, or so your mother tells me. But I'm bloody well proud of you and I've always been." He shifted his gaze to Aulay. "*Always*. You were my thinker, aye?

My adventurer. Forgive me if I didna say it
—"

Aulay's heart lurched. "No forgiveness is necessary," he said, and put his arm around his father's shoulders. *"Tapadh leat,"* he said simply. *Thank you.* Two simple words that could not convey the true depth of his feeling, but said with all sincerity from the bottom of his heart.

Aulay looked again at his wife and son. An hour ago, he would have sworn it was impossible to be any happier than he was. He was beginning to think that happiness was a bottomless well, and if he weren't careful, he'd drink so much from it that he would burst.

GLOSSARY OF TERMS

Twenty years ago, on one of my first trips to Scotland, I picked up *Everyday Gaelic* by Morag MacNeill, in addition to some linguistic texts and a Gaelic-English dictionary. What I learned from those purchases is that Scottish Gaelic is not for everyday use. I don't know how anyone but a native speaker could ever become proficient — it's a tough language. But that hasn't stopped me from sprinkling Scottish Gaelic terms and phrases throughout my manuscripts like a boss. While I've tried to be accurate with gender and grammar, I'm no expert. So please take the instances where I use Scottish Gaelic with the grain of rock salt it deserves. Pronounce the words as you see fit because I don't know how to say them, either. My apologies to Scottish Gaelic speakers everywhere.

In this book, I also used some Danish. The same caveats apply, but should perhaps be viewed with even more skepticism, because I — brace yourself — used the internet and Google Translate. My sincere apologies to the Danish speakers among us, too. Without further ado, a glossary:

Danish:
God nat: good night.
Hun er Dansk: she is Danish.
Hvem: who.
Ja: yes.
Ja meget smuk: very beautiful.
Kvinde: woman.
Mor: mother.
Pige: girl. One source claims it is used as a term of endearment, like lass.
Pusling: a term of endearment, like pookie pie.
Sankt Hans: Midsummer's Eve, the Danish celebration of the summer solstice.
Skål: cheers.
Søde: sweet. One source claims it is sometimes used as a term of endearment.
Todlforvatning: This is the closest I could get to Customs House.

French:
Tout de suite: At once, immediately. My grandmother used to tell us to clean our rooms "toot sweet."

Scottish Gaelic:
An deamhan thu ag ràdh: the devil says.
Athair/màither: father/mother.
Bod an donais: damn it. Not a literal translation.
Bòidheach: beautiful.
Diah/mi Diah: God/my God.
Diah/ dè an diabhal: God of/what the devil.
Fàilte/Fàilte dhachlaigh: welcome/welcome home.
Feill: feast, festival.
Feasgar math: good afternoon.
Gun déid leat: good luck.
Leannan: sweetheart.
Madainn mhath: good morning.
Mo chridhe: my heart.
Slàinte mhath: cheers.
Tapadh leat: thank you.
Tha gaol agam ort: I love you.
Tha thu breagha: you are beautiful/pretty.
Uist: hush.

AUTHOR NOTE

About those rabbits . . . I ran across some accounts of how the Isle of Canna, a small island near Lismore Island off the coast of Scotland, had a significant rabbit infestation a few years ago. Fifteen thousand rabbits overran that sparsely populated island, eating everything in sight, burrowing to such an extent that they caused a mudslide over the main road, and even unearthing some human remains in the cemetery. They were mostly eradicated, so if you dined on rabbit in France about eight years ago, it might have been one from the Isle of Canna. Google it!

While the real problem for Canna was neither amusing nor cute, I borrowed the rabbit infestation to add a little flavor to my fictional depiction of Lismore Island.

For the record, the North Sea was known as the German Ocean by most in Europe in 1752, and was called that by many until the late 1800s. I used the term North Sea in this novel to avoid pulling readers out of the story to wonder about an unfamiliar ocean.

ABOUT THE AUTHOR

Julia London is a *NYT, USA Today* and *Publisher's Weekly* bestselling author of historical and contemporary romance. She is a six-time finalist for the RITA Award of excellence in romantic fiction, and the recipient of RT Bookclub's Best Historical Novel.